The Novel Killings

Kate Shelton

For my dear friend Maggie, who gave me the courage to live fully and my family, who gave me the strength to do so.

Korza Books
www.KorzaBooks.com
1819 SW 5th Ave #293
Portland, Oregon 97201

Copyright © 2024 Kate Shelton
Cover Design By Moonpress | *www.moonpress.co*
Interior Layout By Michael Schepps

First Edition June 2024
ISBN: 978-1-957024-07-3
Distributed and printed by Ingram

PROLOGUE

Flashes of light danced like galaxies in Ana's eyes, stemming from a mass of attention centered on her. "Ana! Caleb! Look this way!" someone called. A click followed by a flash blinded her again.

Ana shook her head; the bursts of light began to fade. She could barely make out the person standing in front of them. The lady's hair was curly, she wore a bright geometric top. She had something around her neck.

With a click, Ana's eyes exploded with bright white stars again. "Ana, Caleb! For the camera!" the woman said. The flash came once more, only this time Ana didn't open her eyes.

"I just need one good one," the woman coaxed. "You two will be front page tomorrow. I'm sure of it."

Another click.

"Ana and Caleb, I'm Suzy. I work for the paper. How do you feel about being famous?"

Ana rubbed her eyes again. The word 'famous' made her panic. She knew better than to think it was something she would ever be. Ana understood from a very young age that she was unremarkable. Fame was out of her reach.

Beside her, Caleb started to cry. He turned his head into her shoulder and whimpered. She put a hand around his back and rocked side to side gently. Ana looked down; his white, blonde hair was dirty, black almost. His shirt and shorts were the same; her brother wasn't wearing shoes.

"Ana? How old are you? How old is Caleb?" the woman asked.

"I'm 14. He's two," she mumbled. The woman wrote something down on her little notepad.

1

A whistling sound made both look up. A camera was right in their faces. Click. The stars returned. "That's it!" The woman said. She began threading another roll of film into the back of the camera.

"I'm just so glad you two are alive," the woman said. A group of people beside her nodded and gave half smiles. "A miracle!"

Ana finally looked up and noticed fire trucks and police cars all around them. Officers in uniform stood off to one side and a group of firefighters were nearby. Ana and Caleb sat on the curb; the rough concrete dug into Ana's thighs.

Slowly Ana twisted to look behind her. A sob barreled through her chest and escaped her mouth. Their home. The home they'd lived in since Ana was a baby was gone. Burned to the ground. All that remained was a smoldering foundation. Smoke mixed with steam as a couple of firefighters doused hot spots.

"Nooooo!" she screamed.

Ana had no idea where she'd been. Her mind had no memory of the fire or the destruction around them. This didn't happen. She wasn't there. She didn't know when or how she came to be sitting on the curb with her brother.

Her mind focused. She was supposed to be watching her baby brother. And their mom.

"Where's my MOM?!" Ana screamed.

The woman from the newspaper looked perplexed. She let the camera hang around her neck with a colorful strap. She came and sat next to Ana and patted her back. It felt forced, like she read somewhere that this is what she should do but she didn't quite know how.

A cop stepped closer to them. He was tall and sturdy; he had a cropped haircut and a big walkie-talkie strapped to his chest. His eyes were ringed red; he hung his head. That's when Ana knew.

"Noooooo!" she screamed again. Ana tried to jump up, but Caleb clung to her legs with more force than she expected his two-year-old body to have.

"Ana, I'm so sorry. Your mom. She uh. She didn't get out in time. The fire started near her in the kitchen; that's where we found her. It was too hot, too fast. She died, Ana."

Ana looked down at her hands; they were red and raw. Small blisters grew along her palms. Her skin felt like it was on fire. Only when she paid attention to them did she notice how much they hurt. Tears rolled down her cheeks. She patted Caleb's back. Her hands exploded in pain.

"But Ana, you were such a blessing to Caleb's life. You saved your brother. There is no way he would have made it out of the house had it not been for you," the cop was saying. The reporter gave an encouraging smile.

Ana rubbed her skinny legs. She'd never been told she was anything but trouble.

A guttural scream echoed off the neighborhood houses and shot right in Ana's ears. Bex. Ana's heart sped up and her cheeks grew hot. She dipped her head in between her legs and tried to keep the nausea at bay.

"Ohhhh, my god!" her sister screamed. She ran down the street, carrying her high heels. Her curled blonde hair fluttered around her face and her red homecoming dress climbed higher on her thigh with each stride.

"Ana! What did you do?" Bex demanded. Soon she was on Ana, pushing her shoulders with both hands. The curb dug further into Ana's calves. "Ana! You had one job. It was your fucking turn to watch Mom! Where is she?"

Tears welled in her eyes and a sob built in her chest. Air refused to fill Ana's lungs. "Ana! Where is mom?"

3

Ana rocked back and forth. She couldn't answer her sister. She didn't know any more than Bex did. It was a blank, black slate where her memory should have been. The night still smelled of smoke.

"I. I. I don't know," Ana said. The words wouldn't come out any faster than her memories did.

The cop stepped between them. He put a hand on Bex's shoulder. "I'm sorry, but your mother. Your mother. She uh," he started.

"She what?! Where is she?" Bex said. She took a step back.

"She. She didn't make it. There was a fire, she didn't make it out. I'm really sorry."

Bex collapsed in the street in a puddle of big hair and red sequins. "Ana! How could you?!"

"Miss, it was just a tragic accident," the cop said.

"Annnnna!" Bex wailed. "You were supposed to watch Mom. It was your night!"

"I'm sorry," the cop offered again. He didn't know the extent of it; that much was clear. It was all Ana's fault. "It's a miracle she was able to get Caleb out, though."

Tears streamed down Bex's face. "But not our mom. Ana, how could you?!"

Ana didn't have an answer.

ONE

Ana's heart thrummed in her chest. Meeting a guy in the woods was a reckless idea. She'd read more than enough thriller books to know that thinking with your heart instead of your brain was the fastest way to land your face on a missing person's poster.

The old beater car chugged up the foothills. Music played softly from her phone and Ana wished once again that she could afford a car that had an auxiliary port. A ding interrupted the melody and Ana dared a glance at the screen.

I'm here! It's beautiful. Good suggestion James texted.

Ana wiped the sweat from her palms on her black yoga pants. A smile broke across her face with anticipation. She was finally going to meet James in person. James. They'd met plenty of times over Zoom and chatted on the phone but meeting him in person - at her favorite place - she hadn't seen that coming when she woke up early to write.

The butterflies multiplied in her belly.

The old Ana would have found any excuse to avoid him. She would have been too shy. This would have felt too forward. This Ana? She was driving up the hill to meet a perfect stranger. A stranger she felt something for.

This Ana didn't even tell her sister where she was going. Some part of her knew they should do something normal like meet at a coffee shop or walk in a park, but the other part of her didn't care. She wanted to show James the best part of her, and that would be easiest in the place she felt most comfortable.

Ana hearted his message and used voice-to-text to let him know that she'd be there in ten. She looked herself over in the rearview mirror. Her blonde hair was pulled back into a pony with loose strands framing her face. Ana pushed them back and did her best to make it look chic. She licked her fingers and pressed the remaining few into her scalp.

The Three Sisters Park sign caught her eye; a fresh round of outdoorsy stickers covered half the letters. Ana drove into the parking lot. It was early but the trailhead already had a couple of SUVs. James wasn't leaning against a car, basking in the sun like she'd imagined. She couldn't tell which was his. She picked a place next to the welcome sign and turned off the engine.

Ana grabbed her backpack off the passenger seat and glanced at herself in the mirror one more time. A knock startled her. She turned and found James standing next to her car. Her heart began to race, she had no idea where he'd come from.

He smiled big and she forced her mind to slow down. He opened the door and said, "Hey," in a quiet voice. His eyes went up and down her, landing on Ana's face. Her cheeks bloomed with heat.

Ana pulled herself out of the car and slung her backpack on her shoulder. "Hey," she managed. Awkwardness killed the butterflies. Disappointment replaced her feelings; she was expecting a big hug, a sweet kiss. Something magical.

She stole a look at him. Skinny jeans clung to his legs, and he wore Converse shoes with the laces tied around his ankles. He had a thin but leanly muscular build, no taller than Ana herself. A vintage Nirvana logo adorned his shirt. His big blue eyes were more intense than she thought. Ana found the way his blonde hair and a little bit of a birthmark snuck out of his Carhartt beanie impossible to resist.

Ana pulled her backpack up higher on her back and motioned toward the trail. "Should we do it? The main trail is an easy loop around a pretty lake. I still can't believe something so beautiful exists so close to Denver."

He shuffled his feet; a plume of dust hung in the morning light. "Let's get to it," he said.

She forced a smile and started walking toward the trailhead. She pushed away the small voice in her head that screamed to stay out of the woods with a stranger.

"Glad this worked out, thanks for thinking of me," Ana said.

"Thanks for meeting me on a whim."

"How was the flight?" she asked.

"Oh fine. O'Hare was busy as usual but no delays."

Ana glanced at the map, three miles around and back. If they walked slowly, she'd have a couple of hours with him. She smiled again.

"So, you're working in Denver?" Ana asked.

"Yeah, just here for a few days. There's a restaurantprenuer that owns a few joints in downtown - LoDo, like you locals call it. He wants to start a podcast so I'm here to help him get all set up and then we'll handle the rest virtually like I do for you and your sister."

"You never came out and got us started," Ana said. She jostled him a little bit with her shoulder. He stepped away. Embarrassment colored her cheeks.

"Well, I didn't need to. You and Bex had already started the show without me, remember? This guy needed me to set up his recording equipment and stuff."

"Oh yeah, you found us. Said you needed to build up your portfolio or something like that," Ana said with a laugh. James smirked.

"Well, it worked. I have more clients than time now," he said.

"Of course it worked. My sister and I have the best true crime pod out there," Ana said.

"I agree."

"No, I'm just kidding. We're nowhere close to those Murderinos or Junkies but maybe someday."

"You'll get there."

They passed by a strong-smelling outhouse and made their way onto the shaded path. The drop in temperature made a ripple of goosebumps break out over her arms.

James stopped and turned his head toward the mountains. "It sure is pretty here."

"I know. That's why I love it. I found this park when we first moved here. I come all the time."

"It's not even busy," he said. His words sent a shiver down her back. She ignored it.

"I know, we're lucky. I guess being a Wednesday morning helps."

"Most people are at work," he said.

"Not us!" she whooped and put her hand up to give him a high five. He kept walking. She lowered her arm and shoved her hand into her pocket.

They walked in silence for a while longer. The trail was narrow between tall pines, forcing them to walk close to one another. Every time their bodies brushed each other, Ana wanted to reach out and grab his hand. He kept them firmly in his pocket.

"So, the show is going okay?" James asked.

"Yeah, it's fine. Bex loves doing it. She wants to make it way bigger. That's why she wants to do that live podcast recording show."

"I can't wait for that. It's a good idea. I'm glad I can come back out for it."

"It'll be here soon," Ana said. She looked off into the trees, suddenly filled with anxiety about the whole thing. She hated the idea of recording a podcast live and didn't want to do it in front of James.

"Do you guys have it planned?"

"Not really, Bex booked the place. That's about it."

"What are you going to record about?"

"I don't know yet. A famous unsolved Colorado case, I think."

"Which one? There are a few."

Ana racked her brain. She couldn't even remember many of the options she and Bex had come up with. "I don't know. Maybe JonBenét."

He looked at her dead in the eyes; his thoughts were unreadable. "That one seems too obvious."

"Okay, then maybe Jennifer Larsen."

He let out a little grumble. "That one is too old, too obscure."

She chewed her lip in frustration. This wasn't how she thought the morning would go. "Okay, then what do you suggest?" she asked.

He rubbed his chin. "The Denver Prostitute Killer?"

"I don't know, maybe. I'll just let Bex decide. This is her thing anyway," Ana finally said. "I'll focus on my books."

"I mean, they go hand in hand, right?" He asked.

"You sound like Bex."

He lifted one side of his mouth in a half smile. His first all morning.

"How are the books anyway? They should be more famous."

Her ears perked. She liked that he was paying attention.

"The books are good. I'm working on a few things. It's just hard. Harder than I imagined. I thought that since I wrote for the paper, writing books would be just as easy. I was wrong though; It's been a slow start. The only reason I can keep doing it is because my sister lets me live rent-free."

"Hey, everyone wishes they had a sister like that," he said.

He looked back at her, his eyes were dark, narrow. Ana realized she knew very little about him or his family. She wanted to know him better.

"Yeah, I'm pretty lucky," Ana finally said. He nodded.

They pushed deeper into the woods. Another shiver spread across Ana's body in the cool air. She suddenly felt very isolated.

"I know what you need," he said after a while. She looked up.

"You need to go viral!"

"That's harder than winning the lottery," she said.

He stopped walking in the middle of the trail and faced her. Ana's heart sped up and tingling broke out across her whole body. His eyes searched hers, and she wondered if he was finally going to kiss her.

"I've seen it for a hundred different authors on TikTok. Something just needs to happen to get people's attention."

TWO

The ding of new meeting invitations, emails arriving unceremoniously in her inbox, and Teams calls filled Bex's days at her Denver startup. She spent the morning training a new report about the ins and outs of their platform - "Product Xponential," a one-stop shop, enterprise-level marketing cloud, designed to bring the future of marketing to mid-sized businesses.

Bex didn't love her job, but she did love the perks. She'd quickly climbed from some laughable sales gig to her role as the lead sales trainer. It was her job to teach all the new sales folks just how to describe Xponential and how to sell it. The more successful her reports were, the more money she brought home. And lately, the team was bringing it home.

Sometime after Bex sent Vance off for lunch, she absentmindedly opened a new tab to check her email. The inbox was filled with hundreds of political ads and online stores promising big sales. She selected them all before an old email caught her eye. It was a message from AncestryAndMe, sent to her over a month ago. "New Match!" teased in the subject line.

She hovered her pointer over the email and wondered if she should open it or trash it. Months ago when she submitted her DNA, it felt like a good idea. Now, with a match waiting in her inbox, she almost regretted submitting her sample.

She and Ana were in a good spot. Ana was writing. Bex had recently started hanging out with the hottest girl in the office. In their last one-on-one, her boss, Theo, teased a promotion soon. What if this match knocked Ana off her progress? Did Bex need to blow all that up in the quest for answers?

Something pulled at her. Bex had to know. They were all adults now and their brother, Caleb, was out there somewhere. Finding him would mean it could be the three of them again. They could have a real family.

Bex opened the email and her eyes rushed over the page. She had a match and that match had sent her a message. She clicked.

The screen took forever to load. Bex chewed her fingernail, fighting the urge to bite down and break the acrylic covering her natural nails. Instead, she looked around the office. She hated how open she felt in the middle of the sea of other desks. Could people see her screen? Would they know what she was looking at?

Bex pulled herself closer to her desk, using her body to shield the page. The dashboard finally loaded. Bex's breath caught in her throat and her fingers began to shake over the keyboard. A red number one covered the little envelope icon on the top, right side of her screen.

She clicked into her inbox. The name Caleb Dukes stared back at her. Over the month, he'd sent a whole slew of messages.

Hey, Bex. Caleb here. If I'm reading our results right, we're half-siblings. Hi. The first one said.

Her stomach jumped into her throat.

The page was filled with messages from him, but Bex's eyes wouldn't focus beyond the first one. Questions clouded her mind. What was he like? Did he look like them? What had his childhood been like? Would he be mad that they'd abandoned him? How would Ana take all of this? Bex wasn't sure that she was ready for any of it.

Bex took a minute to let the reality of finding her brother digest. She sent up a silent prayer that he'd had a happy life, that his adoptive family was so much better than where Ana and Bex had come from. She prayed that he was less messed up.

I was adopted but I've been looking for my birth family since I was 18. My parents didn't give me much to go on, but I remember some stuff. I finally got this match the other day. His next message said. Her eyes welled with tears. Her brother was on the other side of the screen.

I couldn't help it. The next message said. *I looked you up online. I found your podcast. Love that you host with our sister. Cool!*

Bex felt a wave of protection for Ana wash over her. Ana was so much more fragile. If Bex told her sister about their brother, Caleb, that could very well shoot her over the edge. Ana didn't need any more disruptions or drama. For the first time in a long time, she was finally doing okay. Bex couldn't jeopardize that.

And Bex didn't need another sibling to take care of.

Bex debated closing the window. She could feel that she'd just opened a can of worms and she hated herself for it. Why had she let herself even submit her sample in the first place? It was so stupid, and she knew it. Things were moving too fast.

And it's true crime? Even better! The next message said.

Bex's mouth went dry. She felt violated. Of course, Bex knew that a simple search of her name would bring their podcast up on Google results, but still. It felt wrong. She wasn't ready for him to know all that.

And Ana is an author. Getting cooler by the minute.

Bex's hands shook. This all felt like too much. They'd barely matched a few days ago. How did he already know so much?

You there? He asked. Bex wondered if the AncestryAndMe website would tell him whether she'd read the messages.

Bex took a drink of water. The coolness of it slid down her throat. She still didn't know what to say. She and Caleb shared DNA but he felt like nothing more than a stranger. She didn't want to continue reading.

So, can we meet up? I'm actually in Wyoming nowadays. I'm not that far from you two. I could road trip. I gotta get to know my two creepy sisters!

Bex did the quick math in her head. Depending on where he was in Wyoming, he was only a few hours away from Denver. That made her even more uncomfortable. She turned in her seat to see if any of her colleagues were watching. Everyone had on headphones and seemed to be lost in the grind. She turned back around.

"Hey, Bex - I'm back," someone said behind her. She quickly closed her laptop and found her trainee behind her. Bex put on a smile and forced herself to still.

"Hey, Vance. How was lunch?"

"Good, just went to that pho place around the corner, I have a feeling I'll go there a lot." She nodded and he plunked down in the chair next to her.

She twisted her laptop away from him so he couldn't see her messages. She logged out of her AncestryAndMe profile without responding to Caleb. She would deal with him later.

THREE

The lake was even prettier in the morning. The sun caught the seiches, making the water glisten. The snowcapped mountains practically loomed over them. The city sprawled out before their eyes on the plains below. Her face warmed and the shake in her hands finally settled. Ana felt lighter than she had in a long time, she felt like she was right where she belonged. She just wished James felt the same.

James and Ana stood side by side. Something pushed her toward him. He seemed rooted to the ground; he barely looked her way and when he did, the muscles in his face were taut under his skin. She so badly wanted to catch his smile.

"This lake is called Diamond Lake, its name fits," Ana said. His whole body tensed next to her. Questions were on the tip of her tongue. Why did he invite her out here if he was going to give her the cold shoulder?

Ana made herself smile. "Do you like Colorado so far?"

James picked up a rock and threw it into the water. It landed with a splash and a ripple. "Yeah, how could you not? I love how peaceful it is here. If this park was in Chicago, this area would be overrun with people, even on a Wednesday."

Ana's anxiety started talking in her head. Her brain was convinced that this would be the moment that James pulled a knife out of his back pocket and slit her throat. He was bigger and leaner than her, she couldn't outrun him.

Bex came to her mind. Ana wished she would have at least told Bex where she was going and with whom. She missed her sister; Ana needed Bex to help regulate her body.

Ana pushed her palms into her eyes and told her brain to knock it off. She had simply watched far too many true crime documentaries and read a few too many cheesy thrillers. She told herself that their story had just begun, there was no way it would happen. They just needed more time.

"So, how are things with Bex?" James asked. The question came out of left field.

"Oh, fine. She's doing well at work and all that."

"What's she like?" He asked. Ana turned the question over in her mind. It felt out of place.

"I don't know. You've met her through the podcast stuff. She's intense and hellbent on success but she's the most loyal, true person I know. I wouldn't be here without her."

He cleared his throat but didn't say anything. He pushed dirt around until he found a flat rock. Standing, he skipped it across the lake; it bounced once and then twice before petering out.

"Maybe when you're here for the live show, we could do this again?"

"Maybe."

Ana licked her lips and realized she never put on sunscreen. Her skin felt hot and tight across her face. She wished she grabbed a hat at least.

She pulled her hair back with her hands and began to wrangle the wavy mess into a bun on top of her hair. In the process, she dropped a hair band into the ground. It landed next to James as he looked for his next skipping rock.

She pulled her hair back with her hands and began to wrangle the wavy mess into a bun on top of her hair. In the process, she dropped a hair band into the ground. It landed next to James as he looked for his next skipping rock.

"Hey check this out," he said, straightening quickly as he threw a perfect six-skip stone. Ana was impressed. James had a natural athleticism and there was a glint of happiness in his eyes.

"Nice work—you've always got a backup career in rock tossing," Ana laughed.

"I spent a good chunk of my twenties stoned – I've got some experience," James laughed too. He started to walk along the lakeside path in a suddenly brisk pace. Ana hurried to keep up, feeling a quick flash of guilt over littering her hair band but not wanting to be left behind. Her mind clouded with confusion. He'd done nothing but send mixed messages all day. She told herself to relax.

After another couple minutes James stopped, pulled another rock from his pocket and made another throw. Ana used the pause to give herself a hair twist, letting it fall unencumbered down her back. She wondered what James was thinking.

He turned back to her and flashed his widest smile, "I like your hair down better anyway" he said.

FOUR

Bex sat at the kitchen table at home drinking a full pour of a juicy cab from the pantry. She fit pieces of a Denver skyline puzzle into place as she worked. Bex hoped the alcohol would give her the courage to write her brother back. The wine hit her empty stomach and sloshed around; it relaxed her body but not her mind.

The messages hung over her like a dark, foreboding cloud. She knew she needed to respond to Caleb, but she had a sense that nothing good would come from it. Ultimately, the call of being the oldest sister won. She opened her inbox before she could change her mind. Her brother had sent a whole slew of new messages.

Did I chase you off? I just want to get to know my sisters. I don't understand why you aren't replying. I've been looking for you forever.
Bex? Where are you?
Can I please come meet you and Ana?

A tornado of emotions hit her all at once. Tears formed in the corners of her eyes again and the wine revolted in her stomach.

His last message read *Why you gotta be like this? I could even be on your show, we could have an episode all about our fucked up story.*

Bex tried to picture bringing Caleb into their lives. She couldn't imagine it. Just his first few messages told Bex that he was like Ana - unstable. He would completely disrupt whatever little peace they'd created.

Bex's priority was her sister. It always would be. It had to be. Bex never told Ana that she submitted her DNA, and this was confirmation that she made the right choice. Bex decided right then and there that she wouldn't tell Ana about Caleb. The news would set Ana off, maybe be the catalyst for her next spiral. Bex didn't even know if she could handle Caleb herself.

It was decided. Bex had to find a way to keep Caleb from them. She closed the window and decided not to message him. It was painful and the guilt intensified, she just couldn't square her two siblings in her mind, and she couldn't picture them in the same room.

Bex picked Ana.

The wine swirled around in her glass and Bex took another long drink. She picked up a blue piece and tried to match it somewhere in the sky. Bex checked her phone; Ana still hadn't replied. Bex didn't like the feeling of coming home to an empty house. Ana should be there.

Bex paced around the house. Both her siblings were making her feel out of sorts.

The sound of the garage door opening made Bex jump. It only took one look at Ana for Bex to realize that something was up with her sister. Her skin was pink, her eyes were shiny. Her blonde hair was loose, tossed wild around her face. She looked almost happy.

"Where have you been?" Bex asked.

"I just went for a hike at Three Sisters."

Bex took another drink and thought about Ana's answer. That place was special to both of them, and they went often. Always together. It was their place. Bex looked her sister up and down. She was still so thin, so stringy. Everyone always said they looked alike, but Bex couldn't see it.

Ana was the all-natural version of them - no makeup, never fixed her hair, dressed in the same clothes she'd owned since high school. Bex preferred to accentuate their features with the right clothes and hair, and a little help from fillers. Bex hated how gaunt her sister looked. How frail. Bex hated being compared to Ana.

19

"Who did you go with?"

"Just by myself," Ana said. "Wanted to get out of the house." Ana immediately busied herself with filling up her water bottle. Ana didn't dare look at Bex. She was lying.

Ana pulled her backpack off her shoulders and hung it on the rack by the back door. Her shoulders were a little pink and so was her forehead. She must have been gone for a good chunk of the day.

"Why are you home early?" Ana asked. Bex looked at the clock. It was only 2 PM. Bex bit her lip, she'd left work earlier than she thought she had.

"Oh, I was just having one of those days. I blocked my whole day to train a new guy, but it didn't take as long as I thought it would. So, I came home."

"Cool. Did it go okay?"

"Yeah, Vance is his name. He was a quick learner."

Ana hummed to herself as she unlaced her hiking books. The sound hit Bex square in the chest. What had made Ana happy enough to hum?

"You hiked alone? What's gotten into you?"

Ana let out a little giggle. "Actually, James is in town, and he invited me, so I went with him." Her face reddened and a big smile broke her face in half.

"What? James from the podcast?"

"Yeah. This morning. It was spur of the moment."

Bex stood up. The wine hit her hard and she had to put out a hand to steady herself on the kitchen table. "Ana! Are you fucking dumb? You didn't even tell me where you were going. What if he kidnapped you or something?"

"Oh, Bex. Don't be ridiculous. I'm here. I'm fine."

Bex grabbed her sister by the shoulders and shook her. "Ana, really? You gotta tell me where you're going and who you're going with. I need to know."

Ana took a step back. Her face clouded over. "Chill Bex. I'm a grownup. You're my sister, not my mom. I promise I'm fine."

"Oh, for fuck's sake, Ana. We have a true crime podcast. You write murder mysteries. You know how stupid it is to go to the woods with a perfect stranger. You could have easily been made into an episode of your own."

"Bex, take it down a notch. It was just James. We know him." She blushed again.

"Might I remind you - we've never met him in person."

"I have now. It was fun to hang out with him. There might be a little something there," Ana said. Her face warmed with hope.

"Where is my sister? And what have you done with her?" Bex said. Ana busied herself with unloading her backpack.

"So, did he try to kidnap you?" Bex said.

"No, Bex. It was good. I'm glad he asked me to go. It was a little awkward at first, but by the end, it felt right."

"I guess we better have dinner so you can tell me every last detail," Bex said. Anxiety swirled in Bex's mind. She didn't trust Ana's judgment.

Dinner proved Bex correct. Ana gushed about James without bothering to throw one single caution to the wind. The longer they sat at the table, the tighter Bex's stomach cramped. Her sister was dancing into dangerous territory and if experience had taught Bex anything it was that her sister's highest of the highs were just as precarious as the lows.

FIVE

The curling iron felt awkward, useless in her hand. She could not figure out how to twist in a way that made her hair full of effortless loose curls instead of the tight spirals that looked like she just walked out of a perm appointment. Over the years, Ana had watched Bex do it hundreds of times, but Ana could not recreate what her sister was able to do. She unplugged the cord and dropped the tool into the sink.

"Screw it," she said under her breath as she brushed her hair back and clipped it in place. She tugged at the sides of her hair and tried to frame her face angelically as Bex told her to do once.

Ana grabbed an old tube of lipstick and ringed her lips with a shade of muted pink. The sound of Bex's door opening broke the silence; Ana dropped the lid in the sink with a loud clunk.

"Damnit," she said as she fished it out from under the curling iron.

"Whoa," Bex said as she walked past the bathroom. Ana mustered a smile but didn't explain.

"What are you getting ready for?" Bex asked.

Ana put the lid back on the lipstick. She rolled the cord up and put the curling iron under the sink. Ana smoothed down her red dress and fiddled with her hair one more time before meeting her sister's eyes.

"I have plans," Ana said. She pulled her dress down and tried to make it lay right against her midsection.

"I see that. With whom, might I ask?" Bex asked.

"James and I are going to FaceTime tonight."

Bex turned and let out a huff. "I thought we were going to record a new episode today," she said as she walked toward the kitchen.

Ana felt that familiar panic taking over her system. The one where she knew it was her job to make peace with her sister, to keep Bex happy. Ana didn't want to.

"We can record later," Ana said.

Bex grabbed her phone off the counter; a small smile escaped before she put her hard mask back on. "I'll order the Thai now. We can record real quick and then you can do your little date," Bex said.

"No, James and I are already on for 6 PM."

"What is this? AOL Dating from the 90s? People are more flexible these days; he can wait," Bex said. She laughed but there was no humor in it.

"Sure, but I really want to talk to James tonight so we can record our next episode later. Maybe tomorrow?"

"I'll be busy tomorrow," Bex said.

"With what?"

"I'm going out," Bex answered. There was finality in her voice.

Ana pushed anyway. "With who?"

"Just a friend," Bex said. She didn't look up from her phone.

"So, let me get this straight. You forced me to tell you everything about James the other day, but you won't even tell me who you're going out with? What happened to - *we're sisters, we tell each other everything!*" Ana mocked.

"This is different!"

Ana laughed. Hard. Tears threatened in her eyes. Bex couldn't even see how ridiculously hypocritical she was being.

"What's so funny? Pray tell," Bex cried.

"You don't see it, do you. You don't trust me with an inch of freedom, but the rules are nonexistent for you. Why do you care that I'm going to FaceTime with James tonight when you clearly have someone on the side that you won't even admit to."

"I don't have someone on the side!" Bex yelled. Ana could see her sister's face getting redder by the minute, but she couldn't stop. Ana ignored the warnings her brain emanated.

"You have someone, and we both know it. You're texting constantly lately and you're always smiling at your phone. You've been distracted lately. Take the podcast for a perfect example. If you weren't preoccupied, you would have had us all scheduled for tonight instead of vaguely mentioning it in passing," Ana shot back.

"I don't have to answer you!"

"But I must tell you what I'm doing and where I'm going all the time?"

"I know what I'm doing, okay?" Bex said. Her voice was low and cold.

"And I don't? Thanks a lot, Bex."

"Oh, please. We both know you don't have a great track record," Bex said. "If and when it makes sense to introduce you to her, I will."

The word 'her' flashed in Ana's mind. Bex had someone and apparently that someone was a girl. Ana wanted to ask a million more questions but the look on Bex's face told her not to push her luck.

"Well, let me know when that might be," Ana said. Bex's thumbs flew over her screen, intent on whatever message she was drafting.

"I'm going to go call James now. Maybe we'll record after," Ana said as she walked out of the kitchen. She didn't wait for her sister's response.

Ana slammed the door to her room and leaned her head back against the wood. It was cool and the door felt solid compared to her racing mind. Ana needed to get Bex out of her head so she could focus on James.

She messed with her hair and tried out different angles to see which worked best. She clicked James' contact. The video chat connected, and he answered with a smile.

"Sorry, I thought I had a few minutes," he said. His hair was wet, and his cheeks were red. She forced herself to look at his eyes.

"I called early. I just couldn't wait," she admitted. "I can call you back in a few."

"No, no this is fine," he said. He sat down in an office chair, heavily. Ana couldn't see much behind him, but it looked like he was in his room. She felt a pang of desire to be with him.

"How are you?" she asked.

"I'm good. I'm good. How are you?"

"I'm good. Busy day. I just wanted to check in on you and Bex? How's the podcast?" He asked. Something fell inside Ana. Ever since his text asking to FaceTime, she'd imagined a date. Not business.

"Oh, it's fine. Bex wanted to record tonight but I had this with you," she said.

"So, you're going to record after this?" he asked.

"Maybe."

"You should. Your next one is due."

"And what if I don't?" she asked, letting a small smile play on her lips. He didn't reciprocate.

"Well, you'll let listeners down and your show will never reach new audiences."

She rearranged herself on the bed, aiming to get her face into the soft evening light coming from the window. She hoped he noticed.

"I hate to break it to you and Bex, but I fear the show is never going to take off," Ana said.

"Like I said, it will if you go viral."

SIX

The laces of her shoes pressed against her foot; Bex pulled them tighter and tied the strings with practiced efficiency. She shoved her AirPods in her ears and stepped outside. On the porch, she did a half stretch and started running. She couldn't listen to her sister flirt on the phone for one more second.

Every time her foot smashed into the ground, a thought pounded into Bex's head. Ana was being reckless. Bex knew it in her bones, she'd seen this before. If Bex didn't get her sister under control, something was going to happen. Ana's love interests had always been like this - fast and furious, and definitely misguided.

Ana's life imploded the moment her love bomb exploded. Depression hit hard and fast, and her judgment clouded over like a Colorado prairie storm. Bex could already see thunderheads building on the horizon.

Bex wondered if she needed to call Ana's therapist, Dr. Daniels. They'd worked together over the years to handle all of Ana's baggage - her trauma, getting laid off from the paper, and her weird blackouts. Bex thought he might be able to take Ana's manic state down a notch and save them from a deadly fall.

Her path took her past a mom pushing her two young daughters in a stroller. As Bex passed, she heard the little girls singing their ABCs, laughing and giggling. The mom helped them when they got stuck on P. It gave Bex a pang of sadness. The family seemed so happy, so normal. Bex pushed herself to run faster.

It wasn't the run that made Bex's chest ache. It was the missed memories. Bex and Ana, they'd never had the chance to be a normal family with an engaged mom.

As Bex looped around the neighborhood, her mind kept running back to Caleb. She repeated his messages over and over. All these years, she let herself believe that Caleb was adopted and lived a happy, normal life. She hated that his words told a different story. Maybe he wasn't so lucky either.

Her chest heaved and her legs tingled as she rounded the corner back on their street. She checked her watch; Bex had done the whole loop five minutes faster than her usual pace.

Bex pushed open the front door. She collapsed onto the couch, her chest rising and falling. A sheen of sweat layered her skin. She stuck to the leather-like glue. Bex leaned her head back and listened. The house was quiet, Ana was off the phone.

"This kiss, this kiss!" Ana belted out at the top of her lungs. Bex groaned. Ana wasn't the sing-out-loud kind of person, and certainly not the kind that sang love songs. It wasn't a good sign.

The couch made a sick ripping sound as her thighs peeled from the leather. She walked to the hall closet and grabbed the podcast recording equipment. It was time to regain control.

"Ana! We're recording," Bex yelled over the music beating from Ana's room.

"Unstoppable!" Ana called back. Ana turned the music up louder. Bex rolled her eyes.

"It's time! We already decided this."

Bex pulled each of their microphones out of the box in the closet and carried them to the living room. She got to work setting up each of their recording spots as they'd always done. She walked back to her room to grab her laptop, knocking on Ana's door as she passed.

"What? I told you no," Ana called through the door. Bex had a sudden flashback to them as teens, fighting over something stupid like who would watch their mom for the evening.

Bex grabbed her laptop and slipped it under her arm. She walked back to Ana's door and turned the knob. Bex was surprised to find it unlocked.

Ana didn't hear the door open over the sound of Faith Hill screeching through the speakers. Bex found Ana in the middle of the room playing air guitar, her hair wild and the room around her an even bigger mess.

Bex's stomach dropped. This was the manic high Bex feared. Ana was using the curling iron to sing; her eyes and hair were wild, room, total chaos. Ana at her best self was calm and reserved. At worst, Ana was down in the gutter, ready to die. At the very worst, she was like this. Higher than a kite. Not from drugs, but from the high of life. Frenzied and completely reckless. The higher she was, the harder the fall would be.

Ana's complex mental health was a puzzle, and even though she'd spent years in and out of therapy, Ana still didn't think she had a problem. The therapists did though. They had tried to slap all kinds of diagnoses on her over the years. Regardless of the acronyms, this dancing was surely some harbinger of what was to come.

Bex crossed the room and grabbed her sister's arm. Ana stopped mid-riff and turned, breaking her arm free of Bex's grasp in the process. Her face went from pure bliss to red mad within seconds of turning.

"I said I'm not doing it," Ana said between clenched teeth.

"I know, but we have to. We have a schedule to keep."

"I will do it later," Ana said. "Can't you see I'm busy here?"

"You're dancing in your room to a song that came out before Mom died. You're not busy."

"I'm celebrating!"

"What? What do you have to celebrate?"

Ana turned away from Bex and went back to swinging her hips, dancing with an imaginary person in her room.

"I got to talk to James AND I'm nearly at 10k followers on Instagram. I have a lot to celebrate!" Ana yelled over the music.

Bex reached out and turned it off.

"Hey!" Ana yelled. She pulled Bex's hand from the stereo.

"Just record with me tonight and then we'll be done for a whole week. It's easy," Bex said. Ana felt slippery; Bex was desperate to hold onto what she could.

"I don't even have anything to talk about. I haven't researched a case," Ana said. Her voice sounded whiny, like a little kid's.

"Yes, you do. You have plenty in your little notebook. Just pick one. I'll jump in where I need to, it will be fine." Bex spotted the notebook in question on Ana's desk. She plunked it from under the papers and tucked it under her arm as she grabbed Ana by the arm. Bex pulled Ana to the living room. Ana braced herself but she was no match for Bex.

"I don't want to!" Ana screamed as they struggled down the hall.

"You have to. I let you talk to James and now let's do this!" Bex said. Bex pulled Ana to the couch and sat her in her seat. Bex stood near her sister, waiting for her to run. Bex handed Ana her notebook.

"James agreed with you. You two are ganging up on me," Ana said. She turned her face into a pout.

"Really?" Bex asked. She sat in her seat.

"Yeah, he said we need another episode," Ana said. She flipped through her pages, looking for a cold case to cover.

"Well, then let's do it. Two against one."

"Fine. I guess we could do Maggie Long. That one is still kind of fresh in people's minds."

Bex snapped her fingers. Sounded great. "Let's do it," she said.

Ana pulled on her headphones and positioned her notebook in her lap. Bex's jaw unclenched a little. Bex reached for her headphones and slipped them into place.

"Hello and welcome to *The Serial Syndicate*," Ana said into the microphone.

SEVEN

All day long, Ana struggled to focus. The words wouldn't come, and it felt as if there was a block on top of her fingers. She could barely write a sentence. The clock ticked slowly while the anticipation ate at her. When it finally crossed five, Ana called it a day. She abandoned her characters in-scene and found her sister in the living room. Ana sat next to her on the couch.

"It's going to happen today," Ana announced.

"Tell me!"

"I'm going to hit ten thousand followers."

"Whaaaat! Let's go, boo!"

The number changed to 9,999. @authoranadams only needed one more follower for the dream to be real, for the line in the sand to be crossed. Ana was almost there, her fingers tingled with anticipation. She licked her lips; she was almost there and her whole body could feel it.

"Do it! Check now!" Bex cried. Ana looked at her sister. She was as radiant as ever. Everyone said they looked so much alike - blonde hair, big glassy eyes, but Ana couldn't see it.

The phone sat propped between them, illuminating the soft evening dark of the space. They had spent the day waiting for this moment, waiting for Ana to cross the mark.

Ana couldn't wait a moment longer. She jittered in her seat. She slid her finger down the screen and watched the pinwheel twirl at the top of the page. A moment of panic swept over her, sure that all her hard work was going to be Zuckerberged right off the app by the man himself with one too many refreshes. Ana plucked the phone from the table and brought it closer. Just as the panic started to spread, the screen loaded. Her mind couldn't quite grasp what was right under her nose.

"TEN THOUSAND FOLLOWERS, ANA!" Bex yelled. She jumped up from the table and whooped and hollered around the kitchen. "Ten thousand! How many indie authors can say that? I'm so proud of you!"

Ana stared at the screen. Her eyes swam around the statistics listed on the professional dashboard page. The number listed in the total followers category was too good to be true - 10,001. This was the magic number. She'd done it. She reached that golden goose metric that all wannabe book influencers had been clamoring for since the early days of Bookstagram.

"Ana! You did it," Bex said again. Ana set her phone down on the table.

Ana stood and jumped up and down. She laughed so hard that tears of joy rolled down her face.

Bex ran to the kitchen and grabbed the bottle of champagne. "Do you feel like you can handle a bit of this?" she asked. Ana had to force herself to take a deep breath. She didn't get why Bex was treating her like an invalid all the sudden.

"Yes, Bex. One glass isn't going to hurt me," Ana said. She followed her sister into the kitchen.

"Okay, just checking." Bex twisted the lid off with a thunk.

The sweet smell of celebration filled their tiny kitchen. Bex jabbed a glass in Ana's direction, it was noticeably less full than Bex's glass. Ana swallowed another round of annoyance.

Bex pushed her glass Ana's way with a clink of their glasses. "I did it," Ana said after taking a big gulp. She still couldn't believe it. The champagne was sweet; she liked the way the bubbles popped on the roof of her mouth.

"It was all those follow trains," Bex said with a laugh.

"I know. I felt skeezy every single time I posted one, but they worked."

"They worked! Look at you!" Bex grabbed Ana's empty glass from the table. She didn't refill it.

"I do have to say, I think it's the podcast, too. That last episode got like 300 listens. Surely that little blurb James had you add in at the end about your books and social channels helped," Bex said as she washed the glasses in the sink.

"Maybe," Ana said. She found *This Is How We Do It* by Montell Jordan and blasted it from YouTube. Ana let loose and danced around the kitchen. She could feel Bex's eyes tracking her across the room. Bex didn't join. Ana screamed along with the words.

Before the song reached the chorus again, Bex grabbed Ana's phone and paused the music. Ana stopped dancing and tried to grab her phone from her sister's hand. Bex pulled it away too fast.

"Hey! I was dancing."

"I know, but we're talking. I want you to understand this - the podcast is on fire and we both know it. If you would just stop fighting me about it, it would help your author business so much more! You'd get a lot of followers then!"

"Let's flip the track, bring the old school back. This is how we do it," Ana sang as she danced around the kitchen.

Bex poured herself another full glass of bubbly. She didn't even ask Ana if she wanted any. "Hey, what about me!" Ana cried.

"You can have more later," Bex said. Ana hated the way her sister was treating her like a child.

"Wait, I'm not being a very good influencer right now," Ana said. "Can I have my phone back? Give me more champ; we can cheers and post it!"

That tactic worked. Bex handed over Ana's phone and gave her another splash of the champagne. It took a couple of tries, but Ana and

Bex captured the perfect clinking boomerang. Ana put in her stories with a caption that said, "Cheers to 10K, babes!"

Ana posted the story and set her phone back down. It wasn't long before her watch was buzzing on her wrist with congratulations from her followers - she'd reached the Promised Land, and everyone knew it.

"I'm going to make us some dinner to celebrate," Bex announced. She flung open the fridge door and began looking for something inside. All Ana could see were Bex's pre-made meal preps that Ana wanted nothing to do with.

"Let's just order takeout," Ana suggested.

"No way, sis. You've earned a home-cooked meal. You've been doing so well now, for so long, I'm so proud of your progress. Even just a few years ago, I didn't think you'd survive, let alone all of this. You've come so far." Ana's face warmed. For all the anger she'd felt at her sister lately, it still felt good to have Bex's approval. This validation meant much more than the number of followers she had.

Bex pulled out a purple eggplant, a carton of eggs, and some cheese. "How about eggplant parm? I got the stuff today in hopes that we would need it," Bex said. Neither one of them commented on the fact that this dish was what their mom would have made for a birthday or special occasion if she was still here to celebrate with them.

Ana swallowed a lump in her throat.

"Thanks, sis." Ana sat back down at the table while Bex got to work beating the eggs. Ana refreshed her follower count to make sure no one unfollowed in the time they'd been celebrating.

She was already down to 10,000 even. Damnit. She wondered who the one person was that had followed only to unfollow. Ana took another screenshot in case it slipped down again.

"So, what else are you going to do to celebrate?" Bex asked. She prepared the eggplant like she did most things: with precision, ferocity, and skill. Get in her way and you could lose a finger. Or two.

"Oh, I don't know. I might get crazy and get Starbucks tomorrow," Ana said.

"A venti, even?"

"I might."

"Have you talked to James lately?" Bex asked. Heat spread across Ana's cheeks; she wasn't prepared for the question.

"No, just a few text messages."

"Well, I'm sure he'll be glad that you've got so many followers. Turn them into listeners next."

Ana looked down at her phone. She couldn't wait a second longer. She sent the screenshot to James with a row of confetti-popping emojis. She wanted to celebrate with him later once she got through the evening with her sister.

"Isn't it crazy how far we've come since everything that happened? You're a published author and we have a podcast," Bex said. Ana dipped her head. She hated talking about that period of her life.

"Yeah, it's been a crazy few years."

"Aren't you glad you lived to see this life?" Bex pushed.

"Right now, yes."

Bex took a drink. Ana forced the thoughts of the hospital out of her mind. Tonight was for celebration, not memories. Nothing was going to get in between her and this high.

"Speaking of things, how's the next book coming? You have 10,000 invested fans nowadays."

"I'm still filling out my next book outline; I need to spend some time working through some holes."

"You amaze me. You know it? You've always been a writer. Since we were kids. I don't even know how you do it but clearly, you're doing the damn thing," Bex said, clapping in between her words.

"Yeah! *This is how we do it*," Ana sang, the same song looping through her head over and over.

"I'm already there, I know that whatever the story is, it will be-" Bex started. Her phone dinged on the counter next to the stove. Bex stopped talking and picked it up. A little smile played at the corner of her lips.

"Who's that?" Ana asked.

"I was just saying, it'll be good. I'm sure of it," Bex said. She stirred the sauce on the stove. The room filled with the smell of their childhood.

"You didn't answer my question."

The phone dinged again. Bex's hand shot toward the sound in reflex but then pulled it back before giving in. She grabbed the phone and gave Ana a little sheepish grin. Bex absentmindedly swirled the sauce while she typed away with the other hand.

A red rash of color flew up Bex's neck above her tank. A smile played on her lips.

"Okay, spill the beans," Ana demanded.

Bex turned her back to the stove and poured in the noodles. Ana looked around their gray, uninspired kitchen. They might as well live in a hospital for all the color and excitement around here. Ana fought the urge to splash a can of paint on the walls on a near-daily basis but living as a guest came with biting her tongue about Bex's sad monochromatic color scheme.

Ana took a sip of her champagne. The combination of bitterness and bubbles hit her tongue and woke it up. "Bexley Adams. If you don't tell me now," Ana said. A small laugh escaped involuntarily.

"Anabeth Adams, if you don't leave me alone, I will never tell you another secret so long as I shall live."

"My name is not Anabeth!"

"It should have been."

"Our mom only had one exciting name in her, and you got it. I just get to be Ana with one N - a distinction I'll have to make every day for the rest of my life."

"Lucky you."

"No but really, who the hell keeps blowing you up?" Ana asked. She had to ask. Not knowing was eating her up.

"Worry about yourself!"

Ana picked up her phone. There was no response from James. She tried to hold back the disappointment growing in her belly. She forced herself to twirl around the kitchen another time, singing to herself. She didn't want to lose the feelings of euphoria she just had.

She was doing the damn thing. Nothing could stop her. Nothing.

EIGHT

The phone vibrated in Bex's back pocket. She stirred the sauce one more time, trying to ignore the pull of the message. Her lips danced around a smile as her mind conjured up what Aimee said. Bex hoped she sent a picture this time.

Bex opened the oven, and the smell of garlic bread filled the kitchen. She focused on the aroma and forced her hands to stay busy flipping the loaves over.

Her phone went off again. The temptation was too strong. Bex slid off the oven mitt and unlocked the screen.

"Gah. Who is that?! We're having a sister night, remember?" Ana said. This was at least the third time she'd asked.

Bex ignored Ana and tapped her way to her messages. The notification wasn't from Aimee; she stopped responding when Bex offered to come over after dinner. The wind left her lungs and disappointment took its place. Bex thought Aimee would jump at the invitation.

Out of habit, Bex went to her email next. It was probably some junior account rep trying to make a name for themself by working late. Only there were no emails in her work inbox, something almost more alarming than the fact that there was still no response from Aimee.

Bex flicked back to her mail app and saw that there were two messages in her inbox. One looked like it was for the podcast. The other was an email from AncestryAndMe alerting her to more unread messages. Bex deleted it. She wasn't ready to face her brother again.

Clicking the bolded line, she opened the podcast. Bex was sure it was a ploy from some desperate family member begging them to cover their sister or cousin's cold case.

Instead, it was actually from someone at a brand representative management firm. Bex scanned the lines -

Hey, Bex and Ana - love your show, looking for advertisers?

The email went on to highlight some hair dye company, claiming they're the 'Warby Parker' of highlights, looking for up-and-coming podcasters to work with. Bex let out a low whistle.

"What?" Ana asked.

"We just got an email from a brand rep. They have an advertiser for us!"

"*This is how we do it!*" Ana screamed from the top of her lungs after restarting the track. She took another twirl around the room. Bex loved seeing her sister so happy, but she couldn't help but worry about the crash that was to come any day now.

"Yeah, hair dye. Wanna be the guinea pig?"

"No, I rather like my blonde hair, but I'll take their money," Ana said.

"Now we're talking, sis! You're finally getting it. Remember how much you hated the idea of podcasting and how I practically had to beg you to do this? It's paying off now!"

Ana played with her phone; she didn't look up. "Maybe you were right."

Bex jumped and fist-bumped the air. "Louder!"

"You were right," Ana said. Bex whooped.

"See, see what I mean. This podcast *does* have potential. If we take this one, we'll be up to three brand deals. That's going to multiply here soon."

"So, we'll make enough to cover our Starbucks every month?" Ana asked.

"Shut up. We'll make more than that in no time."

39

Bex got out two plates from the cabinet. They looked just like everything else in Bex's house - pure white, clean lines. Simple. Aesthetic. Just the way Bex liked it.

Ana stood and started toward the stove. Bex waved her off with a little flick of her wrist. Bex started scooping spaghetti noodles onto each of their plates. Bex was only a few years older, but she loved taking care of Ana. Their roles hadn't changed that much into adulthood.

"Yum!" Bex said as she filled Ana's plate to the brim with noodles and then topped it with the eggplant parmesan. Bex put a small serving on her plate. The food smelled delicious, and her belly growled but Bex would never let herself eat that many carbs.

"So, I guess I'll go ahead and email back about the hair dye. Neither of us must dye our hair but I think it would be a good advertiser for the show," Bex said. She put each plate in its respective spots.

"*This is how we do ittttt,*" Ana sang.

"Do you know any other words of that song?" Bex asked with a laugh.

"*It's Friday night!*" Ana sang louder.

"Stop it. I need to think," Bex said. "The podcast is way ahead of what I forecasted for us for this point. That's great."

"It's cause we're so good," Ana said.

"I know," Bex said. And she did know it. They were meant for this.

Bex took a bite and her tongue recoiled at the heat. She didn't stop though; the hurt was worth the flavor. It tasted just like their mom used to make.

The smell of dinner made Bex think of Caleb. He never got the chance to eat their mom's home cooking, much less know her. Grief hit her hard. Bex knew she should tell her sister about him but if Ana's dancing and singing was any indication of her mental state, she could not handle it right now.

"So, you doing okay?" Bex asked instead. It was the question she wanted someone to ask her. Posing it to Ana would have to be enough instead.

"Yeah, I'm great! *This is how we do it*" Ana sang. Bex knew that her sister probably really did feel great in the moment, but it wouldn't be long until that was no longer true.

The table shook as Bex's phone vibrated next to her plate. She took one look at the screen and grabbed the phone. It was Aimee; she finally responded - *I'd love to see you tonight.*

Those six words made Bex's face light up. The volley of emotions was intense, and she was thankful for the distraction. Bex could feel Ana's eyes searching but she didn't care. Aimee made her throw all caution to the wind.

"So, you going to tell me who's got you in such a tizzy or do I have to keep asking?"

"Are you going to tell me about James," Bex fired back.

"No."

"Then, that's a no for me, too. I guess we have a good 'ole fashioned standoff."

Ana's face twisted with unasked questions. The feeling of power made Bex smile bigger. Ana shook her head and went back to eating.

Bex finished her plate and put the dish in the sink.

"You're already done?"

"Yeah, it was great. It's been fun to celebrate you tonight, Ana. You're doing big things and I'm so proud of you."

"What? Are you leaving?" Ana asked. She still had a mound of food on her plate.

"Yeah. I'm going to meet a friend. I'll be home later," Bex said. She headed for her room.

"Really? I haven't even finished yet. What happened to celebrating your influencer sister?"

"Sorry, sis. I gotta run but I'm set to record the next episode later this week."

"So, you have to know where I'm at all the time, but you just come and go?" Ana said. She looked like a toddler who didn't get their way.

"Yeah, it's my house. I make the rules."

Silence ballooned between them. Bex fought the urge to apologize, or worse, to text Aimee and say that something came up. Ana looked down at her plate and swirled the spaghetti around halfheartedly. Ana's head slung lower. Bex felt that familiar twinge of sisterly guilt that she'd carried their whole life. Bex worried about Ana's manic state and whether she could be left alone.

A flash of a future fight with Aimee about Ana steamrolled through Bex's mind. Bex needed to start choosing Aimee or she was going to lose her. Ana would always be there, Aimee might not. Bex made a conscious decision to leave Ana.

"I'll be back later," Bex called over her shoulder.

NINE

4:36 PM - Direct Messages from @anasnumberonefan -

Hey, you.

I just finished your bomb-in-a-box-book. Ana, so good.

This is going to sound crazy, but the whole time I was reading that book, I couldn't stop thinking about what would happen if a book bomb really went off in real life. It's such a good way for a person to kill someone. Genius, Ana Adams. You deserve to be famous.

PS - I just saw your 10k story. You and your sister are so cute! Does anyone ever tell you how much you look alike?

43

TEN

Ana reread the Instagram messages from @anasnumberonefan. The rapid-fire responses were frenzied. The words swam on the screen.

With Bex gone and the high of the night fading, Ana missed the happiness she'd felt. She wished it hadn't left so soon this time. She felt the dredges of depression seeping into her bones and she wanted to stop it. She couldn't though. The low was inevitable after the high. There was nothing she could do about it.

Ana sunk further into the couch and let the sadness wash over her. She tucked the blanket around her legs. The house was always so quiet when Bex was gone, the living room felt too dark. Out of habit, Ana looked to the front door to verify the deadbolt was still engaged. It was. Ana hated being alone and she hated that she missed her sister so much.

Whoever Bex found was keeping her out later and later. Ana craved bed but some part of her wanted to stay awake to see if Bex would come home.

Ana looked at her phone, sure that her new number one fan would have another message for her. Her skin crawled with loneliness. She felt jumpy.

Ana checked her other messages. A Mr. Duval offered to be her sugar daddy *No strings attached baby; I just want to see you happy. I can offer you $3,129 a day to be your daddy.* Ana laughed and deleted the message. Every day she got some kind of sugar daddy phishing scam like this. Self-described book marketer extraordinaries promising her the world were a close second. The messages from Ana's Number One Fan felt different. Off.

Ana went back to the Number One Fan's messages. The sender's words about her book rolled around in Ana's mind. She wasn't anywhere close to famous enough to have a number-one fan.

She went to the user's profile. They'd only shared one post earlier in the day. The square image was a picture of Ana's books stacked with a coffee cup beside them, a classic bookstagram post - the kind that Ana had been tagged in frequently. The caption was as unimaginative as the rest - #TwoforTuesday from one of my favorite up-and-coming authors, @anaadamsauthor!

Ana hearted the picture. It was nothing. Just an overzealous book lover who probably didn't think before she sent those messages.

Thanks for sharing! I'm so grateful for your support! Ana commented.

She flipped back to her messages and accepted the user's message request. Ana hearted the first message and left it at that. She didn't want to encourage this fan any more than she already had by commenting on their post.

Several other messages were waiting for Ana in her inbox - the story she posted from dinner cheering with Bex was quite popular. Ana told herself that she should respond as the dutiful author friend her followers knew, but Ana closed out of Instagram instead.

There was nothing on the television that caught her eye. She turned on the Pop Music playlist on Spotify station just to fill the void with some kind of noise.

With the night stretching in front of her, Ana knew she should create the week's email blast. The job nagged on her to-do list since she decided to skip it during her normal office hours to hike with James.

Ana always saw a bump in sales after an email went out, but that fact still didn't motivate her. She hated that being a self-published author meant that she was a book marketer more than she was ever a book writer. Ana didn't want to create emails or answer Instagram messages. She just wanted to write and sell books magically.

The couch cradled the back of her head while Ana tried her best to talk herself into just getting the email done and ready. She wished some of that mania she felt a couple of days ago would resurface. But like always, it was slipping through her hands. That happiness, top-of-the-world feeling felt like a distant memory by this point. Soon the depression would be back with a vengeance.

I love this. I love this. I was made for this. She repeated her well-worn mantra in her head. It didn't work. She thought of her sister instead.

Ana picked up her phone and clicked the "Find My" app. Bex and Ana always shared their locations. It was a safety mechanism. And a coping mechanism. If Ana could at least see where Bex was at any given moment, that string between them would remain tethered. That's what sisters do right? Share their locations and what they're up to.

Ana clicked on Bex's name, but nothing happened. The app wouldn't refresh. Bex's little picture in a circle hung over a soft background. The app didn't give away any secrets. Ana jammed her thumb on Bex's picture. Still, nothing happened. Ana refreshed the app again.

A message popped up - *This user stopped sharing their location with you.*

She swallowed hard. Ana rubbed her eyes and reread the error message; it was still there. Tears formed in the corner of her eyes. Her chest fell. *No one loves you;* her mind told her.

Ana tossed her phone across the couch. It landed on the floor with a thud. A half cry, half groan escaped Ana's mouth. She covered it with her hand, afraid the neighbors would hear her through their paper-thin walls.

Her lip got the brunt of her anger. She chewed and chewed on her bottom lip until she tasted blood. Ana and Bex shared everything; something they'd always done. What was Bex doing that she didn't want Ana to see? Bex had always been her person. And Ana had been Bex's. Or so she thought. Who could have changed that?

Ana grabbed her laptop and forced herself to open her work in progress.

ELEVEN

The bar looked dark and dank like it should smell of cheap college boys and cheaper beer, but instead, it was filled with sterile young professionals sipping thirteen-dollar martinis and chilled pinot grigio, all seeking a sliver of happiness in this trendy hipster den. The color palate was all grays and yellows. The chairs were purposely retro, and the hanging lights and neon signs placed just so pretended to be out of the 70s.

Except all of it was phony, as contrived, and brand-new as any other location in this rapidly changing quadrant of Denver, and not nearly as cool as the old days. Bex just wanted to go back to Aimee's house, but Aimee loved this place, rolling her eyes when Bex called it "a gentrified dive bar."

"Let's do another round," Aimee said as their server approached. Bex loved the way Aimee's dark hair looked, down and curly. It was wild, untamed – and made it hard for Bex to say no.

When people saw them together, no one assumed they were dating. That's partially because neither of them looked stereotypically lesbian but also because Bex still had a hard time with PDA. She still wasn't used to being with a woman, and certainly not in public.

Aimee's wild hair and even wilder personality were everything that Bex had never found in a man. Aimee was fun. Intoxicating. Especially in the bedroom. Bex's insides warmed at the thought of what would come later.

"Let's go home," Bex said. She winked.

"What's the rush?"

"Nothing, I just want to go somewhere quieter."

Aimee groaned and threw her hands in the air. The server, a young man with wire glasses and a mullet tapped the table with the tips of his fingers.

"What'll it be ladies?"

"The check-" Bex started.

"Another marg," Aimee said at the same time.

Bex forced herself to laugh.

"Whoa. House divided," the server said. He didn't laugh, he was in a hurry.

"Well, if she's ready to go, you can bring her a check. We'll go Dutch," Aimee said.

"No, no. We'll stay. We'll both have another," Bex said. He tapped the edge of the table again and nodded.

"No, really. What was that all about?" Aimee asked as soon as he was out of earshot. Bex could see that her smile was forced.

"Nothing, I just want you to myself," Bex said.

"Okay, granny. You ready to go home to your skin routine and a cup of tea before putting on a floral muumuu?"

"Yes, actually. We have work tomorrow. In fact, we have an eight o'clock. You scheduled it, babe," Bex said. She held her smile firmly in place.

"I know but if we're both tired, you can't can me," Aimee said. She made a gratuitous mock yawn.

"Yeah, but the whole team will be in the room, too."

"Oh, Bexley Adams. You're fire in the office. I've seen you rock meetings where the stakes are higher. No one can beat you babe, one more drink won't change that."

"Thanks," Bex said. It felt good to hear. Aimee reached across the table and squeezed Bex's hand. For the first time in a long time, Aimee made Bex feel appreciated.

"Speaking of - when are we going to tell the team about us? I'm bursting, I can't hide you much longer," Aimee asked. She poked her wrist, where a watch would run.

"I don't know, we gotta give it a bit. I don't want to have to get HR involved and all of that. You're my report. Technically, I'm your boss and this isn't allowed. One of us will have to quit."

"No babe, they'll make an exception. We're too cute for all that legal stuff," she said. Her lip turned into a pout.

Bex swallowed. She felt the same; she was ready to scream from the rooftops that she loved Aimee, but she couldn't risk her job.

"I don't know. I don't think they can play favorites," Bex said. "Soon you'll get a promotion, or they'll shift the teams. I promise the minute you're not under me, we'll throw a whole-ass party. The entire world will know then."

The server dropped off their drinks and flipped a thumbs up before scooting off.

"Promise?"

"Yes, of course," Bex said. She needed to give Aimee more. "How about this - let's get through that big meeting in San Fran and then we'll tell them. That way we don't mess up the team's vibe beforehand."

"Oh, so I'd ruin the vibe then," Aimee said with a laugh. She took a big gulp of her drink. Bex noticed how her lips looked through the clear of the glass. She wanted to kiss them so badly.

"No, no. Don't put words in my mouth. It's just a big meeting, we must kill it."

Aimee took another drink. Bex could hardly resist her.

"Let's just go back to your apartment and have fun."

"Ohhhh, I get it. I'm not good for the vibe, and I'm not good enough to tell anyone, but I am good enough for fun. I see," Aimee said. She was laughing but the words stung.

"Baby. Stop. I just want you. You're driving me crazy. That red shirt... It's already been a long week and I just need you."

Aimee took another drink and batted her eyes in the process. Bex was being played but she had no power to stop it. Aimee was going to win, that much was clear.

"Okay boomer, I'll make you a deal," Aimee said. She leaned closer. Bex chewed on her lips and said a silent prayer that this would go her way.

"I'll let you come over tonight if you promise to let me finally meet your sister."

Aimee sat back in her chair and giggled, an almost cruel light in her eyes... Squeamishness tore through Bex. She wasn't ready for that step either. Bex took a big gulp of her wine. It didn't taste nearly as good now.

"I will introduce you two soon. You're my two leading ladies."

"Why not today? Call her up, what's she doing tonight anyways?"

"I can't just call her, she's probably working."

"Working? She's an author - a self-employed author who lives in your house, rent-free. She can't be that busy. She'd probably like to get out occasionally."

"She's probably just settling in for her sprints tonight."

"Sprint? What the hell is that?"

"It's just what she calls writing. She writes 'sprints' for 30 minutes and then takes a 10-minute break and sprints again. It helps productivity I guess."

"So athletic," Aimee said, sarcastically.

"Yes, she's very good at what she does," Bex said. "Hey, did I tell you that she hit 10,000 followers on Instagram? We celebrated earlier. It's a big deal, she's very happy about it."

"Wow, that's cool. I would have loved to have been invited."

"It was a sister thing."

"I just want to meet her. If she's anything like you, I bet she's amazing." Aimee grabbed Bex's hand. "I want all of you, Bex. And that includes your sister. I know she's a big part of your life."

"Thanks, boo. I promise soon. She is great and I think you two would like each other."

"Soon when?"

"I don't know. She's kind of a volatile person. Things can set her off. I just have to make sure she's in the right space."

"Why are you so protective over her?"

Bex looked around the room. Every other conversation looked so easy. She hated the way she always got so heated when it came to Ana, but it was as second nature as breathing. Nothing came between her and Ana. Most especially some fling.

Bex tried a drink of her wine. It got more bitter with each sip.

"We had a really shitty childhood. Our dad used to abuse our mom, and Ana. Yes, in the way you're thinking. Ana needs me," Bex said. She felt tears welling up in her eyes.

"Okay, clearly I've touched a nerve, I'm sorry," Aimee finally said after the silence between them stretched for an awkwardly long time.

Bex took a big breath and forced herself to relax her shoulders.

"It's okay. Ana is just my sister. We're close."

"I know. It's always 'Ana this' and 'Ana that.'"

"No, it's not."

"Yes, it is. How many times have you already ditched me for Ana? I always invite you over and you're recording a podcast with your sister or going on a hike. You know you can invite me to those things too? If we're going to date, I'm going to have to meet your sister. That's normal."

Bex ran her tongue along her teeth. "I know. I know. I'm just not ready. Ana's not ready. I haven't ever been in a very serious relationship. I don't bring people home. That's sort of our sacred space."

Aimee looked across the bar. Bex wondered if she said too much.

"I don't know. You can't live with your sister forever. She doesn't even pay you rent!"

"Her life has been really hard."

"So has yours, Bex."

"Ana got the brunt of it. She had it harder when we were kids and she got laid off from her job when The Rocky Mountain News closed. She needs my help."

"For how long?"

"I don't know. However long it takes. Someday she'll be a famous author and she'll be the one paying my mortgage," Bex said. She looked down into her wine glass.

"And I'll win the lotto."

"I'm just saying - someday things will be different, but this is where they're at for now. I know maybe it's weird, but I love her. I can't explain it. We just need to be close. Our childhood was rough, we needed each other then and we need each other now. This is how we cope."

Aimee finished her beer and waved down the server.

"Will you close us out?" Aimee asked the server as he came up to the table.

"Sure thing. One or two?"

"Two," Aimee responded. Disappointment made Bex's shoulders sag; she couldn't think of anything else to say.

The server brought two checks. "I'll get yours," Bex offered. Aimee waved her off.

Bex took her time filling out the receipt and signing her name. She tried to recall everything she'd said, to find where she went wrong. She didn't want to end on this note. She didn't want to let Ana ruin everything, again.

"Let's go home," Aimee said. Her big smile split her pretty face. Bex's head spun with whiplash, but she didn't protest.

TWELVE

The cursor blinked on the screen, taunting Ana. The words wouldn't come and the questions about Bex wouldn't stop swirling in her mind. Bex was still gone, and her location was turned off. Ana looked at the clock. It was after 11. Her sister never used to stay out this late on a work night.

Ana worked at her lip again, wincing at the taste of blood. She paced the kitchen and tried water and then wine. Nothing stopped the anxiety.

She tried her mantras again. *I'm a writer. I was made to spin stories.* The words didn't block out the thoughts of Bex. It didn't stop her arms and legs from feeling cramped and itchy like bugs were working their way out of her skin.

Ana told herself over and over that it didn't matter where Bex was, that she would come home soon enough but the sisterly thread between them was taut. And Ana could feel the pressure as it pulled further apart. Ana tried to force herself to believe that she didn't need her sister, but she did. Desperately. Ana needed Bex to come home.

The click of her laptop lid shutting in place brought Ana a moment of peace. The blank white page was too much to look at.

A siren sounded somewhere down the street caught Ana's attention. The pull of the night called her outside. Fresh air would do the trick. Ana decided she needed to take a walk down the street to the neighborhood's communal mailbox to get out of her damn head.

Ana slipped on her flip-flops and headed out the door. She tipped her head back and filled her lungs with the coolness of the evening. There was no better place than Denver in late summer.

"Hello, there!" the neighbor called to Ana as she set out toward the mailbox. Ana could never remember his name, but she gave him a small wave back. He smoked on the porch, all hours of the day. Including late at night, apparently.

Ana slid the key into door #12. She turned and pulled the key to open the door. It was stuck, she needed both hands to pry it open. It came clean with a thwack of mail falling to the ground. Their rectangle mailbox was still shoved full of more coupon books, junk mail, and god knows what else even with all that lay on the ground around the box. Ana couldn't remember the last time she checked the mail. Since Bex did everything online, her sister never bothered to grab the mail either.

The mail came out in waves; Ana cradled it all in her arm. She dipped her head level with the box to make sure she got it all. One little white envelope was pressed to the back. Ana shoved her arm, clear up to her elbow to get it. It ripped a little as she pulled it free.

"ADAMS" was written in all caps. The letters were thick and big; her last name yelled at her from the envelope. There was nothing on the back of the envelope, no clue as to who sent it. Ana put the envelope on top of the stack and hugged it all close to her chest. Ana walked back home quickly, careful not to make eye contact with her neighbor.

Tucked inside the comfort of home, Ana spread the mail out on the kitchen counter. The envelope addressed with her last name stuck out amid all the junk mail and mail addressed to Bex.

The fliers and coupons went straight into recycling; the rest, stacked in a neat pile in the middle of the counter for Bex when she returned. Whenever that might be. Remembering that Bex was gone made her feel lonely. She felt unmoored without her sister there.

Ana returned to the couch. The envelope sparked her curiosity, with its lack of a return address and their name in capital letters. Laughing to herself, Ana thought that an unexpected letter like this could make for a good inciting scene for her next mystery.

Slipping a fingernail under the flap, Ana ripped it open. Inside was just one thin lined sheet. It looked like it was a grocery list ripped from the ringed notebook, folded, and slipped inside an envelope addressed to Ana.

Ana pulled the paper free of the envelope and unfolded the paper. The same block letters filled the page.

> IF YOU DON'T WANT TO BE IN MY LIFE, FINE. BUT YOU SHOULD KNOW - TRUE CRIME IS NOT A GENRE. IT'S NOT A HOBBY. IT'S NOT A PASTIME AND IT'S SURE AS HELL NOT A VEHICLE FOR YOU TO MAKE MONEY. LEAVE SURVIVORS AND VICTIMS ALONE. YOU OF ALL PEOPLE SHOULD KNOW THAT. STOP. JUST FUCKING STOP.

Her hands shook; the words blurred in front of her eyes, and she felt dizzy. Ana turned the letter over, there was nothing on the back save for the places where the dark ink had seeped through the thin paper. Questions piled in her mind. Fear.

It was personal. It didn't make sense.

Ana smashed the letter into a ball. That wasn't enough. She uncurled the paper and balled it up again. Ana couldn't decide what to do with it. She shoved it into her desk; she couldn't look at the threat any longer.

Ana fell into bed. The words flashed before her eyes, a jumbled mess but the meaning was still the same.

Had they podcasted about the wrong case? Was this personal? Had she hurt a survivor, or their family, or both? She made the wrong person mad. And they had her address.

A knock at the door dislodged her thoughts and made the fear crescendo through her whole body. Were they here now? Was someone watching her? Waiting for her to find the letter? Fear took over Ana's whole body.

The knock came again. Ana could not pull herself out of bed, even if she wanted to. Her heart was beating too fast and there was no way her legs would have been able to carry her across the house to the front door.

Another knock. Even louder this time. The whole house shook; she was sure of it.

Ana grabbed the covers and pulled them over her head. Her heart hammered against her ribs. No one should be knocking in the middle of the night. Especially when she was alone.

THIRTEEN

A noise outside brought Ana back from wherever her mind had gone. She looked around the room. She didn't remember moving to the couch. She didn't know how much time had passed. Ana stood and looked out the window but couldn't see anything in the dark. The letter came rushing back in her mind. The words. The hurt. The anger. She remembered the knocking. Fear seeped into every cell in her body. She walked to her desk and pulled it from the drawer.

Ana unwound the paper. The hard, angry words stared up at her. Ana read the letter one more time, her eyes stopping on each word, calculating its worth.

This time the hurt was even worse. The words sunk into her; the accusations stoked the shame she'd carried with her since the beginning. She had known all along that the podcast and her books were all wrong. *Ana* was all wrong and always had been. This was proof. Her heart pounded against the walls of her chest.

Ana crumpled the letter back up and threw it as far as she could. It landed just beyond her feet. There was a magnetism keeping it close. She hated it and wanted it far away from her. She picked it up and shoved it back into her desk.

She didn't know why she was having such a visceral reaction to a stupid letter. Ana faced plenty of negative reviews in the past and mean people in her DMs. This was just another version of that.

She couldn't talk herself into forgetting about it though. DMs were removed. They were sent over the Internet. This letter invaded her space. Someone was a hell of a lot closer.

Ana decided she needed to sleep it off. She started to make her way back to her room. Before she'd even reached the couch, a loud knock rang through the house. Ana stopped in her tracks. She dropped to the floor. They were back. Someone was outside. They wouldn't give up. It was far too late, and she was far too alone.

Every single muscle in her body tensed. She put her head in her arms and began to rock herself back and forth. She bit her lip to stifle a cry. Her mind took her to the blackness again. If there was only one thing Ana knew, one lesson she'd learned the very hardest way as a child, it's that she couldn't be left home alone. Bad things happened.

Sometime later, the quietness brought Ana back to the living room. She had no idea how long she was on the floor, in the fetal position but her mind must have sensed safety. They were gone.

Ana forced herself to stand and peer outside. Through the door's glass cutouts, Ana could see the dark of the night. The porch was empty. She wanted Bex to look at their doorbell camera to see who had been on the other side of the door, but then she remembered Bex wasn't there at all. No one was. She'd been left alone. Ana remembered her sister cut her off; Ana didn't even know where Bex was.

Standing on her tiptoes gave Ana a better look. A dog barked in the distance. Ana pushed her nails into her palm and told herself to get a grip. She opened the door just slightly and looked both ways.

Their concrete stoop was free and so was the whole street in front of the house, as far as she could see. Ana almost talked herself into believing that she'd imagined the whole thing. Just as Ana turned to head back inside, she caught sight of a dark figure moving in the shadows down the street. It was far too late for someone to be walking down the street, let alone knocking for that matter. Was she imagining things? Or was someone there?

She stepped out on the porch to get a better look. He walked with confidence; like he deserved to take up the whole sidewalk. A chill ran down her back. She had no way of knowing if that was who came to her door, but she didn't want to find out.

Ana threw the door shut and smashed the deadbolt in place. She leaned her back against the wood and slipped down to the floor. The only thing Ana could hear was her heartbeat in her ears.

Bex. Bex. That was all Ana could think. Ana needed her sister. Bex would know what to do; she would calm Ana down. Ana slipped her phone from her pocket.

Bex was at the top of Ana's favorites list. She pressed Bex's number and gripped her phone until her knuckles looked chalky white. Bex was the only reason Ana was still alive. Bex always took care of Ana, that was the only lesson Ana had ever really learned, deep down. Ana couldn't be left alone. Bad things happened. But Bex was always there for her, and Ana was sure tonight would be no different.

The phone connected and Ana heard the ringing in her ears. Ana's shoulders relaxed just a bit with the anticipation of hearing Bex's voice. The phone rang and then rang some more. Soon Bex's voice filled the line, but it was only her voicemail. Bex's voice sounded robotic, fake.

Ana hung up and tried again. The phone rang through to Bex's voicemail again. Bex always answered Ana. Where the hell was she? Ana redialed. This time the phone went straight to voicemail. Did Bex just turn off her phone or was she out of service?

The phone was slippery in Ana's hand. She had to concentrate on holding it to flip over to the "Find My" app. Ana's finger shook but she finally clicked on Bex's photo, one of the two of them at a park last summer. It wouldn't load. Bex's location was still turned off.

Ana's stomach did a flip. Ana didn't know what to do without Bex. A flash of anger hit her all at once. Who could Bex be with that was more important than Ana? The anger subsided almost as quickly as it came over her, replaced by sadness. Ana needed her sister, she was alone, and Bex wasn't there for her.

The vibration from the door registered in her back before the sound reached her ears. Thud. Thud. Another knock. Fear gripped her and rooted her in place. Ana screamed at herself to move but her body just wouldn't do it. Ana knew that bad things happened when she was all alone, with no one to protect her. They always did. Fear ripped through her.

Ana couldn't do this alone. She opened her phone and clicked on James' name.

James, I need help. She texted. *Someone is at our door. I'm scared.*

Some small part of her mind knew it sounded pathetic, but she didn't care. Bex wasn't answering and James was all she had.

Ana waited for the dots to appear to indicate he was responding but they never showed up. Somewhere in her mind, she knew he was probably asleep but that didn't stop her from desperately craving a response. She clicked her phone on and off, but no response from James came.

Please. She added. Desperation coursed through her veins. She needed a human. She needed someone to talk to. Her phone remained annoyingly silent. James was the only person she knew who kept his read receipts on, and he hadn't read these messages. They were delivered but not read.

A silence fell over the house. Ana waited to hear footsteps on the porch or another knock but nothing. Somehow the silence was almost worse. She couldn't anticipate what was coming next, but she believed, with all her heart, that it would hurt.

There was only one other person she could call. Ana found Dr. Daniel's contact information in her phone and clicked his number. It started to ring. Dr. Daniels had always helped her before.

Dr. Daniels understood her anxiety and propensity to spiral. She just needed him to talk her off this ledge until Bex came back home or James responded.

The phone rang and rang. A recording came on the line that said, "If this is an after-hours emergency, please hang up and dial 911." It wasn't even Dr. Daniel's voice.

Ana looked at her phone. She couldn't call 911. They would tell her that she was imagining things. They'd call her crazy. They would send her straight back to the hospital again. She hadn't been for years, but she remembered enough not to want to go back. The thought of those bright fluorescents, the bullying leers of the cops and smug superiority of the orderlies, the smells of piss and disinfectant, all of it... made her skin crawl.

James and Bex weren't there for her. Ana had no one. She was all alone.

Ana pitched her head back against the door. She was all alone and someone knew her address. Someone took the time to write her a threat. And someone was on the other side of the door. Ana didn't want to live in a world without her sister. Ana didn't want to live in a world, alone. And Ana was alone.

The thoughts hit her like the kids used to do when they played dodgeball in elementary - everyone attacked the poor, motherless girl. Only this time the onslaught was justified. Ana had nothing. The thoughts sped through her mind and grew faster with each spin. She was alone. She couldn't write. No one answered her. She didn't have a house or a job. Ana had nothing.

She rocked back and forth.

A plan swept through Ana's mind. She stood and walked to the bathroom, sure of what she needed to do. She didn't want to be a burden on anyone any longer. She didn't want to have to do this alone.

And she didn't want to be here. She couldn't face whoever was at the door. The voice in her head needed to be turned off. Ana couldn't do it anymore, not by herself.

And so, Ana did a very bad thing.

FOURTEEN

The drive home was long and quiet at this hour. Bex craved Aimee's bed and wanted to waste the day away drinking her in. Bex almost did just that but the eight AM sharp phone call with the East Coast team forced her to drive across town before anyone else was even awake.

Aimee tried to talk her into getting ready together at her apartment, but something in Bex couldn't. She hadn't talked to her sister all night; Ana called but Bex sent her to voicemail. Bex just wanted to check in before another long day.

When Bex came inside, the kitchen was empty, and the house was quiet. The air tasted stale and smelled a little strange. The house was cold. Bex couldn't quite put a finger on what, exactly, but it was obvious: something was off.

"Ana!" Bex called.

"Ana? You here?" Bex called again.

Ana's door was closed. Bex grabbed the handle and pushed into the door with her shoulder. It was locked. Ana never locked her door.

"Ana!" Bex yelled. Something was wrong with her sister. Bex's intuition knew before her mind. She flew into the door with her shoulder. She felt a sick thud but only her body gave way.

"Are you in there?" Bex yelled into the door. She tried to reason that Ana could very well be out for the morning. Hell, she probably went to the farmer's market. Bex grabbed her phone out of her back pocket and clicked Ana's name as fast as she could.

Bex waited. The call rang once. Bex could hear the phone vibrating against the wood of the desk or the side table in Ana's room. Ana never went anywhere without her phone. Bex canceled the call.

"Ana! What's going on? You're freaking me out!" Bex yelled.

"Are you still asleep?" Bex looked at her watch. It was just after seven AM; Ana was always awake by that hour.

Bex ran back to the garage and rifled through the drawers in the workbench, looking for a small metal hook. She looked through the catch-all drawer twice before she found it in the back corner, under a box of nails.

The little L-shape of metal wasn't much but Bex prayed it would do the trick. She raced down the hall, grabbing onto Ana's door to slow her momentum. Bex shoved the metal hook into the tiny hole in the knob and twisted it around. Nothing happened.

"Come on!" she told herself.

Bex pushed it back in and looped it around, trying to find purchase inside the mechanism.

"Oh hell!"

Bex took it out and pumped her hand. She slid the metal in and tried to hold her hand steady. It caught something. She turned once and then again. The lock twisted and the handle turned freely.

The door shoved open with a thud against the opposite wall. Bex's eyes swept around the room and then again. The room was dark and stunk of something foul. Bex gagged, she pinched her nose and looked around again.

There was a wine bottle on the table and Ana's phone sat next to it. The room was a mess. Stuff everywhere, the bed looked like a porcupine made a nest in the middle of it. The comforter was on the floor and pillows littered the floor. Ana's clothes were in a heap and the room stunk.

"Ana! What the fuck is going on?!"

Bex walked around the side of the bed to make sure Ana wasn't in the room. That's when she saw feet. Bex rushed to the bed and threw the covers back. Ana was lodged between the bed and the wall.

65

"Ana! Ana!" Bex called as she grabbed her sister by the shoulders and pulled. Ana was a total dead weight. Bex heaved and bent her knees into it. She finally got some leverage and dislodged Ana's body, pulling her back to the bed.

Bex rolled Ana over and pushed the hair out of her face. Ana's eyes were only open a slit and her mouth hung open. Ana's hair was sticky with vomit and her shirt was tainted with a big red stain down the front of it. Bex couldn't tell if it was blood or vomit.

Ana's arms were sticky but warm. Bex shook her. Ana's whole body convulsed but she did not open her eyes.

"Ana! Ana! What the hell! Wake up," Bex called. She started to cry, big, heavy sobs.

The whole bed rocked as Bex tried to wake Ana up by shaking her. Ana's face remained gray and waxy. Bex looked around the room. This time she noticed the empty wine bottle.

"Ana!!!!"

No matter how many times Bex shook her, Ana didn't move. Bex's sobs came louder. What did her sister do? Bex could not live through this again.

Bex grabbed her phone and dialed 911. "What's your emergency?" the operator asked.

"It's my sister. Something is very wrong. I need an ambulance!" Bex cried in between sobs.

"Ma'am we can help. I need you to calm down. First, tell me your address."

"19224 Cherry Blossom Street, Denver."

"Okay, first responders are on their way. Did your sister get hurt? Is she breathing?"

"I don't know! I was gone last night, and I just got home. She's sick. I think she drank too much wine."

"Okay, ma'am. Please check her pulse," Bex wanted to slap herself for not thinking of that. She put two fingers under Ana's chin. Her skin was sticky, it didn't feel right. Bex's fingers picked up a weak beat deep inside Ana's skin.

"I can feel a pulse but it's weak! Please come!"

"Responders are enroute. What is your sister's name?"

"Ana Adams. Please tell them to hurry."

Bex shook Ana; she willed her sister's eyes to open. Her mouth popped open, and her head flopped to the side. She looked like a fish out of water.

"They're coming. Does Ana have any allergies? Anything the paramedics should know?"

"No, I don't know. Yes, she's bipolar and on medication for that and anxiety."

"Okay, thank you. Has Ana been showing any signs of self-harm?"

"No! I mean, sometimes in the past. She has some mental health issues. Sometimes she does stupid stuff. But I think she just drank too much. She's been doing okay lately."

"Okay, ma'am. The paramedics are in your vicinity. Please open the door for them," the woman instructed. Bex let out a sob as she ran to the door.

The next several minutes passed in a blur of uniformed medics passing by. First with an empty stretcher and then a stretcher filled with Ana's tangle of hair and motionless body strapped down. Bex reached for her as they went by but a woman with a gentle touch held her back.

"Ma'am, I know you're upset but you have to let her go. Your sister is very sick," the medic said.

Bex's breath rang ragged through her body. Bex had watched their mother get taken out the same way and she never came back home. Bex wouldn't be able to survive if it happened again.

"Ana. She's my sister."

"I know," the medic said. "They're going to help her."

"I need my sister."

"I know, sweetie," the woman said softly.

In the distance, Bex could hear the sirens getting quieter. Ana was being driven away and there was nothing Bex could do to protect her.

"It was my fault. I stayed at my girlfriend's house last night and now Ana is dying. I've done it again."

A wail escaped Bex. The woman wrapped her in a hug and Bex let her. The guilt was immense. She didn't think she'd be able to stay standing if the woman wasn't there to hold her up.

Someone beside them cleared their throat. The woman pulled back. Bex looked up and saw another medic. He looked no more than twenty with a pockmarked face and a skinny frame. Bex fought the urge to tell him to piss off.

"We found these," he said, holding up two empty pill bottles with a purple-gloved hand.

With a start, Bex recognized them. They were prescription pain pills, an old, faded bottle of Vicodin from back when Bex had her nose adjusted, and a newer one that Bex thought was from a visit to urgent care last year when Ana had sprained her knee hiking. Ana must have found them in the bathroom. She hated herself for not putting them somewhere safer. She should have seen this coming.

"Administer Naloxone!" someone called into their radio.

The woman next to her put a hand on her shoulder. It did nothing to quell the fear building inside Bex.

"We'll take her to Denver General. It's the closest and they have a great team for cases like this."

"Like what?" Bex managed to ask.

"Overdose."

"Oh, my god."

"We don't know anything yet, but it looks like she may have taken a combination of pills and alcohol. Depending on many things, that can be very dangerous. They'll do their best though, okay."

"What happens after that?"

"Well, it will be up to you. If she survives, I would highly recommend some kind of therapy if you can afford it. She is going to need help to recover from whatever made her do this."

"You think she did it on purpose?"

"In my experience, yes. Something probably happened – maybe a boy broke up with her or she got bad news at work and made a split-second decision to end it."

"She's been doing so great though."

"I know. That's what's hard about it. It doesn't always make sense and it's not always easy to tell from the outside who is struggling the most."

Bex sat down on the couch and put her face in her hands. She didn't want to admit it but Bex knew this was her fault. She saw Ana's mania and she predicted the fall was coming. Bex just didn't think it would have been such a big fall. She'd let her whole family down when they were kids. And now this.

"Listen, go to the hospital, and tell them your sister's name. They'll let you see her as soon as you can."

Bex nodded.

"Is there anyone I can call for you?" the medic asked.

Bex thought of Aimee. She wanted her support, Bex just didn't know how to tell her what happened.

"No, but thank you for everything," Bex said instead.

"Of course. It's our job."

"Okay," Bex said. Bex knew that she needed to call Dr. Daniels. She should have done it weeks ago. She felt the urge to smack herself upside the head for not making the time before.

The medics left and Bex was alone in the house and unsure what to do.

Bex allowed herself one last round of tears and then got to work. She packed a bag for herself and Ana. Bex sent a message to her boss explaining her absence. She texted Aimee and said something came up with Ana.

Finally, she found Ana's phone and unlocked it. She found Dr. Daniels' contact information as she walked out to her car.

He answered on the second ring. "Ana, sorry I missed your call last night. I don't do after-hours calls," he said.

"Hi, this is Bex, Ana's sister. I wanted to let you know that I just got home and found Ana in a bad way. They suspect she took some pain pills with a bottle of wine. I just called 911. I'm on my way to the hospital."

The doctor sucked in a big breath of air on the other end of the line. Bex tried to picture him. She bit her tongue to keep herself from berating him for not answering Ana last night. But then she remembered she didn't answer either. She had woke to so many missed calls from her sister.

"Oh, Bex. I'm so sorry to hear that. I thought Ana was doing so well."

"I know, she was so happy for weeks. I should have done more to prevent a big crash."

"I had hoped we were beyond these big swings. She was making real progress but thank you for finding Ana and getting her the help she needs. I have hope that they will be able to reverse this."

"Yeah."

"Doctors are amazing these days. You'd be surprised how much they can help her."

Bex wasn't sure how to take his optimism. Was he protecting himself? His ineptitude in not watching her closer?

"So, what happens next then?" Bex asked as she barreled out of her garage.

"Well, call me in a couple of days when she's recovered. I'd like her to come to Hillside. As you know, that's where I work both inpatient and outpatient. I think being with us for a few weeks could help her."

"Okay," Bex said.

Bex hated the sound of inpatient, but she was willing to do whatever it would take to save her sister.

FIFTEEN

The room felt clouded with heaviness, everyone shared memories that were so much worse than her own. Ana chewed on her fingernails while she listened to story after story about why her co-residents attempted suicide. The closer the circle wound its way around to Ana, the louder her brain got.

For a person who weaves words for a living, these group therapy sessions were the hardest part of residential treatment. It was the eyes, all looking at Kelly, the therapist leading the session. Ana was better with pen and paper; speaking was never something she was good at.

Pain bubbled in her finger, but Ana couldn't stop chewing away. Her cuticle filled with blood. The girl next to her was talking and then it would be Ana's turn. Destroying her finger was her only defense from her frayed nerves.

"I don't have much to say about myself. I'm kind of boring," the girl next to her said. She was petite but looked like she would fight anyone who came her way.

"This is a safe space, Sarah. If you want to share more, you're welcome to," Kelly said.

Sarah let out a long sigh. "I don't have anymore," she said.

"I won't force you to say anything you're not comfortable with but remember group therapy is part of the healing journey," Kelly said to the group. Sarah just sighed again.

Kelly looked down at her clipboard. She was an older woman with streaked gray hair. She wore flowy clothes and looked like she did pottery for fun.

"Ana, welcome. You're new to Hillside," Kelly said. "Team, let's give Ana a warm welcome." A few people clapped but most did nothing. Ana's brain wanted to explode from awkwardness alone.

"Hi," she said. Ana looked at the ground; she couldn't meet anyone's eyes.

"Ana, Do you want to tell us a little bit about yourself?" Kelly prompted.

"Sure, I guess. I'm Ana. I live here in Denver. I'm a writer and I host a podcast with my sister," Ana said. Someone on the other side of the circle let out a low, grating whistle.

"Ana, do you want to tell us about what brings you here?"

"Uh. I had a little slip-up last week. I spiraled a bit and drank too much wine. And took some pills."

"Ana, thank you for your bravery."

That didn't feel brave. It wasn't the whole truth, there was so much more to the story. Much more than Ana wanted to share in a group setting. Ana just nodded; it was easier than bringing it all up.

"Anyone else we didn't get to?" Kelly asked. Her voice was soothing, kind. In another life, Ana imagined her mom could have been a group therapist like her - they looked alike, with friendly eyes and an open vibe.

No one answered and a loud silence fell over the group. Ana wondered if group sessions were always this way. It didn't feel like much healing would happen in this kind of setting, but she didn't have a choice but to sit here. She supposed the same was true for all of them.

"Today we're going to talk about life beyond Hillside. The goal is, of course, for all of you to get out of here and go on to have safe, productive lives." A few heads nodded.

"So, today, let's talk about triggers," Kelly continued. "These little buggers can come in many different forms, and they will certainly come when you get out of here. They can be anything - smells, particular people, places – that make you either want to slip back into your addiction or make you have suicidal thoughts again. The goal for today is to recognize what triggers you. When you understand what sets you off, you can work to avoid it and minimize the amount it affects you," she said.

Kelly looked around the room. She met Ana's gaze with a little crinkle of a smile around her eyes.

"Think about it, what triggers you? What makes you want to slip back into your old habits?"

Ana moved to another finger. The question was too big for her mind. Ana didn't want to confront it. How could she answer that her whole life was one big trigger? Ana mentally checked things off in her mind: fucked-up childhood, when her sister wouldn't answer the phone, when the words wouldn't come. Living was a walking trigger for her.

Her life always went like this. Peaks and valleys. Waves. Sometimes she could hold it all together for a few months of peace, but then inevitably something would shoot her back down. She missed a lot of time, big black chunks in her memory. The blank spots that had been there since she was a kid.

"Anyone want to share?" Kelly asked.

Some young girl with Addams-Family dyed-black hair raised her hand. The therapist nodded her way.

"Go ahead, Jennifer," she said.

"My stepdad. I hate that motherfucker," Jennifer spat.

"Family is a big trigger," Kelly said, nodding. "And when you're out of here, and presumably have to be around him to some degree, do you have any thoughts about how to deal with the fact that he triggers you? And if you don't, that's okay. We'll be talking about this both in group and individual therapy for some time as we prepare to transition you out of here."

"I'm going to run away," Jennifer said. Ana looked at her and was met with a placid, yet determined, face. Something about the way she set her jaw, made Ana think she was serious.

"Jennifer, I understand the need to get away from those things that set you off. I really do. And in some cases, running far away from them is a good idea. But for some triggers, we simply cannot remove them from our lives. I assume this will be the case with your stepfather. Even if you move away, he will always be there."

"Then I'll kill him," Jennifer said. Gasps rippled across the group.

"Jennifer, that isn't even remotely okay to joke about. Let's do this, you and I will set up some one-on-ones this week and we'll talk through why he makes you so upset, and we'll make a plan to work through it all."

Jennifer laughed. The sound was tinny, high in Ana's ear. Kelly tutted disapprovingly and wrote something on her clipboard.

"Ana let's turn to you. What is something that triggers you?"

Ana sat up straighter in her chair. She wasn't expecting to be called on.

"Uhh, life?"

The group laughed. Ana looked down; she didn't mean it as a joke.

"Okay, I get that, too," Kelly said. "Can you pick one thing to talk about today? A family member? Work?"

"I guess similarly to Jennifer, my sister is a trigger for me."

"Okay, go on," she prodded.

"Well, I get anxious when she's not around, but I am also anxious when she is around. We live together, so it's constant."

"Ana, I'm proud of your insightfulness. Especially with family, it can be hard to see those dynamics. It's even harder to admit them.

Good job!" Guilt swallowed Ana. It didn't feel right to out her sister like that.

"And Ana, what are some things you could do after Hillside to minimize how much she triggers you?"

"I don't know, I probably need some space. I want to get my own place."

"Yes, Ana! You're a newbie but this is incredible. You see your trigger, and you're working on a plan for how to minimize it. Wonderful."

Ana's chest swelled. The therapist was right, it did feel good to confront what she knew to be true for a long time. Ana needed space. She needed a house of her own, she needed friends outside of Bex. She needed more independence.

She had only been at Hillside for a couple of nights, but she already felt so much better. The future was promising.

SIXTEEN

The bowling alley was dark and loud music beat from the speakers. Every few minutes, groups would erupt in loud cheers. It was one of those places that had done a trendy rebrand. It was now a cool and hip place for millennials to hang after work.

"I still can't believe it happened, she was doing so good," Bex said. She grabbed her ball and slipped her fingers into the holes. "I mean. I should have known. She was manic and then depressive. Sometimes she loses time - blacks out, I guess. Goes blank. That's how it's always been for Ana, I was just hoping she wouldn't do it again."

"That's textbook," Aimee replied. "I'm sorry it happened but you've got to be more realistic. Your sister is mentally ill. You can't just wish her to get better."

"I know. I just thought we had it figured out." Bex took a practice swing, then another sip of beer.

Aimee grabbed Bex's arm. "It's not your fault; you've done more than enough for your sister. You just have to support her through each phase. I don't know that you'll ever just figure it out and be done with it."

Bex liked the way Aimee's soft hand felt on her skin; it felt so good to have someone in her corner for once.

"She was writing a new book, she just hit ten thousand followers. She even went on a date the other day. She should be happy."

"Look, I'm sorry it happened. I am, but you gotta quit beating yourself up about it," Aimee said, giving her a little squeeze. Bex's skin tingled.

"I know. I just fucked up. I didn't answer my phone and I stayed at your house and then this," Bex said.

"You're allowed to have a life outside of your sister."

"I do."

"But here we are at the bowling alley and we're still talking about her."

"I know, I'm sorry. It's just a lot to wrap my mind around."

"So don't. You're probably never going to understand. Just forget about it for the night. Let's have some fun."

Bex looked at the pins and squared her shoulders. She wanted to smash down every single one of them.

The server stopped by their lane. "Another pitcher?" she asked.

Aimee nodded. Bex shook her head no.

"What? We just had this fight the other night. I thought we were having fun. Why did you say no?"

"Ah, I don't know. One is probably good."

"I'm practically a whole keg ahead of you? Get on my level!" Aimee laughed.

"They're expensive."

"What, now you're worried about money, too?" Aimee said.

Bex launched her ball down the lane and watched it spin all the way down. It knocked over two pins. She slapped her leg and cursed under her breath. Bex wondered how to answer Aimee without sending her further down the sister-hating path.

"Well, Hillside is going to strap me. Ana has Medicaid but I'm not even sure if that will cover it. I didn't do that much research, I just agreed to send her there because it's where her psychiatrist works," Bex said. She sat on the bench and watched Aimee get her ball.

"So? Ana can pay for it. It's not your responsibility to cover it."

"With what paycheck? Ana lives with me; I pay for it all. That's how we've decided to set it up until her books and our podcast take off. It will be okay; I just have to be conscious for a while."

"Oh my god, Bex. Really? What, you're just going to cover the cost of INPATIENT care until she's better? What if she never gets better?"

"She will, I know it. And you know what they say, 'a little trauma is good for the writing career,'" Bex said. She laughed but Aimee did not. She looked away; her eyes followed another woman as she walked by their lane. Bex felt a stab of jealousy.

"Oh, my god. Stop. You just need to cut her off," Aimee said. "Make her grow up."

The comment hit Bex right in the gut. The beer did a flip in her stomach. The silence stretched in between them. Aimee shrugged as if that was such an obvious answer to the issue.

"I can't do that, and you know it," Bex finally replied.

"And why not? It's your money. Your house. You could kick her out. Or at least make her get a real job."

"She works!"

"Self-publishing books and hosting a weekly podcast hardly counts."

"That's not fair. Tons of content creators make a good living. We just got to give it more time. The podcast will eventually cover the bills. In the meantime, I'll set up a payment plan with the facility. It will be fine."

"Are you going to go see her there?" Aimee asked.

"They asked that I don't for a little while until they get a handle on her mental health. It's standard for patients to have a period of separation for the first while."

"Makes sense, I guess."

"Yeah, it's just hard. Aside from a few work trips, this is the longest I've gone without seeing her ever. I miss her."

"Y'all are something."

"What does that mean?"

"I don't know. I just know that you're both grown adults. She'll be okay, just give her time to figure it out," Aimee said. She walked up to the line and launched her ball hard and fast. Bex couldn't believe Aimee had that kind of arm. Aimee did a little dance when the last pin wobbled and then toppled over. Bex couldn't lose Aimee, either.

"I'm sorry, you're right. Let's have a fun night." Bex waved down their server and ordered another pitcher.

They talked about their next work trip to San Francisco for a big attorney-client and daydreamed about an upcoming summer trip to Cabo. They ate fries and took down way too many beers. Bex loosened up and let the night take her away. She squashed all the Ana-related feelings of guilt with the alcohol and fried food.

"Wanna come home with me?" Aimee asked after a second game.

Bex nodded. There was some solace in the fact that at least Bex knew Ana was safe inside Hillside.

SEVENTEEN

The second she walked in the door; Ana was hit with a strong smell of artificial cherry. The room was messy and dusty. It was warmer and somehow homier than the rest of the building. Compared to how clean and sterile the clinic was, the office felt out of place.

"Hello again!" Dr. Daniels said as she pushed through the door. Something clicked against his teeth; Ana realized it was one of those old-school cherry lozenges. He stood and walked around his big mahogany desk.

Dr. Daniels was a big guy, six feet at least. He had to be pushing sixty with salt and pepper hair and loose jowls around his neck. He wore a navy three-piece suit and a baby blue tie. His outfit also stood out among all the scrubs and soft clothes the patients wore. His face was largely covered by a gray beard and thick glasses.

"Ana, you look better!" he beamed. Ana didn't believe him. Her hair was greasier than a fast-food hamburger.

"Thanks," she said. The mumbled words barely escaped her mouth.

"Sit, sit," he gestured to the leather couch on the other side of his office. He took the chair facing the couch. Ana hated how he always used two words at the same time.

The couch was more comfortable than it looked. She fought the urge to lie down and sleep. She didn't want to be here. She didn't want to talk to another person.

"Welcome to Hillside, Ana. I'm glad you're here. I take that back. I wish you were at home, but given the circumstances, I'm glad you're still with us."

Ana couldn't look at him. She picked at her fingers instead.

"So, Ana, you tried to do yourself harm?"

"I guess you could call it that."

"Your sister called me right after it happened, and I recommended she bring you here since we have a working relationship. Continuity of care is important."

Ana nodded.

"How are you finding it here?"

"Fine."

"I see you're in a chatty mood today," he said. His belly jiggled with his chuckle.

"So just a bit of housekeeping before we begin," he said. "I've been in touch with Bex, and you'll get to see her very soon. Usually, we like to have patients take a break from family, but I know you and Bex have a special bond."

The mention of seeing Bex almost made Ana topple over. Her feelings were complicated, and Ana wasn't ready to face Bex. Ana looked around the room instead. The carpeted floor had a multi-colored rug over it; it looked silly to Ana. There was a little machine in the corner admitting white noise. Dr. Daniel's diplomas hung on the wall, four of them. Dang.

There was nothing personal though. No photos of a wife, or husband. No pictures of kids or a dog. Maybe Dr. Daniels didn't have anyone either. Or maybe he wanted a very strict separation between his work and his family.

"I'm not ready to see her," Ana said.

"That's fine. We understand that family can be hard. We'll get there with time."

"I want to call my friend, James."

"And who is James?" Dr. Daniels asked, rubbing his chin.

"He's our podcast engineer and my friend. I want to be able to call him and let him know what happened. I don't have my phone; he probably thinks I ghosted him."

"Well, Ana. As you know, we have a strict no-phone policy. That's important to help everyone heal and improve without stressors from the outside world. I can't permit you to talk to him now, but I can ask Bex to let him know."

Ana leaned back in her seat and blew her hair out of her face. Ana didn't want Bex in the middle of whatever she had with James.

"I know that's not what you want to hear, but it will be the best for you long-term. Let's move on. So, you've been here a day. Sorry, I couldn't see you sooner, I was tied up with another patient," he said. He paused; Ana didn't say anything.

"Settling in? How are you finding it here?" he asked again. She could feel his eyes searching her face. She couldn't take it. She made eye contact. His eyes were shiny, and he had just a slight smile. He wanted her to match his energy.

She couldn't. "It's fine."

"You did a group session with Kelly, right?"

She hadn't been there for long, but it was already a blur: group, yoga, painting, and outdoor time. And talking. Talking. Talking. They were throwing a whole slew of healing modalities her way, hoping one would stick.

"Yes, group with Kelly," she said.

"And how was it?"

"Fine. She's nice."

"Yes, of course, everyone is nice. But we also want you to find someone that can help you the most. There are a variety of therapists on staff so if you don't feel like you're clicking with Kelly, we can try someone else. That's okay."

"No, she's great. Just not used to this place."

"That's normal. We ripped you right out of your normal life and stuck you in a place where all you have to worry about is taking care of you. That takes a bit of adjustment."

Ana nodded, not looking up from the swirls in the rug.

"Good, good."

"So, my role here is to oversee all the pieces of your treatment and your medication. We want to make sure it is all working in concert so you can get back to normal life sooner rather than later."

"How long do I have to be here?"

"Well, Ana, that depends. You are not forced to stay here. This is a voluntary program, but your sister and I strongly recommend you stay at least for a bit longer. But usually, our patients stay a month. That's long enough to sort out medications and build skills that help you re-enter normal life."

"And as a member of your team, I want to get to know you even better. That's why I asked you here, just to keep a finger on the pulse of your progress. I want to make sure I'm helping you as much as I can."

He gave her a toothy smile. Ana looked away. It was all too much. She didn't want to be his friend. She wanted to go back to her room.

"It's been a little bit since I've seen you. Let's catch up. You're still writing and doing your podcast?"

She nodded.

"Have you been under pressure?"

How could she answer him? He wouldn't get it. She just shook her head instead; her work wasn't stressful compared to most people's.

"I am wondering, do you think the topics of your books contributed to your mental health struggles?"

Ana knew the conversation would eventually wind up here. She still didn't have an answer for him or anyone else who asked why she wrote dark books. She didn't know how to make him see that writing and podcasting about the worst of society didn't make her suicidal. In fact, it was the only thing she had to live for.

When Ana was at her best, she felt like telling victims' stories - shining a light on the underbelly of the world - was her life's work. At worst, Ana feared she was glorifying true crime with literal blood money. Dr. Daniels would never understand.

"Ana," he said, twisting his head to make eye contact. "Your first book, it's about a bomb in a book? Did I get that right? And the one after that was about a woman who jumped off a bridge?"

"Is that correct?" He asked again. "Murder mysteries?"

"More or less."

"Why do you think you're interested in true crime?"

"It's my job."

"Okay, and what is writing a book like for you? I'm fascinated by it."

"I don't know. I find an idea, usually rooted in some true story. I plot it out, and then write it."

"Ana, you're not giving yourself enough credit. Writing a book is hard. I recently read that 97% of people who start writing a book, never finish it. And of those who do finish, only about 20% of them actually publish it. You've done it twice, and you have another book in the works? That's something, Ana."

Ana was surprised by this turn in the conversation. She was certain that he would tell her she needed to find lighter topics to write about.

He leaned forward in his chair. She could smell the cherry cough drop scent on him. She could see that his teeth were yellowed, probably from years of smoking. She tried to sink back into the couch.

"Ana, I'm proud of you. You have a lot going for you and we're going to get you right as rain so you can get back to writing."

She nodded involuntarily this time. She didn't miss home and she didn't mind the space from Bex, but god, she missed her words. She missed her followers, and she missed puzzling plots together. She even missed the marketing - a little bit.

"Ana, you're in good hands here," he said. "You and me, and a little help from your sister, we'll keep you safe."

EIGHTEEN

Excerpt From Obstruction of Correspondence
By Ana Adams

Murder is personal but that doesn't mean it has to be proximal. That realization changed Warren's life. The realization that he could cleanly dissect the problem from his family - without ever going near him again - was the first time he'd felt hope since he was a boy.

It was surprisingly easy. He needed a box. The mechanisms of a gun. And a few shells. He needed a VPN to block his online search queries and he needed to pay for a scheduled post office pickup from the next city over.

He already had the perfect alibi, a surgical residency at UC Davis. More than 1,500 miles from the explosion; an alibi was more than location though. It was a lack of motive. No reason. And as far as anyone knew, their family secrets had always been just that, secret. He didn't even sell his trauma to get into one of the top surgery programs in the country. No one knew their family's history. And no one would expect a doctor-in-training would have the time or energy to pull something like this off.

He also already owned all the gloves, caps, and masks he would need to build the thing, without letting a trace of his DNA slip into the box.

The hardest part was figuring out how to fit his plan between the pages of the book. He watched videos on the dark web, with the anonymity of a VPN, until his confidence grew, and his plan seemed nothing if not reasonable.

He did exactly as the masked man in the video told him. He bought the pieces, one by one, over time. He thrifted. He pawn shopped. He took it apart and put it back together until he created a near-replica design of the one in the video.

He loaded blanks and held his breath. The first time was a miss. The second time the bullet didn't even make it through the cover. He watched the video again and tinkered some more. He pinched his finger and lost his resolve.

Warren set the box on the floor and removed his sterile equipment. He sat on the couch and realized that his dad had been right all along - he wouldn't even amount to much. He couldn't do this.

His phone buzzed in his pocket. A text from his mom.

"He's at it again."

Warren waited but nothing else came through. He knew what his mom meant, that his dad was out in the garage drinking and it would be no time until he was ready to beat the shit out of someone. Since Warren left and his brother overdosed, there was only his mom.

A million responses plowed through his mind. Warren debated calling his mom, hell even calling the cops. He knew all of that would just make it worse for his mom. He'd beat her even worse next time.

The box was the only way.

Warren put his gear back on and set the trap one last time. He closed the lid of the book gingerly and taped the box shut, just as the masked man told him to do a hundred times over by now.

Warren prayed that this time would be it. That he would have finally gotten it right. He opened the box and it clicked. The blank shot went off perfectly. He winced at the sudden noise and felt something inside of him give way.

A mixture of pride and pain caused tears to prick in the corner of his eyes. He'd done it. He'd figured it out. Warren curled into a ball on the floor and let the tears come.

It was time.

Warren picked up the book he picked out for his dad - <u>My Dad Had That Car.</u> It was a heavy, coffee table-type book that his dad would have loved looking at the pictures of if he ever read anything besides car manuals. *His dad couldn't read it now. The middle of the book was carefully cut out in a perfect square to cradle the thing that would end his life.*

He set the book inside a new, crisp box. Warren opened the cover and got to work setting the bomb inside the book just the way the masked man taught him. Warren pulled the three live bullets from the plastic bag hidden in the back of his junk drawer. He took one out and kissed it through his mask.

"This one's for you, Dad," he said into the empty apartment.

He pushed the bullets into place and closed the lid of the box. Warren watched the video enough times to know that nothing could trigger the device unless the book was opened, but seeing it on his dining table, knowing his mom was in for one hell of an awful night was too much.

Warren grabbed his phone. Hold tight Mom. I love you. *He typed back. There was so much more he wanted to say but he knew he couldn't. She wouldn't ever leave him. Saying more wouldn't do anything. This was the only way.*

Warren grabbed his keys and headed to the nearest package drop box. He couldn't wait for the pickup date.

"Fuck you, Dad," he whispered as he put the box in the mailing bin.

—

The ding woke Ruth up from her nap. She hadn't realized she'd fallen asleep but the latest headache from his tirade was taking its sweet time to subside. Ruth stood and the arthritic pain crashed through her body as she moved toward the door.

She knew she was too damn old to subject her body to this much longer.

Ruth pulled open the door and found the stoop empty. A single white box lay in the center of their front porch. Ruth took a half step forward, holding the door open with her foot while she bent down to pick up the package.

It was heavier than she expected. The address was a printed square, sent to Paul. No return address. She knew it was some part for that old piece of junk car he had taken apart in the garage.

She walked it to the kitchen, feeling the sharp pain in her hip where he'd kicked her the other night.

Ruth opened the door between the kitchen and the garage and called to Paul, "Hey there - you just got a package in the mail. I'll set it on the bench for you."

"No, it's the crank I need for the winda'. Open it and hand it to me, will ya?"

Ruth would rather do anything else than spend more time out in this garage with him, but she knew better than to set him off. Ruth set the box on the bench and found an old screwdriver to cut through the tape.

It took her a couple of turns but she broke through the double layers and opened the box. She moved the packaging materials, looking for the crank. Her hand hit something hard.

She put the paper on the bench and peered inside the box. It was a book. A book with old cars on the front. A cold wave washed over Ruth. She didn't want to have to tell him that whatever part he was waiting for wasn't inside this box.

"Give it here, lady," he said from somewhere on the other side of the car.

"It's a book, Paul," she said. She knew he would hate the quiver in her voice.

"What'd ya say?"

She cleared her throat. "It's a book. There's no part."

"You dumb? I asked you to hand me the crank!" he shouted.

Ruth fished the book out of the box. It was heavier than she imagined. Ruth let her hopes rise that the crank was somehow inside the book, and she was indeed just a dumb lady.

Ruth opened the book. An explosion rocketed in her ears. The garage went hazy. She fell to the ground, her hands grabbing for her midsection, blood seeping between her fingers.

The last thing she heard was, "Oh my god, Ruth. What now?"

Her final thought was, Let it finally be over.

NINETEEN

Bex stepped inside the phone booth in the office. As she slid the door closed, the noise of her colleagues faded away. She took one final look around the room, no one was watching her. No one noticed that she'd slipped away.

She said a tiny prayer of thanks and turned away from the team working behind her. The idea of a fishbowl office - open and collaborative - was fun until you had a personal call like this one to make.

Bex found who she was looking for in her contacts and pressed his number. She felt nervous as the line connected and began to ring. Over the last week, this idea was all she could think about. And this was the first step.

"Hello, Dr. Daniels speaking," filled her ear. Bex sat up straighter.

"Hi, there - Bexley Adams, Ana's sister. Thanks for making the time to connect," Bex said. Her heart felt like it was in her throat, making it hard to get the words out as confidently as she normally would.

"Of course, I'm glad we're on the same side for Ana's care. She's doing well here at Hillside. She's been participating in group therapy and has had many one-on-ones with therapists. She's also doing yoga and other forms of self-directed healing."

Something in Bex's shoulders relaxed a little. It was good to hear that her baby sister was okay.

"And I met with her yesterday," he added. "She and I just had a little check-in. Just to see how she's adjusting. We talked about her writing."

"That is very good to hear, I sincerely appreciate that you're taking care of her."

"Yes, of course. I am committed to seeing her through this latest blip," he said. Bex couldn't tell if that was something he was proud of or if he was ready to get rid of her sister.

"How soon do you think she can come home?" Bex dared ask.

He cleared his throat. "Well, as I'm sure you're aware, there are many factors that play into answering that question. For Ana, I'd love her to stay a month or so."

Bex's chest tightened. Quick math ran through her mind.

"I just don't know that we can afford to keep her there for that long," she said.

"I know, don't get me started on mental health care in America," he said. "The cost is prohibitive for most."

"So, can she come home sooner?"

"Yes, of course. I can't keep her here, but I'd like at least a few more days to stabilize her."

"Okay, through the end of the week," Bex said around a lump in her throat. She had no idea how she'd ever pay off that bill, but she had to do it for Ana.

"Thanks, Bex. Your sister is lucky to have you."

Dr. Daniels gave Bex more details about Ana's care. He sounded quite proud of the program he'd built. The pair hung up and Bex let out a loud sigh. She leaned her head against the padded wall and rubbed her forehead. It was a lot to take in.

A soft rap on the door made her jump. Bex turned and saw Aimee peering through the window. She held up her hand in a wave. Bex smiled. Aimee put her hand on the glass and Bex did the same.

Bex pulled the glass door open with a question on her face. She was worried people would notice. She scanned the room behind Aimee, still no one was watching.

93

"What's up?" Bex whispered.

"Nothing, I just wanted to check on you. You looked a little stressed."

"I'm good. I was just talking to Ana's doctor."

"Everything okay?"

"Yeah, just making a plan for her."

"She coming home soon?" Aimee asked. Her hand brushed Bex's; a shiver went down her arm.

"Yeah, end of the week."

"That's good news, right?"

"Yes, I'll be glad to have her back home."

Aimee nodded. Bex couldn't read the gesture, but she appreciated that Aimee stopped her day to check in, especially in front of everyone. Warmth spread across her middle and a smile cracked her face.

"Well, I have a call here soon with that dairy in Erie but I'm glad she's okay," Aimee said. She grabbed Bex's hand and squeezed. "Let's hang tonight and you can tell me all about it."

As she walked away, Aimee turned back and winked.

TWENTY

Her assigned room wasn't big enough for all the pacing Ana needed to do. She craved the outside. Ana couldn't be stuck in this room anymore. She didn't want to talk about her interest in true crime with some quack doctor or why she and her sister were so fucked up. She wanted to be able to write without people looking over her shoulder. She needed to breathe without the smell of cleaning solution filling her nostrils.

The only problem was Dr. Daniels and Bex stood between her and freedom. Sure, this was technically a voluntary hold, Ana could walk out the front door, she just didn't have anywhere to go. Ana didn't have a job or a place to live. She couldn't just go back home and hope Bex would let her back in.

Ever since Ana was let go from the newspaper - followed by a mental breakdown, a half-hearted period of self-harm, and a long stretch of afternoon blackouts - she'd relied on her sister for practically everything. Bex said it was for launching Ana's author career, but Ana knew its real name: charity.

Despite it all, Ana found a sense of freedom at Hillside that she'd never get at home. It wasn't until Ana was away from Bex that she could see it. Ana didn't want to be in residential anymore, but she sure as hell didn't want to go home to her overbearing sister either.

Ana needed to make a plan. She needed to find a way out and into her own place.

Ana's room was small, hardly enough space for a twin bed, a little desk, and one small dresser to put her things on. Everything was bolted to the ground and there was nothing that could do any harm. She did have one small window that overlooked the parking lot; it wasn't much but at least she could feel a little of that famous Denver sunshine.

The sun made Ana think of James and their time together at the lake. Longing hit her square in the stomach. She was sure that whatever they had would be gone after this - poof. He wouldn't understand. Whatever tiny thing they had between them felt like it was slipping between her fingers.

Ana did another lap around the room; she forced James out of her mind. Ana looked out the door, people were milling about. It must be free time, otherwise, she'd be expected to stay in her room until someone told her differently. Ana looked down the hall and decided anywhere was better than there.

The urge to put pen to paper overtook her mind. She needed to be in someone else's nightmare, not her own. Ana needed to create scenes where the main characters possessed agency and control. She needed to write herself out of this place.

Ana grabbed her spiral notebook and the pen one of the group therapists gave her from the drawer in the desk. It was meant to be a journal, not a future book but Ana didn't care. Writing was her drug, and she was definitely having a withdrawal.

The common area was free of other patients; Ana sat down. Set in the corners of the facility, hang-out spaces were designed for gathering to foster organic relationships - only friendships - between patients, one of the therapists told her. Ana only ever used the spaces if no one else was there.

It wasn't her Mac or her desk at home, but the tie-dye bean bag was surprisingly comfortable in a college dorm kind of way. Ana opened the notebook; the smell of paper caught in her nostrils. Ana basked in the ecstasy of a blank page.

The problem with other therapists is their propensity to get caught. I'm not like other therapists, Ana wrote.

Ana didn't have a clue where the story would take her, but she didn't care. The urge to understand Dr. Daniels pushed the words onto the paper. Writing the words was cathartic; it also gave Ana's brain a way to plan her next move.

"Hey, there-" someone called behind her. Ana didn't turn, convinced the person was talking to someone else.

A patient, in a nondescript sweatsuit, rounded the corner and stood in front of her. His hair looked like it was fresh out of a surfing session and some kind of snake tattoo circled his wrist and forearm. Ana thought she recognized him from one of their group sessions, but his name wouldn't come to her.

"Ana, right?" he asked.

Ana didn't move; she wanted him to get the hint. She wanted him to leave.

"Ana? We were in group together."

"Yes?"

He sat down in the bean bag next to hers. The bag let out a swoosh as the air displaced under his weight.

"I'm Kyle Francis," he said. He shoved a hand in her direction. She didn't drop her pen or shake his hand. His hand fell into his lap along with his face. This guy couldn't read a sign from an inch away.

"So, what brings you here?"

Ana snorted. "What kind of question is that? Same as everyone I guess."

"Ha, yep. Me too. Just add in a little addiction to the mix."

Ana didn't want to know more. She looked down at her paper and analyzed her first line. Given the circumstances, she thought it was pretty good.

No, I'm not better than them. In fact, I'm likely worse in a lot of ways. She added.

"What are you working on," Kyle asked. He still hadn't taken a hint.

"Oh, just writing."

"A letter? Got a boyfriend at home?"

"No," she said. She didn't care which question that answered for him.

"No letter, okay. What about a boyfriend?"

A vision of James crossed her mind, flooding her with memories of the budding relationship they had. A smile broke out on her face.

"Oh, you do have a boyfriend. We're going to have to go ahead and get rid of him."

"Yeah, his name is James and he'd be pissed that you're talking to me this way."

"Don't worry about him. I'll handle it," he laughed and made a gun sign with his fingers. Ana cringed.

"So, you don't want to talk about your boyfriend. I get that. Let's talk about what you're writing then?"

"Just a book," she said between her teeth.

"That's right, you're the author!"

"I guess you could say that."

"What do you write?"

"Serial killers," Ana said.

"Really? That's cool. I'm really into true crime."

Ana forced herself not to roll her eyes at his originality. An obsession with true crime was nothing special: one look at the bestseller list and the top podcast charts proved that. Everyone has that sick need to soak in all the gory details and imagine themselves caught in the crosshairs of a killer. Most just didn't admit that they too lived in the nation of freaks.

"Yeah."

"And you have a podcast? That's hot." He leaned a little closer.

"What's it about?"

"True crime."

"Siiiick," he said.

Ana looked down at her notebook. She willed him away.

"What's the name of your book? I wanna read!" he said.

"Uhh. I have a couple. My first one is called *Obstruction of Correspondence*."

He leaned over and yanked her pen from her hand. He wrote the title on the back of his hand in sloppy, third-grade writing.

"I'm allowed to have my iPad here - expanded privileges and shit. Thanks, rich parents. Imma download it right now," he announced. Questions swirled through her mind. Why was he allowed tech when no one else was?

"Thanks," she mumbled.

"A podcast and books. You're living every crime junkie's dream."

"Not really, if I was - I wouldn't be here."

"Oh, whatever. The best creators are the ones that have a little trauma of their own. They're relatable. They write better stories because they have experience."

The hairs on Ana's neck stood up. She didn't like his vibe; she didn't want to have this conversation any longer. Ana rocked to stand up out of the bean bag chair.

He grabbed her arm and held her back again. "Ana, I like talking to you. Stay."

"I have to go," she said. He stood too, but never let go of her arm. She shrunk in comparison to his sturdy build.

He smiled wide and wrapped her in a big hug. He squeezed just a little too hard. "I like a creepy girl," he whispered in her ear.

TWENTY-ONE

Bex sat down on the couch and turned on the television. She flipped through Netflix, looking for anything to take her mind off all of it. Aimee ditched her for some rave party filled with vapes and seizure-inducing lights in LoDo and Ana was still at Hillside. Bex was alone. She didn't like being home without Ana. The air around her felt permeated with loneliness.

Work weighed on her mind. Keeping her relationship with her direct report under wraps was harder than she imagined it would be. People were starting to notice the way they shared banter in the hallway and went to lunch together. It wouldn't be long before HR was involved.

Bex landed on some kind of mindless romance reality show where contestants had to forge a relationship without ever seeing the other person. Bex watched connections fumble through conversations with a wall between them. She didn't think she could commit to someone without knowing their appearance. Bex worked hard to look good, and she wanted a partner who did the same.

As she waited for some kind of action on screen, Bex flipped through the apps on her phone. She landed on her email. Between a day packed with meetings and sneaking around with Aimee in between, Bex hadn't checked her personal email all day.

She cleared out the junk and found an email from a podcast listener.

Hey, Bex and Ana - when are you releasing another episode? Love your show. Don't quit now, okay? The message said. It was signed by someone named Veronica.

Bex sighed. If Veronica noticed that they were behind, who else had? The podcast was suffering with Ana away. Bex couldn't carry the show alone, she hadn't even tried.

She picked at her split ends in the light of the television and thought about their upcoming podcast event. Bex and Ana were supposed to host a live recording in just a few weeks. She prayed like hell that her sister would be up for it by then.

A ding from her phone broke through her thoughts. An email from AncestryAndMe.com arrived in her inbox, alerting her to new messages in her dashboard. Her stomach cramped.

Bex clicked on the link in the email and logged into her account. As she feared, a new landslide of messages from Caleb waited for her.

So, Bex. You there? You going to talk to me or what? I'm your brother, you know that right?

Bex squeezed her phone tight. She needed to get him off her back and soon.

Caleb, yes. I see your messages. I'm going through something right now with Ana and I need to focus on her.

Three little dots appeared in the chat box. Caleb was writing her back.

What's going on with my sister? He asked.

She's sick. I need to take care of her. Bex wrote. She felt a sense of purpose. She was being completely honest with Caleb. Ana needed her right now and Bex was going to do everything she could for her sister.

The chat quieted. Bex thought that maybe that was enough, maybe Caleb would get the hint easier than she feared.

You know, I came by your house the other night? I knocked and knocked. No one answered.

Did you not answer the door because you got that letter? I'm sorry I sent it, I really am. That was uncalled for. I was drunk; I wrote it in the heat of the moment. I came to apologize.

Bex sat up straighter on the couch. She wanted to throw her phone across the room. A million questions made her thumb dance over the screen. She couldn't decide which to ask first.

How do you know where I live?!

What, like it's hard? You own the place. I know how to look at property records. You haven't given me your phone number, so I couldn't call first. I had to drive to Denver for work. I came by on a whim after I checked into the motel.

Bex's heart skipped in her chest. He might be her brother, but he wasn't welcome to barge into their lives like this.

When did you come? She asked.

Uhh. I don't know. I think it was last Wednesday? He wrote.

Fear coursed through her body. That was the same night that Bex went out with Aimee. That was the night that Ana tried to kill herself.

I stayed and waited for you for a while, but no one ever came home. I had to get back to the hotel. I just want to talk, Bex. I'll come back. Please.

Something cemented itself in Bex. She needed Caleb out of her life. And fast. Not only did he look up their address and show up at their house uninvited, but he was the catalyst for Ana's attempt. She hated him.

Please just leave us alone. Bex responded.

TWENTY-TWO

The walls of the place closed in on Ana. She could feel eyes on her anytime she left her room. Her whole body was on edge, she couldn't seem to relax. Ana didn't think she would be able to manage if she had to stay much longer.

The only thing she could do to keep her mind from eating itself from the inside out was to let the words flow. She grabbed her journal and began writing.

> *The fire is burning from the inside of the building, out. The heat is intensifying, and the oxygen is disappearing by the minute. This place is flaming my anxiety and the fire inside me is suffocating my soul. Ana will burn up and my ashes will float away unless I can create a fire break, and then an escape plan.*
>
> *I'm wearing normalcy like fire-resistant clothing. Showcasing my saneness sews my fire trench coat together inch by inch. Pretending to be healed is my escape plan. I just have to show the fire marshals - Bex and Dr. Daniels - that the fire is under control and it's safe for me to run.*

The prose was unnatural in contrast to her normal plotlines, but writing helped her see the way out. Her words understood before her mind, but there on a paper was a plan. The sooner people believed she was sane and happy, the sooner she could get a place of her own and have true freedom.

'On the paper, Ana wrote:

To do:

- *Participate in group*
- *Play nice with others*
- *Rest well*
- *Take medications*
- *No outbursts*
- *Smile!*

Ana could do these things. She could check them off one by one and show great progress. She could show Dr. Daniels that his efforts were working. She just had to fake it until she could make it.

First up, go to a group therapy session and act normal. She could do it. Freedom would be hers sooner than later.

"Ana! Ana!" Kyle called from across the circle as soon as she walked into the meeting room. "Come sit by me!"

The voice inside her head screamed at her to ignore him. Ana looked up and saw Dr. Daniels watching her. Normal, she reminded herself. Ana walked across the room and sat next to Kyle.

"I'm sitting by the famous author," Kyle announced to the group. Ana's face flushed and heart raced. Her cloak of normalcy threatened to fall off as she had the urge to tell him to leave her alone..

"And I'm sitting next to you!" She said instead, adding a big fake laugh. Ana caught Dr. Daniel's smile out of the corner of her eye.

"Ana, I started your book. Insane. I love it," Kyle said. His eyes were bright, and she could tell he believed every word. Despite herself, Ana sat up a little straighter.

"Yeah, I got it yesterday and read half the night. You're so good!"

"Thanks," she said. She tucked her chin; she didn't want to talk about it here.

"Okay, group. Let's begin," Dr. Daniels said.

Kyle reached over and squeezed her knee. It took everything in Ana not to recoil and punch him in the face. Instead, she patted his hand and turned her knees away from him. She added a mental checkmark to her list: a normal reaction.

"Today, we're going to talk about goals. Goals are so important for healing," Dr. Daniels said. The cough drop in his mouth clinked against his teeth. "Specifically, we're talking about what goals you have set for yourself. And are you accomplishing them? If you don't have any goals, let's talk about developing them."

The sun shone through the window and warmed Ana's cold skin.

"So, my questions are - what goals have you accomplished since being here? And how have you been able to do that? Who wants to go first?"

Ana motioned that she was ready to talk. Dr. Daniels gave her a wide smile and nodded to her. He leaned forward, ready to listen. Ana needed him in the palm of her hand, she was getting close. She could feel it.

"I'll admit, when I first got here, I didn't have any goals. I didn't even want to live. But slowly, over time, I set a goal to write a few sentences a day -"

"I told you! She's a famous author!" Kyle interrupted. The room erupted in conversation. Ana's face turned beet red.

"Let her finish," Dr. Daniels warned.

"Not that famous," Ana started again. "After I got back into the habit of writing, my goal became to write a few paragraphs a day. I'm still writing every day, and now my new goal is to work my way out of here."

"Wow, Ana. To go from wanting to end your life to writing again, incredible. How have you been able to do it?"

105

"Well, the help and support here have been life changing. Especially from you, Dr. Daniels," Ana said. She gave him another big smile. He ate it up. "And sorting out my medication probably helped. Also, being away from home made me realize that I have a good life, I have a good sister and a career."

"Ana, I know you will be able to accomplish your goals. Let's talk more after this," he said.

Ana dug her fingernails into her palm. She smiled and looked him right in the eyes. "I'd love to," she said.

"Anyone else? I know Ana is hard to follow but goals are one of the things that heal us," Dr. Daniels said.

Kyle raised his hand and Dr. Daniels nodded. "My goal is to marry Ana Adams!" The whole group laughed.

"Kyle, that's inappropriate. Let's talk real goals, what are you working on here?"

"My parents say I'm an addict, but I don't think so. I think I'm just in love," he sang.

Kyle put his hand on Ana's knee again. She could feel his sweaty palms through her thin pants. Ana's whole body tensed. She hated the way he'd laid claim to her. Ana kept her smile and brushed his hand away, but not before he got one final squeeze in.

The conversation wound its way around the circle, people sharing goals and celebrating wins. Ana kept a smile on her face and worked to stay engaged. She did not jump every time Kyle touched her and she did not shrink under Dr. Daniel's stares. Normal.

A cacophony of metal chairs being folded and stacked along the wall coursed throughout the room as soon as the session ended. Ana did the same with hers. Kyle grabbed it out of her hand and winked. "I'll take this for you, and as payment, you'll go to lunch with me?" he said. It was more of a statement than a question.

"Ana, you got a few minutes before art class?" Dr. Daniels asked, saving her. She could smell his cherry cough drops.

"Sure."

Kyle walked off, head down like a scolded puppy.

"Let's go to my office," he suggested.

Ana followed, keeping her breath even and her body fluid. This meeting would make or break her plan for an easy exit and Ana was all in.

"So, you're feeling good? Writing again?" He asked, shutting the door behind them. The room was claustrophobic. Ana took a deep breath and told herself to be cool.

She sat down and crossed her ankles.

"Yes, I think I'm ready to go home. I've been here a while now and I've learned a lot."

He sucked in a big breath, whistling slightly against his yellow teeth. "Are you sure this is not about that Kyle kid? I noticed him being a little forward in group this morning."

"No, he's just trying to be funny. I'm ready."

He lectured her about the importance of proactively taking care of her mental health. She tuned him out as much as she could. Finally, he asked, "Do you feel like you can manage at home?"

Ana gave an emphatic nod. She was getting somewhere.

Dr. Daniels did his usual throat-clearing tic before saying, "Okay. Ultimately, it's your call."

TWENTY-THREE

Seeing Ana for the first time felt like coming home. Bex's body relaxed the instant she saw her sister and her face broke out in a smile. Ana stood at the front of the facility, bag packed and zipped at her feet.

Ana gave Bex a wave as she pulled up next to her under the facility's carport. Ana was wearing a blue tracksuit and tennis shoes, the same clothes Bex had dropped off for her sister after intake. Ana's hair was in a messy bun on the top of her head.

The clarity in Ana's eyes was the first thing Bex noticed as she walked around the car to her sister. Ana looked good. She was alert, in control. She looked more alive than Bex could remember. Maybe this stay was worth it.

"Sister!" Bex yelled, enveloping her in a big hug. Ana's body stiffened for just a split second before Ana relaxed and returned the hug. Bex noticed how Ana smelled chemical, like a hospital.

Bex pulled back and looked Ana in the face, searching her eyes. The lucidity was still there. Bex didn't imagine it.

"You look so good!"

"Thanks, I'm ready to go home."

Bex ran inside the facility and signed the documents they put in front of her. She didn't want to leave Ana for long, so she didn't take the time to read it other than noticing the big bill for Ana's care in the stack of paperwork. She made a mental note to call about that later.

"Okay, let's go!" Bex said. She tried to pick up Ana's bag, but Ana got to it first. Ana's new-found independence practically hit Bex over the head.

Bex popped the trunk and Ana put the duffle inside. Bex walked around to the driver's side and got in. Ana slipped into the seat on the other side. A million questions for Ana rushed through Bex's mind. She told herself to take it easy and give her time to adjust.

Bex finally landed on, "So, how was it?"

"It was good. Or as good as a place like that could be but I do feel better. Thank you for helping me get the care I needed," Ana said. Bex couldn't read her sister's expression.

"Of course, that's what sisters do, right?"

"Sisters," Ana said. She looked out the window.

After they merged on the interstate, Ana announced, "I want to move out, I want to live alone."

Bex's whole body tensed. There was no way Ana could live alone. Bex couldn't let that happen.

"Why?" Bex asked, hurt competing with fear in her mind.

"I've never really been on my own before. I think it's what I need."

Bex couldn't picture it. She had just signed something about Hillside relinquishing care of Ana to Bex. Ana wasn't ready.

"We'll discuss this more later," Bex said. She rolled her shoulders back and let resolve set over her. Ana needed her, she just couldn't see it yet. Whatever sense of relief Bex had felt before was replaced with worry.

"In other news," Bex started. "I got an email from a fan the other day. They wanted to know when we were going to release a new episode. Can we record a new show soon?"

Ana didn't respond.

"And remember, we booked that live recording show. That's coming up. We have to start marketing to people about it. What's your schedule like? We could even get one done tonight if you think you have a case you could cover that soon?"

The buildings on either side of the highway flew past them. Ana looked out the window, she didn't engage. Bex's annoyance flared.

Aimee's words crashed before her. Why did Bex have to put in all the work? Why couldn't Ana just meet her halfway sometimes?

"Ana, did you hear me? Can we record tonight? We have taken a long break. It's time to get back after it."

"I don't know. It just feels like a lot," Ana said, tripping over her words.

"Okay, we don't have to do it tonight. I can also do it tomorrow or Thursday, but the sooner, the better."

Ana rocked back in her seat and popped her back; the sound reverberated loudly. The pop sounded too loud to have come from Ana's petite body.

"I'm saying I don't want to do it at all. Not tonight, not later this week."

"What? Where is this coming from?"

"I just want to work on my own projects for a while. I had some good ideas strike me in there," Ana said. She leaned her head against the window and sighed. Bex did not see this coming.

"And not to mention, I've been thinking - I'm not sure we should do true crime anymore," Ana added.

"Since when? Is this something you learned in therapy or what?"

"No, I just don't feel like it's right anymore."

"I don't even know what you're saying."

"I'm saying I want to be done with the podcast. I'll find another way to make money, I don't want to record anymore. I want to focus on my books."

"You don't just get to decide that, Ana," Bex said. Her words came out cold and hard. Bex didn't bother softening them.

"If you want to continue, you can but I don't want to be a part of it."

"It's a sister show. That's what people love. I can't do it alone."

"Find someone else then."

"What the fuck, Ana? Where is this coming from? Help me understand!" Bex put a hand on Ana's knee. She thought out how their stepdad used to do that, too. She didn't squeeze though. Bex saw Ana flinch out of the corner of her eye; Ana probably remembered it, too.

"Before I went to Hillside, I got a letter in the mail. They demanded we stop profiting from victims' stories. The sender had our address. Someone was knocking on the door. Don't you see how much danger we're in?"

"Ana, why didn't you tell me?" Bex asked, lowering her voice. Caleb's messages reverberated around her mind. He said something about a letter, and he said he was sorry for sending it. Things clicked into place. Maybe Ana wasn't crazy. Maybe this whole thing was a result of their shared DNA.

"I tried. The night I got it, I called you. You didn't answer. No one answered that night. Not you. Not James. Someone kept knocking. I was home alone. That's what pushed me over the edge, not so much the letter but the fact that I felt like I had no one."

"I'm sorry, Ana."

"I know what I did was stupid, but I still feel like the letter has some merit. I can't shake the feeling. That person is still out there."

"Well, I'm sorry that happened, but the show must go on. You realize that right? We're too far into this?"

"I'm going to use a coping skill I learned at Hillside, I'm going to step away from this conversation. We can talk about it more when we've both had time to process."

Bex turned into their neighborhood. This was the most honesty they'd shared between them in years, but Bex didn't know how to deal with it. She wanted the old Ana back. The one that didn't have it in her to stand up for herself. Bex pulled into the garage; Ana got out of the car and walked into the house without another word.

111

Bex slammed her car door shut. This wasn't how she imagined Ana's return. Ana needed to remember whose house she was living at and who paid the bills. Ana needed to remember whose world she was living in.

TWENTY-FOUR

Ana noticed the made bed and clean space before she was fully inside her room. One part of her was relieved that she would not have to relive that night through the process of cleaning up her room; the other was annoyed that Bex had been in her space.

The door shut with a thud behind her, and Ana leaned against it. Her room smelled of a mixture of stale air and Clorox. The bed and the pile of unread books on the nightstand called her name. Ana wanted to disappear into a world of words, not of her own.

Her computer on the desk reminded Ana of all that she ignored in the last few weeks. Ana compromised with herself, she brought her computer to her bed and pulled her comforter up over her legs. The Mac groaned to life and took far too long for the update bar to slide across the page.

The thought of checking her social media accounts was enough to send Ana right back to Hillside. She opted for her email instead. The account loaded and the bold '435 unread emails' blared at her from the sidebar. A quick look told Ana that the majority of them were spam emails to be deleted.

A handful were from fans and the rest were marketing requests - *pay for book reviews!* the emails screamed. Ana rolled her eyes and filed them into the trash.

One email caught her eye. It was from James. Ana figured it was some kind of check-in after her recent attempt. She considered deleting the email, she wasn't sure she could face his words, his disappointment. The desire to be close to him again won. She opened the email.

Subject Line: Read this. Please.
Sender: JamesShaw@TrueRecordings.com

Ana,

Bex told me what happened. I'm sorry. You have to stay;
we're not done yet. This story isn't over.
And I know this is weird given everything, but I need you
to see this. Awfully close for comfort.
James
PS: See you soon.

The word "this" was highlighted in blue. A link. His email didn't make sense. Ana's mind struggled to re-engage in real-life things after being in a curated world, free of stress for so many days.

Ana picked at her thumbnail, deciding if she should click the link. The desire to know far outweighed whatever reservations she had. Ana clicked and waited for the page to load.

An image of a refined older woman filled the screen. Her hair, short and gray, looked like she got a weekly perm treatment. She was wearing a pretty lavender shirt and a set of pearls. Her eyes looked kind.

Woman Killed by a Bomb in a Box

Chicago - A woman was killed at her Englewood
home late Tuesday. Reports indicate that Ruth Banks
opened a package addressed to her husband; inside was a
homemade bomb lodged in a book.

The woman was found shortly after the explosion
by her husband. She was rushed to St. Bernard Hospital
but succumbed to her injuries. This is a developing story,

and The Chicago Tribune will publish more details as they
become available.

If you receive an unfamiliar or suspicious
package, police recommend calling the non-emergency
line for further instructions before opening. If you have
any information regarding the package, we urge you to
call the Chicago Police at (888) 201-6000.

Ana's body went limp; her central nervous system was no longer in control. She felt herself fall out of the chair, onto the carpeted floor, but there was nothing she could do to stop it. She didn't want to. Literally grounding herself was the only thing she knew to do. Ana willed her heart to slow down, for her breath to return to normal. It was no use. The image of a bomb exploding into that sweet woman kept intruding.

She forced herself to sit up and look at the screen again. She studied the woman's face, she took in the details - the wrinkles, her gray eyes, and her gray hair. Sure, she'd written a book about a bomb in a box but that was a coincidence. That was it. Simply a coincidence.

James was wrong. He had to be.

Ana read the story again. Details shot off like fireworks in her head - Englewood, bomb... they were all key elements in her *Obstruction of Correspondence* book. The words clouded in front of her.

Ana closed her laptop and pushed it away from her. She told herself that this had nothing to do with her.

Tears rolled down Ana's face. She slunk to the floor. The last time Ana got like this, it sent her to Hillside. Ana couldn't do this again. It was too much. Too big.

Whoever wrote the letter was right. Her focus on true crime meant real-life consequences. Ruth was gone because Ana wrote a murder well enough for someone to copy. Nausea boiled in her belly and Ana craved oblivion.

She lay on her stomach and put her hands flat on the carpet. Ana grasped at anything she'd learned at Hillside to get her through this moment. A mantra came to mind - *I'm only responsible for me.* She repeated the words over and over. No matter what the article said, this wasn't Ana's fault. It couldn't be.

In and out. In and out, she breathed.

Ana focused on the facts. *Obstruction of Correspondence* was published more than a year ago. The readers were few and far between; the reviews were dismal. There was no way that her crappy debut had anything to do with Ruth's murder.

Terrorists sent bombs in boxes. Extremists. Hate groups. Someone with evil in their hearts. James was too quick to jump to conclusions. This article was in no way related to Ana.

TWENTY-FIVE

A Bomb in a Box... a Weird Coincidence?
By @crimebythebook • 4 days ago

My bad if I'm reading too much into this but I just came across something weird.

Have you all heard about the bomb in the box that went off? Some asshole killed a sweet old lady named Ruth Banks last week in a Chicago suburb by putting a bomb into a book and mailing it to her.

When she opened the book that was included in the package, some mechanism inside went off. It shot three bullets into her abdomen. She was taken in for surgery, but the damage was too extensive.

That's not the weird part though, the book used to make the bomb is what has me questioning it. The police put up a few <tasteful> pictures online asking for anyone who recognized anything to report it.

I zoomed way in on one of the photos and found the title of the book in the upper corner.

Of course, I looked up the book. It's called *Obstruction of Correspondence* by some indie author named Ana Adams. I'd never heard of it. I looked at the synopsis of the book, it's all about a son who mails a bomb in a box to his dad. Only the mom opens it up, and it kills her.

It's a little bit of a coincidence, no? A book about a bomb used to make a bomb in real life. It gets weirder though. The book is set in - you guessed it, the same 'burb of Chicago.

I've heard from my sources on some other forums that the cops have almost nothing to go on but whatever idiot sent this box, left traceable DNA evidence.

Dead gut shot grandma? A bookstagram hottie as the suspect and/or the victim? This case has EVERYTHING. Thoughts?

TWENTY-SIX

Bex knocked on the door once. There was no answer. Bex knocked again. "Ana? You okay?"

Bex put her ear closer to the door and listened. She knew Ana was in there, but the room was silent, in stark contrast to the wails she'd heard minutes ago. Something had set Ana off. Again.

"Ana?" Bex tried once more.

From inside the room came muted shuffling. Bex stepped back.

The door swung open. Ana's eyes were puffy, and her face was beet red. Ana had lost whatever glow she amassed during treatment. Her eyes looked crazed; her mouth set in a grimace.

"What's going on?" Bex asked.

"Sis it's bad," she cried. Ana wiped her nose on her sleeve.

"Please tell me what's going on." Bex moved toward her sister and tried to wrap her in a hug. Ana reeled backward. Bex's hands dropped to her side.

Ana sat on her bed heavily and put her face in her hands. Bex's heart began to beat faster. What was it? Taxes? The death of a friend? Something to do with Ana's Amazon author account?

"James sent me an email. He said someone copied my book."

Bex searched her sister's face. It was covered in worry and disgust. "Well, that's not the worst thing. People post pirated copies of books all the time. We can send them a cease and desist and tell them to take it down. It will be okay."

"No, Bex. I don't mean someone copied the words. Someone copied the murder in *Obstruction of Correspondence*. Someone killed a sweet old grandma named Ruth with a bomb in a box. Just like in my book," Ana said.

Bex stood a little straighter.

119

"That's not even possible."

"It happened, Bex!"

"How do you know that it is related to your book? I'm not trying to be mean here, but not that many people even read that one."

"I know. I fucking know. I just looked it up. I've only sold like 200 copies."

"Whatever. It's a coincidence. It has to be. You don't have to feel guilty for someone doing a sick thing."

"You don't get it, Bex. The main character in the book lives in a small suburb of Chicago. This just happened in the same town."

Bex's body tensed. It was a little weird but weird things happened all the time.

"It gets worse though," Ana cried. She jumped up from the bed and went to her computer.

Ana clicked a few buttons and pulled up a photo. She zoomed in. "Look at this!" Bex moved to her sister's side. It took her eyes a few passes to categorize what she was looking at, but she could see the title of *Obstruction of Correspondence* in the top corner.

Bex took in the rest of the page. She skimmed the Redditor's post. They noticed the similarities between Ana's book and this case and then they noticed that the sender used an actual copy of the book. This wasn't some figment of Ana's imagination. Someone copied Ana.

"What the hell?" Bex asked.

"Someone on Reddit found a picture of the crime scene. They used my book to send a bomb. The sender used my fucking book."

Bex took a step back. She jammed her heel into the corner of Ana's bed; she let out a sharp yelp of pain.

"You okay?" Ana asked.

"Fuck. That hurt!" Bex admitted. She sat on the corner of the bed and rubbed her foot. Ana sat next to her sister.

"I just don't understand. Why would anyone do this?" Bex asked.

"God. I don't know," Ana said. She pulled her knees up to her chest and buried her face.

"I don't have any clue. James sent me the email and said it looked like someone was copying my book. I didn't believe him, but I think he's right."

Bex rubbed her heel again.

"Who would even do this? I'm just a nobody author. No one even knows my books. Why not copy someone like James Patterson or Alice Feeney? Their books are so much better," Ana said.

"Maybe that's the point. Maybe they picked someone obscure to make it harder to figure out the connection."

"But then why send the bomb with my book?"

"I don't know," Bex admitted.

"And the other thing, I don't even know how they did it. When I wrote the book, I didn't include how to actually make a bomb. I kind of glossed over that part," Ana admitted.

"Well, someone figured it out."

"I know. But who?"

"Anything strange happen lately?" Bex asked.

"I don't know. I sometimes get creepy messages on Instagram but nothing much more than spam."

"Nothing else?"

"There was this weird guy in Hillside. He kind of latched on to me. He read the book during treatment and decided I was his new favorite thing. Maybe him."

"Really?" Bex asked.

"I don't know. I think he was just trying to get into my pants."

Bex laughed. Her hand flew to her mouth.

"It's not funny!"

"Do you think he could have done this?"

"I don't know. I got a weird vibe from him, so I tried to avoid him. But he is smart. And he got to go home some weekends. It would have been a quick turnaround but maybe."

Bex ran her hand through her hair, pulling out a handful of loose strands in the process. Seeing her hair laced between her fingers reminded her of something. "Hey, wait, didn't that Reddit post say something about DNA evidence?" Bex asked.

Ana turned back to her computer and scanned the page. "Yeah," Ana read.

"Well, just as soon as they do, they'll clear your name. This too shall pass," Bex said.

"Yeah. Yeah, you're right. But what should I do in the meantime?" Ana asked.

The best answer Bex could come up with was, "I say we record a podcast episode about it."

TWENTY-SEVEN

Ana watched Bex pull the heavy mics and digital recorder they used for podcasting from the hallway closet. Apprehension grew in her belly; this didn't feel right. She pulled at a thread on the couch.

"I don't think this is a good idea. I don't need another Reddit post about me," Ana finally said.

"I don't see any reason why we shouldn't?"

"Well, for starters, remember the letter I told you about? They want me to stop with true crime or they'd put a stop to me -"

"Do you still have the letter?" Bex interrupted.

"No, why?"

"I was just thinking we could read it on the show. The letter combined with this book bomb case would make dynamite."

Ana scrubbed her face harder. Her mind couldn't picture sitting in front of the mic to discuss either one.

"No really, Ana. Do you have the letter?"

"I don't know what happened to it. I haven't seen it since I got home."

"I had the cleaners come, maybe it's still in your room?" Bex jumped up and ran down the hall. Ana followed her and watched as Bex started pulling out the desk drawers, one by one.

"What did it look like? What am I looking for here?" Bex asked as she wrenched open the middle drawer. Ana's nerves frayed a little more with each move her sister made. Ana hoped she wouldn't find it.

"I don't know. I don't even remember. I think it was like a grocery shopping list maybe."

Bex continued going through Ana's things. Ana picked a finger and got to work, chewing it to the quick. She'd picked up this habit while she was in residential, and it was impossible to stop. Ana needed something to stop her from her racing thoughts.

"Here!" Bex exclaimed. She pulled a piece of paper from a stack of bills and envelopes from the desk drawer. The letter stuck out the side. "The cleaners didn't throw it away." It was wrinkled and worn but the words were still clearly visible.

"Oh, my god. This letter is just pure insanity; they probably sent one to every true crime host. I can't believe you let this push you over the edge," Bex said. She stood with one hand on her hip, her face screwed up in indignation.

A wash of shame flooded over Ana. Bex would never understand; it wasn't just the letter. It was the person knocking. It was the fact that no one answered her when she called. She'd been all alone and couldn't rely on herself. With all the work that Ana had done at Hillside, she realized not much had changed for Bex. She still saw Ana as the same, scared, and dependent girl she'd always been.

Bex read from the letter, "True crime is not a genre. It's not a hobby." Ana tuned the words out. Hearing it all over again was a little too painful. She didn't need to be reminded of how this letter and her reaction to it almost cost Ana her life.

"Ana, we have to record. This is all too good. People will eat it up."

"We can't. Did you and I read the same letter?"

"Ana don't be silly. They aren't going to do anything to you. It's not illegal to talk about true crime. We're doing those victims a favor by bringing a voice to their stories."

Anxiety forced her mind to race. Ana didn't want to fuel the fire, but there was something to what her sister was saying. Ana always believed it too - writing true crime was a way to give victims a voice again. Podcasting was an extension of that.

"And anyways, Ana. How are we going to figure out who sent that bomb in a box? We have to bring more attention to that case for it to ever get solved."

The image of Ruth filled Ana's mind. The sweet grandma. The woman who opened a package sent to her, just like anyone else would have. Ruth Banks did not deserve this, and it was up to Ana to give her a voice.

"Okay."

"Okay as in you'll record with me?"

"Yes," Ana said. As soon as the words left her mouth, Ana second-guessed herself.

Bex let out a whoop and jumped up from the desk chair. "I'll finish setting up!"

Ana paced in her room. She knew Bex would be furious if she backed out but the thought of recording a show right now made her want to puke.

The little leatherbound notebook - Ana's podcast planner - was on the table next to her. Ana knew she should pick it up and jot down a few notes for the show. Ana couldn't.

She sat with her knees pulled up and her head in her lap. She tried to remember the breathing exercises she'd learned. She tried to do whatever she could to slow her mind from closing in on itself.

Instead, all she could think was that this podcast would be the death of her.

—

"Hello and welcome to *The Serial Syndicate*, I'm Ana," Ana started the show. Her stomach rolled with fear. Her heart couldn't catch a rhythm, but at least the intro part of the show came easily for her.

"And I'm Bexley Adams. We're sisters, and we share a love for true crime. We also share a love for wine. We both have this cool thing called trauma-induced humor. We're glad all of you freaks feel the same."

Ana took a deep breath. She couldn't get the jumble of words in her mind to stand in a line.

Bex caught her. "Today, we're talking about a case you probably haven't heard of yet. It's not a cold case, in fact, it just happened. And it's personal," Bex said.

The weight of this story was crushing Ana, one word at a time. She couldn't contribute anything to the show. She couldn't help Bex.

Bex looked at Ana over her computer screen. She waved with her hand, indicating that Ana should pick up the slack. Ana looked down and swallowed the bile that rose in her throat. She coughed once and grabbed her water bottle.

A clicking noise filled the silence. Bex pulled her headphones off and made a cutting gesture across her throat. Ana pulled her headphones off, too. "I paused it," Bex said.

Ana nodded.

"Are you going to be able to do this?" Bex asked. "I need your help."

"I don't know. It feels wrong."

"Remember what we said? We're doing this for Ruth."

"Are we? Or are we doing this for clicks and downloads?"

"Both."

Ana wrapped the microphone cord around her finger. Every instinct said to stop recording and walk away.

"Ana, we have to do this. You get that right? Your silence will make you look involved somehow. You need get out in front of this."

Bex's words twisted in Ana's mind. She never considered that someone might think she played a role in Ruth's death besides penning the inspiration. Bex was right. Speaking up was the only thing she could do.

"Okay, I'm ready."

"For Ruth," Bex said. She clicked a key on her laptop and pointed at Ana.

"For Ruth," Ana mouthed. Ana pulled her headphones back into place.

"But that's not all. Let's go back to the beginning," Ana said into the microphone. "A few weeks ago, I got a strange letter in the mail. Someone threatened me to stop profiting off of true crime. So let me say this - for one, we're not making a big profit here. We make barely enough to buy a cup of coffee every once in a while, and for two, I'm telling their stories. Victims have no voices anymore. It's up to people like me to give them a chance to talk and a chance to be heard. That's all I've ever wanted to do."

Ana looked at Bex. She nodded and gave a thumbs-up. Ana felt her power surge as she took agency over the situation.

"Here, let me just read the letter," Bex cooed into her microphone. She pulled the note from the table next to her and repeated the vitriol for the recording.

Ana shuddered. The words were even more menacing when they came from Bex.

"If that wasn't enough, someone copied my book," Ana said.

"And we're not talking about plagiarizing, folks. Someone carried out the murder Ana detailed in her first book, *Obstruction of Correspondence*. Word for word."

TWENTY-EIGHT

They pulled their headphones off in unison. Bex's excitement multiplied as she thought about publishing this episode. Their podcast could have died with Ana's mental health crisis, but this would revive it. This episode was full of the drama and curiosity that true crime junkies lived for.

Bex knew the letter came from their brother Caleb. The writing style was the same and it was the only thing that explained his last message. The world didn't have to know that though, and especially not Ana. Keeping the identity of the sender a mystery would up the ante and keep Ana fearful enough to stay home.

She just hoped Caleb wouldn't listen to the episode. It would be blatantly clear that she either didn't read his messages or didn't care. Some small part of her feared that if he listened, he'd become even more erratic. Her worries weren't big enough to stop her though. The show needed this recording and so did she.

Bex shook her head and pushed the fears away. She'd deal with Caleb and his reaction later. Going viral with an episode like this was worth the risk.

"That was good," Bex said. Ana nodded; she looked a little shell-shocked.

Ana wrapped the cord around the base of her microphone while Bex exported the audio file and uploaded it for James. The sooner they could post it, the better. They needed to get out ahead of this story. If they were the first to cover this story, it would make *The Serial Syndicate* podcast as big as Bex had dreamed of since they started.

"I'm sending this to James now. I'm going to ask him for a rush job," Bex said.

"Thank you-" Ana started but a knock at the front door interrupted her. Ana closed her mouth and knit her eyebrows together.

"Did you order something?" Bex asked.

"No, did you?"

The knock came again, louder this time. Bex set her computer on the couch cushion next to her and walked to the front door. "Someone is probably here to save our souls," she announced. Bex hoped the joke covered the fear she felt that Caleb was back.

Ana laughed. "Good luck to them."

Bex opened the door. Aimee stood on the porch. Aimee was wearing yoga pants and tennies. Her black hair was in a low ponytail and her face was fresh. Bex looked her up and down; Aimee looked hot.

A wide smile broke on Aimee's face. She stood tall, looking proud of herself. Bex opened the door a bit wider. "Aimee! What are you doing here?"

"Just visiting my girlfriend, I hope that's okay. We've hardly seen each other this week!"

Bex heard Ana shift on the couch behind her. She cleared her throat. "Yeah, of course. Did I give you my address?" Bex asked, confused.

"Oh, I saw your address the other day when you bought something on Amazon at my house."

A lump grew in Bex's throat. She wasn't ready for this. She hadn't prepared to introduce Aimee to Ana, especially given everything. Aimee dramatically batted her eyelashes and gave a pointed look. Bex had no other choice.

Bex opened the door and gestured for Aimee to come in. Aimee walked across the threshold and gave Bex a peck on the cheek as she did. Bex's cheeks burned hot. She closed the door and wiped her sweaty palms on her pants.

129

"Aimee, this is my sister Ana. Ana, this is Aimee," Bex said, motioning to each of them.

Ana set her computer on the side table next to her seat and stood up. In comparison to Aimee's tall, athletic build, Ana caved into herself, looking like a scared bird. Ana's eyes were wide; she flapped her hands against her pants awkwardly.

Aimee threw up a hand to shake; the gesture stopped Ana in her tracks. She didn't reciprocate; Aimee dropped her hand back down. "I'm Aimee, Bex's girlfriend. I'm so glad to finally meet you. I've heard so much about you."

The room went silent. Bex ached for her sister to be normal for just once. Instead, she just stood there, ratcheting up the awkwardness by the second.

Ana finally stepped forward and gave Aimee a limp, dead-fish handshake. "I'm Ana, Bex's sister. I have heard nothing about you," she said. Bex's mouth went dry.

"Well, that's no surprise," Aimee said. She giggled.

Bex couldn't handle the tension any longer; her hands needed a job. She grabbed her computer off the couch and cleaned up the rest of the podcast equipment. "We just finished recording a new episode," Bex said as she moved it all to the coffee table.

"Here, sit, Aims," Bex said. She motioned to a spot on the couch. "Can I get you something to drink? Wine, water?"

"Wine would be great," Aimee said.

"Ana, do you want anything?" Ana shook her head no and Bex headed to the kitchen, relieved to have a second to catch her breath.

Bex felt annoyed at Aimee for showing up uninvited. And then at Ana for existing. Bex pushed those thoughts down. She could not return to the living room wearing all of that on her face.

The cork stuck in the bottle of the Shiraz Bex chose. She could hear murmurs from Ana and Aimee in the other room, but she couldn't make out the words. Bex considered smashing the bottle on the counter to expedite the opening.

It took a knife and a second attempt for the smell of the wine to fill the kitchen. Bex poured into three glasses, splashing some of the red liquid on the counter as she did. It pained her a little to leave the stain on the marble but the pull to get back to her sister and her girlfriend was much greater.

Bex walked into the living room. She felt the ice-cold tension between Ana and Aimee before she even handed out glasses. Ana was looking down at the floor, chewing on her finger - her tell that she was uncomfortable. Aimee's eyes searched the whole room, taking it all in.

Bex's teeth ground into each other as she took in the sight of the two of them. Her knees felt weak. These two women were the most important in her life; she needed the two of them to get along.

"So, you two getting to know each other?" Bex asked.

Ana didn't respond. Aimee let out a "Ha!" under her breath. Bex sucked in her cheeks.

"Here you go my love," Bex said. The words were foreign in Bex's mouth with Ana in the room. She immediately wished she hadn't said that last part. Aimee smiled. Bex wondered if she'd just won some brownie points. She handed Aimee's glass to her and sat next to Aimee on the couch.

"Ana just got home from treatment. Wild timing," Bex said, nervously. It was stupid but it was the best she could come up with.

"Ana, Aimee, and I work together, we're on the same team, actually," Bex kept going.

"Yep, and we have a big work trip together next week," Aimee added. Bex bit her tongue. She hadn't told Ana that yet.

"We're going to California. We have a big sales visit. Bex is going to kill it," Aimee added. Ana looked into her wine, swirling it. Bex willed her to ask a question, to join the conversation but she did neither.

Bex put a hand on Aimee's thigh. She took a drink of her wine and fought the urge to down it all at once.

"So, you recorded a new episode? That's exciting," Aimee finally said, breaking the silence.

"Yeah, it's been a long time coming. It felt good to get back into it. Ana is a natural," Bex replied.

Bex looked at her sister. If Ana heard the compliment, it didn't register. Bex chewed on her lip. She wasn't sure why Ana was being so cold toward Aimee. It was completely obvious that after just a few minutes with Aimee, Ana already iced her out.

"What was it about?"

"Well, actually," Bex said. She cleared her throat. There was no way to put this that wouldn't make the room even more tense.

"Someone copied my book," Ana said. Bex was surprised she spoke up.

"So, you recorded about that?" Aimee asked. She rolled her eyes like a junior high school student.

"Yeah, it's a big deal."

"Is it though?" Aimee asked.

"It is a big deal," Bex interjected. "It's not like copying as in plagiarizing. It's copying as in someone copied the murder."

Aimee's eyes went wide as she understood the implication. "Oh, I take that back, that is a big deal," she said, emphasizing the last few words.

Ana nodded. "Yeah, and it's an even fucking bigger deal when you're the author of the book. People online have already started to figure out the connection. We recorded an episode about it."

"Oh my gosh, tell me everything!" Aimee said.

Bex spent the next few minutes catching Aimee up. Aimee's face grew more animated with every word and Bex could see that Ana was simultaneously getting more uncomfortable. The more Bex detailed the story, the more she knew they were on to something. She couldn't wait for the episode to come out and she could only hope that people were half as interested as Aimee was.

"Wow, so that really happened?" Aimee asked. Ana and Bex nodded.

"What are you going to do about it?" Aimee asked.

"Publish this podcast episode?" Ana said.

"No, I mean, what are you going to do about the killer?"

"What can I do? I don't even know why someone would copy my book. I'm an indie author who has barely sold any copies," Ana said.

"I think you should try to catch them," Aimee said.

"What?" Ana asked. Her face filled with confusion; it was clear she didn't understand.

"I think you should try to catch the killer!"

TWENTY-NINE

Aimee's words had rolled through Ana's mind over and over all night, the idea polishing with each turn. Ana could catch the person who brought her plotline to life. She had to. Ana lay in bed and stared at the wall, imagining how to do it.

A ding from her computer interrupted Ana's thoughts. She woke the system up and found an email from James waiting in her inbox. **Episode #63 Ready.** They just recorded the show the day before, she couldn't believe James already had it mastered for publication.

His email is short and to the point:

> *Wow! Quite the show there, Ana. It didn't need that much work; it's ready for ya. Glad you're back.*

Ana reread his message. She would have expected James to say more. Maybe ask how she was doing with it all?

She shoved the thoughts from her mind and uploaded the episode. *The Serial Syndicate* didn't have that many subscribers, but all 184 of them would get a push notification. She posted a link to her social channels next.

Ana went back to the only thing she knew how to do - writing. The book she'd been working on since before her residential treatment. The plot was hazy, but she knew she wanted it to be about sisters - the way sisters live and die by one another. The idea seemed clear in her mind, but the story wouldn't flow from her fingers.

She put her computer to the side and pulled the covers up to her chin. With everything, she didn't have the words in her to write another sentence, let alone a whole twisted mystery.

A jarring sensation from her phone woke Ana from her stupor. She must have dozed off. Ana rubbed her eyes and noticed how the light changed in her room; it was early evening. The day passed her by quickly. She didn't remember how she had spent the time.

On her phone, she found messages from James and Bex -

> *Holy shit, Ana. The ep is going viral - already at 5,000 downloads.*

> *Thanks for posting the episode! It's on fire. Do you see the comments on Facebook?*

Ana rubbed her face again. She strained her eyes to make sure she was reading the messages right. The most listens their show ever got was somewhere around 1,000. Ana didn't even want to know what people were popping off with on social. How long did she sleep? Did she black out? She hated that she couldn't remember.

When she opened the Facebook app, Ana was shocked to see just how many things she'd missed.

Fear tore up Ana's spine. Her podcast post had hundreds of comments already. It didn't take long to find what Bex meant. The comments turned unbelievably mean.

> *I had never even heard of Ana Adams until today. Is this some kind of publicity stunt?*

> *You cannot tell me that someone picked a random book by a random author and sent it to someone. It had to come from the author. Prove me wrong.*

> *Ana sent that box. Who else would do this?*

Ana sat up straighter in bed, her heart pounding. From the moment she saw that Reddit post, Ana knew people would blame her for writing the story - for giving the killer the idea.

But Ana never imagined people would think she built a bomb and sent the box.

THIRTY

Bex pulled out a blue suit and a black suit. She folded them carefully and placed them into her carry-on. Bex's whole body ached from holding so much stress. Leaving Ana in the midst of the podcast aftermath felt wrong, but staying wasn't an option.

The tension was written all over Ana. She was even more quiet and withdrawn than before, the weight of the news hunched her shoulders over her computer. She was down a rabbit hole of subreddits and conspiracy theories. Leaving Ana made Bex feel like she was leaving an appendage. Bex thought through every possible excuse to stay, but she didn't have one.

Bex and her team were all flying to San Francisco to woo a big client. They were some big law firm that needed a cloud marketing system to keep in touch with their thousands of clients. Landing this contract would make Bex's career.

In her suitcase, Bex included her red-bottomed Louboutin heels, a couple of cocktail dresses, and her secret weapon - condoms. She had been to enough of these meetings to know that sometimes, you just have to do what you have to do.

Bex zipped the bag and looked at herself in the mirror. She looked every bit the boss bitch she wanted to be. Her slicked-backed pony and red blazer made her look sexy and powerful. It was the perfect combination to wear to head straight to their client's office after the flight.

The clink clink clink of Bex's heels reverberated around her as she walked down the hall. She stopped at Ana's door and listened. She could hear Ana click click clicking away on her keyboard. Bex breathed a sigh of relief. At least Ana was stable enough to write. That was a good sign.

Bex rolled her bag to the kitchen and made herself a cup of green supplements with her electric frother. She gagged as she swallowed the concoction on an empty stomach. She threw back her handful of vitamins and made an iced coffee to go.

The sound of her heels clicking on the floor was the only sound in the house. Bex knocked on Ana's door once, waiting for a response.

"Ana? Are you awake?" Bex asked even though she knew she was. Her sister did not respond.

"Ana?" Bex asked as she pushed the door open. Ana was in bed with the covers pulled up to her chin. Her laptop sat on her lap. The room was dark, the only source of light came from Ana's screen, illuminating her pale face.

"Hey, you-" Bex said. "Writing?"

"Yep."

"I'm proud of you."

"Thanks."

"I'm heading to the airport," Bex said. She smoothed her dress down. "I'll be back in a few days, just as soon as I get the contract inked."

"Okay," Ana said.

"Will you be okay?"

"Yes, duh. You travel all the time for work. I'll be fine."

"I know. But it feels different now. There's so much going on."

"Yes, I'll be fine. We'll stay in touch. Go, don't miss your flight."

Bex held onto the door. Telling her sister goodbye felt impossible. She was being ripped between her two main priorities - work and Ana. Staying wasn't right. Leaving was all wrong.

"Just go, I'll be fine. I promise," Ana said, dragging out the last word.

"Okay, please just don't do anything stupid."

THIRTY-ONE

The house was quiet and still without Bex. For the first time in days, Ana felt like she could breathe. She closed her laptop and made breakfast. As she ate, Ana felt a sense of peace she hadn't known in years. She was on her own. And she liked it.

Ana suddenly wanted more. An idea materialized in her mind and took shape almost faster than Ana could grasp. This was her chance. Freedom was in front of her. Bex was gone. There was no one to stop her. Ana could leave her problems behind her - her sister, the creep who knew her address. All of it.

Cupping her coffee mug, Ana let the idea blossom in her mind. She didn't have anywhere to go, and she didn't have much money to her name, but all of that paled in comparison to getting away from it all. It was now or never.

What about one of those cheap motels on Colfax? A room could serve as home for a few nights. With a little space and clarity to make her own decisions, Ana would be able to figure it out from there.

Ana jogged to her room and found a bag. In less than ten minutes, she was packed and ready to go. She took one final look around her room, expecting to feel sadness, or maybe even a little bit of guilt. She felt neither. Ana slammed her door shut, excited to get on with her life.

Ana nearly opened the front door before remembering the doorbell camera Bex had installed last year. Now that Bex was watching her every move, chances were good that Bex had her alerts turned on. If Ana walked out that door with a bag slung over her shoulder, Bex would get on the next flight home.

Ana shut the door slowly, hoping the movement didn't trigger the camera. She set her bag down, worries filled her mind. If she went out of the garage, the camera at the back of the house would capture her just the same. She couldn't risk Bex catching her.

She sat on the kitchen table and tried to decide what her best option was. If she went out a window, someone might notice. If she went out either door, Bex would notice. Ana decided to take her chances with nosy neighbors.

The window in her bedroom faced the front of the house. The camera could pick up her movement if she went out that way. The window in the kitchen opened wide and the distance to the ground was short. It was on the side of the house, away from the cameras and away from the main street that ran in front of their house. Ana decided that was her best bet.

She pushed up the blinds and pulled the window open. It took a couple of pushes to get the screen to dislodge from the window. She nearly ripped through it before it gave way. Ana leaned through the window as far as she could and set the screen on the side of the house.

Ana grabbed her bag and lopped it through the window. It landed on the grass with a thud. Ana first put one leg through and turned to lower herself to the ground. The drop wasn't far, but it looked like it would hurt. She hauled herself back inside and looked up and down the street.

Her stomach flipped. She couldn't quite tell from here, but she was pretty sure the porch-sitting neighbor was out again. She wondered if he could see her from his vantage point. Ana sat on the windowsill with both legs dangling.

Ana sucked in a big breath and launched herself forward. She landed in the grass on her hands and knees. Her right leg exploded in pain. She grabbed it and realized she'd landed right on a rock. She counted to ten, working to catch her breath.

She stood and clasped her hands together. She did it. She was nearly free. Ana walked back toward the house. Without a stool, she couldn't quite reach the window. It felt wrong to leave it open, but she didn't want to draw more attention to herself by trying to close it.

"Fuck it," she said under her breath. She grabbed her bag and walked to her car, careful to avoid the front of the house.

That's when she noticed it. A black car with dark-tinted windows was parked just across from her car. It had a perfect line of sight to their house.

Ana did a double take. She was home all the time. She noticed who came and went in their neighborhood. She generally knew what kind of cars her neighbors drove. This one was out of place. She couldn't see who was inside the vehicle.

The beating of her heart drummed in her ears. Her hands shook as she tried to find the right key to her car. Ana told herself to chill.

She couldn't shake the feeling though. Something about the car made her nervous, like she was being watched. In a rush, she opened the door, pushed the key into the ignition, and revved it to start. Her old car chugged to life.

Ana sped out of the neighborhood. She didn't have a plan, she just needed to get away from all of it. Her car pulled onto the interstate and on instinct, she headed toward the mountains.

A couple of songs later, Ana was back at Three Sisters Park. Her special place. Ana breathed in the mountain air deeply and relaxed. She was outside and she was free from her sister, and everything else for that matter.

Ana did a slow loop around the lake, taking in the beautiful day. She snapped a picture of the lake and sent it to James.

Wish you were here with me this time <3 she said.

Ana put the same picture up on her Instagram story. She'd all but neglected her followers since her stay at Hillside but today she felt like she'd turned over a fresh leaf. She was ready to take control of her life and control of her work. That included her social media channels. Ana twirled around in the meadow and let the sun bask on her face. She was back. She was free.

A rumbling stomach interrupted her thoughts. She needed something to eat, and she needed a place to stay. Ana walked back to her car, hoping that she'd find a granola bar stashed somewhere inside.

Ana stopped in her tracks as soon as she made it back to the parking lot. A black sedan with tinted windows was parked near the end of the line of cars. She wouldn't have noticed it had she not seen one near her house. One was weird. Two was no coincidence.

Her feet refused to move forward, and her mind raced with questions. Was it the same car? Did it follow her here? Ana couldn't remember the license plate of the car in her neighborhood. She couldn't be sure it was the same one she'd seen earlier.

Ana ran to her car and locked herself inside. Her heart refused to slow down even as she pulled out of her parking spot. The steering wheel got sweaty under her hard grip. She turned back toward Denver and forced herself to try the five senses technique she'd learned in group therapy. It didn't make a difference in the speed of thoughts rushing through her mind.

A buzz from her phone paused her mind. She grabbed it and looked as she drove. It was James.

As pretty as I remember. James wrote. She couldn't deal with him right now. She needed to get out of there.

Ana looked in her rearview mirror. There were plenty of cars on I-70, but she didn't see the black sedan. She told herself that this wasn't a movie. No one was following her. Seeing a black car at the trailhead was nothing.

As she drove on, her tension began to fade. Ana dreamed about the burger she was going to get from McDonald's and planned to find a hotel as soon as she had something in her belly. Ana even pictured a new scene for the book she was working on. By the time she was back down in the city, Ana had the music blaring, and she liked herself.

Ana pulled through the drive-through line and ordered a McDouble. There was almost nothing Bex hated more than fast food - "That'll make you fatter than any ice cream" - she loved to say. But Bex wasn't around to tell Ana what to do.

The server handed Ana a large Coke and a bag full of her food. Ana's car exploded with that signature McDonald's fry smell just as soon as she rolled up the window. Ana's mouth watered as she drove toward freedom.

Ana pulled out of the drive-through and merged onto the road. She braked at a stoplight and put a fry in her mouth. It tasted even better than she remembered. Ana looked in her rearview mirror out of habit.

"Oh, fuck no!" she screamed. Ana smashed her foot on the gas and ran right through a red light, barely missing a truck coming the other way. The black car followed behind her. Ana pushed the pedal in as far as she could, racing through the city streets. Every time she looked, the black sedan was only a couple of car lengths behind her.

Ana pulled into the alley between two buildings and shoved the gear shift into park. The black car did not follow her into the space. Ana's head throbbed with each pound of her heart. Ana was just a writer; she had no skills for dodging trouble in real life.

Images of kidnappers and mob bosses flew through her head, but Ana knew the stalker was much closer than any fictional villain. Whoever was chasing her had to be the person who sent the letter. Maybe even the person who was knocking down their door the other night.

Hell, maybe it was even the person who sent the bomb.

Ana felt paralyzed. She looked in the mirror every other second, but she didn't see it yet. If someone was out to get her, she was a sitting duck right in this dark alley. She knew she should keep moving; instead, she just sat there, dumbstruck. Tears rolled down her cheeks.

She hit her hands on the steering wheel. Fear and self-loathing enveloped her. Ana wasn't cut out to live on her own. She could barely get lunch without losing herself in some black car coincidence head trip. There was no one after her. They would have nabbed her by now. It was all in Ana's head.

Maybe she was as crazy as everyone said.

Ana put her car in drive and turned toward the familiar streets that led to Bex. Who was she kidding? She couldn't live on her own yet. She needed her sister.

THIRTY-TWO

Bex traced slow circles on Aimee's thigh as they lay in a tangled mess of sheets in the hotel room bed. When Bex snuck down to Aimee's room, she felt like she was James Bond on a mission. She slunk through the halls and avoided being caught by anyone on the team. Bex couldn't resist; Aimee was worth the risk.

They spent the day locked up in their client's conference room teaching the team how to use their new system, Product Xponential. For a bunch of lawyers with salaries to match, Bex was annoyed that she was forced to cover such basic stuff as undeliverables and opt-outs.

Bex also hated that she'd had to watch Aimee crush it in that boardroom all day without giving an ounce away about their relationship. Aimee was the lead trainer and Bex her boss, that was all. There was nothing Bex could do to disrupt the sales call.

"Today went better than I thought it was going to," Aimee said.

"Really? There were a lot of tense moments. They just didn't seem to get it. I'm worried about their understanding of the product. I think it might be too much for them."

"They're getting there. I think a couple more days and they'll be good," Aimee said.

"I just want to get home," Bex whispered.

"I know, I'm sure you're worried about Ana. But I won't lie, I don't hate being here with you," Aimee said. She squeezed Bex's hand.

Bex smiled. "Me too," she said.

"You are so good at this. You love putting men in their places. I nearly spit out my coffee when you told that CFO guy 'The data doesn't lie, sir.'" Aimee laughed.

"I probably shouldn't have said that, but I couldn't take another mansplain. He did shut up after that though," Bex replied.

Aimee traced a heart on the back of Bex's hand; goosebumps rippled up her arm.

"How's Ana?" Aimee asked.

Bex swallowed down the panic that had been growing all day. "Honestly, I'm a bit worried about her. She hasn't answered my texts all day. I called her after the meeting, but she didn't answer then either. I'm talking myself out of catching the next flight."

"Why?"

"I don't know. There's been quite a bit of chatter online, I just want to know she's okay."

"People are talking about the podcast episode or what?"

"Yeah, Ana published it and it's kind of blown up actually - that part is great. But the comments online are foul. I'm going to try to call her again soon."

"What are people saying?"

"That Ana did it. That she sent the bomb."

Aimee pulled away and sat up. "Wait. Do you think they're right?"

"What?" Bex asked. She searched Aimee's face.

"Did Ana do this? Did she send the box?"

Bex shot up and faced Aimee. "No, of course not!" Heat expanded in her chest. Her hands balled into fists.

"What? I'm just asking."

"No, she did not send the box. For one thing, she was in residential treatment when it happened. She couldn't have made an explosive device while she was fighting for her life. And secondly, Ana would never. She's the sweetest person on the planet. She's my sister."

"Sorry, it was just a question."

"I can't believe you could think that."

"Really? It's not that far-fetched. Who else would do it? And you're always saying that Ana is a little 'off.' You won't let us near each other, I had to force my way in to meet her the other night."

"She's 'off' as in fragile," Bex said, making air quotes as she did. Bex leaned back against the bed frame. Her heart kept its clipped pace and her head throbbed. Pressure from all angles weighed her down.

"It wasn't Ana," Bex said after counting to ten.

"Okay, I got it."

Aimee leaned back against the frame, too. Their bare shoulders touched. Aimee rested her head on Bex's shoulder. Bex worked to relax her stiff body. Aimee was just asking what everyone else on the internet wondered, Bex shouldn't blame her.

Bex's phone vibrated on the glass side table, the noise breaking the silence between them. Bex leaned sideways to grab the phone. Bex braced herself for bad news from the client or worse, another email from Caleb. She hadn't heard from him in days. She didn't know if that meant he'd given up or he was plotting something bigger.

It was a text message from James.

"It's our podcast engineer," Bex said to Aimee.

"Okay," was all Aimee replied with. She grabbed her phone and began playing some stupid match game.

You home with Ana? She okay? James wrote. Bex rubbed her temples. This message did nothing to help ease her tension.

I'm in Cali for work. Why?

I can't get a hold of her. She texted me earlier but now she's not responding. James said.

She hasn't answered me either. Hoping she's just lost in her words. Bex responded.

Maybe the comments on the podcast?

Probably. They're a bit rough.

Three little dots filled the screen. James was typing. While Bex waited, she put a hand on Aimee's thigh. She didn't look up from her game.

The dots stopped. James changed his mind.

Bex turned to Aimee and ran a hand over her leg. "I'm going to call Ana, okay?" Aimee just nodded. Bex dialed her sister; the phone rang and rang but Ana didn't answer. Bex checked Ana's location. She was at home.

Fear seeped through Bex's mind. Was Ana successful this time?

Bex's phone dinged again. Another message from James.

Don't freak but I'm worried. Ana told me that you have a doorbell camera the other day. I took a chance and tried your Apple password to log in. It worked - you use the same password. She hasn't come or gone all day. Do you have cameras inside the house? I couldn't see inside.

Bex reread the text message again. Did James just break into their cameras? Bex had already checked them quickly but didn't notice anything suspicious.

"Oh my god," she said.

"What?"

"James is worried about Ana. That's what he's been texting me about, he hasn't heard from her either. He just said that he logged into my cameras at the house to see if she's okay. He's asking if there are cameras inside."

"That's creepy as fuck!" Aimee said. She set her phone down and looked at the messages on Bex's phone as if they were radioactive. "How did he log in?"

"I guess Ana told him we have a doorbell camera system. He knows our Apple password for podcasts and stuff. I use the same one," Bex said.

Bex's mind raced. Why didn't he just ask her to check the cameras? Why did he even think to use her Apple password? Why did she use the same dumb password on all her logins?

"Why does he care about Ana all that much?" Aimee asked.

"They kind of have a weird thing going. I swear he and Ana have an elementary-school-style crush on one another, or at least Ana does. They text quite a bit; she just met him for the first time the other day."

"So, they're dating?"

"No, not officially. I'm not sure if he feels the same but he lives in Chicago and works for podcasts across the country."

"He lives in Chicago?"

"Yeah."

"Isn't that where the box bomb went off?"

"Yeah, a suburb I think."

"And didn't Ana say he was the one that first told her about the bomb?"

"Yep. He's like a true crime sleuth. He saw it online and sent it to her."

"That's a lot of weird things in a row," Aimee said. "That guy is *sus.*"

It was almost as if a lightbulb went off. She sat up and looked at his message again. Bex's gut understood before her mind, her sister wasn't safe with James.

THIRTY-THREE

Whatever shred of independence Ana had gained was stripped away by the black sedan. Shame beat Ana down; the only thing she could do was sit on the couch and watch mindless television. Dissociation took over and her mind went black.

Somewhere around sundown, Ana's brain clicked back into place. She worked to convince herself that it was just a coincidence. Black cars were as common as stoners and Patagonia vests in Colorado. She was drawing conclusions where there were none. She was home and safe. In a day or so when her mind was right, she'd try moving out again. Ana had time. Bex wasn't due home for a few days.

Ana checked her phone. James and Bex had blown up her messages; she could see their worry increasing by the text. She smiled a little. It was nice that they cared about Ana enough to check in on her. Ana decided to let them both wonder for a bit longer.

Ana turned to her computer. If she was going to live on her own, she had to get serious about her work.

She logged into her Amazon account to check her sales report. The line shot straight up, nearly off the chart. Ana double-checked that she hadn't somehow logged into some other author's account. It was hers.

People might have decided she was guilty, but the accusations were doing wonders for her book sales. More than 300 copies of her *Obstruction of Correspondence* book were downloaded in the last couple of days. Print sales were in the double digits as well. She'd sold more copies of her book over the week than she did the whole previous year.

In her Amazon account, Ana saw a sales figure she didn't even think was possible. Her next payout would be $1,109.12. Ana read the number again. For all the hours she toiled at the computer screen, she had some income to show for it.

Her mind doubled with excitement. The title of "best-selling" author was now her's. Ana smiled and made a little hoot. She clapped for herself. This meant once the money hit her bank account, she really could move out.

Ana opened Instagram. She said a silent prayer that somehow, she wouldn't find carnage. Her notifications were higher than usual. She bit her bottom lip and clicked on her latest post. Comments flooded the screen. Words swirled in front of her eyes. *Coincidence*, and *killer*, and *guilty* washed right off the screen and into her face. Ana didn't want to see more.

She closed the app and opened TikTok as a Hail Mary. Along with every other starving author out there, Ana recently opened an account where she posted occasionally about her books and her life as an author. She only had a handful of followers and her views hovered somewhere around 200 per video.

Ana prayed that of all places, her anonymity would remain on this platform. She was wrong.

The first video that popped up in her feed was by @TexasTrueCrimeChick. Ana never saw her face before, but the petite brown-haired girl had green-screened herself in front of the cover of *Obstruction of Correspondence*. Ana gulped. The algorithm was algorithm-ing way too hard. How was this the first video on her For You Page?

Ana was afraid of what this Texas girl had to say, but the fact that the video had 27,000 hearts and another couple thousand comments made her press play.

"Ohh boy, I have a story for y'all," she said. Her southern twang filled Ana's ears.

"The author of this book," she pointed behind her, "wrote this all about a bomb in a box. And a few weeks ago, someone copied the plot of this book - same victim name, same location - and sent a bomb in a box to a poor woman who opened it up. The explosion killed her."

The creator looked stricken. Ana's whole body tensed, knowing what was next.

"And that's not all. Someone on Reddit figured out that the book used in the crime was a copy of this book," she pointed to Ana's cover behind her. The cover was a dark background, a brown, cardboard box in the front where you could just make the word 'misdelivered' on a box. Ana designed it herself in a free plug and play graphic design website. At the time, she loved it. Now, seeing her cover behind this TikToker's head, Ana wanted to puke.

"So, we have a book copied in real life and the sender used a very specific book. And worse yet, the author of this book hosts a podcast with her sister. It's called *The Serial Syndicate*. Today, they dropped a new episode where they discuss this case. If you haven't listened, you should."

The virality of this video explained why the podcast blew up and why her book sales were off the charts.

"I know I'm always preaching about innocent until proven guilty and all of that, but I'm not the only one going here - Ana Adams is guilty as hell. Just listen to her show, she is robotic, and she doesn't sound like she gives a damn. I think she sent this package. She is the only one with motive and clearly, she did the research to write her own book. It's not that far of a stretch to think she brought her plot to life."

Ana sat up and rubbed her forehead. She couldn't believe this was happening.

"Time will tell, but I have a feeling this is only getting started. Make sure you give me a follow to stay in the loop."

Ana closed the app. This was so much worse than she thought. She could deal with a few insensitive comments on Facebook - an app fit only for dinosaurs at this point - but the possibility of going viral on TikTok scared her. TikTok was a whole new animal and if that video earned that many views, there were others. There had to be.

The vibration of her phone broke through Ana's racing thoughts. She looked at the screen, Bex again. Ana let it go to voicemail.

Ana grabbed her notebook. She didn't know what to write but the urge to put words on the paper was the only way she knew how to process it all. Ana opened it to a new page. Her pen hovered over the lines, trying to decide where to start. She wrote *The List* at the top of the page and underlined it.

Ana chewed on the end of the pen, a habit she picked up in elementary school, something she did when she needed to think. Ana needed to put her theories to pen and paper. Who did this? Who framed her? Names swirled around her head, but she couldn't be sure of any of them.

This exercise made her realize just how sad and small her world was. There were very few people in Ana's life. There were very few suspects.

She forced herself to stay away from the black hole of self-pity. Ana didn't have the luxury of wallowing anymore. She needed to figure out who did this and make it right. For Ruth. But also, for herself.

Ana thought of Kyle. His name crossing her mind sent goosebumps down her arm. The way he latched on to Ana and made her feel suffocated. His propensity for true crime. Ana wasn't sure that was enough to commit a horrendous murder, but it was something. She wrote his name on the list.

Another name came to mind, Dr. Daniels. Ana never particularly liked the man; he was too friendly and too invested. What would be Daniels' motive? Ana questioned herself. Maybe he wanted to make her feel crazy so she would have to come back to Hillside? Maybe he wanted to help jumpstart her author career with a big splash? Ana wasn't sure, but she wrote his name anyway.

Ana didn't have any other concrete suspects. The only people she spent time with were James and Bex. They would never do something like this to her.

She thought back over the last few days. There was someone else. The person who sent the letter. Based on the hate spewed from their words, the sender wasn't an unreasonable suspect. She knew nothing about the person, but she added them to the list.

The other thought that came to her mind was the person who had been beating down their door in the middle of the night. Out of everything, that made her the most scared. Someone knew where she lived, and they were willing to practically beat down the door to get to her. She didn't know who they were or if they were related to the person who sent the letter, but she wrote them down just in case:

Kyle

Dr. Daniels

Letter writer

Door knocker

The list was sparse. Reading it filled Ana with doubts. None of these people were strong candidates. She didn't even have a name for half of them. And the ones she did, neither of them had a solid reason to do this to her. Ana forced herself to consider that it was none of them.

The only consistent thought Ana could keep in her mind was what Aimee said. She couldn't live like this until she caught the killer. The fear was too great. It clouded her mind and ruined her judgment.

She wouldn't be able to live on her own until the killer was locked away.

Ana needed a way to catch the killer. And she needed to do it fast. But how? Writing a murder mystery was much easier than solving one in real life.

Absent-mindedly, Ana flipped through her journal, looking for anything that might trigger an idea. Ana landed on a page with the words 'Live Show!' written at the top. Her eyes skimmed the page; she found the notes were from when she and Bex planned their upcoming live recording.

A plan materialized in her mind. The live show. That was it.

She could see some of the suspects in person. It would give her a chance to gut check them. Ana was sure she would be able to tell which one had done this to her. To Ruth.

If Ana caught the killer on a live recording, she would really go viral. And when the killer was caught, she would be free.

THIRTY-FOUR

2:16 PM - Direct Messages from @anasnumberonefan -

> Hey, you. You never responded to me the other day. Too busy cause you're BLOWING UP? Killing it, lady. I don't know why more authors don't bring their stories to life. It works. Can't wait to see what will happen next! Keep going. You'll be the next Colleen Hoover here soon.

THIRTY-FIVE

39 South was a high-end, modern restaurant that overlooked San Francisco Bay. The lighting was dark, the drinks strong and the portion sizes almost enough to feed a hungry mouse. Young professionals clustered around intimately lit tables and inviting booths deep in negotiations - for sex or business, or both. The room buzzed with deals being made, soft laughter, and the crystalline clinks of overpriced cocktails.

The spot lit center table Bex sat at with her teammates and the clients they were courting was charged with big egos and even bigger sales goals. Bex and her team had spent the week with the client building rapport, especially Aimee. She went above and beyond to help the law group dream of all the possibilities of a new cloud-based system.

Now, it was time for Bex to go in for the kill. The client was close to signing a year-long contract. The first year was always the hardest; if her team could get this first one signed, they'd be golden. And Bex would get her bonus.

Bex wore her tightest black dress and signature red-bottom pumps to dinner, hair worn up and swept off her neck to show off her diamond studs and white gold Cartier choker. Bex purposely sat on the opposite end of the table from Aimee, next to the key decision-maker of the group. Bex knew how to close a deal; she was ready to do whatever it would take.

Their CMO was a man named Dave. He was at least twice her age - mid-sixties - and too ignorant about cloud marketing to be the man in charge of their whole customer recruitment and retention program, but in charge he was. Dave wore a classic Rolex, and his salt-

and-pepper hair was slicked back. His tailored suit, taut around his arms, told Bex that he still spent a fair amount of time in the gym.

From the first moment they arrived at the client's office earlier in the week, he latched onto Bex. She let him. They flirted between meetings, and he winked at her enough times to make Bex wonder if his eyes just naturally twitched.

Bex liked the way he made her feel. Not his attention, but rather the fact that she could so easily persuade him to sign the contract. Or at least that was her plan.

"So, Dave," she said, taking a measured seductive swallow of the expensive wine he ordered for the table. "Ready to sign the contract? Ensure that you get to work with all of us for years to come?"

He laughed heartily. She looked around the table. Her team - mostly young account executives - had big eyes and nervous, jerky movements, their inexperience at odds with the natural arrogance of the good-looking 20-something professionals. Aimee fit right in. Bex looked away and returned her focus to Dave. Her job was to get him buttered up, pen in hand.

"What's in it for me?" he asked. His voice was loud, the whole table heard.

"Well, obviously the great platform we offer allows you to stay ahead of your customer's needs and top of mind when they're ready to refer someone."

"No, no. I get that. You've pounded that into our heads all week, what else can you add to the deal?"

Bex was used to this little dance. She thought quickly on her feet, "We'll add in some extra features to your platform at no cost. And we will give you those additional information fields your head of customer service wanted."

He took a long drink; a little red wine dribbled down his red face. His hand shook as he replaced the glass. He was drunker than she realized. Dave's eyes roved around the table; this was a man who was used to getting what he wanted. Dave knew what he wanted. And Bex knew, too.

"Bexley, that's your full name, right?" She nodded. He gave a big toothy grin. His teeth were stained from the wine.

"David, is that your full name?"

"Ha! It is."

"Well, David, let's sign the contract, and then we can go out to celebrate," she said with a wink.

"It's a deal!" he yelled.

The tension in Bex's shoulders dropped. Now that they had a verbal agreement, it wouldn't be nearly as hard to get it inked on paper. She couldn't wait to see the bonus check she'd get this quarter with this group in her column.

"A round of shots!" Dave yelled as he flagged down the server with his white linen napkin. Bex shoved her embarrassment aside. Shots were always a good sign.

"What'll it be?" Dave yelled her way.

"Tequila!" she said. The server looked at everyone across the table. Everyone nodded in agreement except Aimee. Bex purposely avoided eye contact; she could feel Aimee seething across the table, but Bex didn't have the bandwidth to deal with her.

The tequila went down burning. Dave whooped. Bex smiled through the fire in her throat. She felt Aimee's stare, but Bex kept her eyes on Dave and kept the fun rolling.

Dave launched into another one of his success stories, some big litigation against a tech giant. Bex snuck a look at her phone. Ana had finally responded that she was fine. Relief flooded Bex's mind, but she forced herself to push it away to focus on the clients at hand. She would call Ana later and see what had kept her silent all day.

159

As dinner wrapped up and the bill was settled, the group stood. Dave hung back and waited for Bex. As she met him, he brushed her hand with his. Dave's skin was smooth, it had the softness of a guy who'd never done manual labor.

With the rest of the group up ahead of them, Dave grabbed her hand and twisted his head toward the side door. He smiled wide. Bex knew exactly what he wanted.

"How about we sign the deal tomorrow and then a date will be in order," she whispered in his ear, her voice light and happy. She made sure to give him a big smile and the full front of her cleavage. He laughed. He cocked his head toward the door again, pulling her hand - harder this time.

"Let's go," he said. His words slurred together.

"I can't go tonight. Sign the deal and I'll call you for that date," she said. Prior to Aimee, she would have left with him in a heartbeat, but something reined her in. She couldn't just yet.

He let go of her hand and huffed out of the restaurant like a petulant little kid. He didn't turn back to any of them before he hailed a cab. The move worried Bex. She didn't care if he didn't like her, but she very much cared what would come of the contract.

Bex and her team took an Uber back to the hotel where they were staying. The ride was cold, everyone looked tired and worn out from a long week.

"Great job tonight!" she said in the car. "Those dinners are never easy, but you all did a nice job carrying the conversation. Thank you." She got a few nods, but no one said much. Aimee wouldn't even look at her.

Back at the hotel, the others filed to their rooms quickly. Bex caught Aimee alone just before she shut the door to her room.

"Can I come in?" Bex asked.

"Why?"

"I want to see you."

"I don't."

"Aimee, what's going on? What did I do?" Bex said. Her voice cracked.

"Oh, shut your mouth. You know what you did. Flirting with those guys right in front of me."

"I wasn't going to do anything," Bex said.

"Tell that to the condoms in your bag," Aimee sneered. She shut the door in Bex's face. Bex stepped back, shocked. Aimee took that dinner worse than Bex thought she would.

Bex went to her room, annoyed that Aimee couldn't see that sometimes you needed to forgo your emotions to close the deal. Bex cracked a little bottle of prosecco from the room fridge.

Fuck Aimee. She was ready to celebrate a big win. Even if she was to do it alone. Driven by anger and pent-up energy, Bex left the hotel in search of a good time.

—

The next morning, Bex dressed, making sure to look the part of the high-powered tech product manager that she was. She just needed to get one signature and she could be out of there. Then she could repair things with Aimee. Bex possessed the confidence that she could do both.

They arrived at their client's office and the admin took them to the conference room where they spent the last week showing the team all the ways that their business communications and marketing could be improved with a proper sales cloud.

"Colin will be here shortly, he texted to say he's on his way. There's coffee and bagels, feel free to make yourselves at home," she said. She was a petite woman, no more than twenty-five but she looked like she was good at her job.

"What about Dave?" Bex asked. Her mind was solely on him.

"Oh, I'm sorry, did he not let you know? He's come down with something and won't be in."

"I hadn't heard that," Bex said. She worked to keep her face calm. She had checked her email several times already. There hadn't been a change in plans.

"Yeah, Colin will be here soon, and he can answer any questions for you."

"Do you know if Colin can sign the contract?"

"I don't, sorry."

Awkwardness filled the space as Bex's team waited for Colin to show up. Bex had been in enough of these meetings to know that Dave's sudden no-show was a bad sign. She tried not to let it show but she could tell her team sensed it too.

She looked around the room. The table was designed to intimidate, big plush chairs around a massive, lacquered redwood slab. The walls featured giant paintings with thick modern paint swirls which gave them a textured look. From the height of the boardroom, you could just make out the vast arch of the Golden Gate Bridge in the distance.

Colin entered in a huff. He looked all business, not like the funny easy-going guy from the night before. "Sorry, I'm late," he said."

"No worries, sorry we kept you out late last night. Apparently, last night was a little too much fun," Bex responded. She gave a jovial laugh, but it didn't seem to crack Colin.

"Ah, yeah. It was a good night, thank you and your team for taking the time to be here." He was stiffer than someone after their first yoga class.

"I'll just get down to business," he said. "We've decided not to move forward with the contract."

The full force of his words hit her in the gut. She was counting on this sale. She was counting on the bonus she would receive when the deal was signed.

"Oh goodness, why?" Someone on her team asked. Bex would have normally taken up that line of questioning but for once she was glad someone else stepped in.

"We just took a closer look at our budget, and we don't feel it fits," he said. Bex didn't listen to the rest of it. The opulence of the room told Bex it had very little to do with money.

She finally found her voice. "Is there anything we can do? We can work with you on budgeting or see where we can cut features."

"No, no. I don't want to take any more of your time. We're not interested in moving forward."

Her brain ached with whiplash and disappointment clouded her judgement. Last night, they were so damn close, and now this. This was all her fault. She should have just gone home with Dave last night. If she was in his bed this morning, things probably would look a whole lot different now.

"I have a full day. I'll let you all get going," he said. "Feel free to take a bagel for the road." He might as well have said, don't let the door hit you on the way out.

Bex and her team packed up their laptops and work bags. Their flight wasn't until later in the day. They would need to go back to the hotel and pack up. And Bex would need to update her boss. Bex would rather pull her nails out one by one before she made that call.

The Uber back to the hotel was nearly unbearable. Bex didn't bother saying anything. She couldn't. She somehow lost the biggest deal of the quarter and pissed off Aimee in less than twenty-four hours.

It was all she could do to keep the bile from spewing across her colleagues.

Bex escaped to her room. She couldn't look at her team for another minute, especially Aimee. Not that Aimee would have ever met her gaze anyway. All Bex wanted to do was talk to her sister. Bex just hoped she would finally answer.

"Ana, finally," Bex said when Ana answered. "Where have you been?"

"Sorry, I just got into a weird headspace. I needed a minute."

"Are you okay?"

"I mean, I haven't tried to 'unalive' myself if that's what you're asking."

"Are you okay otherwise?"

"Well, this thing has blown up. The good news is our podcast has been downloaded more today than all other days combined and the same for my book sales."

"Hey! That's great," Bex said. The pain of the last day roared up in her mind. "We're going to need the podcast now more than ever. Hell, I just saw an article that some crime podcast sold for some twenty-five million. I think I could settle for selling ours for a million five."

"Why do you say that?"

"I fucked up, Ana. I thought I had a major sale out here but it kind of went to shit. And I messed things up with Aimee, big time."

"Oh, sister. I'm so sorry."

"It's my fault. I just tried to do too much."

"Is there anything I can do?"

"No, just don't leave me, too. I need you. And the podcast."

THIRTY-SIX

"I ordered Thai!" Bex called from her room.

The sound of her sister shocked her. Ana thought Bex would have locked herself in her room for the evening. Ana hoped she would have had the night to refine her plan to catch the killer. Thai meant Bex wanted to hang out instead.

"Yum! Thanks!" Ana called back. She wasn't ready to let Bex in on her plan yet. She needed to act normal.

Ana stared at her work in progress; instead of adding new scenes she imagined confronting Dr. Daniels and Kyle at the live show. She could almost imagine one of them confessing. Ana's daydream was interrupted by the doorbell. "I'll get it," Bex called.

The smell of hot peppers hit Ana as soon as she walked into the kitchen; her stomach growled. She didn't remember eating anything after the McDonald's she panic ate. If she was honest with herself, Ana couldn't remember much of the last three days. Had she blacked out again? She wasn't sure. Ana didn't want to think about it.

"Thanks for dinner," Ana said as Bex unloaded the brown paper bag.

"Sure. I'm starving and I needed something to go my way." Bex handed Ana the Styrofoam box labeled 'pad see ew' in tight, neat handwriting.

Ana sat at the table. "That bad, huh?"

"Probably worse," Bex said, joining her at her usual spot.

"Sorry."

"Yeah, me too. I don't even know what happened with the client. We were at dinner; it was going so well. He was flirting with me, and I flirted back. That's why Aimee is pissed at me, I guess."

Ana swallowed. She didn't know what to say.

"And then, it didn't even pay off!" Bex said, indignantly.

"What do you mean?

"Well, the dick was trying to get me to leave with him and I said no. I thought I was playing coy, and I'd call when he signed the contract. He didn't even show up for our final meeting."

Ana took another bite. The food tasted a little funny in her mouth. Ana always knew that Bex was a go-getter, but she felt for Aimee. Just watching your boss sink to that must feel gross, let alone your girlfriend.

"I just don't understand why you were flirting with him in the first place."

"That's just what you have to do. Tech is filled with gross old men who need to have their egos stroked. I wasn't planning on going on a date with him. I thought I could get the contract without going that far. Flirting usually works, I don't know why she didn't see that."

Ana thought she was lying. She took a bite and chewed slowly. There had to be more to the story.

"I'm sorry you didn't have a great trip."

Bex stood and grabbed a bottle of wine from the rack on the counter. She held up the bottle in an invitation to Ana. Ana nodded; Bex poured each of them a glass. One glass held a noticeably larger pour.

"I'm mostly annoyed by Aimee. I didn't even do anything. She's acting like I killed a kitten in front of her."

"Are you exclusive? Have you entertained that conversation?"

"I mean, yeah. Basically. We haven't defined it necessarily but neither one of us is dating anyone else. We still haven't told that many people though, so it's a little gray. The client didn't know we were together."

"But I see her point, if she thought you were an item, seeing your boss who happens to be your girlfriend flirt and agree to a future date probably hurt."

Bex set a wine glass in front of Ana.

"Yeah, I just didn't do anything wrong. I was trying to close the deal. Aimee should understand that."

Ana took a drink of the wine. It was surprisingly good. The liquid warmed her chest and Ana was glad to have something to take the edge off this conversation with her sister.

"Have you tried talking to her?"

"We flew home together but she iced me out, only talking when necessary. And now the team probably fucking knows that there was something between us. Ugh."

Silence filled the room. Ana didn't like this version of her sister. This manipulating, gaslighting version of Bex came out when she didn't get her way. With a little space from her sister, Ana could see it all so much more clearly.

"I just need Aimee to get it together, I'm not the cheating type. Work is a priority, and you are a priority. She needs to understand that and quit bitching all the time."

This conversation made Ana's hair tingle. Bex didn't like that Aimee wasn't going along with her schemes. When Bex found out that Ana wasn't playing her role either, Bex would turn just like she had on her girlfriend. Ana could only watch the transformation take over her sister, she had nothing to say.

"And now, I have a one-on-one with my boss tomorrow. What a nice 'welcome home' to me. I don't know how much shit he's going to throw at me. I lost the biggest client of the quarter."

Ana swallowed. She closed the lid of her container as quietly as she could.

167

"Hopefully it will all work out," Ana finally said. She wanted the conversation to end.

"Ugh. So, what's up with you? What did you do while I was gone?" Bex said.

"I was just in my head. Nothing crazy. The words aren't coming as easily this 'round."

"Are you okay?" Bex asked. "Do I need to worry about you too?"

"No, I'm good. Nothing like before. I am just a little stressed about everything going on. And our live show coming up."

"Yeah, on the live show. I was thinking on the plane home that we need to record an episode and put out all the details to invite people. Maybe we should do that tonight?"

Ana wanted to do anything but record another show.

"I don't know if we need to record a whole show. I can just create a Facebook event," Ana said.

"Let's do a show. After the way the last one blew up, we need to capitalize on that momentum. The podcast is all I have left," Bex said with a self-deprecating laugh. "And you of course," she added.

Ana ground her teeth. "You sure? I don't think we need to give everyone more to talk about."

"That's exactly what we need to do! It's now or never."

Ana's mind came up with a million excuses, but she knew that for everyone she gave, Bex would shut it down. It wasn't even worth the fight. Bex's mind was made, they were recording a show tonight. Ana needed to *get in line*, as Bex would say.

She put her leftovers in the fridge and downed the last of her wine. Ana rinsed the glass in the sink. Watching the blood-red liquid run down the drain did something to her. She wanted out.

"Let's just record so we can get to bed. I'm tired and I'm over all of this," Bex said.

THIRTY-SEVEN

"Hello and welcome to *The Serial Syndicate*. I'm Ana," Ana started, just as they always did.

"And I'm Bex," Bex filled in.

"Well, first let me say thanks to all of our new listeners," Ana said. "I still can't believe how many of you listened to the last show. We're blown away by your support."

"And secondly, thanks to all the new haters out there! Because of all of you commenting and talking shit about us - Ana especially - we're reaching more and more people. So, keep at it," Bex said. She was spewing fire and ready to blow this show up even bigger than the last.

"Today, we're talking about JonBenét Ramsey. What? Did you think a couple of Colorado true crime podcasters wouldn't ever get to that one?" Bex laughed loudly into the microphone.

"But first, we have an important announcement - you're invited to our live recording! Next week, we'll be at the Lioness Lair Denver. We'll record a podcast episode live from the stage and you'll be able to see the magic happen for yourselves."

Bex looked to Ana, ready to pass the invitation off to her. Ana was picking at her nails, not paying attention. Bex felt annoyed. She couldn't believe how disengaged she was.

"The live show will be held on June 12 at 7 PM. Lioness Lair in Denver on Market Street. We'll be recording by 7:15 and then we'll do a Q&A after the fact, off-air. Ana and I will stay for drinks - and autographs - afterward. You can also buy the hottest commodity of the year - Ana's books."

It was Ana's turn. That's how this worked, she should have jumped in by now. Instead, they were recording an awkward pause.

Bex looked up, Ana was still in her own world. Bex paused the recording and took off her headphones, slamming them on the table. She snapped at Ana.

Ana finally registered; her head jerked up. When she saw Bex's headphones were off, she took hers off as well.

"Are you going to record with me or what? Remember, we agreed on JonBenét; you know everything there is to know about that case. I need you to get to it."

Ana didn't look up. Bex ran her tongue over her teeth, ready to force her sister into this. They had to record. There was no question about it.

"Sorry, okay. I'm ready," Ana said, finally giving in. Bex pulled her headphones back on and counted down to her sister.

The first few words out of Ana's mouth were mechanical and forced. Bex's whole body tensed. She needed Ana to get it together. Thankfully, after a few sentences, Ana finally found her groove. Her voice leveled off and she lost herself in the details. She led listeners through JonBenét's story in that factual and fascinating way she was so good at. Bex relaxed and leaned back in the chair. She added colorful comments as warranted, but mostly let Ana do her thing.

"That was a good one," Bex said after she ended the recording.

"Yeah," Ana replied. She wrapped the cord around her mic.

"I'm excited for the live show. You're going to sell so many books-" Bex started to say before she was interrupted by a sharp, quick knock at the door.

Bex looked at the clock. It was after eight. "Who is that?"

"I don't know," Ana said quietly. A look of pure terror clouded her face.

Bex considered just letting it go. It was probably some door knocker selling that Colorado sunshine line about solar panels, but then she heard some kind of yell outside. Their neighborhood was usually quiet, the noise was concerning.

Ana and Bex looked at each other; it was clear that Ana was paralyzed. Bex crossed the room and opened the door.

The first thing that registered was the bright orange color, vibrant against the dark night sky and then the smell hit her hard Smoke. Something was burning at their feet.

"Oh fuck!" Bex yelled. "Get water!"

Bex could feel Ana at her back and then she was gone. Bex kneeled closer and realized it was a book. The pages, engulfed in flames.

"Hurry, Ana!"

Bex tried to kick the flaming object, but she only wore her house slippers. She could feel the heat before she ever got close enough to boot it off the porch. Finally, Ana returned with a salad bowl of water. Bex grabbed it from her and dumped it all over the burning book.

The porch erupted in sizzling steam. The smell intensified. Smoke and dirty steam filled their whole porch. Someone called from the street, "Everything okay?"

"Yeah, thanks!" Bex managed to yell back. The fire was out but her nerves were shot.

"What the hell?" Ana asked. She bent down to get a better look.

"My god," Ana said, her voice low and quiet.

"What?"

"It's *Obstruction of Correspondence*."

"What?!" Bex asked, louder this time.

"It's my book."

Bex bent down. Sure enough, the cover was burnt three-fourths of the way, but you could still make out the graphic of the box, and part of Ana's name at the bottom. Ana was right.

171

"Who did this?!" Bex asked.

Bex looked around the porch, hoping to see any other signs of who could have left the book. Under the porch mat, Bex noticed the corner of a piece of paper sticking out. She moved closer and pulled it free. It was an index card, the kind she used to study with in college.

In bold, black marker someone wrote, *Get Fucked!*

Bex held it up and showed Ana. She shuddered; her face looked stricken. Bex stood and wrapped Ana in a hug. Ana was shivering. It was one thing to write a mean comment behind a screen, but this was personal.

Bex grabbed the mostly burnt book and scooped what she could into the bowl. There was a huge black mark on the concrete where the book had burned. It looked like someone performed an exorcism on their front stoop.

"C'mon. Let's go inside."

"Check the cameras," Ana said as she opened the door.

Bex set the bowl on the counter and pulled out her phone. She opened the app. The feed was black. Bex thought it was a weird glitch, but restarting the app did not turn on the live feed. She scrolled back earlier in the day; the camera was working then. Bex sped it up; as of about 8:45 PM, all was normal. Ana watched over her shoulder.

She hit play and waited to see if there was anything that caused the camera to stop working. After about two minutes of a dead street in front of the house, Bex saw movement in the peripheral of the camera.

It was hard to tell, but it looked like someone in a dark outfit, complete with a mask, was walking along just where the camera could reach. Then they sped up and raced up the steps of the porch. Within two seconds, the screen went black.

There was nothing. Bex rewound and tried it again. Same thing happened - someone rushed the porch then the camera stopped working.

"They broke the camera!" Ana yelled.

Bex threw her phone on the couch and went back to the porch. Sure enough, there was a piece of electrical tape over the camera. It was so simple but effective. Other than the approximately four seconds on the screen, there was no way to tell who covered the camera or set Ana's book on fire. Bex ripped the tape off the camera.

"Well, shit," Bex said as she came back inside. "Whoever that was covered the camera. There's no footage."

Ana sucked in a big deep breath. "That means, whoever did this knew where we live and that there is a camera on the porch. They've been watching us."

The fear was written all over Ana's face. Bex knew it all too well herself.

"We should call the cops," Ana said.

Bex looked at the mess on the porch. On some level, she knew her sister was right. The fear of inviting the cop's scrutiny into the mess their lives had become was too real though. Bex didn't need them looking closer at either one of them.

"I don't know. It's just a book," Bex said, hoping it was enough to assuage her sister.

"This wasn't just a little high school prank, this was serious. This could have done some serious damage to our house. They could have killed us," Ana said. "Maybe it was the same person who sent the bomb?"

"We're okay. The cops won't do anything anyways," Bex said. Ana paced around the living room.

Bex sat on the couch and rubbed her forehead. It had to be Caleb. She couldn't think of anyone else. Bex couldn't tell Ana about their brother though. That lie of omission was too far gone. If Ana knew about him and his letter, not to mention his visit, she would lose her shit. Bex needed Ana to be sane and knowing about Caleb would do the exact opposite.

Bex had to think fast.

"I don't know. I did have a weird thing with James when I was in California, maybe it was him?!" Bex said.

"What? What happened? James wouldn't do this."

"Well, he was worried about you and couldn't get a hold of you, so you know what he did? He used my Apple password to log in to the doorbell camera app to see if you'd left the house or not."

"That's creepy as fuck. Why didn't you tell me?" Ana said. Bex could hear the panic rising in her voice with every syllable.

"I was worried that you weren't answering, I didn't know if you were okay. I couldn't add something more to the mix." Bex answered. She cracked her knuckles.

"He lives in Chicago. He wouldn't have done this," Ana repeated. She paced around the living room. "And anyways, if he has the password to our camera, he could just stop the feed. Why use tape."

"He's coming for the live show, right? He could have come early."

Bex could see the wheels turning in Ana's mind.

"I don't think it was James, but there is that guy from residential," Ana said. "Maybe him."

"Does he know where you live?"

"I don't know. Possibly. If someone wanted to figure our address out, they probably could."

Bex pushed her knuckles again, looking for more relief. She was jittery and her mind was running in ten different directions. Her own home had been invaded. She didn't feel comfortable here anymore.

"The problem is it could be anyone," Ana finally said.

THIRTY-EIGHT

Ana's eyes shot open. Her heart pounded and her head stuck with sweat. Ana sat up in bed, the clock read 4:21 AM. She was tense with anxiety. It took her several eye rubs for her brain to catch up to what her body already knew. It was the day of their live show.

Her mind raced and her whole body clammed up at the thought of walking on stage. Dread consumed Ana. She didn't want to be awake this early. She didn't want to have to think about it all day.

The pillows caught her as she laid back down. Ana tossed and turned. She was unable to fall back asleep with the worry sitting squarely on her chest. At 4:57 AM, Ana decided to just get up for the day.

She walked to the kitchen. She started the Keurig and waited for it to fill her cup with the Costa Rican blend she picked. Ana trailed the steam rising from the machine; her eyes caught sight of the bowl on top of the refrigerator. Ana wondered why Bex hadn't gotten rid of it yet. She reached for it.

Ana took the book from the bowl and held it over the sink. Little black flecks of ash danced to the metal basin below. The book crunched in her hands. Ana turned it over, the back was largely intact, but the front was pretty burned.

As gingerly as she could, Ana opened the cover of the book. The pages were burned around the edges, but the center of the paper remained mostly intact. On the title page, Ana was met with a note. She squinted to make out the words.

Maybe this will help - The note started. The rest of the sentence had gone up in flames. She threw the book in the sink and stepped away from it. She would recognize that handwriting anywhere. Bex.

Whoever set it on fire was close. That knowledge was nuclear, it changed everything.

Ana opened the book again. This book was Aimee's. It was the only explanation. Ana became more and more convinced of that fact by the minute. Why did Aimee set it on fire? And how did Bex not see this level of crazy in the woman she was dating?

Ana thought of the list she started. If Aimee was crazy enough to light a book on fire on their porch, what else was she capable of? Ana walked back to her room, the cup of coffee warming her icy hands. Ana's heart raced.

From the drawer in her side table, Ana pulled out the list she started. It was elementary and the kind of shoddy police work she'd written about in some of her books, but it was all she had. It was the only thing she could control.

She reread what she wrote the other day –

Kyle

Dr. Daniels

Letter writer

Door knocker

Underneath Dr. Daniels, Ana wrote the name, *Aimee*. The names taunted her.

Under that, Ana wrote *James*. It hurt to include his name, but she had to. He was watching her. Something was off. She was just as suspicious of him as any of the rest of them.

Ana knew the only way she could truly move past this would be to find the person who sent the bomb. It was now or maybe never.

The live show would give her the chance to see some of them in person, to view them in a newly suspicious light. The event was an opportunity. She wouldn't get a confession but at least she could give herself a chance to get a gut feeling one way or another. It would give her a chance to cross James off the list.

Ana sent a text to James - *Can't wait to see you today.*

She penned an email to Dr. Daniels and said - *Hey, there- I just wanted to check in. I'm doing great outside of Hillside. My sister and I even have a live podcast recording tonight. I'd love for you to come if you're free.* She included the details.

Finding Kyle proved to be a bit harder. She hadn't talked to him since residential and she didn't have his contact information. Ana debated crossing him off the list but something about him gave her pause. He was such a creep. She knew that wasn't enough, but if he came to the show, she would get a better sense of him and what he might be capable of.

Ana looked through her followers on Instagram. It took a few searches, but she finally found the right picture of Kyle. She clicked his profile; weird artist renderings of blood and beaten women filled the page. Ana nearly gagged up the coffee in her otherwise empty belly.

Ana couldn't look. She clicked the message button and quickly typed - *Hey, it's Ana from Hillside. I'm doing this live podcast recording with my sister tonight and wanted to invite you.* Ana included the details.

That just left Aimee. Ana had no way of getting in touch with her. Ana listened, the house was still completely quiet at 5:14 AM. Ana set her laptop and phone on the counter. There was only one way to invite Aimee, and it was in Bex's room.

In the hall, Ana made no sound. At Bex's door, she stopped and listened. Nothing. There was no light under the door. Ana turned the knob as quietly as she could and pushed the door open. Ana snuck inside and closed the door almost behind her.

Ana stood near the door and waited for her eyes to adjust. She could hear Bex's steady breathing, even from several steps away. Ana moved closer and waited again. Bex still slept. Ana thanked her lucky stars that Bex slept like the dead, she always had.

Bex continued to sleep as Ana crossed to the room. Ana picked up Bex's phone and typed in her password. It had always been 3431 - the street number from their first home. Ana found Aimee's contact. Bex didn't move.

Ana didn't have time to think about what to say, instead, she wrote the first thing that came to mind. *I'm sorry for all of it. I'd love to see you tonight at Ana's and my live podcasting recording. Maybe we can go out after and talk?* Ana included the details and hit send.

Ana deleted the message.

THIRTY-NINE

@TexasTrueCrimeChick on TikTok

"Heeyyyyyyy there true crime crazies - it's Becca here and I'm back with a small update about that unhinged author story.

"For all of those who don't know, there's a little indie author named Ana Adams out of Colorado who wrote a D-grade book about a murder that's done through a bomb in a box. Don't bother reading the book, it is clearly self-published.

"That aside, someone copied the book and killed a real-life person. In the most horrific way. And now we have to talk about it.

"This whole thing is rather novel. I don't know that I've ever heard of a killer copying a book. Sure, maybe a famous book, but not some self-published garbage. I don't know. It just doesn't sit well with me.

"I've dubbed this unknown perp 'The Novel Killer.'

"There's been no arrests and honestly, not much else. Since this was a mail crime, it's already a federal case but I don't see the feds staking out Ana or anything.

"Some people on Reddit have said that the cops have hair evidence but so far, they haven't confirmed that.

"Anyways, the real reason you're here - today's news! Ana and her sister share a podcast called *The Serial Syndicate*. They're hosting a show tonight in Denver and live streaming the whole thing. Not only is that insensitive as hell, given everything but it's sick how they've taken it a step further to profit off the tragedy.

"Listen, I know that I am also in the business of true crime, but you best believe if the entirety of the internet thought I shipped someone a deadly weapon, I'd lay low. You wouldn't catch me making content out of it.

"Who knows what will happen tonight, but I'll keep you posted. If you're in Denver, do me a solid and go. Take some video cause it's going to be interesting as hell to see how they address this whole thing.

"Like and follow to be sure you get a front-row seat to this trainwreck."

FORTY

"You good, boo?" Bex asked. They were in Bex's little red Audi, a car that wasn't made for Colorado winters but fit Bex's aesthetic - beautiful and fast, decidedly high-maintenance - perfectly. Bex was driving them to their live show. Ana picked at her nails. Little flakes of her black polish chipped around the edges. Ana was nervous as hell.

Ana cleared her throat. "I guess so."

"Well, we look damn good," Bex said. She'd picked out their outfits, 'sultry business' as she called them. They both wore black, fitted dress pants and discreetly sparkly blazers so they would shine just slightly under the lights. Bex wore a purple, sequined crop top under her blazer but she could not talk Ana into the same. Ana wore a plain white shirt instead.

Of course, Bex donned her power red-bottomed shoes whereas Ana opted to wear sensible black flats. Ana made some joke about needing running shoes just in case, Bex didn't really think she was kidding.

"So, remember, the goal of the night is to sell more of your books and grow the show - got it?"

Ana nodded. The back of the car was filled with a folding table and a good number of signed copies. They also brought stickers and pins to sell after the show. Bex was confident this event was another step on the road to becoming big-time.

"You didn't answer me."

"That wasn't a question. Sell books, push the podcast."

"I don't want you to do anything else," Bex warned.

In the corner of her eye, she could see Ana swallow hard. "Like what?" Ana asked.

"I don't know, flirt with James too much or worse, freeze up on stage."

"I'll try my best."

"Good. This is going to be good. All the big podcasts have live shows. We're going to be the next big thing, Ana Adams. I just need your help getting there."

Ana rolled her eyes. "Is Aimee coming?" Ana asked.

Bex closed her eyes for a split second and tipped her head back. Thinking about Aimee was number one on her annoyance-list. Work was a close second. The tension in the office was thick between the lost client and the way Aimee made a show of avoiding her. She would barely look at Bex and only responded to the emails that needed immediate attention.

"I doubt it. I'm pretty sure she's done with me," Bex said. Ana nodded.

A tear threatened in the corner of her eyes. She never cried; just the thought of it pissed her off. Bex quickly wiped it with the back of her hand. She told herself to knock it off. No one needed red, puffy eyes on stage.

As they neared the Lioness Lair, there wasn't a single parking space in sight. There was a line wrapped around the venue, waiting for the doors to open.

"Holy cow," Bex said. Ana slid down in her seat.

"Is that for us?" Ana asked.

"I guess so. Jesus, I was hoping a handful of people would show. That's a lot more than a handful."

"I'm going to be sick," Ana said. She put her head between her knees. Bex laughed and clapped her hands together. She found a parking spot several blocks away.

"Let's do it," Bex said as she exited the car. Blood pumped through Bex's body as she buzzed with excitement. Bex walked around the car and knocked on Ana's window, waiting for her to get out.

Bex couldn't tell what Ana was doing. She was gripping and folding a small piece of paper in her hand. It almost looked like she was saying a prayer, something they hadn't done since their mom died. Bex knocked on the window again. Ana shoved the paper into her blazer pocket. She opened the door slowly.

"Let's go, did you see that crowd? They're waiting for us?" Bex said; she grabbed Ana by the hand and pulled her out of the car. Bex filled Ana's arms with book boxes and supplies for their merch table. She grabbed the rest.

"Yeah, I saw it. There are way too many people, Bex. They're a mob." Ana said. She looked green in the cheeks.

"They're not people Ana, they're *fans*. And when there's this many they're not a 'mob,' they're an *audience,* and that can never be too big."

They walked to the venue, loaded down with products. Bex hoped the way back to the car would be much lighter. The closer they got to the venue, the louder the crowd got, full of animated talk and laughter. The energy was good, it made Bex's chest swell with pride. They were all there for *The Serial Syndicate.* The night was already off to a fantastic start.

Bex led Ana around to the back of the building, so they didn't have to walk in front of their fans with all this stuff in their hands. The artist's entry was unlocked and unmanaged. Bex let herself inside. The venue smelled of beer and cigarettes, but it was quiet inside.

She led them down a hall and found a room labeled *Talent.* Bex assumed that was for them. She pushed open the door and set her boxes on the table along the wall. Ana did the same. Bex turned and realized they weren't alone.

"James!" Ana said.

James looked just like Bex remembered him from their Zoom calls. Skinny, ripped jeans and Converse shoes. He wore a faded black hoodie that was about three sizes too big for his thin frame and a different Carhartt beanie pulled low, just over his eyebrows. He could have been any other 20-something dude in the city aptly dubbed 'Menver' - filled with those who didn't want to grow up, opting for the mountain slopes and beer instead.

"Hi!" he said. He shoved his hands into the pockets of his jacket and took a step back.

"You made it," Bex said.

"Of course, I wouldn't miss this."

"How was your flight?" Bex asked.

"Which one?" he laughed. "I've been all over the country for work lately. I came here from San Francisco, more flights next week."

"Oh, I was in San Francisco last week, too," Bex said.

"Yeah? We should have met up."

Bex smiled. Seeing James during her week from hell would have shot her right over the edge; this was plenty.

"It was kind of a hard week," she said instead. "I didn't have time for any fun."

"Me neither, it was a lot of work for me too. These podcasts just keep popping up."

Ana let out a nervous laugh; Bex noticed Ana's furiously blushing cheeks and took a deep breath. Bex wanted to get to know James better, but all she could see was him breaking into their cameras without so much as asking. Looking at them. Intruding on them. Being in the same room with a person who lacked boundaries made her uneasy.

"But this one is my favorite," James was saying. Bex forced herself to listen. "You guys are really on the cusp. I can feel it."

Ana nodded and a wide smile spread on Bex's face. He was right. This podcast was full of potential. It was nice to see that someone else thought so as well. Maybe he wasn't so bad after all.

"How are book sales?" James asked Ana. "If they're like podcast downloads, you're probably *rich* rich by now."

Ana's nervous laughter filled Bex's ears again. Ana's face was cherry red. Bex realized that Ana's crush was much bigger than she let on. Bex needed to keep a better watch on her sister.

"Book sales are good. Actually great," Ana said. "I've sold more in the last few weeks than I have all year. I guess you were right about that 'going viral' thing."

"Now we just need another murder that follows book two," Bex said to silence. Both Ana and James gave her a long look. A shiver ran down her spine when she realized she said that out loud.

FORTY-ONE

Ana's chest constricted, forcing all the oxygen from her lungs. Ana needed air; she tried to will her lungs to move but fear held them in place. A big booming cackle from James broke the moment but it did nothing to ease the tension in the room.

"You got a dark sense of humor Bex, I love it! I agree! Another murder would do wonders - especially a gory one. We would really crack the charts. It's been a thrill to see your books and show take off, that's all. It's every author's dream - and podcast engineer's," James said.

"I. I. I don't know. I don't want to sell books or get downloads if this is what it takes," Ana managed. She took a step back; his words reminded her that he was as good of a suspect as any of them.

Bex clapped her hands together and said, "Sales are sales." Ana didn't understand why her sister agreed with James.

"Are you ready for tonight?" James asked. He stood there, still cool. He didn't see that his words paralyzed Ana.

"I need some air," Ana said through gritted teeth. She no longer wanted to be trapped in this tiny green room with either one of them. She rushed through the door.

"Be back in five!" Bex called after her.

Ana was met with a dark hallway with more doors; they were labeled with old band names - *Kiss*, *The Beatles* - but she didn't know what they held inside. She tried the knob on the *Kiss* door; it was locked.

At the end of the hallway was an exit sign. It wasn't the same door they came in; it was toward the back of the building. It looked promising. She walked as fast as she could on the slick floor in the shiny slip-ons. Her feet craved her Birks.

The door was heavy, and Ana wasn't sure it would even open. She pushed the metal bar and shoved it with all her might. Ana tumbled outside. The cool spring air met her with a crispness she desperately needed.

The space was marked as employee parking. There was a small group of people smoking in the corner of the lot but otherwise, it was quiet. Ana leaned against the brick of the building and closed her eyes.

Taken by anxiety, she started to cry. Ana didn't want to be on stage. She couldn't be around James. Or Bex. The thought of the audience was even worse.

Ana's mind turned to her plan. She chastised herself as she realized just how impossible it was going to be. She couldn't trust her intuition. Not with James, not with any of them. The realization made her tears flow even harder.

Stupid. Stupid. Stupid. She told herself. How did Ana ever think she would be able to tell who the killer was? Her emotions: too high. The list: too long. Ana's gut: too volatile. All of it: too hard.

Tears rolled down her face, leaving warm streaks as they did. Ana would never be able to figure out who sent that bomb in a box. She would never get out from under Bex. And worse, everyone online had already convicted her. Worse than all of that, Ruth might never know justice.

She sucked in a loud sob, some of the smoking crowd turned to look at her. Ana twisted away; she wanted to be alone with her thoughts.

A touch on her back made Ana jump. She smashed her hand into the brick wall, pain exploded in her knuckles. "Jesus Christ!" she yelled.

"Whoa. Sorry!" the person said behind her.

Ana spun around. The voice didn't match Bex or James. Her eyes blinked a couple of times, trying to place the face in the darkness of the night.

"Ana! It's you. Hey, are you okay?" He added as his eyes searched hers.

She blinked again.

"Kyle?"

"Yeah!"

She looked him up and down. He looked so different than he did at Hillside, wearing black scuffed Doc-Martens, rhinestone-caked, acid-wash jeans, and a clearly expensive and still stiff leather jacket. He might as well have stepped out of some punk-rock music video from the 90s, the affected vintage outfit screaming 'try-hard.' He was such a contrast to the relaxed and scruffy hipster look James had perfected.

"What are you doing here?"

"What am I doing here? You invited me! I wouldn't miss this for the world. I can't wait to see you do your thing, babe." He winked.

"No, what are you doing back here?"

"Oh, I was just trying to come find you. The stupid bouncer at the front door wouldn't let me back to you, so I came around the building. I don't know why there's no security back here, but hallelujah I found you. Why are you crying though? What's up, my love?"

A shudder rippled through Ana. She hated herself for ever inviting him.

"What's going on?" he tried again.

"Oh, just nerves, I guess."

He stepped closer and wrapped her in a big hug. He smelled of weed and too much Axe Body Spray. Ana tried to move away, but he held tight. He stroked her hair.

"Kyle!" she growled.

He pulled back reluctantly but did not let her arm go.

"What's going on? I thought you invited me because you were finally ready to give this a chance?" he said. His watery eyes looked exactly like the ones on that pleading face emoji. She wanted to slap it away.

"Kyle, don't take this the wrong way but I invited you here to ask you a question."

"Ohhh, I like the sounds of this," he said, stepping closer to her once again.

"No, nothing like that."

"Okay, then what?"

"I don't even know how to say this. A few weeks ago, someone sent a bomb in a box to a woman named Ruth. It killed her. The murder was awfully close to my book that you read in treatment. I just need to know."

"Whoa. Know what? Ana Adams invited me here to discuss the news? Yeah, I heard about that. Sucks, but I'm not going to lie, you're even more badass in my eyes now!"

"No! I need to know if you had anything to do with it! It had to be someone close to me."

He licked his lips and smiled. Kyle grabbed Ana by both of her arms and tried to pull her in. It was clear he wanted to kiss her. "Are you saying we're close then?" he whispered in her ear, kissing it after the words slipped from his mouth.

She put both hands on his chest and pushed him away. Ana wracked her mind with ways to get through to him. She knew he was a drug addict and depressed, but maybe he was a narcissist under it all. She didn't have the answers. She couldn't get him to take it seriously.

"Kyle! Answer the question."

"Sorry my love, you're just too much. Too perfect."

"DID YOU SEND IT OR NOT?" she said through clenched teeth.

"I'll only tell if you let me kiss you."

189

Ana pulled back further; he still had one hand on her arm. Her skin crawled and she hated the fact that he wasn't vehemently denying it. How could he equate Ruth's life with a kiss? Ana backed into the wall, there was nowhere left to go. Kyle's cheeks went rosy, and his eyes roamed her body up and down.

"Ana, what do you say?"

"I say no fucking way. If you sent the box, just tell me. You're freaking me out."

"Ana. Ana. My love. Don't you see it? We could make such a perfect couple. You come up with the ideas, I help you execute them. Quite literally," he said. His laugh was deep and sinister. She couldn't believe what she just heard. She stepped back, running into the brick wall behind her.

"I'm kidding. You don't get my sense of humor yet, do you love?"

"This is not funny."

She turned to leave but he threw out a hand and anchored himself to the wall. He trapped her. Ana's heart raced. She considered her options, she could duck and run. She could yell for help and hope one of the smokers would come to her rescue, or she could kick him in the balls.

"Kyle. Just stop," she said, hoping she didn't need to use one of the other methods.

"Ana, I'm kidding. I just think you're so fucking brilliant. Your dark mind and even darker heart draw me in. You make me crazy."

"Kyle, I don't want to make anyone crazy."

"Well, the good news for you is I have always been crazy. That's why my parents keep sending me to Hillside, but you make me crazy in a good way."

Ana swallowed. Her mouth was dry, and her mind raced. She needed a minute by herself to think through all of this. Kyle was more disturbed than she originally thought.

"I've got to go get ready for the show."

Kyle looked at his watch. It was some fancy silver thing that looked incongruous with the rest of his outfit. "No, babe. You're not on for another twenty minutes. We have time."

Ana tried to find another excuse. The door next to them opened with a thud.

"Ana! There you are!" James called as he rounded the other side of the big metal exit.

"James," she said, relieved.

"You better come back inside," he said.

FORTY-TWO

The last person Bex expected to walk through the door was Aimee, but that's exactly who came in as Bex set up Ana's books on the merch table.

"Aimee, hey -" Bex started. A big smile spread across her face.

Aimee looked beautiful. Hot. She was wearing this colorful jumper that shouted '70s remix' with big colorful flowers up and down it. Bex's whole chest swelled at the sight of her; Bex hadn't let herself admit how much she missed Aimee until that moment.

"You're here," Bex said. She still couldn't believe it.

"Yeah, I was hoping to talk to you," Aimee said, not getting too close.

Bex wanted nothing else. She grabbed Aimee's hand and pulled her away from the growing crowd in the concert hall toward the dressing room.

Aimee followed slowly. Bex opened the door to find James sitting on the cracked leather couch, fiddling with some piece of equipment. It wasn't the private moment Bex wanted but there was nowhere else to go.

"I'm incredibly glad to see you," Bex said, moving to the corner of the room.

"I'm here because you invited me," Aimee said. Bex racked her mind. She was sure that she invited Aimee at one point or another, but Bex thought that chance was long gone.

"Well, thanks for making the effort," Bex said.

"I'm just here to clear the air. We have a lot of shit we need to discuss - mainly your sister. And that dinner," Aimee said. She squared her shoulders.

James jumped up and fled out the door. Bex didn't blame him.

"You're right. We do have a lot to work on."

"We?" Aimee laughed.

"Okay, me. But I promise, I'm always trying to do the best I can for everyone."

"This relationship isn't me, you, and Ana," Aimee said. "I get that you have to take care of your sister and I've tried to be patient with that, but I can't keep competing with her. I need to be a priority in your life, too. Same goes for work. If you don't think you can commit to that, then there's nothing left for us to discuss."

Bex pinched the top of her nose. She closed her eyes and forced in a couple of ragged breaths. This was the last thing Bex wanted to hash out before their big live show, but she knew - and loved - Aimee enough to know it was now or never.

"Look, babe. I'm so sorry about it all. You're right and I've missed you more than I can say. I want to make it right."

Aimee moved away from Bex and crossed the room. Aimee sat down heavily on the couch. Bex went and sat next to her. She put a tentative hand on Aimee's knee. Bex could feel how sweaty her palms were the instant her hand touched the silk fabric of Aimee's outfit.

"I can't believe you flirted with that guy so hard at dinner," Aimee said. Bex could hear the hurt in her voice.

"I'm sorry, I was just trying to close the deal," Bex said. She hung her head.

"It shouldn't have to come to that. Our product should speak for itself."

"I know. I just have big sales goals and I was willing to do what it took. For what it's worth, I never had any intention of doing anything."

"It doesn't matter to me. You still shouldn't have even thought of it. You were flirting so obviously in front of me. And the rest of the team. You even brought condoms on the trip."

193

"I know. I'm sorry and it didn't even work."

Aimee twisted a chunky gold ring around her finger. Sitting next to Aimee made Bex realize that she wanted to keep her there. She had to find a way to balance Aimee and Ana in her life.

"I'm sorry. Can we try again?" Bex asked. "I love you; I do. I know that with certainty. I'm sorry I didn't make you feel that way enough."

Aimee gave a tentative smile. Bex grabbed her chin gently and pulled Aimee's face in for a kiss.

The door crashed open, interrupting them. Bex dropped her hand from Aimee's face and looked up. The first thing Bex saw was Ana. Something wasn't right.

"Ana! Are you okay? What happened?" Bex said. She jumped up from the couch and went to her sister.

"Oh my god," Aimee said from behind. Bex turned to look at her. Aimee's serene face turned from a light bronze to red.

James came back into the room. He stood off to the side, looking between them.

"What?" Ana asked. Bex froze.

"Bex invites me here to clear the air and start over, and we almost do just that, but then here you are again, Ana Adams. You're here to make a big drama-queen entrance and ruin our moment again," Aimee hissed.

"Me?" Ana asked. She looked perplexed.

Aimee's words finally registered in Bex's mind. "I didn't invite you here to clear the air."

"Yes, you did. And now this? I should have known," Aimee said. She reached for her purse on the couch.

"Wait, Aimee. Let's talk. I'm sorry if you thought tonight was for us. I do want to make things right with you, but Ana and I have this show. I have to make sure she's okay before we go on stage."

Aimee opened her sequined clutch and dug out her phone. She tapped a few things on the screen and then Aimee held it up. Bex's eyes landed on the last text that she sent Aimee, just that morning.

"I didn't send that," Bex said.

"Oh, please, now you're calling me a liar. What, did I invite myself and come so that I could be humiliated again? No, Bex. I thought maybe you'd changed but I was wrong. Your sister is still your number one and always will be. You've made your priorities loud and clear."

Ana stepped in between Aimee and Bex. "I invited you. I sent that text," Ana said. Her voice was low, cold. She stood with her head up.

"You what?"

"I invited you," Ana repeated. "I took Bex's phone while she was sleeping and invited you."

Bex put a tentative hand on Aimee's back. She shrugged it off. Bex didn't understand the exchange between the two most important people in her life.

"I wanted you to come so I could get to know you. Bex never gave us a chance, but I've seen all I need to," Ana said. She had a small smirk on her face that Bex had never seen before.

Bex felt physically pulled between the two of them. Her mind told her Aimee, her heart screamed Ana.

Aimee tilted her head back and laughed. "Oh, you some kind of detective now? You want to check in on your sister's girlfriend?"

"No, but you're doing all the legwork for me. Thanks," Ana said. She took a step toward Aimee.

"You two are fucking lunatics. I should have known better than to come tonight, no matter who invited me," Aimee said.

FORTY-THREE

A knock deflated the tension in the room. Everyone turned and looked; Aimee backed away. A tall, gangly-looking guy stepped into the room. He wore all black and an earpiece slotted discreetly in his left ear. He looked like a wanna-be FBI agent.

"Ready? On in two!" he shouted into the room much louder than necessary. Ana wondered if his hearing was poor from all the mosh pits this place held or if he just liked the sound of his own voice.

"Yes! We sure are," Bex said, coming forward. She put on a totally placid face. She looked ready to walk into any boardroom, despite what just happened.

"Great, follow me!" he yelled.

Bex looked around the room, she found her purse and quickly applied a fresh layer of red lipstick to her Botox-filled lips. She grabbed Ana's arm and slapped a round on Ana's face, too. Ana fought the urge to wipe it off just like a little kid whose mom dolled her up for a pageant.

"I'll record," James confirmed.

A lump grew in Ana's throat. She hadn't let her mind go to the on-stage part of this whole thing, but it was time. She faltered.

"I'll talk to you after the show, Aim. Okay?" Bex called behind her. Ana didn't look to see her reaction.

Bex grabbed Ana's hand and pulled them after the stage manager. He led them down a dark hallway, passing signed posters of all kinds. The lump in Ana's throat grew along with the sound of the crowd.

"Wait here," the man ordered. Bex and Ana did as they were told. The only thing that separated them from the stage was a flimsy velvet curtain. Ana couldn't make out individual words, but it was clear from the buzzing conversations, the crowd was ready. Bex gave Ana a big smile and patted her back once, then twice.

"I can't believe Aimee," Ana said. "Do you know what she did?"

Bex shook her head. "Not now. We'll talk about that after the show."

The man came back and gave them a thumbs-up. Neither of them moved. He pushed both Ana and Bex through the curtain. The crowd exploded in applause.

The showroom was somehow even more dark and musty than the hall they just came from. The only lights were pointed directly at the stage, a glittering disco ball hung from the middle of the ceiling. The walls were lined with deep red velvet curtains. Ana could practically smell all the weird shit that had gone down in there.

Bex led Ana by the hand onto the raised stage where two metal stools were waiting for them - Ana would have never made it if Bex's grip wasn't so firm. Ana kept her eyes down to keep the bright lights from blinding her. The crowd roared as Bex and Ana made it onto the stage. There was a wild energy to the room. It was nothing like anything Ana ever experienced before.

A small smile formed in the corner of her lips. She was terrified but yet, this was the sort of thing she had always dreamed of as an author. She could see her books lined up on the merch table, she could see the people's faces, agape with the excitement of the night. Ana knew that any indie author would trade her places in a heartbeat.

The sisters positioned themselves on the stools and Bex handed Ana her microphone. Ana dared look up again. Her eyes took the crowd in. She blinked a few times, sure that she was seeing double. She wasn't, they were all there for her.

Every single room in the venue was taken. Ana looked around the room, very few faces were familiar. She spotted Kyle in the back corner, Aimee along the other side. James was stage right, headphones on.

Ana remembered the list; her plan came crashing back through her mind. The only one who wasn't there was Dr. Daniels. Self-loathing threatened to collapse her confidence right there on the stage. Why did she think she would ever be able to determine the killer here? If anything, she was more confused than before.

"Hello and welcome to *The Serial Syndicate* Podcast," Bex said. That was typically Ana's line; Bex started without her.

"I'm Bex and this is -"

"Ana," she said. She cleared her throat and tried again, this time more forcefully, "Ana!"

The crowd whooped as if they were some famous musicians, not sisters - wannabe podcasters - with a half-baked show about the most famous Colorado cold cases.

"Now that you're all seeing us in real life, you can see what I mean. She's the brains and I'm the beauty," Bex said. The crowd laughed. Ana ground her teeth. She always hated that line.

"We're so glad you're all here," Bex said. Ana nodded.

She couldn't look up. Her mind centered on the list, on her stupid plan. She couldn't contain Aimee, Kyle, and James in her mind. She realized she couldn't trust her instincts and hated herself for it.

"Tonight, we're doing things a little differently. Our podcast engineer, James," Bex said, pointing to him off stage, "is here recording. We're going to talk about the most famous unsolved case in our state's history and then we'll do a little Q&A. After that, there will be time to chat with your favorite podcasters and buy Ana's books!"

The crowd whooped again. Ana felt like she was standing on the edge of a cliff. The energy from the crowd threatened to wallop her like a single churning wave. She didn't know if she could meet their demands with what she planned for the show.

"Take it away, Ana!" Bex said.

"When I say Colorado's most famous unsolved case, what comes to mind?" Ana asked. People leaned in closer, like they couldn't hear her. She tried again, infusing her voice with as much charisma as she could manage.

The crowd screamed in unison, "JonBenét!"

"You'd be right about that. The Ramsey case is probably the one that got the most media attention, how could it not? Beautiful little girl. Mysterious family. A brother we don't trust. But there's been another, more deadly killer out there that has never been caught. Anyone know?"

A few murmurs echoed around the room, but Ana didn't hear anyone with the answer she was looking for. This made Ana's worries diminish a touch. She hoped this case would be interesting enough to hold their attention all night.

"The Denver Prostitute Killer!" she sang into the mic. The crowd clapped and cheered.

"The Denver Prostitute Killer murdered at least seventeen women in Denver, Colorado between 1975 and 1995. Worse yet, experts agree, there were probably many more victims that were never able to be connected through official DNA sequencing. And worse still, despite the advancements in DNA analysis, the killer has yet to be identified," Ana said into the mic.

Murmurs cascaded across the crowd. Ana stood and walked to the center of the stage. She pulled her shoulders back, ready to give them every gruesome detail they came for.

Just as Ana was about to launch into the case, a little commotion broke out in the back of the room. Ana strained her eyes against the intense lights to see what was happening.

Someone stood and pushed through the crowd, making their way to the end of the row. Ana worried that they were having some kind of emergency. The man broke through the row and rushed up the aisle.

"Ana, are you The Novel Killer?!" he yelled as he got closer. Ana took a step back.

The audience erupted, louder than before. Ana's stomach dropped. She felt like she was the butt end of a joke that she didn't understand. The words "novel" and "killer" bounced around the room as others picked them up and tried them on for size.

"What did you say?!" Bex asked. Ana looked back at her sister, desperation in her eyes. Ana needed Bex to help get the show back on track.

"That's what they've dubbed this on TikTok!" someone from the crowd yelled.

"The Novel Killer!" another echoed.

The name detonated the powder keg energy of the room. Soon all Ana could hear was an explosion of noise, the words "The Novel Killer" repeated over and over. The sound hit Ana square in the chest. The crowd took over. Ana and Bex lost control. Everyone was talking at once.

The phrase rolled over in her mind, growing and expanding. It was the only thing she could think of. It was such a clever name, so catchy. But somehow that made it all worse. It was a name people would remember.

Bex took over, going into manager mode. "Oh, come on," she said. Bex let out her best podcast laugh. "Is that why you're all here? You think Ana sent that box? No way. Just look at her."

The crowd heckled at her response, but Bex was undeterred.

"Look, this whole thing has been hard on Ana, but even more so for the family of Ruth, I'm sure of it. Let's all remember that there is a real victim out here and it's terrifying. Creatives should be able to write fiction to their heart's content without worrying that some sick freak will copy their work."

Ana was encouraged when she looked back up and saw some nods in the crowd.

Ana finally found her voice. "I didn't want to get into this tonight, but she's right, guys. I did not do this. Someone has copied my book and I aim to find out who. Justice for Ruth!"

Ana was surprised by the strength in her voice, but she meant every word of it. The passion that ripped through her was powerful, addicting. She wanted more of that feeling of being in control, having a purpose.

Bex took the newfound energy in the room and seized it. "Justice for Ruth!" she called into the mic.

Soon the whole room was chanting, "Justice for Ruth!" Ana felt an incredible rise of emotion fuel her. She could find out who The Novel Killer was, and she could bring Ruth and her family the justice and peace they deserved.

Ana always dreamed of a moment like this - all authors do - a moment where a mass of individual readers found a collective voice, all those single waves of energy and passion for the author coming together in a great surging tide. Ana finally had a fandom.

"Thanks for coming, and thanks to those who will listen at home. We appreciate your support and I know that together, we can give Ruth the justice she deserves," Ana said.

"I'm not the killer. I'm a writer of fiction and that's all it's ever been. But now I have a much more important responsibility. My job is no longer simply to create works of fiction. This is real - as real as it gets. This is nonfiction now and my job is to bring Ruth justice," she added. The crowd roared; her heart swelled.

Ana took a deep breath and prepared to launch back into the story of The Denver Prostitute Killer. She cleared her throat and worked up the courage to start.

"It's happened again!" Ana heard someone yell, just before she stopped hearing anything at all.

FORTY-FOUR

Ana opened her eyes. She couldn't see anything beyond Bex's face. The room tilted and twisted. Ana tried to sit up, but she didn't have enough strength. Bex grabbed her arm and helped Ana upright herself.

She blinked several times for her eyes to focus on the swirls of color in front of her. Ana recognized the posters on the wall, the wrinkled leather sticking to her hands felt familiar. She was in the dressing room, but she didn't remember walking there. Her mind tried and failed to recreate memories of where she had been.

"You're awake," Ana heard someone say. Her mind felt fuzzy; had something happened or did she black out again? She couldn't trust herself to answer. She waited for someone to fill in the blanks for her.

"You short-circuited sis," Bex said. "Did your old 'blank-stare, slack-jaw, zombie-walk,' routine. Black-out Ana, back again." Ana looked up at her sister and studied her face. Bex looked tense, worried. So did James. Aimee was still there, too. Why hadn't she left?

"Nooo," she whispered.

"You don't remember what happened?" Bex said. Her voice was intense. Ana's head snapped back. The movement made the room twist again.

"There's been another murder," James said. His words swam in Ana's mind. Another murder?

It all came rushing back. Ana's mind exploded with lights, colors, the fear she felt. Ana was on stage, someone yelled that there was another murder. She remembered the way her body physically recoiled at the news. She could still feel the way the information crushed her. After that, she couldn't remember a thing.

"I don't know what happened," James said. "Maybe it was the lights. Maybe the news? Bex and I saw you start to get weird at the same time and got you off-stage, I don't think anyone else noticed."

"What about the show? Should we go back?" Ana asked.

"They all left," Bex said. "It's over."

"But did we record enough?" Ana asked.

Bex's disappointment was written all over her face. Ana cowered. She hated making Bex upset. Heat raced up Ana's neck. She couldn't look away from her hands, she couldn't face the room of people who expected so much more from her than she was able to give.

"We did get some good clips. If you put those on social media, people will eat it up. No doubt," James said. Ana's stomach lurched; she didn't want this anywhere online.

"No. We can't post this," Ana said. She put her head between her knees; she felt like vomiting all over the green room floor. Ana forced herself to focus on the grounding techniques she'd learned in residential. She focused on taking slow and steady breaths.

"Ana don't do this," Bex said. The irritation in her voice was growing. "We will have to. That's all we have from tonight.

Ana wished she had it in her to fight her sister, but she didn't have the stamina to stand up to Bex, not now. Probably not ever.

"It's already online anyway. People were filming," James added.

Ana laid her head on the armrest. The cracked leather under her skin was rough and pieces stuck into the skin of her cheek. She just wanted it all to stop. She didn't think she could endure another minute of this life.

"Here's what we'll do," James said. Bex nodded, clearly glad that a plan was coming together. "Tomorrow, you two will record the bit about The Denver Prostitute Killer at home. I'll splice it with what I got tonight. Then, you'll have a full show. We can use the clips about the naming of the killer and the announcement of another case to build interest. It'll be good."

"This is marketing gold," Bex said, snapping her fingers after each word.

Ana visualized what it would be like for someone to post her fainting online. Seeing the clip in her mind's eye made it all come crashing back to her - she could see herself on the stage. She could see the crowd. And then Ana saw the person who made her world explode. It was Kyle.

Kyle was the one who yelled, "It's happened again!!"

Ana's brain became loud with questions. How did he know? Why hadn't he told her earlier when they were talking outside? Her skin began to crawl.

"Is there really another victim?" Ana asked. She didn't care about James or Bex's plans for the show. This was far more important.

A phone appeared in James's hand. His thumb moved over the screen faster than anyone she'd seen. He cleared his throat and began reading.

"San Francisco - An unidentified body has been rescued from the San Francisco Bay. Police have not yet said much but they did release a single photo of a necklace the victim was wearing to help identify her. The necklace is on a silver chain with a citrine stone."

Ana heard enough. Her mind instantly understood the gravity of his words and her brain manufactured adrenaline faster than ever before. The necklace. The bridge. These weren't coincidences.

James kept reading. Ana covered her ears like a scared child. The words still seeped in.

"The police are seeking the public's help to identify Jane Doe. If you recognize the necklace or the tattoo below, please call the tip line and make a report. This is a developing story, and we will continue to update our readers as more information becomes available."

205

Ana sat up quickly. The room spun; blackness clouded her vision. She began to rock back and forth. Tears ran down Ana's cheeks. She didn't even try to stop them.

One murder might have been a coincidence. But two? A pattern.

"I need you to go!" Ana yelled. The overwhelm was too much, her body was too unregulated. She couldn't stand to have them look at her for a moment more. She needed silence. She needed to be alone with the news.

"Ana, you can't be alone. You just passed out," Bex said in a patronizing voice.

"I'll take you home," James offered.

Her mind revolted at the idea. She didn't want to be near either one of them. "No. I'm okay. Just leave. I can take an Uber home. Just leave me alone!" she demanded. They all looked at her with disbelief; none of them were used to Ana standing up for herself.

"You don't have to tell me twice," Aimee said. She grabbed her purse and put a hand on Bex's back. Bex looked between her sister and her girlfriend. Bex wavered. Aimee pushed her forward.

"You sure you're good?" Bex asked one final time.

"Yes, I'll see you at home," Ana said.

Bex grabbed her purse and Aimee's hand. She nodded once before the two of them left. The room lost some of its claustrophobia the minute they walked out.

"Let me take you home," James said quietly. For a second, Ana considered it. It was the opportunity she was looking for to be alone with him, the chance to see if there was something there. Something kept her from saying yes. Her mind was too full. She was too upset. Ana didn't trust herself.

"No, it's okay. I'll catch up with you later. I just need a minute to process all of this."

"You sure?"

"Yes, I'm sure," she said.

He argued his point, but she wouldn't give him an inch. She couldn't be alone with him. Not with everything. She needed a new plan. She needed space. He finally walked out.

Alone in the green room, Ana knew she'd made the right decision. The quiet felt like a balm to her burned soul. Ana looked around the room. She didn't know what she would do but Ana knew she didn't want to be there any longer.

Ana left the venue out the back door. The cool air hit her, and chills flew down her arms. Ana looked around; she felt the urge to walk and clear her head. She walked away from the venue, putting space and distance between it all.

"Ana!" a voice yelled from behind. She recognized it. Blood drained from Ana's face; her hands shook. She started walking faster. She could hear him jogging behind her. He caught up and stepped in front of her, blocking Ana's path.

"Kyle. How did you know there was another murder? And why didn't you tell me before?" Ana spat. She could barely stand to look at him.

"Whoa. Chill love," he said, stepping closer to her.

She backed away, into the hard brick of the wall of the building on her right. Ana looked around but they were all alone. He must have waited for her.

"Don't call me that. Answer my questions."

"Geez. Slow your roll. I didn't know when I was talking to you before the show. I have an alert set up for you on my phone. I get an email anytime someone mentions your name. Sometime around the time that the show started, someone put it together. Your name started popping up in forums and my email blew up with alerts."

"You have an alert set up for me?"

"Yeah, of course. I have to know what my favorite author is up to. That's how I knew about the bomb, too." He winked.

He pushed her back against the wall, sliding his hand up her shirt. "Stop!" Ana yelled. Her whole body baked with heat.

"What? I'm just giving you a little of what you asked for."

"I didn't ask for anything!" she yelled. She looked around the parking lot, but the place was deserted.

"You invited me here!"

"I just wanted to talk to you."

"We can talk, let's go to my car." His whispers snaked into her ear. Kyle grabbed her wrists and pulled her through the lot. There were no lights, no one to see. No one could hear her cries.

Her vision went black.

FORTY-FIVE

Excerpt From Falling is Easier than Jumping
By Ana Adams

The wind whipped her hair as her life whipped through her mind. There was nothing left to live for after all he had done to her, yet the cold ocean wind slapping her in the face did something to her. The elements on her skin, the blood pumping through her veins made the desire to live bigger than she'd felt in years.

One foot in front of the other, she walked the length of the bridge. She fingered the citrine necklace her grandmother gave her. November. Citrine was the color of the month her daughter was born. And coincidentally the month her grandmother died. Not even two weeks after meeting her great-grandmother for the first time.

She thought about life. She thought about him. If Megan jumped, he would win. It would give him an out and he could go on with his life, further declaring himself the victim.

People would send cards and flowers. He would get all the sympathy for the wife that could not stay. Sympathy for the wife who took her own life from the top of the Golden Gate Bridge. He would get to continue living, looking for his next victim, while she lay dead in the cold waters below.

Megan walked on. She reached the point of the bridge where they began construction of the net. The system was designed to catch jumpers like her. She turned and walked back to where access to the water lay open.

The necklace was cold in her fingers, the metal absorbing the night. Megan considered jumping again. She leaned as far over as she could. Through the fog, she could not see the water below. She could only see the allure of the black peace that awaited her if she jumped.

She couldn't see it, but she could sense the water, just as the victim could sense their killer. Just like a mother could sense her daughter. Megan should have been able to sense her daughter; he took that from her, too.

Megan couldn't see the water but knew it was as hard and frigid as a block of ice. It would break her bones and steal her breath before she was even ten feet under. She could feel the hardness of the water, even from up here. The peace she craved would come at a price.

The same knowing washed over her. She sensed him before she saw him. Megan looked down and prayed the sea would rise up and take him instead of her. She could be seen as the real victim for once.

She didn't have to turn to know he was moving close. He cut through the night air just as he'd cut through her heart time and time again. His hands were on her, wrapped around her throat. Megan couldn't cry over the noise of the sea.

The cold rendered her hands useless; the wind whipped the fight right out of her. His last words caught in her ears between the sadness of the sea "- Go. Go be with our daughter."

Megan would never know if he pushed her or if she leaped to her fate. It didn't matter. She was finally free. She was finally with their daughter.

FORTY-SIX

"Heeyyyyyyy there true crime crazies - It's Becca here and I'm back with a big update. There's been another Novel Killing.

"I'm not going to lie, when people first started talking about the bomb in a box case, I was intrigued but I sort of thought this would be a little blip in the news about some small-time Colorado author. I'm here to admit I was wrong.

"The Novel Killings, as I've named them, are picking up speed. You heard me. Stick around, y'all. This is a big fucking deal. And if you don't know what I'm talking about, go back and find my older videos.

"Here's what we know so far - a woman died by falling from the Golden Gate Bridge. She's been identified as Ella Jones. Her family says she was not suicidal, and they are certain that she would never have jumped. Apparently, Ella was terrified of heights, and they were shocked she was even on the bridge to begin with.

"That alone does nothing to tie this to Ana Adam's book, but here's what does. Ella was recovered with a citrine necklace. Her family says she did not own the necklace, nor would she pick out something like that on her own.

"You know what else has a very specific citrine necklace described in the book? Ana Adam's second book - *Falling is Easier than Jumping*. In that novel, a woman is murdered by being pushed from the Golden Gate Bridge. She's wearing her grandmother's citrine necklace.

"The novel goes on to detail how the victim's husband has to live with what he's done, and the past comes back to haunt him but that's neither here nor there. All you need to know is Ella wouldn't have

211

jumped and she didn't own a citrine necklace. Someone copied the murder in Ana Adam's second book.

"All I can say for certain is this - we'll be talking about The Novel Killings for a long time. Buckle up and follow along."

FORTY-SEVEN

Every time the live show popped into Ana's head, another wave of shame crashed over her. The whole night from beginning to end was a disaster. Her body hurt and her mind was doing its best to protect her. The memories came back in fits and starts, everything was hazy and clouded in confusion.

She knew the news of another murder broke during the show. She knew she blacked out. And she could tell that something happened after the show. Beyond that, she couldn't grasp the details.

Ana fingered a bruise on her wrist. She had no idea if the blood vessels under her skin broke in the aftermath or sometime before. She didn't want to think about it. She turned to the internet to drown out the self-hate threatening to force her back to Hillside. If Ana was going to save herself, she would need to catch the killer. Fast.

She fixated on learning everything she could about the case. For every Reddit post Ana read, another thread popped up. There were dedicated Facebook groups to discuss the case and #TheNovelKiller quickly became a trending hashtag across the web.

After hours of reading all she could find, Ana's eyes crossed. She rubbed her face and felt her stomach growl. Ana looked around her room; it was messy, and it reeked of that faint BO that came with being holed up under the covers all day.

It had been two nights and Bex barely checked in over text a couple of times. She still hadn't come home. Ana assumed her sister had taken up residence at Aimee's house so Bex could prove her undying love to that dumb girl. That was fine with Ana, she was glad to have space.

Ana pulled the list out of the drawer next to the bed. Hot embarrassment flushed her cheeks red as she realized what a sham that idea was. She was no closer to figuring it out than she was days ago.

The names taunted her. It could have been any one of them. She ground her teeth, annoyed at herself that her instinct wasn't stronger. She couldn't trust herself. Ana slapped her forehead. Why did she ever think that would work?

Ana opened her author email. She was shocked to find hundreds of unopened messages in her inbox. Her eyes slid down the page, clocking names like SelfPublishing.com and 9News Denver. The chick from the Crime Junkies podcast had even reached out. The subject lines varied but all of them indicated they wanted to hear from Ana herself.

Ana read the first email from a producer at the local Denver news station. *Ana, I'm Paul and we'd love to get you on a segment - all about your books and get your take on The Novel Killings. Let me know your thoughts.* He wrote. It felt oddly informal for what he was asking. Ana didn't know how to respond to Paul or any of them. She didn't want to be on the news. Especially not after her last public appearance. She couldn't faint on live TV. Ana closed her inbox, leaving the rest of the emails unopened.

A buzzing under the covers jolted her. She thought she'd silenced all notifications. How did this one get through? She rooted around under the covers, looking for her phone. It kept buzzing. Ana found it under one of the pillows.

"Hello," she said tentatively. Ana didn't even know why she picked up the phone.

"Ana. It's James."

"I know. I have caller ID." A small laugh escaped them both at the same time. Ana snapped her head up. She could not let the way she felt about him get in the way of her work. James was on her list. She needed to be careful.

"I was just calling to check on you. Are you doing okay?"

"Physically?"

"Well, all of it."

"I'm hanging on by a thread. I have read everything there is online about The Novel Killings and I still cannot wrap my mind around it."

"This is probably so scary for you."

"Tell me about it."

"I just can't believe the killer is back," he said. Ana picked at her lip. "I really thought the bomb in the box was crazy but this? The necklace. I've always had a thing for true crime. This is nothing like I've ever seen."

"Why me? I'm not even a good author, everyone knows it."

"Oh, Ana. Stop it. You are good. Clearly, your plots are worth stealing."

"Hardly," she said. She pushed her hair out of her face.

"What are your sales like now anyways?"

Ana told herself it didn't matter but she was just as curious as James. "I don't know, let me look."

"The reason I called was I wanted to ask if you and Bex had a chance to record the missing part about The Denver Prostitute Killer?

The microphone on Ana's desk caught her eye. In all that happened, Ana forgot they were supposed to record the rest of the show. It seemed like the least important thing on her list right now.

"Not yet. We planned on doing it tonight," she lied.

"Great. Good. I think we should strike while the iron is hot."

James' words lit something in her. Ana knew he was right, now was the time to really slam down the gas pedal but the other part of her was paralyzed by insane guilt for even considering exploiting these deaths like this.

Ana logged into her Amazon account. The numbers jumped off the screen; she blinked twice before her mind could grasp what they meant. "Holy shit," she said, barely above a whisper.

"What?"

"Book sales. They're insane. I've made $14,771.22 to be exact in the last month."

"Ana, that's incredible!"

"Thank you. I never thought I'd see numbers like that in my dashboard. Just wish it wouldn't have come at such a big cost."

"Let's do it again," James said. His voice was earnest.

"What?"

"Another murder."

Ana's heart threatened to stop right in her chest. She didn't trust that she heard him correctly.

His laughter filled the line. "Ana. Ana. I kid. Don't pass out over there again. I'm 1000% kidding. It was a bad joke."

Ana picked at her lip again. She tasted a little bit of blood, but she didn't stop. She needed the pain to ground her.

"That's the second time you've said that James," Ana finally said.

"Really? Okay, it's a bad AND tired joke. I get it," he said. She couldn't detect remorse in his voice.

The only thing she could think of was his name on the list. It was now or never. "James, is there something you're not telling me?"

Another boom of laughter found Ana's ear.

"Ana, no. I promise I'm just joking. I'm just having a little fun," he said.

Ana pulled out the pen from the metal of the spiral notebook. She circled James's name on her list. And then she circled it again. A big, thick line formed around the letters.

Ana knew what she had to do.

FORTY-EIGHT

Bex pushed her foot into each step harder than the last. She'd only been at it for 23 minutes but sweat dripped down her back. Her calves burned and her chest heaved. Only 37 minutes left on the stair stepper.

The whole live show had gone worse than Bex could have ever imagined. She planned on Ana being awkward. She figured there would be low attendance. Never in a million years did she think someone would interrupt the show with news of another murder, however.

The only silver lining of the evening was that it drove Aimee back to Bex. Maybe it was the fact that Aimee could see this thing was already much bigger than the two of them. Maybe it was that Aimee felt bad for Bex for having such a crazy sister. Or maybe it was the fact that Bex left her sister and went home with Aimee after it all.

Either way, Bex wasn't complaining. Spending the weekend at Aimee's house, away from the world, away from all the hype had been something special. They'd barely even left the house; they lay wrapped up on the couch watching old movies and eating ice cream. It was perfect. And just what their relationship needed.

Coming to the gym wasn't easy. It was the first time they'd been apart from each other since the whole thing happened. Bex didn't want to break the spell, but her body craved movement. She needed to work through all these thoughts while her legs burned.

Bex looked up from her feet and caught another woman starting the machine next to her. There were four machines in a row; Bex felt annoyed that she picked the one right next to her.

"Hey, there - good morning," the woman said. She was a little older than Bex, but her body looked dang good. Toned and tan. She wore a maroon crop top and bike short set. She turned the machine up faster than Bex's was going. A feeling of competitiveness burned through Bex. She turned her machine up faster, too.

Bex unstuck her sweaty palm from the handrail and gave the woman a small wave. Bex turned up Adele in her ears and kept grinding. She still had nearly thirty minutes left on the machine. She took a swig of water and forced everything out of her mind.

She made it up another flight of stairs on the machine; a hand on her arm interrupted her thoughts. She looked up and saw the woman next to her had paused her machine. Bex did the same. She pulled out her AirPods and looked at the woman.

"Is that you?!" she asked and pointed to the television in front of the row of machines.

Bex looked at the television and nearly fell backward off the steps.

The TV was playing 9News with a cell phone clip of Bex and Ana's live show. Bex couldn't hear what the anchor was saying but she knew the clip was taken just moments before Ana fainted.

The text at the bottom said, *The Novel Killings - A Denver Connection?*

FORTY-NINE

Ana was desperate to escape her mind. Her thoughts were loud, all-consuming. She needed to take a break. She needed sunshine. Ana laced her tennis shoes and walked out of the house.

With no plan or purpose, she turned and walked toward the park down the street. She just couldn't be home alone anymore. The spring day was popping with sunshine and green everywhere she looked. It was a stark contrast to the dark corners of her mind.

The walk woke something up inside her. She could practically taste the anonymity the outside world offered her.

Ana walked past a Starbucks and went in on a whim. She ordered a venti chai and for the first time, didn't feel guilty about paying the $5.28. She finally had money of her own and she could spend it however she wanted.

While Ana waited for her drink, she studied the community posting board.

"Basement Studio for Rent" popped out on the board. The poster included a picture of a small basement room with a bed and kitchenette. It was just down the street from her. The rent was $1,100/month with the first and last month's rent due at signing.

Ana took a step closer to the poster. With the royalties due her, she could afford it. A place of her own. Ana took a picture of the poster and decided she would call as soon as she was home. Ana felt a burst of hope explode in her chest.

"Venti chai for Ana!" the barista called. Ana cringed. The whole cafe looked toward Ana as she walked to the counter. They knew. Ana's face went red, and her whole body shook. She felt eyes boring into the back of her head. Ana grabbed her drink and raced outside.

The drink warmed her ice-cold hands. She walked down the street a couple of blocks. She decided to stop and sit on a park bench along her walk. The sun warmed her face and Ana tried her best to hold onto the hope she'd felt about a place of her own.

A man walked by; he seemed incongruous for the area. He was tall and stocky. He wore a crisp suit and dark glasses. He looked like a lawyer, walking into the courtroom. Only he was in a park in the middle of the day, misplaced.

He passed Ana with determination in his step. As he neared her, the man looked her way and nodded. Ana was barely able to lift her lips for a small smile. Something about him made her nervous.

She turned away and took a sip of her chai. A glint in the trees on the other side of the greenbelt caught her attention. She narrowed her eyes and squinted. She was sure there was some flash of light in the middle of the leaves. She leaned forward to get a closer look. The light disappeared.

Something registered in her mind. It was a camera. Someone took a picture of her. Ana stood and started walking. She felt contaminated, violated. The story was big, but she never thought it was big enough for some half-rate paparazzo to want a shot of her.

Ana became desperate for the safety of home. She began walking in that direction. As she turned a corner, Ana looked up and saw someone duck and run down an alley. All she could see was their back. Male. Dark jeans. Beanie. Her hand clenched her cup harder. Was she seeing things? She walked toward home and stayed alert. She passed the alley, but the person was nowhere to be seen. Ana looked up and down the space. Something about that man seemed familiar but she didn't know why.

Ana kept walking. It took everything in her not to run. Another man in a suit caught her eye on the other side of the street. Something stuck in the lapel of his suit caught the sun. She saw a holster on his hip. Ana ducked her head. There were two men out of place in their residential Denver neighborhood. People didn't wear suits here.

The chai in her stomach turned to cement. That wasn't paparazzi. Those weren't businessmen. Ana understood that they were cops. Cops doing surveillance.

Ana turned the corner and walked up their street. A black sedan with deeply tinted windows was parked just a few blocks from her house. It was the same car she had seen a few days before. She was sure of it.

Fear exploded in every cell in her body. Ana dropped her chai on the sidewalk. The lid flew off and steaming liquid covered the sidewalk. She ran home.

FIFTY

r/TrueCrime · reddit.com

The Not So Innocent Ana Adams
By @truecrimemaven • 12 hours ago

Folks, I have some serious intel for you.

Ana Adams comes across as this sweet little 'pick-me'
writer, all 'I'm so deep and dark and damaged' on her
Instagram and podcast, but we've gotta take a harder look. I've
done some digging and I've found out some serious shit.

And to be fully transparent, I did a lot of questionable
searches - a little bit of a creeper move on my part, but once I
started, I couldn't stop. And hey, it's Reddit, right? Would you
expect anything less?

Here's what I learned.

Ana was born in a little piss-poor town in Kansas, called
Atchison, to Sandy and Frank Adams. It looks like her mom and
bio-dad were married in 1983. They had Bex, her sister and
podcast co-host, in 1984. They had Ana in 1986. They're like a
couple of years apart– check out the pics from their most
recent episode. Those two sisters are hot for a couple of elder
millennial cougars!

 Would you? You know I would.

Bex and Ana's dad, Frank, was a real douche. He got
arrested multiple times for domestic violence, and that's only
what I can find in the police records. Who knows what else the
bastard did at home?

But then in 1989, he got picked up and was jailed for beating the shit out of their mom. I couldn't find much but it looks like she went on disability later in 1989. So, he must have fucked her up. He got convicted for 12 years - which is practically a life sentence for domestic violence.

There's not much between 1989 and 1991 that I could find but Sandy got remarried in 1995 to some guy named Henry. This is where it gets interesting. There were a couple of case reports in the early 2000s that accused Henry of sexually assaulting Ana. I couldn't find much because the records were mostly sealed, but what I did find seemed legit.

Henry and Sandy also had a baby of their own in 1999. A little boy they named Caleb. Get it? Ana, Bex, and Caleb. Some neighbors quoted the mom saying, "I don't know much, but I still know my ABCs." That was just before she died.

Then in 2000, Bex was in high school. She went to prom and Ana was home with Caleb and Sandy. Reports say that Sandy was left unattended and the whole house went up in flames. Sadly, Sandy died in the fire. Ana and Caleb barely escaped through an upstairs window. Henry was at work according to the newspaper article I found.

After that, it looks like Ana, Bex, and Caleb went to live with Henry in some apartment across town.

*** And this, my friends, is what I want you to read - Henry died suspiciously not even six months later. They found him passed out on the couch, beer in hand. Deader than Digg. It looked like a heart attack, but they found a wildly sus amount of blood pressure medicine in his bloodstream. He was on an angiotensin receptor blocker and had just refilled his prescription according to the pharmacy. But the bottle was never found. Did someone crush up his pills and put them in his drink?

It doesn't look like the police investigated his death all that hard and who can blame them? But who knows, this all might have been stopped from the start - if they had.

Ana and Bex went into a foster home for teen girls. Caleb was adopted by another family. I looked and cannot find his records - sealed adoption. Ana and Bex have never publicly mentioned Caleb in any of their shows (yes, I did go back and listen to them all). And they've never referenced his birthday or any anniversaries on social.

Weird right?

TLDR: Ana had a fucking hard childhood; I won't take that from her. But what happened to her stepdad, Henry? Maybe she's not as innocent as she says. Has she been playing the long game? Who knows what we'll find out if they ever announce anything new about that DNA evidence.

FIFTY-ONE

Pushing the door open was like going back in time. It hadn't been that long since she was at Hillside, but it felt like a lifetime. Ana wasn't the same person she was back then. She barely even recognized the place, her stay here felt nebulous in her mind.

Once inside, the smell of the hospital was overpowering. Ana thought about ducking and running but she knew that a condition of staying free was regular check-ins. Ana held her breath and walked up to the reception desk.

"Ana Adams, here for Dr. Daniels." The clerk nodded but didn't say anything to Ana. She clicked a few things on her computer and then pushed some kind of notification button. She motioned for Ana to wait in the lobby.

Ana was alone in the big space; she wasn't sure if it was because the day was late or if she happened to have an appointment on an off day. Ana picked up an old *Woman's Day* magazine and flipped through it. Her eyes couldn't focus long enough for the content to be absorbed in her mind. She put it back down.

The door leading to the offices opened. Dr. Daniels held it open and smiled big. He was wearing his usual plaid wool suit coat, despite the warm day. Everything about him was just as Ana remembered, down to the growing pit she felt in her stomach when she saw him.

"Ana! Good to see you, come right this way," he said. Ana stood and followed him.

"So how ya been?" he asked as soon as he shut his office door behind him. The room was hot, and it smelled of those artificial cherry cough drops he popped throughout the day.

"Good. Good. Just here for a check-up," Ana said. He motioned her to the couch in his office. She sat and he took the chair next to it.

This was a typical therapist setup, yet he was too close. She hated being in his space, in this power dynamic.

"So glad to see you up on two feet. Your eyes are bright. You look good, Ana." He smiled again. His coffee-stained teeth stuck out against his pale skin.

"Yeah, I'm doing good. I just need a med recheck and then I'll be out of your hair."

"Whoa. What's the big hurry?" he asked with a laugh.

"No hurry, I just don't want to bother you. I'm doing alright."

"Well, tell me about it?" He asked.

"Just working, getting into the swing of things."

"Still living with your sister?"

"Yep," Ana said. She didn't want to give him any bit of rope to hang her with.

"And how's that going?" he asked. Dr. Daniels leaned in closer to her. She could see the wrinkles around his eyes and the way his skin hung loosely on his old, jowled cheeks.

"It's fine."

He leaned back and crossed his arms. Dr. Daniels' eyes penetrated Ana's. It was clear that he'd had years of practice in getting people to talk. She looked down, unable to hold his gaze.

"Ana, the news," he said before stopping. He didn't need to say more. She chewed her lip. He was the last person she wanted to get into this with.

"Ana, I'm sure things have been tough. I want you to know, I'm on your team."

"Thanks," she mustered.

He leaned forward and patted her shoulder. His hand was too hot, she could feel it through her shirt. Ana wanted to shake his hand off. She dug her fingernails into the palms of her hands instead. She just needed to play her part until it was over.

227

Dr. Daniels gave her a small squeeze and then leaned back in place. "I'm worried about you. How are you really doing? Talk to me, Ana."

"I know it sounds like a lot, but I promise I'm doing okay. It's kind of given me something to live for - to fight for justice for the victims," she said, hoping it was what he wanted to hear.

He rubbed his chin.

"Speaking of things, I saw your invitation to the live show. I'm sorry I couldn't make it; coming would have crossed the patient-provider boundary. How was it?"

Ana swallowed. "It didn't go as planned."

"And how are you feeling about that?"

"Well, embarrassed. I can't believe I blacked out. But more than that, I'm still heartbroken that the killer has taken another victim."

"Me too," he said quietly.

Silence filled the room. Ana felt Daniels' eyes roving over her face.

"These blackouts... they are a little worrisome."

Ana considered denying it, but it was clear it would do no good. She hated herself in that moment.

"No. No. I'm okay."

"What happened that night, Ana?" he pressed.

"Just the show. And then I ran into Kyle after the show."

"Kyle from group therapy?" he asked. He cleared his throat.

"Yes, I invited him, too. I thought we could be friends."

Dr. Daniels held her gaze. He knew there was more she wasn't saying.

"And then what? What happened when you ran into him?"

"Well, I was just really upset by the news. Freaked out. I don't know. It was too much. I didn't want to hang out with him anymore. It's a bit hazy after that."

"How do you feel about that? About losing time?"

"Mostly mad. I hate that it happens, but I can't seem to stop it."

"Are you ready to work through this thing, these fugue states and lost time, you keep experiencing? I think we can fix it - or at least understand it - but it will take some time."

"No."

"You sure? It's not exactly productive to lose big chunks of time. I'm worried about you, Ana."

"I said, no," she spat.

"Okay, we'll come back to it," he said, palms out signaling he'd back off. "How's everything else?"

Silence swarmed around them as Ana decided how to answer. She didn't want to talk about her memory lapses. She wasn't even sure they were as big of a deal as everyone made them out to be.

"Okay, just trying to finish my next book."

He snapped his fingers and jumped up. The sudden shift of energy sent Ana off balance. "Your books! My wife bought them after all the news broke out. She read them in just a couple of days and then gave them to me. She obviously doesn't know you're my patient, but Ana, they're good."

She nodded. Something about her doctor reading the innermost parts of her brain was worse than any therapy session.

"I can see why someone copied them."

Ana felt the color drain from her face.

He put his palms up and said, "Sorry, that was terribly off base. I just meant they're unique. Not run-of-the-mill plots. I can see why a killer would pick your work over someone else's *if* they were going to do this. I'm not condoning, just noting."

His little speech didn't make Ana feel any better.

"Enough about that," he said, putting the books down. "How's your medication treating you? You still liking the Celexa and

229

fluvoxamine? How is that combination? It can take up to six weeks to work, so it's possible you're not there yet."

"Yes, I'm still taking them. I'm feeling fine."

"Do you feel like your mood is improving? Do you feel like the blackouts are increasing in frequency or duration?"

"No, but I'm not getting worse."

He wrote something down on his notepad. "Ana, I'm proud of you for continuing life at home, but I will say - I'm still very worried about you. Blacking out and losing time is very concerning. Your mental health is still very fragile, and you require significant care."

Ana popped her knuckles. She just wanted this appointment to end.

"You know, it's always an option to come back here?"

FIFTY-TWO

Ana stormed in the front door; she didn't even bother to say hi to Bex before she flew off the handle.

"Oh, my god. I hate Dr. Daniels. I need a new therapist," Ana said. She threw her purse on the counter and huffed to the fridge. She yanked out a Coke and ripped the can open. Bex tensed. Her sister was worked up; good things never came from an agitated Ana.

"Hello to you, too."

Ana took a big gulp. "Sorry, hi. I'm just pissed."

"What happened?"

"He's just all up in my business. With everything going on, he thinks I should come back to Hillside."

Ana paced around the kitchen, like a caged animal plotting an escape. Bex felt her panic rising.

"He's your therapist, Ana. Dr. Daniels is supposed to be up in your business. We pay him a lot of money to literally monitor your health."

"Not like this! He's not sure about my diagnosis and medication. He's worried about how I *lose track of time*." Ana said, putting air quotes around the last bit. "He thinks I need more support."

"Well, maybe he's right. Maybe I should be around more?" Bex asked. "This is a lot for anyone to take in, let alone..."

"How many times do I have to say it? I'm fiiiine," Ana said. Her voice bordered on shrill. She sat heavily at the table and put her head in her hands. Bex saw just how much Ana still needed her.

Bex pulled out a cup from the cabinet and stirred in her green supplement. It was clear that Ana was still dysregulated. Guilt overtook Bex.

"You sure? I know I've been spending a lot of time with Aimee. I should be home more," Bex said. She gulped her chalky drink. It didn't help the lump in her throat.

"No, I don't need you here and I don't need Dr. Daniels to lock me up again," Ana replied.

"How are things with Aimee anyway?" Ana asked, clearly changing the subject.

"We're getting there. We've sorted through some things."

"Aimee hates me," Ana said.

"She doesn't, I swear. I think she's threatened by our relationship. She doesn't have any siblings. Her childhood was normal - totally vanilla. I don't think she gets it."

"Sorry, I invited her. I just wanted to see her," Ana started. This didn't make sense to Bex.

"Why? Why did you want to see her?"

"I need to show you something."

Ana stood from the table and walked across the kitchen. She stood on her tiptoes and pulled the silver metal bowl down from the top of the refrigerator. Ana walked the bowl back to the table. Inside, the charred book still lay. Between the water and the fire, it barely held its shape anymore.

Ana took the book out and opened the cover with a crackling sound.

"Look," she said. Bex set her drink on the counter and walked to her sister. Ana held the book up and pointed her finger at the cover page. Bex could see her own writing. Ana figured out what Bex had known all along. Aimee set the book on fire.

"You gave my book to Aimee, huh?"

Bex thought through a handful of lies but she could see it in Ana's face. She already knew the truth. "Yeah."

"Aimee tried to kill us, Bex."

"She didn't. This was just a way to get back at me for what happened in San Francisco. She found some condoms in my bag and lost her shit."

Bex paced the room, running her hands through her hair. Bex knew that what Aimee did was unhinged but it was in the thick of their argument. Aimee just wanted to make a point; she could have done something so much worse - like tell their company HR about the relationship. The book wasn't all that bad.

"I know it sounds crazy, but she was just mad. She wanted to get back at me."

"You expect me to believe that Bex? Don't be dumb. She set *my* book on fire on our porch. What kind of sick person does that?! And why didn't you tell me you knew it was her? That's off base, too."

Ana stood and threw the book in the trash. Bex could feel a chasm just starting between them. It wasn't wide yet, but Bex feared this was only the beginning. Someday, it might be impassable. Bex needed to keep Ana close.

"Ana, she was just mad that I flirted with our prospective client. She wanted to get back at me. It had nothing to do with you. I didn't want to worry you."

"Then why the fuck did she use my book? She could have used a dictionary!"

"I guess just because I gave it to her," Bex said. Bex knew in her heart that Aimee was a good person. She burned the book in the heat of the moment. Bex was impressed that Aimee cared enough to do it. She liked that her girlfriend was so passionate.

"I can't believe you don't see it, Bex. I invited her to the show so that I could get a sense of her. I wanted to see what my gut felt when I confronted her about the book that she lit on fire on our front porch!"

"Ana, you're blowing this out of proportion."

233

"And you're not taking it seriously enough. I didn't get the chance to corner her, but something isn't right with your girlfriend. What else has she done?"

"Ana. Don't."

"Don't be so blinded by your love that you can't see her for what she is."

Bex paced around the kitchen. She forced herself to have another sip of her green drink. She couldn't have this conversation with her sister. It was going nowhere, and it wouldn't help anything.

"I'm done talking about this," Bex said with finality. "We need to record the rest of our live show tonight. I'll order Thai." Ana started to protest. Bex held up a hand to stop her.

"I'm not recording," Ana said. Bex grabbed her phone to order.

"You are. We are going to talk about The Novel Killings, and we'll finish the last bit for James. The show is hot right now and we're not going to miss this opportunity. I won't let you," Bex said.

Ana sat at the table and picked at her cuticles. She didn't argue but Bex could tell she was seething inside.

"Look, I'm sorry Aimee set the book on fire. That was uncalled for. She and I sorted things out, I promise it won't happen again," Bex said. Ana didn't look like she believed Bex.

Bex finished the order. "I cannot get over how big this has gotten," Bex said, trying to get through to her sister any way she knew how.

"It's everywhere," Ana said. She didn't look up.

"I know. I saw 'The Novel Killings' mentioned on the homepage of Yahoo today."

"You were using Yahoo? That's serial killer behavior if I've ever seen it," Ana said, finally laughing. Bex relaxed and the tension drained from the room.

"Hey! It was something for work. And it was awkward because my team was in the room. I didn't need a big story about my sister to pop up right during a meeting. Oh, and someone recognized me at the gym, that was a new level. The woman next to me stopped me because I was on the TV in front of us."

A big smile broke on Ana's face. "Someone from the news emailed me. They asked me to be on their program."

"Ana! Why didn't you say something? What an amazing opportunity! For your books and our show."

"Are you kidding me? Do you not remember me blacking out? I'm not doing that on the news for the rest of the world to see."

Bex scrubbed her face. God, she wanted to be on the news - on television! - but she knew she shouldn't push Ana too hard just yet. "Hmm... I'll make you a deal - you don't have to decide tonight but we will be looking into the news soon, okay?" Bex said.

Ana nodded. It felt like a win.

"You've worked hard for this," Bex said. "You deserve to be on television." She stood and poured herself a glass of wine after finishing her greens.

"I think it's some bit of sick luck. Some freak decided to copy my work out of all the millions of published murder books out there," Ana said.

"Well, sometimes luck and hard work marry each other," Bex said, repeating a phrase their mom used to say before she lost her ability to say things like that.

"Our podcast will blow up next."

"We're all over Facebook and TikTok. And Yahoo apparently," Ana said. Her laugh was full, she couldn't hide her delight any longer.

"And we're the talk of the office and the gym. Hell, probably every office and gym across America," Bex added.

"We manifested this shit," Ana said. They gave each other a high five with a loud clap.

Bex leaned against the counter, feeling relieved that she and her sister were on the same page again.

"But don't think I've forgotten about Aimee," Ana said as she walked out of the kitchen. Bex froze. It felt almost like a threat. Bex wanted to fight it, but she let it go. Soon enough, Ana would see that Aimee just did it for attention, nothing more.

Ana showered and their Thai was delivered. They shared a quick dinner and planned out the show. A twinge of unease danced in Bex's belly. When they released this show, there would be no going back.

They set up the recording equipment in the living room. Bex held back hope, fearing that Ana would back out at any minute. She sat and put her headphones on first. Bex closed her eyes and dreamed of the reach they'd have.

"Hello and welcome to *The Serial Syndicate*. I'm Ana and this is _"

"Bex! We're glad you are here. Hello to all our new listeners and much love to the OGs that have been with us since the beginning."

"If you're listening, chances are probably quite high that you've heard of The Novel Killings. And chances are even higher that you're probably here because of that. This episode is going to be a little bit different," Ana explained.

"Yep," Bex interjected. "We started a live podcast recording the other night at a show in Denver. Unfortunately, the show was cut short when we learned that there was another Novel Killing. There has been another murder. So, when you hear the recording from the show here in a bit, you'll get an insider's look at just how that all went down."

"We originally planned to finish recording this show with a look at The Denver Prostitute Killer, but it makes more sense to delve into the details of the newest Novel Killer case. If you'll allow it, we'll save the Prostitute Killer case for another day," Ana said into the microphone.

Bex smiled. This felt right. This episode was going to be a turning point for the show, she could feel it as certain as the tide. They'd go from the periphery of the news on sites like Yahoo to the dinner table, to prime time. It wouldn't be long before they were asked for interviews and spots on the Today Show. It wouldn't be long before more advertisers were knocking on their door. She could feel the wave pulling back, building. Readying for a big crash.

"So, let's do it. Here's what we know so far," Ana said into the mic. Bex watched her work. Her voice was captivating, and she had a way of putting words together that worked. Despite her flaws, Ana was an amazing host. Bex could admit that she was made for this.

Ana expertly took listeners through every chilling detail of the case, down to the citrine necklace and the claims from the family that the victim did not have a necklace like that. Ana pulled in speculation that the victim must have been drugged, detailing how the girl's family is convinced she would have never jumped. She made the case that this real-life murder followed the first part of her book, *Falling is Easier than Jumping* to a T.

They wrapped up the show and started cleaning up their equipment. "That was amazing. I can't wait for James to master it so we can publish. It's going to be big," Bex said.

"It felt good to get it all out," Ana said. She wrapped the cord around her mic.

"I still can't believe that girl was pushed while I was in the city for work. It's a creepy coincidence."

Ana stopped in her tracks. She looked Bex square in the eyes. "What?"

"Yeah, I was in San Fran for work the same day the girl was pushed. My whole team was there. You didn't know that? Crazy, right?"

FIFTY-THREE

After wrapping up the show, Ana escaped to her room as fast as she could. She needed space; she needed air. The door closed behind her with a thud. She leaned against the door, her chest constricting. Bex was in San Francisco when Ella died?

Her mind danced around the idea, not yet ready to let it fully take shape, not wanting to believe. Even if her mind couldn't admit it, her body knew enough to know she wasn't safe. Ana reached down and did something she had never done before. She locked the door to her bedroom.

San Fran. Work. Same day. Ella. The words cycloned around her mind. Bex was in California when Ella was pushed from the bridge. Bex was in the same city when Ella was murdered. Aimee was there, too.

Something took shape in Ana's mind. She dashed to her bed and ripped open the drawer of her nightstand. Her notebook was right under a new layer of junk. Ana wrestled it out and flipped the pages.

The list. She read it over again.

> *Kyle*
> *James*
> *Dr. Daniels*
> *Letter writer*
> *Door knocker*
> *Aimee*

Ana pulled the pen out of the coil binding of her notebook and tapped it on the empty line below Aimee's name. With a shaky hand, Ana added Bex's name to the bottom. Her heart jumped up into her throat and made it hard to breathe.

Bex and Aimee had motive. They were in the right place at the right time, and they were smart enough to pull this off. Aimee could be behind The Novel Killings just as easily as the rest of them. And Bex could very well be complicit.

In the corner of the page, Ana drew circles with the pen making some kind of angry tornado drawing with wide black loops and furious scribbles. She felt swept up into some destructive force that she could not escape from, a glowering storm that obliterated the safe and familiar landscape.

Ana didn't want to be a victim of this storm anymore. She needed to take things into her own hands, and she needed to make this stop. An idea popped into Ana's head. She looked at it from every angle, it was crazy as hell but the longer she thought about it, the more convinced she was that it could work.

From under the mess of papers on her desk, Ana pulled out her laptop. She clicked through to her folder of graveyard starts that never saw the light of day. If the killer was going to strike again, they needed more material to copy. If Ana was going to catch the killer, this folder held the outlines of their next move.

She clicked around and reorientated herself with the bones of works in progress that she loved at one point or another. None of them were good and none of them were complete, but that didn't matter. One of these stories would have to do the job.

With each new document she opened, Ana evaluated the short story. She no longer cared if the prose was good or if the plotline was original enough. But instead, she tried to answer the questions - would this be enough to bait the killer? Would this storyline keep the community safer than that one? Each story contained both danger and potential.

Ana chewed on her lip. Finishing any of these stories and writing these events into action was crazy. No matter what her mind told her, Ana couldn't stop herself from typing. Only Ana could write another story for the killer to copy, and only Ana could lay the trap to catch them.

A story she'd written months ago about a Denver woman caught her eye. It would be a hard case for the killer to replicate. Would it work? Would the killer take some poor woman from the streets? This was the only way to find out. It was dangerous but the rewards were tempting: certainty around Bex, more evidence for the authorities and, of course, it would drive sales.

If someone killed a Denver woman, Ana would know - The Novel Killings were not a figment of her imagination.

Ana posted the short story to her old Wattpad account - the one she never used anymore. She didn't tell anyone or post about it on social media. She figured the killer would be watching her every move. The killer would see the story.

If another person turned up dead, she would know for sure that the killer was close. Her first plan was full of plot holes, but this would work. It had to.

FIFTY-FOUR

Excerpt of Whistle in the Woods

By Ana Adams

    Finding a kill was like winning the lottery. You not only had to have the right numbers, but they also had to be in the right order too. Winning the lottery was getting harder and harder. People on their guard. Cameras everywhere. Narcs on Facebook.

    That made the killing all the sweeter. Just thinking about it made him hard. He couldn't wait another day. He needed to play his odds and he prayed like hell that the numbers would line up just right. He needed to win; he couldn't stand to see another woman walking down the street. He couldn't stand to see another woman ignore him. The urge was too strong. The desire to win was all he could think about.

    He tried to distract himself with images online. They took the noise in his brain down a notch, but the urge soon rushed back. He needed something real. He needed to feel the soft skin in his hands. He needed to hear the screams. He needed to whistle.

    Thump. Thump. Thump. Went his hand on the desk. He was twitchy and anxious. His mouth watered and his groin smoldered with heat. He couldn't wait.

    He pulled on sweats and slipped on his worn, gray shoes. He went out to the garage in the back of his house and unlocked the door. Under the cover was the old red pickup he drove only for this work. When he was done, he'd cover it back up and keep it under lock and key. This was one of the many precautions he took to keep his persona as Mr. Gates, Principal of Lindon Elementary in Denver, Colorado intact.

Everyone knew him as a fun-loving, fair-minded leader. Parents loved him, teachers respected him. He'd held the job for nearly ten years without so much as a second glance. Only he knew himself as The Whistler.

He revved up the truck and headed a few blocks south of his house. He knew that if he was going to win the lotto it would be in the poor neighborhood, the kind where women worked during the day and weren't at home peeking through curtains. The place where the people looked the other way and avoided trouble. The place where doorbell cameras were an unaffordable luxury. The place where he'd gotten lucky before.

The night was just starting to darken. His confidence grew with each street he crossed; so did the feeling in his belly. He was going to win the lotto tonight. He could feel it. He licked his lips and tightened his grip on the steering wheel. He was getting closer.

He pulled to a stop on the periphery of the neighborhood. He noticed a group of kids playing ball in the middle. He drove a couple of blocks over. He waited. Walkers came and went, but none were quite right.

Waiting was the hardest part. He knew that if he moved too soon, he'd lose the jackpot. He needed to be patient. The night was almost pitch black, cars came and picked up girls one by one. He licked his lips. He waited some more.

"There!" he yelled in the confines of his old Datsun. He saw one petite woman, not yet hardened by the streets. She wore a short black dress with cutouts along each side. It was enough of a tease to light him up all over again. He pulled the truck down the corner from her.

He waited. He heard her heels clinking toward him. She came into view. Her hair slicked back into a high pony. Her blonde hair swung behind her. There wasn't a john in sight. She was pure perfection.

With the skilled practice of many lucky nights, he got the girl in the seat of his truck by holding up a hand. He rolled down the window and showed her a wad of hundreds. She slipped right in, smelling of sex and cheap perfume.

They were well out of the city before she got worried. It was too late. The Whistler had won the lottery, and he was going to cash that check. He picked a deserted campground that wasn't yet open for the season.

He pulled into an RV slot off the main road, hidden from view. He yanked the woman out of the truck and pushed her down on the mattress in the bed of the truck.

His whistles echoed around the woods the whole time he worked. The Whistler hit the Powerball. Jackpot.

Before he left her lifeless body in the woods, he put a whistle around her neck - his signature sign that he had blown another.

FIFTY-FIVE

Something woke Ana up. She listened but did not hear it again. Ana rubbed the sleep from her eyes; she didn't know how long she'd been out. She didn't remember what she had been doing or when she fell asleep. The gray of the room told her it was early, her mind was a cobweb of bad dreams and exhaustion. She rolled over and pulled the comforter back over her head.

Just as she drifted back off to sleep, her plan rushed back into her mind. Ana had posted her story last night to her website. She wondered how many times it had been read so far.

She heard the noise again. Someone was knocking on the front door. Ana waited. Bex didn't answer. Ana willed whoever was on the other side to go away.

The knock came louder this time; Ana's bedroom window shook. Adrenaline coursed through her body. Thoughts of the night she tried to kill herself ran through her mind. The door knocker on her list was back again. Angry and determined. Ana pulled the comforter over her head; it was her only defense.

Through the thickness of the wall, she could hear a gruff voice, "Ana Adams, open up! FBI."

Fear clutched her, had one of those Reddit freaks swatted her? She calculated her options. Continue to hide and hope they go away? Get them to help her finally find the killer?

Anger swept through Ana. Why were they at her door? She was innocent! Why weren't they looking for the killer?

Her anger was replaced by unexpected guilt. She'd posted new material for the killer just last night. Did she go too far? Was another person already lost in his sick game? Fear clashed with self-hatred. The cops thumped on the door again, louder this time. She wondered if they were here to arrest her for posting a new story. She wondered if they'd just kick the door open and shoot her.

Ana pulled herself out of bed and pulled a hoodie off her chair. She caught a whiff of herself as she raised her arms to put on the sweatshirt. She smelled like a hangover, only minus the fun. Ana rolled on some deodorant and hoped they wouldn't take her appearance as a sign that she was an unstable drunk.

The knock came louder. "Coming!" she called as she dashed through their house to the front door. Ana took one big deep breath to calm herself; it did nothing to slow her heart down. She pulled the door open anyway. The morning sun blasted her eyes and made them tear up as she winced. She wanted to raise her arm to shield her face but stopped, afraid of what might happen if they saw her hands make sudden movements.

On the porch were two besuited white men in their thirties. One wore blue; the other, gray. They both wore American flag pins on their lapels. Dark sunglasses and close-cropped hair rounded out their heads. They were solidly built; they might as well have been brothers for all Ana could tell.

"Ana Adams?"

"Yes."

"I'm Agent Delcore and this is Agent Fredricks. We're with the FBI," said the one in the blue suit; he held up a badge, just like they did in the movies. For a brief second, Ana wondered if it was real. She wondered if they were some kind of rent-a-cop, tricking her into believing the FBI was really on her doorstep. She shoved those thoughts away. The men looked so much more official, more real, than any actor she'd ever seen.

"How can I help you?"

"We're investigating a couple of cases, they've been dubbed 'The Novel Killings.' I'm sure you've heard of this by now. It must be scary," the other one - Fredericks - said, sympathetically.

"Yes."

"Well, we'd like to take you to the field office for questioning if that alright with you?"

"Field office?"

"FBI Field Office here in Denver. The first murder was carried out through the mail, making it automatically our jurisdiction," said Delcore. The hard set of his jaw told her she didn't have another choice.

A horn honked somewhere down the street. She wondered how many of her neighbors were peeking behind their curtains, watching all of this unfold. Ana cleared her throat. "Okay." She nodded.

Some part of Ana screamed 'Get a lawyer!' but she quieted the voice in her head. She didn't have anything to hide. She was innocent and in possession of knowledge vital to the investigation. They needed her and she needed them. They had to act as a team.

Ana followed them down the porch steps. There was a black, sedan with tinted windows parked on the street. She recognized it immediately. Her stomach dropped and she felt faint. The FBI had been watching her for days.

Delcore opened the back door of the car and held his hand out, inviting her inside. Only it wasn't an invitation. It was a command. He got in the driver's side and Fredricks took the passenger side. He looked back at Ana and gave a small, encouraging smile. The doors locked automatically.

Ana watched the big buildings of downtown go by, noticing the playful curves of the giant Cash Register Building as they got on I-70. Construction traffic slowed them as if it were any regular commute.

247

The agents didn't say a word. Not to her or one another. The silence stretched on. The air felt stifling. Ana's heart raced. Her stomach did flip after flip. Ana rehearsed the case over and over in her mind, eager to get started, eager to help solve these murders.

They arrived at a tall building with a fence around it and a wall of teal-colored windows wrapping the whole thing. It was designed with a weird overhang that looked like a fancy carport off one side located in some random development in Aurora next to a Walmart and a Ross. The hardness of the area - graffiti, unhoused people, and loud music - played into the suburb's harsh reputation.

Ana didn't spend much time in this sector of the city, but when she'd come before, she never noticed the small sign that read Denver Division with the FBI logo in the background. Compared to the building, the sign almost didn't want to be noticed.

Nausea built in Ana's stomach as they drove through the gated entry. They parked and took her inside the huge building; Ana felt like she was being watched through all the windows. There were tons of people striding about, most in suits, on a mission.

The agents brought her through the metal detector and then up an elevator. Neither one of them left her side. Fredricks put a hand at the small of her back to guide her along. They showed her to some small, nondescript space on the second floor. The room was interior and there were no windows. It was soundproof; none of the hustle and bustle of the place could be heard once they shut the door.

Fredricks motioned her to sit at the lone table in the center of the room with a half-smile. The chair was cold, hard metal. The two of them sat opposite her. With their glasses off, she could see that their facial features were different. Delcore sported a thick, white scar above his eye and through his eyebrow. Fredricks wore deep wrinkles around his eyes like he'd spent most of his life squinting.

"Thanks for coming, Ana," Agent Fredricks said. His voice was warmer, it almost sounded as if she had a choice. She wondered what his first name was but didn't dare ask. Ana felt woozy. Her head spun and black stars danced in her eyes. She grounded herself by putting her hands on the table. She couldn't black out now.

"Ana, as you know, we're investigating a murder on the outskirts of Chicago and another in San Francisco. They may be related," Delcore said. "Being that the bomb in Chicago was sent via the US Postal Service and that this is now a multi-state investigation, the FBI is handling this, with assistance from local precincts."

"I can promise you they are related," Ana answered, with a voice whose strength and clarity surprised even her. This was it; she was going to be part of the team.

"Yeah?" Delcore asked. He rubbed his forehead.

"Well, the first one followed my first book basically to the letter. And if that wasn't enough, the bomb itself was sent along with a copy of my book," she felt her confidence growing.

"So, we've heard," Fredricks said. "Tell us more."

"And the second murder, same thing. Down to the stone in the victim's necklace. Someone is copying my books," she argued. Ana put her hands on the metal table and leaned forward, a small, satisfied smile on her face. This was good. They needed her help.

"And why do you think someone is copying your books?"

"I don't know. I don't. None of this makes sense, I was nobody before this. Hardly anyone had read my books. It has to be someone close to me."

"And now?" Fredricks asked.

"Now what?" Ana asked. She didn't understand the look between the two of them. It was someone she knew, why didn't they care?

249

"And now are people reading your books?" Delcore said. He gave her a disapproving look.

Ana swallowed. She didn't like the leading tone he used. Her confidence deflated as her stomach dropped. She'd expected them to be on her side and wanted their sympathy. She'd assumed from the beginning that, once they realized what was happening, they'd want to help her, and they'd want her help. It was becoming very clear that she made the wrong assumption.

"Yes, well people are reading my books," Ana replied after taking a pause, "but that's only because this case is getting a lot of attention online."

Agent Delcore leaned back in his chair; his eyes narrowed. "Yup. Looks like you're getting a lot of attention. Everyone is talking about you, Ana. I bet that must feel nice after so many years grinding away in small-time obscurity, being a 'nobody.' That's what you said right? You were just a nobody but now, here you are, selling all those books, bringing a little money in, making a name for yourself. Yes ma'am, everyone sure is talking about Ana Adams. That's why we brought you in."

"How long have you been watching me?!" she demanded. If she had seen them a few times, only God knew how long they'd been following her.

"We're just doing our jobs, Ana. Same as you," Delcore said. He shared a look with his partner. They let Ana bake in the silence.

She thought back to the day that she'd gone for a walk to get a chai. That was the day she was certain she was being followed. Something caught in her memory. She thought about the person she'd seen in the alley. Why did he seem familiar? It hit her like a speeding car. James. James always wore a beanie. Why was he following her too?

Ana couldn't take it anymore.

"You didn't answer my question!" she yelled. She was losing it. These pricks, with their insinuations and pointed looks, were getting to her. She popped her knuckles one by one and tried to slow her mind. Neither agent talked, they were letting her fill the silence.

"Well, here are some people to follow," she said, her voice strained after counting to ten with each knuckle pop. "There are several people who have opportunity and motive. Someone sent me a threatening letter. I've also had someone knocking on my door at all hours. Not to mention, my sister's girlfriend is crazy!"

Fredricks leaned back, he gave a small smile. She knew he was playing good cop, but it was hard not to gravitate toward him.

"Ana, listen to yourself. A knock on the door? You don't like your sister's girlfriend? A mean letter? Come on now, don't be stupid. You're not dumb, are you? A brilliant bestselling author? No, It's obvious. It's *you*." Delcore said, pulling her back in the other direction, hard.

"What?!" she choked. Did he not hear her?

"You just gave us motive - your books are selling in a way that they weren't before," he clucked his tongue, looking smug, assuming he'd just caught her in a lie. "You're the only one who has benefited from all this attention. You've carried out The Novel Killings. Just admit it take a bow and get the movie adaptation started."

"No! No, it's not like that." She stood up and started pacing the room. Why couldn't they see it?

"When the bomb in a box was mailed, I was in a treatment facility. Go back and look at the records. I couldn't have sent that. I was barely alive," she yelled.

"We have, but we have reason to believe it was sent just before you went in. You know some physical evidence was found with the bomb right, a piece of hair? Surely a true-crime junkie like yourself has heard about that. We're going to connect it to you. Why not save us all time and the taxpayers some money and just admit it?"

Ana paced faster. The walls were closing in on her. She tried her breathing exercises. She bit her lip. It didn't work, Ana couldn't calm her racing heart or mind.

"I had nothing to do with this! I am a victim! I told you about the hateful letter I got in the mail. It could very well be whoever sent that. Or there's Kyle, this little date-rape freak who was in treatment with me and he's batshit crazy, his Instagram is nothing but pictures of battered women. He's obsessed with me! There's also my doctor, Dr. Daniels. I wouldn't put it past him at this point either, he'd love to make *his name* from this case."

Ana wanted them to get out a notepad and write all this down. Instead, they both just watched her march back and forth. She realized how desperate and crazy she must look. Ana forced herself to sit down at the table. She took a big deep breath and counted to twenty.

Once she felt a little more in control, Ana continued. "It could be our podcast guy, James. He's said some suspicious things to me lately and then he broke into our doorbell camera to check on me. Tell me that's not stalker-ish. And he has motive - if our podcast blows up, so does his business. But wait, hold on - Aimee set a book on fire on our porch! My sister's girlfriend committed arson!"

They shared another look. Ana could see something pass between them, but she didn't know what. Ana took another deep breath and made herself slow the words coming out of her mouth.

"And I'm starting to wonder about my sister, Bex. She and Aimee were in San Francisco when the second murder happened. She is hiding something, I can tell."

Delcore crossed his arms in front of him. Frederick flipped through a folder. Neither talked. It was like they had some unspoken agreement to let the silence do the work for him. Ana told herself not to fall for it; she bit down hard on her tongue to keep from saying anything else. It was standard: let the suspect fill the silence, make them feel like they have something to prove.

It was a textbook criminal interrogation, familiar to her from a thousand podcasts, blogs, countless afternoons spent watching endless reruns of Law and Order. Every murder mystery she'd ever picked up ended this way. Unfortunately for them, this was a book she'd already read.

She felt confidence surge through her. They were fishing, they didn't have a thing. "Am I under arrest?" Ana asked.

"Ana, we're just asking friendly questions," Fredricks finally said after another long pause.

"I save my friendly questions for my friends. People who don't accuse me of murder." She walked to the door of the interrogation room and tried the handle, surprising herself when it turned.

Agents Delcore and Fredericks were standing, each talking over the other. "Ana, wait!" she heard.

"Nah. You've already made up your mind about me. But you'll see," Ana said. Her voice rose, "I'm going to catch the killer myself."

Ana walked out. If they wouldn't write the ending, she would.

FIFTY-SIX

As Bex's boss droned on about sales goals and key performance indicators in a meeting with the whole team, packed in the conference room, Bex tried to focus. After he'd reminded them for a third time that sales needed to pick up, her phone buzzed. She snuck a glance, and saw that it was her doorbell camera app.

Bex cleared the alert and silenced her phone. Ever since she'd fumbled the sale in that disastrous trip to California, Bex had been on thin ice with leadership. She couldn't be distracted during the meeting. She put her phone on do not disturb.

The meeting took most of the morning; by the time Bex was back at her desk, she'd forgotten to check the camera footage.

Bex found her work email full of requests from clients and status updates from her team. She flipped over to her personal email in the hope of something easier to focus on. The bulk of the emails were from online stores and political campaigns. She quickly cleared her inbox until she found a message from AncestryandMe. She winced.

The office was quiet with most people out for lunch. She clicked email to find that she had new messages waiting for her in her account.

Dread consumed her; she didn't have the bandwidth for her brother. Bex's gut screamed that Caleb was disruptive at best, dangerous at worst. She should have never opened this line of communication. She needed to find a way to get rid of him - for good.

With a shaky hand, she opened her messages.

Ohhh my sisters are famous now! Caleb's first message said.

The Novel Killings, huh? That's clever as shit. When you left me in the dust as kids, I wondered where you'd end up. I didn't imagine this, but

I'm not going to lie, it's better than I ever thought. I even saw your sick mugs pop up on Good Morning America *today.*

I think it's time I paid you both a little visit. I want to meet you two this time.

Bex clenched her jaw and closed the screen. She would not dignify his taunting with a response.

FIFTY-SEVEN

Rays of sun beat down on Ana while she waited for an Uber in the parking lot outside the field office. It was one of those Colorado spring days that felt like the state skipped from winter right into the middle of summer. Even with the heat, Ana's hands still felt cold and clammy. She couldn't quite warm up.

Her interrogation steamrolled through her mind again and again. Her emotions ranged from sheer terror that they'd zeroed in on her to absolute disgust and indignation that they weren't considering anyone else.

The area was busy with everything from delivery trucks to people walking their dogs. Not one of them looked like Ana felt - like her whole world had just been turned upside down. Ana chastised herself for being so dumb. Of course, they suspected her. She hated herself for letting her mind run on autopilot.

Ana thought about her interrogation. She was proud of herself for standing up to them and for walking out, but she wondered if it was too little too late. She was a suspect. That fact sat like a heavy boulder square on her chest. How could she ever push it off and get them to look for the real killer?

Before she could change her mind, Ana punched James' number on her phone. She held it up to her ear, squeezing it hard enough for the phone case to dig into her fingers. "Ana. What's up?"

"Have you been following me?" she shouted into the phone. She looked around to see who could have just heard that, but she was alone on the sidewalk in front of the FBI office.

"Ana, whoa. What's going on?"

"Answer me! I think I just figured it out. You were following me the other day, weren't you? First our doorbell camera and now this?!"

James cleared his throat. She heard a door shut behind him; Ana imagined him leaving some meeting to talk to her.

"Okay, back up. Where are you?"

"I am at the fucking FBI Denver Division," she said, reading the sign. She tripped over the words as they came out of her mouth.

Ana looked around. She took it all in. This place scared her. The security was tight, and the fence stood several heads taller than her. There were men in dark suits coming and going, women who looked like they could take you down in heels. The building was full of secrets. Ana shivered.

"What's going on?"

"I want to know why you were following me!"

"Ana, I wasn't. I don't know what you're talking about. And the FBI is just doing their jobs. It's all over the news, they have to talk to you. It would be negligent if they didn't."

"They think I'm the fucking Novel Killer."

He sucked in a breath through his teeth; she could hear it even through the phone. She wondered why he wasn't jumping to her defense.

"You didn't answer me. Why were you following me?!"

"I wasn't."

"Do you think I'm the killer? Is that why I saw you the other day? You're following me!"

The phone grew slippery from the sweat on Ana's hands. Her heart raced up and anger coursed through her veins. Ana wanted to jump through the phone.

"Ana, you know true crime is a big part of my life. It's not only how I make a living but it's also how I spend my free time. I've been a true crime junkie since way before it was cool. This is my passion," he said. "Want to know what I think?"

257

Ana paced the sidewalk in front of the building, anger sizzling in her belly. He needed to start talking a whole lot faster. She didn't even want to listen to him. She wanted to chuck her phone across the parking lot and never hear from him again. Something kept her from doing it.

"I'm worried about you, Ana. I know you're not the killer but that means someone close to you is. I think it's Bex."

Ana's head snapped up. His words refused to register in her mind.

"Did you know she was in California at the time of the bridge murder? When Ella was pushed off," he said. He waited. Ana couldn't respond. "And the box bomb hit sometime when you were in residential treatment, I'm sure they'll run DNA on it so as soon as they have something, we'll know. I'll table that for now," he said.

Ana wondered why that physical evidence hadn't already triggered an arrest. Surely it was a smoking gun.

James kept going, "Back to Bex. Did you know she took out a big line of credit recently? I found that out when I was looking into her. It took me a bit to figure out why, but I think she took out the money to pay for your treatment."

Ana's whole body froze. Bex never mentioned anything of the sort. A lump of guilt stuck in her throat. Did Bex really do that for her? Guilt weighed her down and nearly made her crumple, drained by the emotional swings of the last hour. Ana would never be able to repay Bex.

"She needs the money, Ana. And you know as well as I do that the best way to make a living from podcasting is through downloads. You know how you get downloads? Something big has to happen. I don't need to tell you, this is big. Don't you see it, Ana? Bex has reason, motive, and the capability to pull this off."

"This wasn't Bex," Ana said quietly. "I think it was her girlfriend, Aimee." Ana's loyalty to her sister was too strong. They'd been through too much together. Ana couldn't sell Bex out that easily.

"Why?"

"She set a book on fire on our porch the other day. Not just any book, my book."

"That's nuts."

"And she hates me."

"Okay but is that enough?" he asked. Ana thought so.

"Well, I don't know about Aimee, but my money is still on Bex."

"How did you know she took out a line of credit?" she asked.

"I pay for a membership to a monitoring service where I can see if someone's credit score changes. It's a little creepy but I have her social since we had to file tax paperwork for the podcast. I just used it to look her up."

"James! What the hell?!"

"I know. I know. But I don't trust her. I had to look at her. You need to be careful, Ana. I think Bex is up to something."

"No, James. The one I should be careful of is you. You used Bex's password to get into my doorbell camera without asking, you've said some awfully weird shit, and now this? And I still think you're following me. You're blaming Bex. She is the best sister I have. She took out a loan to pay for her sister's treatment. Who does that? Not the kind of person who turns around and murders two people."

"Ana-" he started.

She watched a black SUV pull into the field office lot. The windows were tinted, and the car drove so slowly that it must have precious cargo inside. She wondered if whoever they were bringing in was related to The Novel Killings or some other nameless case that hadn't garnered nearly enough attention because every eye was on her.

"Ana don't do this," he said.

259

"Don't do what?"

"Don't go looking for killers."

"I don't have to look very far," she said.

"Ana, please."

He breathed heavily into the phone. Ana could hear his challenge in the silence that spread between them. She squared her feet and shoulders. She would not let James threaten her out of her suspicions or try to scare her. Two could play that game.

FIFTY-EIGHT

Caleb's messages just didn't sit right with Bex. He seemed unstable, maybe dangerous. Bex opened her AncestryandMe account back up and returned to her brother's messages.

Caleb, I've told you before, but I'm done playing nice. Leave us alone. Do not come to Colorado. Do not send me any more messages.

Bex hit send. It felt cathartic. She felt powerful, sure that Caleb would get the point. Bex always carried a lot of guilt for the fact that she couldn't take care of him when he was a baby, but not anymore. She was free of that weight. He'd survived. He'd grown up. He was an asshole. He was no longer her burden to carry.

Three little dots appeared in the chat. Bex waited for his response, chewing on the inside of her cheek as the seconds ticked by.

Or what? You're going to abandon me all over again? Nah, bitch. You can't hurt me anymore, he responded.

Bex sucked in a sharp breath. No one talked to her like that.

Come and find out, she wrote.

Bex closed out the tab for the last time. She was done with Caleb, and she wouldn't let herself waste another minute on him. She took a big drink of her water and pulled her hair back into a ponytail, ready to get back to work.

As she did, Aimee walked by. She shot Bex a smile and then a wink. Bex's whole face broke out in a big grin. Her once rigid muscles melted as she saw Aimee. She wanted nothing more than a big hug.

Some part of Bex knew it was irrational. Aimee had displayed red flag after red flag, but Bex still loved her. She loved that Aimee was willing to fight for her and fight for them. Even if she did it with crazy shit like burning a book.

261

Aimee sat down at her desk across the room. It took all Bex had not to go sit on Aimee's desk and flirt like they were both back in high school. They caught eyes and Aimee batted her thick, black eyelashes at Bex. A flutter ran through Bex's body.

The computer woke up and Aimee focused on her screen. Bex was forced to do the same. She returned to her personal inbox and saw an email from Author Ana Adams amid the podcast requests and junk.

Bex set up notifications for her sister's Wattpad a long time ago. Anytime something new was posted, Bex got a notification. This time, Ana had posted a new story on her account.

It was easy to get lost in her sister's words. Bex assumed that with all the pressure Ana was under, her writing would suffer but the opposite happened. Ana's work had sharpened, like a diamond. It was beautiful. Harrowing and sad. Just the kind of thing that Ana's fans would love to read.

Bex fired off a quick succession of texts to Ana. She was so proud of her sister for continuing to write, despite it all.

Something in front of her shot Bex's head up. Her boss, Theo, stood in front of her. He snapped his fingers to get her attention.

"Hey," she said, setting her phone on her desk. She felt like a middle schooler who had just been caught texting under the desk.

"Hey yourself. We have a two o'clock with the people from Denver Recycles Daily. You're late."

Bex snuck a look at the time on her computer. It was 2:12. She was late and worse, she'd done nothing to prepare.

"So sorry! I got wrapped up in working on a deck for a meeting next week. Coming now," she said. Theo wasn't the forgiving type.

"Don't screw this up," he said under his breath as they walked to the conference room.

FIFTY-NINE

When Ana returned, the house was dark and quiet. She'd only been gone for a few hours, but she felt altered forever. Her eyes scanned the room; it was all the same and all different at the same time. She felt like a stranger in her own home. In her own life.

Ana sat at the table heavily. She put her head in her hands and rubbed her temples. Her brain throbbed and her whole body felt like the muscles would be constricted forever. Ana forced herself to unclench her jaw and relax her forehead. It barely worked.

She was the FBI's main suspect. The realization was too much to comprehend. Ana felt a pressure to prove her innocence so heavily that she was rooted to the kitchen chair. She had to figure this out.

Only it felt like she was trapped in a jail of her own writing. Ana crossed her arms on the table and cradled her head. She couldn't see a way out; she was so alone. Somehow her life's dreams finally came true, but the cost was so big and so wrong that Ana was physically sick to her stomach.

Ana's phone buzzed on the table next to her. Ana picked it up; a text from Bex. *Just read through your story!* Followed by three champagne-popping emojis. Ana knit her brows together; why was she sending a champagne pop at a time like this? About a story like that?

The three dots appeared underneath her emojis. Ana chewed on her lip and waited; she knew her story was nothing good. It was probably the worst piece she'd ever crafted. Ana tried to tell herself that the point was only to catch a killer, not impress her sister, but she still waited for her response with bated breath.

Can't wait to see the killer pull this one off, Bex sent. She followed it with a cry-laughing emoji.

Ana's heart dropped out of her chest and into her stomach. Ana stood and paced the length of the kitchen.

What the hell did that mean? Ana searched for a logical explanation to excuse her sister's words, but she didn't have any. What made Bex think that was funny? Ana could come up with nothing. Bex was clearly watching Ana's website and her reaction was... off.

Ana walked to the living room and looked out the window. She caught a glance at the black box of the doorbell camera and wondered if James was still watching her come and go. She couldn't stop thinking about how he had tried to accuse Bex.

She sat on the edge of the couch and picked at the pilled edges of her pants. Maybe he was right; maybe there was something there. Ana didn't want to believe it but who sends that kind of text message? Who makes light of a very serious case? No one should want another human dead.

Ana knew what she needed to do. Ana stood and charged down the hallway. It was now or never. Ana looked at her watch, there was less than an hour before Bex would come home from work. She had to find out one way or another.

The door opened easily. Bex's room was spotless; the bed was made, not a single thing on the floor. The smell of cleaner hit Ana as soon as she took a step inside. The room felt sterile and contained.

Ana quietly closed the door behind her. She listened; the whole house was quiet save for the small hum of the air conditioner. She swirled around and took it all in. The centerpiece of Bex's room was a big bed in the middle. There was also a little reading nook in the corner and a desk along the opposite wall. The room featured a big walk-in closet and an ensuite bathroom.

The bookshelf seemed like a good place to start. Ana wasn't even sure what she was looking for, but she took a few books down and flipped through the pages. She returned them gingerly so Bex wouldn't notice the snooping.

Ana looked up and down the shelf and around the chair. There was no journal or manifesto, nothing in plain sight. Ana walked toward Bex's bed and pulled out the drawer of her side table. It was filled with some cords and a few toys that she did not want to think about.

The desk was completely free of clutter and everything in its spot; she knew the drawers would be just the same before she even opened them. Ana worried that if she were to leave a sign that she'd been in her sister's room, it was here.

On the shelf, there was a framed photo of Ana, Bex, and their mom. They were sitting on the front stoop of their house. Their mom was in the middle, flanked by a daughter on each side. They all wore shorts and summer tank tops; all barefoot, with big, happy smiles for the camera. Things had been good before everything in their life went to shit. The pain intensified in her stomach and made her double over. Ana never let herself think of their mom or before the accident.

Ana had seen this picture before but seeing it now, while she was snooping in her sister's room hurt. She just wanted a mom to call. A mom to help her through this. She wanted a mom so that neither of them would have had to turn out the way they did. It hurt to look. She focused on Bex's desk instead.

She opened the long skinny drawer in the middle of the desk. Inside were pens, notepads, and odds and ends. She pulled out the side drawer next and found nothing but a row of filing folders with tabs labeled - car insurance, house, and so forth. She closed it.

Ana's eyes landed on Bex's computer. Ana knew that's where she would find anything of value. She just didn't know her sister's password. Ana opened the lid, and the lock screen came into view. The background was a picture of Bex and Aimee from some concert at Red Rocks.

She typed in various password combinations; each time the bar in the middle of the screen shook, telling her she'd gotten it wrong. Ana was worried the whole machine would lock up. Finally, she tried their mom's name. The computer came to life. Typing 'Sandy' hurt.

The desktop was clean and neat. Ana opened Bex's email. The folder labeled 'Ana' caught her attention first. She opened it and a whole slew of emails related to Ana's care. A billing statement from Hillside was the first she opened. The balance at the bottom jumped off the page. The total owed after Ana's insurance was $29,987.23.

Ana's eyes swam across the screen. She felt her stomach roil. James was right. Bex probably was stressed about money. Ana didn't understand why Bex hadn't talked to her about this. They could have figured it out together. She couldn't think about it any longer.

The travel folder was Ana's next move. Bex kept very detailed records of her work trips over the years. Ana flipped back through emails and found her flight plans for her last trip - San Francisco. Ana checked the dates. It was confirmed; Bex and Aimee were in California during the murder of the woman on the bridge.

Ana knew the trip had gone terribly for Bex. Some small part of Ana wondered if Bex's fight with Aimee during their time away had been about something much more sinister.

She stopped. Ana thought she heard something but when she stilled, the house was quiet. Ana told herself it was all in her head. She carefully returned the folder to its spot and ran her eyes along the rest of the folders.

Receipts seemed like the next logical choice. The folder contained thousands of emails, going back almost 15 years to when she'd started her first Gmail account. Bex kept all her receipts for every single thing. There were email receipts in there from shopping trips, dinners, and coffee. Ana didn't know a thing about taxes or money management, but this was over the top.

Ana flipped through a few. Nothing stood out; it all seemed like normal purchases for Bex. Ana didn't know what she was looking for. She scrolled back to before this whole thing started.

An email from AncestryAndMe.com caught her eye. She opened it. There was a little green leaf growing out of the words. Ana scanned the page; around Christmas, Bex purchased a DNA testing kit. Questions rolled through Ana's mind. She wondered what Bex had found. Ana knew she needed to come back to that.

The only other place to look was Bex's desk. She opened the middle drawer to find it neatly organized with pens and office supplies. The next held more supplies and a handful of notebooks. She opened the big filing drawer and found it neatly organized with hanging folders. They were labeled taxes, mortgage, and so forth. Ana looked through a few, but it all seemed very normal.

The last folder was full of paper receipts. Ana pulled it from the drawer and flipped through the stash. Shoes. Makeup. Dinner. Just as she was about to put the folder back, Ana found a slip from Pinecone Gun & Hardware. Ana did a double take; this was out of character for Bex.

Spring. Bullets. Nails. The total came to $81.37. Paid in cash. Ana read the list again. The items were purchased in early February. Just before she went into treatment.

It hit her all at once - these were bomb-making supplies. Ana's head spun and she felt sick to her stomach. The timing was right. She knew enough about improvised explosive devices to know this receipt was suspicious.

The words on the paper seared into her eyes. Her whole body began to shake. She folded the piece of paper as if it were as explosive as the bomb itself. Ana's mind began to race. She must take this receipt to the police. This was proof.

The whir of the garage smashed her back to reality. Bex was home. Ana shoved the receipt in her pocket. She stood and pushed the chair back into place and looked around the room. It all looked the same.

SIXTY

The first thing Bex saw when she came into the office was a new client meeting added to her calendar for 10 AM. She took a drink of her to-go coffee and let the hot liquid hit her belly. The caffeine made her anxiety shoot through the roof, but she kept drinking.

Bex passed the morning in a blur of emails and completing over-due deliverables from their task management software. Her computer dinged and reminded her that she was due in their conference room in ten.

Theo controlled the meeting room with his no-nonsense tone. He detailed a new reminder setting product feature and dryly provided the information about its release. Bex couldn't focus. All she could think about was how Ana snooped in her room the day before. The framed picture of their mom was slightly askew, and her desk rifled through. Bex's room even smelled like Ana. Bex was the type of person that had a spot for everything. And she knew when something had been moved.

Bex could understand that Ana was grasping at straws, but snooping was a new low. Instead of listening to Theo give use case examples, Bex imagined ways to finally confront Ana when she got home.

"Earth to Bex," someone said. Bex snapped her head up. Her face went red, and a big, sheepish smile worked double time to cover up the gaffe. She looked around the room. Ten sets of eyes looked back at her. Embarrassment made her wince.

"Sorry, what was the question?" she asked. Bex could feel all eyes on her, but especially Theo who kept showing up in her meetings after Bex lost the big client in California.

"Stop thinking about your sister," Aimee said under her breath. The room fell completely silent, tension laced the air.

"What was that?" Theo asked.

"Nothing," Aimee said. She cleared her throat.

"No, tell us," he demanded. "I'm sick of whatever this is."

"Let's all cut her some slack," Aimee said. "Her sister is at the center of a murder investigation right now. Have you heard of The Novel Killings? Yeah, the author who wrote those books the killer has copied is Bex's sister."

The stares intensified. In the stillness, Bex finally understood what that saying meant - you really could have heard a pin drop. Bex's neck felt like it was on fire. Her hands balled at her sides, and she had to consciously keep smiling. Things had been so good with Aimee, what had gotten into her head?

"Everyone knows. Everyone. What I don't understand is why this is affecting your work so much," Theo said "You *do* still want a job here, right Bex? Or are you waiting until your podcast tour starts? Or your sister goes on 60 Minutes? Are we a backup plan to you or are we a career?" His face was the only one in the room redder than Bex's. The energy in the room felt like fuel enough to send the meeting up in flames with a single spark.

"Bex and Aimee, just go. We'll finish up here," Theo said, after a moment's silence spent mastering his aggravation. He pointed to the door. Bex looked him square in the face; his words were so far from okay. He tipped his head in the direction of the door.

She gathered her laptop and walked out. She didn't look back for Aimee. It was the worst walk of shame she'd ever taken in her life.

Bex got back to her desk and sat down. She fumed. None of this was her fault. The one thing that Bex had always been good at was work, ever since she was 13, taking jobs under the table to support her mom and sister.

She punched her hand down on the desk; barely registering the pain that shot up her arm. The rest of the team in their fishbowl of an office turned and looked. Bex needed to get out of there before she did something stupid.

Bex didn't ask for permission or tell anyone where she was going, she just got up and went, slamming the glass door closed as she left the building. The satisfying force of those reverberations was the only thing that took the edge off. Slightly.

The last place Bex wanted to be was home. She didn't feel like eating. She wanted to sweat and struggle. Bex walked a couple of blocks to the gym. She unlocked her locker and changed into the spare clothes she kept at the gym for emergencies. This counted. Bex tried to take her frustrations out on the stair stepper, but she couldn't keep pace with the machine. She tried the treadmill and then the punching bags. None of it cooled the hot anger in her belly.

She found herself in the gym's bar instead, thankful for the combination of low-level community alcoholism coupled with intense fitness culture that made gym bars common in Colorado. People here might day drink but that didn't mean they weren't ready to climb a 14,000-foot mountain at any moment. She kicked back Bombay Sapphire gin and tonic after gin and tonic. The dulling weight of the booze was the only thing keeping her from walking back to work and telling them all to fuck themselves.

Anger simmered just below the surface. Bex had only ever gotten positive annual reviews at work. She had never been written up, let alone having been kicked out of a meeting. She was angry at Aimee for making a scene, but she was even madder at Ana for setting this all into motion. If only Ana had never written those books, Bex thought over and over.

Fear underscored the anger, though. Her job was all that she had to her name. It was her identity. It was how she paid for their life. If she lost her job, Bex would have nothing. And neither would her sister.

Bex couldn't say how long she sat in the bar, but the sky turned dark, and she was as drunk as a marathoner after a big mountain race sponsored by Coors. She spent the day spinning arguments in her head and drowning her worries in booze. The gym bar was closing, and the server made frequent passes to tell her as such.

"Okay, ma'am. I gotta close up this space. You gotta go home," he finally said. He looked like a gym bro that only worked there for the free membership.

"The gym is open twenty-four hours a day!" she whined.

"Yes, but the bar closes at eight. I gotta lock it up, protocol and all that."

"Fine," she said.

She stood and the room spun around her. The booze in her belly, unaccompanied by food, sloshed and threatened to come back where it came from. The bartender grabbed her arm and walked her to the door.

"Do you want me to call someone?" he asked.

"No, no. I'll Uber home."

"Take care of you," he said. He gave her a sad look. She supposed she deserved it. She got drunk alone in a sad and sweat-stained excuse for a bar on a Tuesday afternoon. Bex hated feeling his pity.

She stumbled out of the gym. The cold air of the night sobered her, but only a measure. Bex looked up and down the street; she was downtown, and her car was still back at the office parking lot. She knew she shouldn't drive anyway. It took her a couple of tries before she got the ride-share app open.

The app said it would be 17 minutes before someone could come pick her up. Bex did the math; it was only a couple of blocks to walk to Aimee's downtown studio. The pull was too strong. Bex wanted to confront her. Bex needed to vent the anger somewhere. She closed the app and put her phone in her back pocket.

People she saw on the street gave her a wide berth. Maybe from the way she weaved back and forth on the sidewalk, or maybe it was the scowl on her face. With each step, Bex planned insults she would hurl at Aimee: *How dare she burn that book on their front step? How dare she bring up the Novel Killings at a work meeting?!*

The closer she got, the faster Bex walked, almost jogging by the end. She found the building and only remembered she needed a badge to open the door when she got there. Bex was forced to wait a few minutes before some other sucker arrived home.

"Hey, there–" she sweet-talked him. He looked at her suspiciously.

"My girlfriend lives on floor three; in apartment 304. I wanna surprise her. Will you please let me in?"

Bex thought he was going to say no, but he buzzed in and held the door for her. He dashed for the stairs and left her in the lobby without a word. So much for building security, Bex decided with a laugh. She couldn't wait to surprise Aimee.

She stumbled her way into the elevator and pressed the number three. Bex thanked the heavens that Aimee didn't live in one of those penthouse suites that required the keycard to allow the elevator to go that far. Bex looked at herself in the mirror. Her pony was pushed to one side and her baby hairs stuck out on either side. Makeup was smeared under her eyes. She looked as rough as she felt.

The elevator reached floor three with a ding. Bex exited, tripping over the threshold as she did. She laughed at herself. She was drunk. Bex looked up and down the hallway, it was empty and quiet.

273

She walked to Aimee's door, practically frothing at the mouth. She passed 302 and 303. When she got to 304, the first thing Bex noticed was the door was slightly open. Not all the way, but the door didn't click shut. It wasn't locked. That was very unlike Aimee.

Bex knocked once. The door pushed open just a bit more. A foul smell hit Bex. She pushed the door open all the way.

Aimee lay in a pool of blood. Her face was gray. Eyes open, glossy. Understanding hit Bex all at once. She sobered instantly.

Aimee was dead.

SIXTY-ONE

Bex crawled to Aimee and pulled her body into her lap. Aimee's head slipped to one side and blood seeped through Bex's yoga pants. She wasn't thinking rationally, all her body could do was scream and pant and cry.

Time stopped. Bex stroked Aimee's hair and her tears landed on Aimee's waxy skin. Minutes or hours could have passed; Bex had no way of knowing. The only thing that tore Bex's eyes from Aimee was a hand on her shoulder.

Blue latex gloves grabbed her from behind and pulled her to a standing position while another pair gently set Aimee's body back down. They pulled Bex into the hall and swarmed the apartment. Blue and black uniforms gathered and pooled in front of Bex's eyes.

She couldn't stop the wails. All the people between her and Aimee weren't enough. Shivers wracked her body and the magnetic pull between them kept her lunging for the corpse. A gloved hand held her in place.

"Noooooo!" she screamed over and over. It didn't make a difference. Aimee didn't move. She didn't wake up.

Someone pulled Bex away, away from her love. Bex saw the knife that took Aimee's life. It was long-bladed and heavy-looking; all the silver was tainted a dull red. The blood around Aimee had already begun drying; it looked more like a splotch of paint than the life force that had just been stolen from such a vibrant young woman, leaving her a cooling, empty heap.

"Ma'am, ma'am. I need your help. Please come this way," someone said, pulling her harder. She didn't move. Someone else gave her a slight push from behind to get her moving. They brought her down and around the corner, by the stairwell.

Two people stood right in her face.

"Ma'am. I'm Marion Stevens, I'm with the Denver Police Department. Someone called when they heard you screaming. I'm here to help figure out what's going on. I need your help though, okay? Let's start with your name," the woman said.

Bex looked her square in the face; she was older, and her salt-and-pepper hair was slicked back into a bun with blue-tinted glasses pushed up on her head.

"Please help me out here. What's going on?"

"I came. I found her," Bex said. The shock of the words doubled her over.

"Okay, what is her name?"

"Aimee. Aimee Phillips. She's my girlfriend." The cop jotted it down.

"And what is your name?"

"Bexley Adams."

She turned away from Bex and walked down the hall. She said something into her radio, but Bex couldn't hear her. Bex tried to move closer, she needed to know what was going on. Another cop stopped her and held her in place. He was young and looked like he should still be playing high school baseball, not attending a murder. His hair was jet black and his face was still blanketed with baby fat.

Bex swallowed. Her whole body began to shiver.

The policewoman came back to Bex. "Okay, tell us what happened, Bex," the woman coaxed.

"I. I. I don't know. I was at the gym, and I walked here. I was just going to talk to her, but her door was cracked open a little, that's not like her. I knocked and then it opened a bit more, I could see her foot on the floor. So, I opened it all the way. I found her like this."

A look passed between them. Bex felt sick. Their disbelief was written all over their faces.

"I swear!" she yelled. A neighbor popped his head out of his door.

"I just got here, and she was like this. You can check the time I left the gym. I got kicked out of the gym bar because it was closing. The bartender saw me out, he'll remember. And then I walked, I will be on camera. You can check the time of death; she was long gone by the time I got here."

Bex wailed. She sank to the floor. The effort was too much. The weight of Aimee, her job, the podcast, and Ana, pushed her right down. She could not bear it all on her shoulders. She covered her face and wept for all of it.

The cop knelt in front of her. "Ms. Adams, are you okay?"

Bex just sobbed.

"We just need to ask you a few more questions. Would that be alright with you?"

She tried to nod. It was the best she could do.

"Did you see anything suspicious when you got to the building? Anyone that seemed out of place?"

"No, someone let me in because I don't have a badge for this building, but he was nice. He didn't even say anything to me."

Bex watched as more officers filled the space. A few were covered in head-to-toe medical-looking smocks. Bex willed them to find enough forensic evidence to determine who killed Aimee.

"Okay, and did you know if Aimee dealt with any kind of issues with anyone? Did she tell you that she was having trouble at work or with an old partner? Anything of the sort?"

"We work together," Bex said. She let out a moan thinking about how she was going to have to break this to her team. Things were piling up on Bex. Everyone would remember the way Bex and Aimee got kicked out of the meeting. They would all remember the way Bex was fuming. She groaned. This looked so bad.

"Okay. Is that how you two met?"

"Yes."

"But you don't know anyone that Aimee had problems with?"

"No, I don't think so. We love each other."

The cop jotted something else down.

"And what about her family?"

"I've never met them. I don't even think they know Aimee is gay. They live in St. Louis." Another line was added to the notepad.

"Tell me about Aimee."

"She is lovely. Her personality is so fun. We love to dance, eat new food. Our relationship moved fast, but I love her."

The cop scribbled a few more things. Marion's glasses started to slip off her head; she shoved them back up without breaking stride.

"And repeat what happened tonight," the baby boy cop said. A sudden urge to punch him in the throat crowded Bex's mind. She wanted to take all her anger out on him, another presumptuous male authority figure. She followed the swirled pattern of the hall carpet instead.

"I was at work and then I left a bit early. I went to the gym and worked out for a while, and then I went to the bar at the gym. It's just like a little cafe inside the place, they serve food, smoothies, and drinks. I had a few and then I walked here. I found her..."

He cleared his throat. "I'm going to ask you again, please think. There's no one else we should be concerned about?"

"No. I mean, she is. She was the best."

The cop rubbed his chin. Bex felt the inadequacy of her answers. There had to be someone. Bex grasped at straws. "She and my sister hate each other but it's nothing. It's not this." The female cop took note of that.

"Tell us about that," she said.

"There's not a lot to tell. My sister lives with me and she's kind of difficult. Aimee always felt like my sister Ana took too much of my time and attention. It kind of came to a head recently but they're okay."

"And what's your sister's name?" the cop asked.

"Ana. Ana Adams."

"Do I have this correct?" the female officer interjected. "Your sister is Ana Adams, the author?"

"Yes," Bex said. She rubbed her eyes with her thumb and forefinger.

"Got it," the cop finally said. Bex traced the design in the carpet with her shaky finger. Through it all, Bex had been the one to keep it together but now, her mind was broken in two. Her whole body hurt, and she did not have it in her to fight anymore.

"Thank you for your help. We're going to need to take you in for forensics and some further questioning, Ms. Adams."

She looked up. A neighbor was just a few feet away with his phone covering his face. Bex jumped up and lunged toward him.

"Don't record this! My girlfriend is dead! What kind of sick bastard are you!" The cops flanked her on either side and pulled Bex away from the man. She continued to yell obscenities until he ducked behind his door and shut the door with a whack.

They took her down the elevator and out to the car; she didn't resist.

279

SIXTY-TWO

Ana and Bex sat on the couch together, Ana stroking Bex's hair. The only words between them for the last several hours were "She's gone," and "I know." Ana didn't know how to comfort her sister. Their roles were reversed, and Ana was unpracticed.

As she tucked her hair behind Bex's ear, Ana said, "I love you, I'm sorry."

"I love you too," Bex said. Another hiccuping sob escaped Bex. Those three words didn't leave their mouths very often. Maybe it was their childhood, devoid of hugs and affection, or maybe it was the way they were forced to form a hard exterior from a young age. Either way, affection didn't come all that naturally to either one of them.

Love was all Ana had though. She couldn't take the pain away from Bex and she certainly couldn't bring Aimee back.

Ana stroked Bex's hair and thought about Aimee. She had been antagonistic and downright mean. Burning Ana's book on their front porch? Disgusting - especially knowing how their mother had died.. But no one deserved this kind of death.

During the press conference, the cops said that someone got into the apartment and knocked on Aimee's door. As soon as she answered, the killer attacked with a sharp knife. They've reviewed all the footage; one person came into the building with a medical mask and sunglasses. The person was of slight build and indeterminate gender, with pale hair escaping from the sides of a wide brimmed bucket hat.

On the grainy security camera footage, it was enough to hide their identity. No real identifying features. No DNA was left behind. No trace of the person.

The killer was in and out in less than five. Five minutes was all it took to snuff someone's life out. Ana sniffed. She didn't like Aimee, but she never thought it would come to this. Ana watched the footage of the killer entering the building over and over. There was something about them. She couldn't put a finger on it.

Bex's phone buzzed on the table. She'd been getting messages from teammates and friends all day. She just kept ignoring it. The phone shook the coffee table again. "Want me to get that?" Ana asked.

"No, it's fine," Bex said. She pushed out her legs and stretched her arms. "I have to go to the bathroom."

She stood and hobbled down the hall; her body stiff from laying on the couch for the better part of the day.

The phone buzzed again. Ana couldn't stand it; she grabbed the phone to silence it all together. The messages caught Ana's eye instead. They were from a number that wasn't saved in Bex's phone.

She unlocked the phone with Bex's password. Ana opened the messages.

Ut oh. You two are in the news again.
Only this time it's you, Bex.
Couldn't be outdone by our middle, huh?
So proud to be in this family.

Ana's heart raced. Bex's phone felt hot in her hand. Ana's mind sped through possibilities. Was it the wrong number? She searched the screen; the person knew Bex's name. They knew her name. The sender knew them.

The toilet flushed down the hall. Ana read the messages again to make sure she understood what she was seeing. Her eyes landed on "our middle". That struck a nerve. *Our middle.* She flew through the rest of the words. *In this family.*

281

Ever since their family imploded as kids, there wasn't anyone but Bex and Ana. Their mom was dead; their real dad was a ghost. And that bastard of a stepdad - dead, too. Good riddance. They were never close with grandparents or cousins. Those people wrote them off a long time ago. That only left one person.

Caleb? Was Bex talking to their brother? Things clicked into place. Ana remembered the DNA kit receipt she'd found in Bex's email. Had Bex found their little brother and not told Ana? If so, why were his messages so... so... strange?

Bex landed on the couch with a thud. She pulled the blanket up to her chin before realizing Ana had her phone. "Did someone call?" she asked. Her voice was gritty from too many tears.

"No, but who is this?" Ana said. She flipped the phone so Bex could see.

Bex's face turned even whiter; something Ana didn't think was possible. Bex snatched the phone and powered it off.

"Who was that? Caleb?"

Bex sucked in a big breath of air and laid her head back down in Ana's lap. "No, no. Caleb? No."

Ana didn't believe her.

SIXTY-THREE

Fear sliced through Bex so hard she thought she might bleed out like Aimee. Bex turned her phone off and threw it across the room. It wasn't far enough. Caleb knew where they lived and now, he had her phone number, too.

"Who was that?!" Ana asked again.

Bex couldn't bring herself to say his name out loud. Judging by the look of pure panic on Ana's face, her sister knew. She read enough of the messages to put the pieces together.

"That was Caleb, wasn't it?"

Bex looked around the room wildly. There was nowhere to run, she couldn't get out of this conversation.

"Answer me, Bex," Ana said, firmer this time.

"Bex!" Ana yelled.

"Yes, okay. It's him," Bex said at last, after blowing her nose loudly into a tissue. "I think. I don't know how he got my number, but I think it's him. I don't even know why I did it, but I sent my DNA to AncestryandMe a few months ago. We matched as half-siblings. He started messaging me through their website."

"Why didn't you tell me?"

"I don't know. I couldn't. It just all happened so quickly. We found each other right around the same time as all of this started. I can't deal with him right now."

Ana tried to get up off the couch. Bex grabbed her arm and held her into place. "Stay!"

Ana was speechless."Then answer me this - why is he so angry?" She said, after a moment's thought.

"I don't know. I think he wanted to meet us, and I just didn't have the energy for him. He took it terribly. He's been harassing me ever since."

"What do you mean?"

"The letter, someone knocking. All of that was him. He messages me all the time. He's getting more belligerent."

"I don't understand," Ana said. "What do you mean 'the door knocking'?"

"Remember when you got the letter and you thought someone was at the house? He told me he sent the letter. He said that we never responded so he came to visit. I think it was just a coincidence that they were the same night."

"We don't check the mail," Ana said. "And he was knocking in the middle of the night. Is he crazy?"

"I know."

"I didn't answer because I was scared. And you weren't here," Ana said.

"I know. I've tried to reason with him, but he doesn't understand why we left him as a baby or why we can't just pick up and be loving siblings now."

"That's crazy. We have to go to the cops!" Ana said. She sat up straight. "He's harassing you!"

"And tell them what? They already don't trust us. We can't add this. It will just be more fuel to the fire," Bex said before another sob racked her whole body.

Bex laid on the couch and pulled the blanket over her head. She couldn't deal with all of it. A buzzing sound intruded. Bex could have sworn that she turned her phone off. She peeked out from under the covers and saw Ana reach for her phone on the table. Had Caleb found Ana's number, too?

"It's James," Ana announced.

Bex relaxed. "Are you going to answer it?"

"No. I don't want to talk to him."

"Why?"

"I don't trust him anymore. And I can't trust myself to remember that if I heard his voice."

Bex thought about that for a second. "Why?"

"He broke into our camera app, and he keeps saying weird things. I am also convinced he's been following me," Ana said.

"What? He's following you?"

"I don't know. I thought I saw him the other day when I was out for a walk. I'm not sure."

Ana silenced the call and looked at her screen. "Oh shit! I gotta go. My appointment with Dr. Daniels is soon," Ana said. She jumped up from the couch, letting the blanket fall as she did.

"Ana! Don't leave me. We need to talk about James. He's following you?! Don't leave now," Bex said. She felt her panic rising at the thought of being home alone with her thoughts.

"I have to. Dr. Daniels is looking for any reason to commit me, I can't add unreliable to his list," Ana said. She grabbed her purse from the hook by the door.

"I don't want to be alone!" Bex moaned. She meant every word. She'd barely started going to the bathroom alone since finding Aimee's body, let alone spending several hours by herself.

"I'll be right back," Ana said. She walked to the door.

Bex felt a pain so sharp in her chest that she had to shove the palm of her hand into her ribs. "I'll be home as soon as I'm done," Ana said. She closed the door behind her without so much as waving.

A panic attack took hold in her belly. It felt like her heart would explode on the next beat. Ana was all she had; watching her walk away solidified that Bex needed her sister.

Losing Ana would be the death of her.

SIXTY-FOUR

The waiting room felt more like a medical spa than a therapist's office. There was even a little babbling fountain in one corner. No wonder the place cost so much, Ana thought. She crossed her legs and bounced her foot up and down. She counted from one to one hundred to pass the time. Then she did it by twos and by tens. Dr. Daniels still hadn't come for her.

Ana looked at her watch, he was twelve minutes late. Her anxiety shot through the roof. She just needed to get this appointment over with so she could get back home to her sister.

The door opened slowly, and he pushed through. He offered her a toothy smile and swept his arm across the lobby. "Ana! My apologies for the delay. Come this way."

She stood and slung her quilted purse over her shoulder. Ana followed him down the hallway. The place was dark and quiet. She wondered if anyone else was still in this wing of the facility besides the front desk lady. That thought made her shudder. She caught a whiff of his signature cherry smell.

He opened the door to his office and said, "Have a seat, Ana."

She took up her usual residence on his couch and he took the seat opposite of her. He ran a hand through his hair; he somehow looked older than her last visit.

"So, how are things?"

"Fine."

"Ana," he coaxed. She didn't say more. She couldn't. It would open a floodgate. "I saw the news yesterday. It looks like there's been another murder?"

"No. NO. That has nothing to do with my books. I did not write anything like that."

"Ah, but your sister? She was there?"

"Yes, Bex found her... found Aimee. Aimee is... was my sister's girlfriend."

"This all must be so unsettling for you, Ana."

"It's worse for my sister. She feels so guilty that she didn't protect Aimee."

"And how are you doing with it all?"

"I'm okay. It feels good to take care of her for once."

He smiled. "I bet it's still hard to see her as a suspect though."

"I'm pretty sure they cleared her. Someone came in wearing a mask and glasses. A hat, too. Bex came in later; they can see it all on the security tapes. She was at the gym when it happened."

He rubbed his beard. "But some are saying they look like they could still be the same person? That's what the news said this morning."

"No, my sister would never," Ana said, feeling defensive.

He looked out the window.

"Ana, I want to be straight with you - all of this could very well derail your progress. I fear that you could have increased episodes with the added stress and all."

Ana needed to get home to Bex. To make her soup and take care of her. She couldn't afford more time wasted.

"Thank you for your concern, but I think I'm doing quite well given all of it."

"And your meds?"

"Yes."

"You're taking them? They're working?" He looked her up and down. She picked at her fingernail. "Ana, you're taking them, right?"

"I don't feel like I need them right now."

He sucked in a big breath and crossed his arms. "Ana. Listen to me. You cannot, under any circumstances, simply stop your meds.

That is very dangerous to your health. You could have severe withdrawal symptoms. Not to mention, you need that medication."

Ana pursed her lips together; she didn't need a lecture. She didn't need to be drugged into compliance. For the first time in a long time, she felt like herself. She wouldn't be medicated back to whatever that was.

"Ana. Did you hear me?"

"Yes! I am good. I don't need to take all those chemicals. And I'm not having withdrawals, I'm stepping down my dosages slowly. I'm not dumb." Her blood pressure rose; she could hear the beating of her heart in her ears.

"I will respect your decision to reduce or change your medication, but only if we do this the right way."

"I am doing it my way and it's working."

He stood and walked around the room. She could hear him taking big deep breaths, trying to calm his own body down.

Ana looked at him, really looked at him for the first time since she'd gotten there. He was under so much strain: his hair whiter, the wrinkles around his eyes deeper. His shoulders sagged and his brown suit was rumpled, not crisp, and pressed like normal. He didn't look like the same calm, reasonable man she'd known for years.

He sat back down in his chair and put his hands on his knees. His eyes searched hers, he looked like he was about to say something she didn't want to hear.

"You might not be able to tell me this, but do you know where a former patient named Kyle is? Is he back in treatment? We kind of became friends here and I saw him once after treatment, but I haven't heard from him since. I've messaged him a few times," Ana said, hoping the change of topic would get her out of trouble.

A shadow crossed over Dr. Daniels' face. He clasped his hands together and stood up again. The mood changed in the room with that one single question. Daniels knew exactly why she was asking.

"Oh, Ana. Normally, I would not discuss other patients with you but since it is all over the news, I assume you have seen it."

"What?"

"As I've said, we're at a delicate balance here. This could be the thing that tips your scales."

"I can handle it. Please, I need to know."

He paced around the room and went to the other side of his mahogany desk. He said and looked over the papers and trinkets on the top.

"I worry that you haven't heard about this yet. Are you engaged? Have you been having more blackouts?"

Ana wracked her brain. What was he talking about? What had she missed?

"I have been trying to stay away from the news. It's healthier for me if I don't get riled up," she said.

He looked out the window again. The silence ratcheted up the unease she felt.

"I think you really should consider coming back to Hillside. At this point, you'd be a lot safer here. And if you black out, staff would be here to monitor your actions."

"I don't want to come back. I'm managing on my own. And with the help of my sister. I don't need to be locked away. I need to work through this. I need to figure out who is copying my books - who is killing those people!"

"Ana. That's not your job. That's for the police."

"And they're not doing it. I must finish this."

"This is all making me very nervous, Ana. If I have reason to believe you're a danger, I could place you on an involuntary hold. It's a rare step taken in the American mental health architecture but given the interest in the events surrounding you, I could likely make the case."

Ana stood and turned away from him. She looked at his bookshelves lining the way. She needed to stay calm. She needed to prove to him that she could be on her own.

"Dr. Daniels. I appreciate your concern. I don't need this right now. I need to help my sister. And I need to be available for the investigation."

"What about time? Your blackouts? Have you had any more?"

"I don't know why you keep bringing that up! I've told you I'm fine. I'm managing."

"Ana, might I remind you that losing time is a serious concern? We're going to have to identify your triggers and work on your reactions," he said.

She slapped her hands down on the table in front of her. "Tell me what happened to Kyle!"

"Ana, he was murdered."

SIXTY-FIVE

@TexasTrueCrimeChick on TikTok

"Heeyyyyyyy there true crime crazies! It's Becca here and I have a big update on The Novel Killings for y'all. It's a doozy so be sure to like and follow me so you can stay in the loop.

"So just to catch all you newbies up - if there is a single person who hasn't heard by now - there's this small, self-published author in Colorado who has written a couple of books. She barely sold any, but for some reason, someone started copying her stories.

"The first book was a bomb in a box and in the second, a chick was pushed off the Golden Gate. Both murders have been carried out in real life now. Don't believe me? Some creepy details aren't a coincidence. Go watch my other videos to see what I mean.

"But anyways, I have more news for you! Ana was in a residential treatment program right around the same time all this started happening. Apparently while in Hillside, she made a friend named Kyle Francis.

"Well, guess what? Kyle ended up dead. Stabbed in a dark parking lot in a kind of crappy part of Denver.

"I know what you're thinking - coincidence, right? Well, wrong. His parents were able to access his phone and his accounts. Ana invited him to their live podcast recording just before he was killed.

"And guess what, he died sometime that night after the show. The parking lot was just a few blocks down from where they held the recording.

"Bodies are starting to add up, my friends."

SIXTY-SIX

The television rolled the intro music for an old episode of *Criminal Minds*; Bex worked slowly through another bowl of popcorn. They'd been on the couch all day and Ana was antsy. She needed to get up and move; she needed to write.

Ana pulled the blanket off her legs and scooted to stand up. "Where are you going?" Bex asked. She looked as startled as a raccoon caught by the porch light.

"I'm just going to get up for a while. I can't do another one."

"This one is so good! It's about some cult murders in Oregon. If I remember right, all kinds of goodies - incest, rituals. You'll love it."

"I've probably already seen it."

"Watch it again," Bex said. She folded her bottom lip over, making a puppy dog face.

"I'll be right there," Ana said, gesturing to the kitchen.

"Annnna! I need you."

"Sis, I just need a break."

"I know. But I just can't do this alone. I need you to stay by me."

Bex laid her whole upper body over Ana's lap so she couldn't get up. "Just stay with me for a few more minutes?"

Annoyance flared inside Ana. She wanted to write; go for a walk. Do anything besides sit on the couch for another round of Special Agent Penelope Garcia, gracing the screen with her wit and oddities.

Bex didn't move. It was clear that Ana was to be glued to the couch along with her sister. Ana imagined them rotting in place, the way people would find them dead, arms linked. Ana leaned forward and grabbed her phone from the coffee table. She gave into sitting on the couch a while longer.

Ana's thumb hovered over her screen, not knowing where to get her dopamine from. She was tired of crushing candied jewels but was scared to look at any of her social apps.

Penelope droned in the background. Ana couldn't watch her either. She clicked the Facebook app, deciding to risk it in favor of drowning out the show on the television. The notification counter in the corner simply said 99+. The app didn't even bother trying to count beyond that. Ana hovered over the blaring red number. She couldn't make herself click.

Ana scrolled for a few minutes, averting her gaze anytime she caught a glimpse of something that could be related to The Novel Killings. Whatever people were dissecting in true crime groups, she didn't want to know.

After a news story about a blob of seaweed heading for the coast of Florida, Ana landed on a picture of Aimee in a Denver true crime group. Ana closed the app before Bex could catch a glimpse. If Bex saw that, it would set her off all over again.

Ana would kill to know what they were saying but she knew better than to look with her sister next to her. Bex would eventually fall asleep on the couch, Ana just needed to hang tight for a while before she could be free of her sister for the night.

The next thing Ana saw in her feed was a video from the Denver news station. The clip rolled before she could scroll on. Kyle's face filled her screen. Ana's heart felt like it might race out of her chest cavity. "Hey, pause that for a second," Ana said to Bex. A look of confusion crossed Bex's face, but Agent Garcia's face froze on the screen.

Ana started the video over and turned up the volume. "A Denver family is asking for answers after their son was found killed in a parking lot outside Lioness Lair," the newscaster said. The video panned to a couple sitting in a beautiful home. They were framed by big windows and long curtains.

"I'm here with Sherri and Robert Francis, the parents of the victim," another reporter said. "Tell us about Kyle."

"Kyle was the sweetest kid. He had some issues, but what kid doesn't these days?" Robert said directly into the camera. Sherri stifled a sob. "But he was so funny and full of life. He was just getting started."

"And what can you tell us about the night Kyle was killed?"

"We still don't know much. We do know that Kyle got a message on Instagram the morning of his death from someone he met in a residential treatment facility," Robert said. Ana chewed on her lip and waited.

"Not just anyone," Sherri said through her tears. "It was Ana Adams. You know that author that wrote the whole Novel Killer thing? Yeah, her. Ana invited him to her live podcast show. Kyle went and then he ended up dead!"

"We think they're connected," Robert added.

"They have to be!" Sherri cried. Ana couldn't watch anymore. She swiped out of Facebook and forced herself to breathe. Her whole body ached for Kyle and his parents. The guilt she felt was immense. They weren't exactly wrong, she did invite Kyle and he ended up dead. It didn't matter if his death was related to the serial killer, it was still her fault. Another life was lost because of Ana Adams. Kyle's parents knew it and so did she.

"I can't believe they both died," Bex said. Ana looked up from her phone. Bex was staring straight ahead, her eyes glassed over.

"Yeah, it sucks," Ana said. They kept having the same conversation. It was like Bex couldn't hold it all in her mind.

"Don't you think they're connected?" Bex asked.

"Kyle and The Novel Killings?"

"No, Aimee and Kyle. Both stabbing deaths. Fairly close together. Both in Denver."

Ana didn't know what to think. It felt like it was all connected somehow. She just couldn't see through her guilt. The pieces were in front of her, she just couldn't fit them together in a way that made sense. It was driving her mad.

The cops cleared Bex, but she did admit that she was blackout drunk when she came to Aimee's house. Maybe there was something more to the story. And Kyle? Did he even know Aimee? None of it fit into what Ana had been telling herself for weeks: *These killings were related to Ana but not Ana's books.*

"Don't you think?" Bex said again.

"I don't know, Bexie. Denver has a lot more crime than people think. It could just be a really sad coincidence."

"There are no coincidences."

Bex leaned her head back on the couch and closed her eyes. Ana looked her up and down. Bex looked skinny, really skinny, matted hair and greasy skin and her face didn't have that smooth glow to it anymore.

Ana needed space. She needed time to think and process. She couldn't do that with Bex next to her. The urge to move out on her own rushed through Ana. In the chaos, she had briefly let that dream go but now, it was back with a vengeance.

"So, can I go write now?" Ana asked, hoping Bex would have changed her mind.

"No, just stay until the end of this episode," Bex said. She started the show again.

Ana leaned back into the couch. She didn't have it in her to fight her sister. Not now. Ana went back to Instagram.

The little number '124' in the top corner blared at her. Ana clicked through all the reviews and was so happy to see that her books were met with such positivity on the app. She hearted and commented, *thanks for reading!* On every single one of them. Ana was on cloud nine. She couldn't wait to check her Amazon dashboard for updated sales reports.

One unopened message in her inbox gave her pause - @anasnumberonefan again.

Ana clicked on the name. There was a whole new string of messages waiting for her.

They'd come in late the night before. Probably when she and Bex were zonked on the couch.

11:11 PM - @anasnumberonefan

> *Hey Ana. I wanted to be the first to tell you -*
> *Denver woman missing.*

The message included a link to *The Denver Post.*

Ana debated clicking on the link. Was it phishing? Would they somehow get her password and steal the followers she'd worked so hard to curate? The pull for information was too great.

She clicked and was taken to a Denver Post story. The details were sparse, but Ana learned a woman had gone missing from the Montebello neighborhood. She was only 25. The story insinuated she was a sex worker. Her name was Patricia Almont. She went by Trixie. Her lifeless body was found by hikers in the Three Sisters Park, just west of Denver.

The phone fell from her hands. Tears sprung from her eyes and crashed down her face.

"The Novel Killer is back."

SIXTY-SEVEN

@TexasTrueCrimeChick on TikTok

Ambient music playing in the background.

"Heeyyyyyyy there true crime crazies. It's Becca here and I want to be the first to tell y'all. It's happened AGAIN!!!!!!!

"If you haven't heard, I'm the leading creator keeping you all up to date on The Novel Killings. I have a whole playlist; watch 'em and get caught up. Be sure to interact with the videos and follow me while you're at it.

"At any rate, here we go. Oh my god. This is huge. Believe it or not, it's happened again. There's a new case that police suspect is related to The Novel Killings. You know how the author Ana Adams is out of books to copy? Well, she posted a short story to her Wattpad account. Yep, verified... definitively her account.

"I'll read the story in the next video but here's what you need to know - in the story, a woman goes missing in Denver and ends up dead.

"I'm so incredibly mad, sad, disgusted to say this but a beautiful girl - long black hair, bright eyes, full of potential - went missing from Denver. Hikers found her yesterday. She wasn't even 10 steps off the trail. Her name was Patricia Almont. Trixie Almont.

"And before you even go saying it wasn't related to Ana's story, there's proof in the pudding. Ana Adams posted that story and in it, the killer's signature is to leave a whistle tied around his victims' neck.

"You know what Patricia was found wearing? A whistle around her neck.

"It can't get worse than this. Whoever is committing The Novel Killings is a fucking monster.

"Like and follow for all updates on this case cause there's bound to be more."

SIXTY-EIGHT

Bex spread her fingers over the fabric of the couch and watched the way the upholstery danced around. She willed herself to hear Ana's footsteps coming back to the couch, but all that met her ears was the clack clack clack of her sister's computer keys.

The news had hit Ana hard. For days, all Ana could do was cry, the pair of them nearly catatonic in their shared grief, but now, Ana was finally up and writing. Bex hoped she was in the kitchen processing it all through a blank page.

Bex started another episode of *Criminal Minds*. The only thing keeping her alive was the inspiring quote at the beginning and end of each show. She was halfway through season eight. She told herself that when she got to the end, she would go back to work and life.

She rarely took so much as a day off, let alone an entire week. Work was her passion, but even the pull of the one thing she was good at could not convince herself to get off the couch.

Since Bex was the one to find Aimee and since the shit with her sister had become national news, work tried to be understanding. Bex wondered how long they would give her before they ripped the rug out from under her.

The pressure to return and put on a brave face was big - big enough to keep her glued to the couch instead. She imagined walking through the front doors and badging into the creative team's fishbowl a hundred times. No matter what she pictured herself wearing or how she thought people would react, she couldn't bring herself to get up.

It wasn't Aimee so much as it was all of it. Aimee, Kyle, the victims of The Novel Killer. Not one of those cases had so much as an arrest. The killer or killers were still out there; they were no closer to solving the cases than they were days ago. Fear swirled around Bex's head, growing larger with each pass.

The credits rolled. Bex leaned back into the couch and committed herself to another episode.

Bex's phone buzzed on the cushion next to her; she silenced it. Her anxiety told her not to answer, to avoid it like everything else in life she was ignoring. Not even a minute later, it started ringing again. Bex grabbed the phone; she didn't recognize the number, but it wasn't a Colorado area code. That gave her pause.

With a shaky finger, she slid the bar at the bottom before she could change her mind.

"Hello," she said quietly, barely above a whisper. She paused the show.

"Bexley Adams?"

"Speaking," she said.

"Hey, Bex - I'm Zane. I'm glad you answered," he said; his vote instantly going more casual. He sounded young, energetic. Maybe a slight Southern accent. She relaxed some. She couldn't place him.

"How can I help you?"

"Well, Bex. I work for an ad agency out of New York, Seventeen Eleven. I'm at the Denver satellite. You heard of it?"

"No."

"Well, our niche is helping companies land great ads on even better podcasts. And you obviously have the hottest podcast in America right now. We have some high-dollar brands looking for killer placements."

A tiny laugh escaped from Bex's mouth. The sound was strained after days of crying.

"Sorry, what's so funny?" he asked, innocently. This was probably the hardest part of his day; Bex envied that.

"You said 'killer,' it just made me laugh given the nature of what's going on at the moment."

"Oh god. I'm so sorry. I'm an idiot."

"No, it's fine really."

He sucked in a big breath.

"So, like I was saying before I made a fool of myself - we have two maybe, three brands that would pay top dollar for a spot on your next episode," he said. Bex sat up a little straighter. A part of her was starting to feel alive again.

"We don't exactly have plans to record again," she finally admitted.

"What?! There's been a new case, and all that other stuff," he said, enthused. "You have to record!"

"I guess I can talk to my sister about it, but it feels a weird. I'm not even sure we're legally allowed to - it's still an open investigation."

"I get that, I do, but people are expecting it."

"Yeah, maybe. I don't know if my sister will go for it."

"I tell you what, if you record and let my partners have exclusive rights to the show's spots, I'll throw in a bonus."

"How much are we talking?"

"Would ten thousand do it?"

Bex swallowed. They could use the money to cover a big portion of Ana's treatment, especially now that Bex wouldn't be getting any big bonuses this quarter.

"Yeah, I think we can do that."

They discussed a few details and Zane promised to send over a contract. It gave reason for Bex to smile for the first time in days. This was the break they needed; she couldn't wait to see the dollar signs in the bank account. She couldn't wait to pay off Ana's medical bills and get that boulder off her back.

301

Bex leaned her head back against the couch again and looked up at the ceiling. She wondered how she would convince Ana to record another show. She imagined them sitting down and turning on their mics. She imagined Ana going over Patricia Almont's case, detail by detail. She imagined talking about Aimee. Her throat constricted.

For the thousandth time, Bex wondered who could have done this to Aimee. She missed her so badly, her whole body ached.

Bex pinched the bridge of her nose to staunch the tears. It didn't work; they streaked her face and dripped on her chin. She rubbed her face. What a mess. She knew things were very bad. Knowing it wasn't the same as being able to do anything to fix it, though.

A memory of Aimee popped into Bex's mind – "Normal sisters don't have an unhealthy addiction to one another as you and Ana do. Y'all need some space. You need some independence from one another," Aimee had said.

The thought ripped Bex in two. All of this was proof that Ana and Bex needed each other, now more than ever. She missed Aimee but her girlfriend had been wrong about that. The only thing Bex needed was to be near her sister. She would never let go of another person she loved. Not Ana. Never again.

SIXTY-NINE

Patricia's beautiful face plagued Ana's every single thought. Her dimple on the right side, her big dark eyes. The way her dark hair framed her face and fell down her back. Even the bright yellow dress she went missing in.

Patricia Almont deserved better than this. Even if she did sex work, she more than deserved to do it safely. She deserved to grow into an old woman. The rest of them should still be alive too. And Ana deserved to write whatever the hell she wanted to without fear that some sick bastard would carry it out in real life. Her emotions swung from pure red rage to debilitating sadness.

She read everything she could on the case. The police didn't have a single lead and so far, no one had come forward with any information. Trixie was simply there and then gone. Alive and then dead. And it was Ana's fault.

The whole world hated her for giving the killer more material, but none of them came close to hating Ana as much as she hated herself. Her plan was absolutely stupid, and it got another person killed.

The only silver lining was the fact that Ana now knew the killer was close - it wasn't random. He was watching her and was familiar with her old Wattpad account. The killer put Patricia's body in Three Sisters Park. Ana purposefully didn't include a location in her story. This was personal.

The killer knew her. They were taunting her.

Ana thought back to all the happy memories she'd had there. Dates with her sister. Picnics. James. Understanding exploded in her mind. James knew about Three Sisters because of Ana. Her whole body began to shake once again.

303

Ana's mind flipped. Bex knew the park, too. Three Sisters was a place the two of them shared often. Maybe James was right. Maybe it was Bex.

A woman had died to get this information. Ana had a responsibility to her and her family to make sure that life hadn't been lost for nothing. She knew now, beyond any doubt, that the killer was focused on her personally - not her books. That might be the first step in stopping them.

Ana couldn't stand the sound of the television looping through another *Criminal Minds* episode, or another one of Bex's deep sighs. Ana scooped up her computer and relocated to her room. It was dark and the air was stale, but the solitude scratched an itch inside her brain.

She could finally think. She could find the killer. She must. For Patricia. For Ella. For Ruth.

From her side table drawer, she pulled out her list. Ana looked it over. She blotted out the guilt over publishing another story - regret wouldn't bring Patricia back and it wouldn't solve a thing. She was no closer to having a clue than she was weeks ago; she was more confused than anything. Ana rubbed her forehead and chided herself for being so dumb.

With a dark black marker, Ana crossed off Kyle's name. He was killed long before Patricia was taken. Ana's pen hovered over Aimee's name. The timeline was nebulous. Aimee died after Patricia was taken but she was missing for nearly two days before her body was found. Maybe someone saw Aimee take Patricia; maybe they killed her in retribution.

That line of thinking didn't ring true. If they saw Aimee take Patricia, why didn't they stop her in the moment? Why didn't they call the police? And could Aimee lure a person into their car and kill her?

Next to Aimee's name, Ana put a big question mark. Even in death, she still didn't trust Aimee. She could have been the mastermind behind all of this, she hated Ana enough to sabotage her, but did she hate her enough to kill again? Ana wasn't sure.

That left James, Dr. Daniels, and Bex. And the door knocker and the letter writer. Ana scratched out the last two. She wrote 'Caleb' instead. He was the person that had been harassing her. He could be behind this just as easily as the rest of them. Her brother.

Ana thought about each of them. James had motive and was as well-versed in true crime as anyone. Ana remembered something. James said in passing that he'd been in San Francisco when the bridge murder happened. He very well could have been in Denver to take Patricia. If anyone could get away with the perfect crime, it would be him. Worry grew in her belly.

Her pen landed on Dr. Daniels. Ana nearly crossed his name off the list but then a thought struck her - what if he was setting her up to force her back into Hillside? Was he that obsessed with her, with her mental illnesses and her burgeoning fame? Ana wasn't sure. She left his name just in case.

It hurt to look at Bex's name at the bottom of the list. Bex was the only constant in Ana's life. They weathered so many storms together. Ana just didn't want to believe that her sister could be responsible for something like this. Bex as the killer was incongruent with the depressed Bex who sat on the couch cycling through an old crime show.

Ana thought back over the last few weeks. Bex was the most unstable Ana had ever seen her; she was under a lot of pressure at work and from Aimee. Maybe Bex took a gamble and orchestrated this whole thing in hopes that the podcast would finally blow up and they'd finally have the success Bex yearned for. Maybe Bex decided that to reach their huge goals, they must take equally huge risks.

That didn't explain Aimee though. Did Bex kill her because she found something out? Bex had been drunk, she'd already admitted to that. Maybe in the heat of the moment, Bex snapped. But if that was the case, why hadn't they found any forensics to support that? Why hadn't they arrested her by now?

And who was the masked person who walked into Aimee's building? Ana had seen the CTV footage dozens of times. The height and build were right for Bex, but the angle was bad, and the quality was poor. And then Bex came on the screen later wearing something else. Did she change? What about her alibi?

Ana circled Bex's name. Something in her gut just wouldn't let it go. Bex wasn't herself. It was clear that she snapped somehow. Maybe this was what snapping looked like for Bex? Ana couldn't clear her sister's name yet.

Then there was Caleb. It was too weird that the killings started not long after Bex sent in her DNA. He sent that awful letter and knew where they lived. Maybe she ought to look at him more seriously.

In the corner of the page, Ana doodled a peace sign. Their whole life, they never knew peace, but she craved it so badly now. She just wanted to be a normal author with a normal life. She wanted to write with abandon and not fear who would take her words and twist them into reality.

Ana needed a distraction. She grabbed her computer and logged into her Amazon account. She blinked in shock, shook her head then looked again. In just the last week alone, she'd broken a six-figure sales record. The number at the top of the page was a beacon of hope. The report said she earned $102,381.23 in sales in just the last few weeks.

Ana refreshed the screen just to make sure there wasn't a glitch.

In just time since it took the page to reload, the number went up by another $200 some dollars. Ana could not believe it. She leaned in close to the screen to make sure her eyes weren't playing tricks. It was real.

Tears rolled down her face. Proof of her negligence stared back at her from the screen. Her guilt multiplied. Ana finally had something to her name, but it was nothing more than blood money. She'd reached the level of sales she'd dreamed of, but it came at an unforgivable cost.

On one hand, she had the money she needed to get away from her sister and forget about all of this. On the other, the only reason she had found success was through the death of so many innocent people. People would still be alive today if she never wrote those words.

Her emotions volleyed between absolute guilt and pops of happiness. She couldn't center herself. Ana couldn't make sense of how both could be true at the same time. The money was a first step. She couldn't outrun her past, her guilt, but she was facing the right direction. She could make amends later, give money to the victims and those who were neediest.

But for now, the only thing Ana felt like she could do was to keep moving forward. She needed to get to the bottom of this and figure out who the killer was. And she needed to do it fast. But first, she needed to get away from it all. She needed space and time to think. She needed to get away from her sister.

Ana opened a rental search page on the web. She keyed in her area and found several studios in downtown Denver that she could afford now that so many people had bought her books. Ana applied for several places. Soon she'd have the freedom she desperately needed.

Ana opened a blank page on her laptop. Inspiration hit her like a jolt of electricity - something only creatives know. She had a burning urge to get it all out before the feeling zapped someone else.

The only thing she could now do was pen another story. Writing was her only weapon, a killer was watching her, and she needed to pen words sharper than a knife. It was time to write her own ending.

SEVENTY

Sororicide

A Short Story by Ana Adams

They shared a womb. It set them up for a lifetime of competing for space, competing for oxygen, and of course, competing for survival. They vacated the womb but this rivalry between the sisters never stopped. It intensified.

With a lifetime of ugliness and parents who were no parents at all, it was fate that their sisterhood would end in sororicide, the killing of a sister. The only question was who would do it first.

Cora was the sweeter sister, but she possessed a hidden mean streak a mile deep. She would cut Clara down any chance she got; she was quick and clever about it. Clara never saw her sister's wit coming. Clara was mean, nothing hidden about it. She came out of the womb fighting for air and she never stopped. Look at her wrong and it will be over for you.

The fight always sizzled just below the surface, every few days threatening to break the crust and violently explode. The sisters kept the volcano at bay for years, that was until prom night. Cora had a date, Clara did not.

"Stay home and watch Mom," Cora ordered.

"Why?"

"Because she has the mentality of a three-year-old, thanks to your dad."

"Your dad too, bitch," Clara spit back.

"I'll be back later and then I'll take a shift."

"I'm going to go out," Clara said. She pulled on her huge army combat boots.

"Dude. You literally can't. I'm going to senior prom. You're not. And it's your turn anyway. I do it all the time."

"Call CPS, then," Clara said. She pulled her backpack purse off the back of her desk chair in their shared room. They both used the desk as storage; neither one of them bothered to study at it.

Cora pulled on her dress and looked at herself in the mirror. The dress was $20 at the local thrift store; she thought she still looked damn good.

"Alright, I'm out."

"Clara, stop. You know mom can't be home alone. Please just stay with her for a couple of hours. Watch the baby."

"I told you. I have plans!" Clara shouted.

"So do I!"

"Then leave Mom. She'll be fine." Clara stomped out the door. "She can watch Christopher for once."

It was a tough decision to make. She could cancel on her date and miss prom to keep their mom and brother safe or she could pull a Clara and take off. For once, she chose herself. She finished her makeup and met her date at the park where all the other, engaged parents were there to take pictures.

She danced the night away just like she loved to do when she was a kid. Not the responsible daughter who always cared for their mom after their dad beat her stupid. Cora didn't even think about her mom or sister once as she swayed to the music.

The dance quieted and the prom court was soon to be announced when a group of firemen walked in the door. The room stilled, and everyone turned to look. One of them cleared his throat and said, "We're looking for Cora Williams." Her face turned bright red, and she felt naked in front of the crowd as everyone looked at her.

Cora knew something happened to their mom. She walked forward and they took her outside.

"Sweetie, your mom had an accident. The house."

"What happened?" she cried. Tears were already running down her face.

"We think maybe she was cooking. There was a fire. She didn't get out in time."

"My brother?! Where is he?" Cora screamed; her words were swallowed up by the music.

Cora sunk to the ground; her pretty pink sparkly dress flowed around her. The tears came. The waves of grief washed over her, first fueled by sadness at the life she didn't get to live. Sadness quickly turned to anger. Anger for her sister, anger at their mom for being the way she was, and anger at their dad who put them all in this situation and then danced right on out of their lives. The anger turned to rage.

Through the thick of night, with the beat of prom reverberating in the distance, Cora walked home. The rage built with every step of the way.

When she made it to their dilapidated house in the center of town, the first thing Cora saw was her sister's smug face. The bitch dared to wear a half smile on her face. Their baby brother was nowhere to be seen.

The heels went flying and she grabbed her dress and hiked it up. Cora ran full throttle at her sister. She threw herself into her wombmate's body and they both flew to the ground. Clara's head hit with a thud.

People rushed toward them and pulled Cora off her sister's lifeless body. Taking her sister down unlocked something in her brain. Clara deserved the humiliation of it; she'd killed their mom. And Cora was going to make sure she paid.

Cora waited until the cops were gone. Until the sisters were moved to some shit group home. She waited until her sister was fully asleep. Cora unhooked the bra strap carefully without turning on the light. She fingered the smooth elastic fabric in her fingers.

It was time. Their mom deserved better. Clara had to pay.

Cora slipped out of bed and padded to her sister's where she slept, snoring softly. Cora snuck into bed next to her warm body, just like they did as kids. She slipped the bra strap around her neck and pulled and twisted.

Clara woke and put up a fight. It was too late. The oxygen, too far gone. It was easier than Cora thought it would be.

Their twin bond was finally severed. It only took sororicide.

SEVENTY-ONE

"Hello and welcome to *The Serial Syndicate*," Ana said into the mic. Her voice wasn't the strong, announcer-like tone she usually pulled out for the start of the show. Her heart raced and her hands stuck to her bare legs with sweat. It didn't feel right to record considering Patricia's death - or any of the rest of them.

That letter she'd gotten in the mail might as well have been sent a lifetime ago, but it was still fresh in her mind. With every new episode, Ana wondered if her vigilante brother would come and make good on his threat. Maybe Caleb was right. Maybe she and Bex were profiteering off the pain.

It was clear Bex had zero hesitation or regret. The prospect of their big break with this episode woke her up. She'd showered and applied makeup for the first time since Aimee's death. Her eyes were bright, and she couldn't stop tapping her foot.

Bex raised her glass of wine to Ana. Ana could feel Bex urging her to rise to her level. This episode needed energy if they were going to get that bonus from Zane. It was obvious that's all Bex wanted.

"I'm Bex, your loyal co-host, and this is my sister," she chirped into the mic.

"Ana. I'm Ana, your other co-host," Ana said. Her mouth was too dry; she pushed her tongue up to the top of her mouth and tried to squeeze out whatever saliva she could to wet her throat.

"We host a weekly true crime podcast where we discuss cold cases and shine a light on the victims who have been forgotten," Bex said.

"Only, we've been a little distracted lately," Ana added. "You've probably heard by now, there's a serial killer out there copying my books. The media has dubbed the case, The Novel Killings."

"Ohhh you've upgraded them to serial killer, eh?" Bex said with a laugh. "Three does make a pattern."

Ana's face went hot. She didn't know what part of that Bex found funny. "Well, yeah. The definition of a serial killer is someone who commits a series of murders with a predictable behavior pattern. If copying my work THREE times doesn't classify this as a serial killer, I don't know what does.

"Serial killer it is," Bex said. She took a loud gulp of her wine. "And if he's a serial killer inspired by your work, all I can say is 'slay, sis.'"

Ana looked up at her sister. That was such an unhinged thing to say, and viewers would certainly pick up on it. If this was going to air, Ana needed to get the show back on track.

"Anyways," Ana said forcefully. "If you're paying attention to this case, you know there's been another murder."

Bex smacked her lips after another long sip. "Denver is just full of bodies!" Bex said, with an inappropriate laugh. "Like this Shiraz," she slurped loudly, "blood-red, full-bodied and giving... death."

Ana bit her lip, working to steady her voice. Bex wasn't going to be any help, she sounded loopy and more than a little drunk. It was up to Ana. She didn't want to cry on the recording; stopping it was almost impossible. After waiting to see if Bex would follow up Ana continued: "I didn't plan to publish anything new publicly until the FBI captured The Novel Killings suspect. However, I couldn't sit back and do nothing any longer. In a moment of absolute stupidity, I posted a story on my old Wattpad account about a woman who got kidnapped and killed in Denver."

Ana fought a rush of guilt. Her plan had yielded nothing. She was no closer to the truth and Patricia died because of her. She couldn't wallow in that mistake. She had to move forward.

"And, worse yet -" Bex cried. She sounded a little drunk. "My girlfriend Aimee was also killed and so was another person named Kyle who was in residential treatment with Ana. He was Ana's friend. The body count is exploding, and the police aren't even doing their job. Who killed all these innocent people? Why are people close to us dying?"

Ana cringed. She didn't want to take the focus off Patricia in this episode. She made a cutting gesture on her throat, telling Bex to pause the show. Bex clicked a few buttons on her computer.

"What?"

"I don't know if we want to go there," Ana said.

"Why the fuck not?" Bex said. She stood and swayed a little. She walked over to Ana's side of the table and got right in her face. "We have to. Their stories deserve to be heard, too."

Ana considered fighting her sister on this. One look at Bex's balled fists made up Ana's mind. Bex was too fragile, too drunk and this whole thing was already too explosive. It wasn't worth the fight.

"Remember the bonus money coming our way?" Bex yelled much louder than necessary. "This is what they want - a show people will listen to. And the people want it all, every gory detail."

Bex sat down and counted down with her fingers. She restarted the recording.

The episode was quite possibly the most choppy and ill-prepared thing they ever produced. In Ana's opinion, they didn't spend nearly enough time on Patricia or any of the rest of the cases. They talked about Aimee at length, and Kyle filled up the rest.

Bex speculated wildly about scenarios that could have led to Aimee's death; Bex was suspicious of all and had no better idea of who killed her girlfriend than the police did. Ana asked questions where she could and interjected to keep them on track. James would have to work some serious magic on this episode to keep their advertisers happy.

315

After they cleaned up, Ana retreated to her room. She dialed James's number. It was late in Colorado and even later in Chicago.

"Hey, Ana-" he said after the second ring. His voice was strained, and she knew that whatever they had was long gone.

"Sorry for the late-night call, if you're not working, I can send you an email."

"No, no. You're good. I'm still up, I'm finishing up my last episode of the day."

"How do you feel about another one?"

He laughed. "Like tonight?"

"Or tomorrow. But sooner rather than later would be good. Happy to pay your rush fee. Bex and I just recorded a new show but it's going to need some finessing on your part."

"Yeah?" he asked. A new note entered his voice. Nervousness.

"Yeah, Bex is upset about everything, she blabbered a bit. I think you'll need to cut some. But I want to keep the parts focusing on Patricia Almont."

"I cannot believe that happened," James said.

"I know."

"How are you not freaking out right now?" James asked. It was a valid question.

"Oh, I am. I just don't know what to do. I am running in circles trying to figure out how this happened again. Not sure if releasing another episode is the right call but I have to do something."

"Like what?" he asked.

"I don't know - publish this episode. Hope the killer makes a mistake, help find this evil man?"

"I hope it works," he said. Ana could hear him shuffling something in the background. Being on the phone with him hurt. She couldn't square the man she'd fallen for with the man she feared. Her stomach rolled.

316

"How are things on your end?" Ana asked, wanting to keep him on the line.

"Oh fine. Thanks to you and your sister, everyone wants to work with me now.

"Really?"

"Yeah, it's been great. Business has never been better. Maybe podcasts should turn real life more often," he said. Ana knew they should have gotten a new podcast engineer weeks ago.

SEVENTY-TWO

The podcast dashboard almost didn't look real to Bex. Their latest episode had more downloads than all their others combined. So many that it had shot up to the top of the true crime category. A small smile played at the corner of Bex's lips. She zoomed in and stared at the numbers.

Bex leaned her head back and savored the moment. This had come at a big cost, but they had something to show for it. Bex guessed that when the new episode was posted, the numbers would triple. She couldn't wait. They were doing it.

Her phone vibrated from the side pocket of her yoga pants. Bex let it go; she assumed it was more Google alert notifications or maybe even more sponsors with new ad offers. She'd get to them soon. For now, she just wanted to center herself and let the good news soak in.

The phone went off again. And then a couple more times in quick succession. Someone wanted to get a hold of her. Bex thought of her sister. She'd left early in the day to work at a coffee shop. Visions of Ana hurt or worse, murdered, shot through her mind like a sharp shock.

Bex yanked her phone out of her pocket, hoping maybe it was the police. Instead, she found a heap of messages from an unknown number. Bex didn't recognize it.

She sucked in a breath and unlocked her phone, opening the messages. Bex only had to read one message to know who they'd come from.

Another show, huh? I wondered how long it would take you. The first message said.

Caleb.

You and Ana are miss popular now. He added. Her heart sped up and it felt like the bottom of her stomach gave way.

You have time for everyone else in the world but not me, I see.

Bex reread the texts over and over. They didn't make sense. If Caleb hated them so much, why did he keep texting her? Bex didn't want to find out.

What do you want from me? Bex finally responded.

I need you to see me. He shot back instantly.

Bex twirled a piece of her hair around her finger and pulled it out of her scalp.

We can arrange a meeting sometime, but I can't go back and change what happened when we were kids. Bex responded. She knew it wasn't the right thing, but she didn't have anything else to give.

Don't force my hand any further, Bex. The words practically jumped off the screen; they felt like a threat.

Just let this all blow over and then we'll figure it out, she said.

It's too late for that. He responded.

A hundred responses filled her mind, none of them were right. She couldn't be who he needed her to be. She didn't have it in her to show up for him the way that she should have all those years ago.

Bex swallowed hard. Caleb just wanted love, but he was looking in the wrong place.

She blocked the number.

SEVENTY-THREE

The email sat in her inbox, drafted and ready. Ana's finger hovered over the trackpad. Sending this final story out might cause another murder, but it could also help finally catch the killer. It was a dangerous plan, but it was the only way she could think of to make this stop.

Ana looked around the Starbucks. Everyone was quiet, going about their daily life. No one knew the pressure she was under. Or the guilt she felt. Their lives looked so easy.

Refocusing on her email, Ana told herself to just get it over with.

She planned to send this new short story - only a couple of pages - to James, Bex, and Dr. Daniels. She'd password-protected the document so only their three email addresses could access the text.

And if a woman ended up dead in bed, strangled, Ana would know that the killer was one of them. Ana could go back to the FBI with proof that they were the only three with access to her words. Narrowing it down would mean that the cops only needed to look for three sets of DNA evidence, three phones to track. One in three - the odds were better than ever.

If no one ended up dead, then Ana would know it was someone else. She could at least begin to trust her inner circle again.

Before she could press send, Ana looked at the clock and realized she was going to be late for her weekly appointment. She slung her quilted satchel over her shoulder and ran out of the coffee shop. Ana raced the clock to Hillside; she arrived just five minutes late. It felt like she had just been to see Dr. Daniels, but more than a week had already passed.

She sat in the waiting room, her chest heaving from rushing. The room was empty, save for another young guy. Ana did a double take, thinking it was Kyle, but the man in the waiting room had no facial piercings. Ana felt the little piranhas of paranoia swimming through her veins, nipping at her nerves. She needed to get it together.

The door opened, releasing a humid wave of cherry-cough drop smell, while Dr. Daniels gave his biggest smile.

"Ana, please," he said and motioned toward the couch. She sat as directed.

"Hi, Ana. Nice to see you."

"Hello," she said, curtly. She wanted to get back to her plan; she didn't want to be stuck in his office.

"I'd like to do something a little different today if that's okay with you?" he asked, scratching his beard. She nodded. What choice did she have?

"With all the intense focus on the killer right now, I can't imagine a whole session about it would help. I think it might trigger you. I'd like to go back in time if that's okay?"

She nodded again. Ana felt her body relax. She could do that.

"So, tell me about your childhood. You've never said much."

"Well, where do I start?" Ana asked; her whole body tensed.

"Wherever you want."

"Well, it was fucked up if that's what you're wondering. My parents had my sister and then me. My real dad was a piece of work who beat my mom all the time. He hit us too whenever he felt like it. He was cruel and petty, emotionally abusive. A real loose cannon who could go from calm to screaming from just a gesture."

Dr. Daniels made quick, scratchy notes on his pad.

"When we were just kids, he found out that Mom was trying to leave and beat her bloody. A neighbor heard and called the cops. Mom went to the hospital and all that, but he gave her a terrible traumatic

321

brain injury. After that, she was just... slow. Thick, you know? Always afraid and skittish and forgetful, always ready to break. Never the same. Dad went to jail but only for a few years; we never saw him again. Good riddance."

His hand raced across the notebook to keep up with Ana's story.

"So, my sister and I grew up fast, she got a job, and I started taking care of my mom. It was dangerous to leave her alone because we never knew what she would do. Sometimes she'd be fine, sometimes she'd forget to do things like turn off the iron, sometimes she'd piss her sweatpants and spend the whole day wearing them in a cloud of stink. We just never knew. We tried to split our time, so someone was with her. When we went to school, my mom would go to the neighbor's; I think that lady felt bad for us.

"After a couple of years, my mom got a boyfriend. She wasn't out there looking though. He found us. It was no secret in our little town how messed up our situation was, how weak Mom was, and how vulnerable we were. I think Henry wanted an excuse to get close to a couple of traumatized little girls without any guardian."

Dr. Daniels nodded again; his face betrayed nothing.

"It didn't take long before Henry moved in. At first, it was kind of nice because he helped with the bills, and he did a little bit to take care of our mom. For like three whole weeks, I was a kid again."

Ana rubbed her eyes with her palm. She couldn't believe she was telling him all of this.

"Not even a month later, he started sexually abusing me. It was awful; I can't go into details. Probably ever. But whatever you're imagining, it was probably worse. He was sick. The worst of it was that my mom couldn't stand up for me. I'd tell her and she'd just... go blank. Bex was always working. I was just a kid and I had no one. I didn't tell Bex for a long time because I didn't want her to have more to worry

322

about." Ana's throat constricted. These words had never left her mouth before. She fought the urge to turn around and see if Henry was in the room with her.

Daniels' face was open, and he gave a small smile to encourage Ana to continue.

Ana couldn't. "That's about all I can get into now. I don't want to dredge this all up."

"Do you think remembering that abuse is why *you* blackout sometimes? Is your mind trying to protect you?" he prodded.

"No! I don't know why that happens. My body just does that stupid thing."

"It's not stupid. It's what we call 'dissociative amnesia,' your brain just shuts down as a defense mechanism. I have noticed that it happens most often when you're under stress. The reaction might have developed from your childhood, it might have saved you from even more trauma. It's not stupid, it's smart."

"It's not a big deal, I don't know why you always bring it up!" she said. She hated that he kept pushing her.

"Okay, I see you're still not ready to talk about it. So how did you get out of your childhood home, then?"

"Well, I didn't. Not for a long time. My mom and Henry had a baby together. And everything changed again. Baby Caleb was so cute but something about having another mouth to feed sort of set Henry off. He got sloppier. Couldn't hide the violence like he used to, he got meaner and worse to live with.

"Not long after Caleb was born, there was a fire in our house late at night. Henry was at work and Bex was at prom. I got Caleb out, but I couldn't get back in the house to get my mom. She died of smoke inhalation. It was my fault."

"Oh, Ana. That is so much for such a small kid. Don't blame yourself; I'm sorry."

Ana blushed; she didn't want his pity.

"Anyways. Things got worse from there. We went to live in an apartment with Henry and the baby. With my mom out of the picture... Henry didn't even need to hide it anymore."

"And what happened?"

"A few months later he died in his sleep. The police said it was an accidental overdose of his blood pressure medication. He must have gotten drunk and kept forgetting he'd taken his pills. Kind of suspicious but he was a known problem in town, so I think they were glad he was gone and didn't look all that close."

"Do you think it was an accident?" He asked.

"No," Ana answered. "I don't. Some people just aren't that lucky."

"If it wasn't an accident, who could have done something like that?" he asked.

"I don't know. Probably someone else he pissed off along the way."

Dr. Daniels' eyes narrowed in confusion.

"And you and your siblings?"

"Bex and I went into the foster system. We bounced around houses; you know the drill. Caleb got adopted because he was a cute toddler by then. I haven't seen him since; I don't even know how I would find him."

A part of Ana winced at the lie. Bex had found him, and he was as awful as the rest of them. Ana didn't bother telling Dr. Daniels that part. It was too complex - too scary to look at in the light of his office.

"So, the story continues," Ana finally said.

"And what about your medication?" he asked. She tensed; Ana knew this was coming but she didn't want to have the conversation.

"I don't need it."

He scratched his forehead.

"As I've said, I'm not comfortable with this."

"I'm feeling good. I'm coming off it fine."

"With all this around your books and the murders, I don't think we should make any drastic changes," he started; she interrupted him.

"I'm telling you, I'm fine. My mind is clearer and I'm in control. I am still stepping down my medication dose so it's not like I stopped cold turkey!"

"I know, but I still think you need it. Are you having more periods where you lose time?"

"No, I'm fine!"

"I'm also going to offer again - you can always come back here. If the world gets too loud or you're too tired of the fight. Inpatient might be a haven given everything."

"No fucking way!" she spat. "I'm done here!"

When she got home, she fired off the email with a link to her latest story. It was the only thing Ana felt like she could control.

SEVENTY-FOUR

Bex steeled herself, throwing back her shoulders and checking her makeup and hair in the reflection of a window. Walking back into work felt like quite possibly the hardest thing she had ever done. Reminding herself it wasn't going to get easier; she flung open the door. All eyes turned and looked at her, a couple of conversations stopped dead. Everyone was sitting together.

She fought the urge to turn and run; to spend another day on the couch with Agent Penelope Garcia and the rest of the *Criminal Minds* team. But Bex didn't give up. She wasn't a quitter.

Bex offered the room a small smile and a wave as she stepped down into their office space. She got a few waves mixed with sad and sympathetic smiles. There were some shocked expressions, one of the junior members of her sales team stared at her frankly with an open mouth and goggled eyes. Her cheeks burned; she hiked her purse up on her shoulder and kept walking. Bex fought back the tears; Aimee should be sitting at the junior desk near the corner. She should have headphones on, head slightly bopping to whatever Taylor Swift song blared in her ears. Now instead of hearing "Blank Space" there was one where she should be...

It was weird to walk into a place defined by absence. Everything was where it was supposed to be, except Aimee. She'd never be anywhere, anymore, except lying in the cold hard ground. Bex blinked rapidly and tipped her head back just slightly to prevent gravity from wreaking havoc on her face. She just needed to make it through the minute first. Then the hour. Then the day.

Bex rounded the corner and found her desk covered with two vases. The sight of them offered some comfort. Bex never received flowers at work, let alone two. She set her bag down and grabbed the cards. A vase of daisies and yellow blooms was from her boss.

The other set of white roses was from her team. The card simply said, "Sorry for your loss." Bex figured that meant her colleagues all knew about her and Aimee. She cringed a little and then let it go. Aimee was dead, who cared who knew now?

Bex attacked her inbox first. The safety email from the head of HR struck her hardest. Sarah danced around the fact that someone on their team was dead. She offered safety tips and encouraged people to report anything suspicious to the police. The email felt sterile and flat like it was written by an AI robot.

She sighed. In Sarah's defense, there wasn't a standard operating procedure in the handbook for comforting an employee after finding their co-worker/lover's murdered body.

Bex deleted the email and moved on to the hundreds of others she'd missed. Her hands shook and her mind could not settle into one task. She missed Aimee so much. She kept reflexively looking for her name on Slack to send her a private kissing face or to ask about the latest office gossip. Every time someone passed her desk Bex looked up, ready to wink at Aimee as she walked by.

It was too quiet in the office. The somber mood only reminded Bex of everything she'd lost.

Bex's Outlook dinged. It was a meeting request from Sarah. Included in the invite was her boss. The meeting was set to start in the one private conference room in just fifteen minutes. Her stomach dropped even further.

The meeting wasn't a good sign.

SEVENTY-FIVE

Lightning arced through Ana's brain, an electric throbbing that seemed to shake her bones. Ana recognized that this as 'brain zaps,' one of the side-effects of stopping her medication. For a moment, she considered taking the dose her body was used to, but the pull of freedom from the orange bottles was enough to keep her rooted in place. Her mind, her's alone. The symptoms would subside soon enough. She fought through another jolt.

Ana was fighting for her life. The only way she would survive this was to be totally in control of her thoughts and actions. She didn't need the medication clouding her creativity or her judgement. She no longer wanted to be wrapped in the warm comfort of an SSRI. She needed to be at her best, her sharpest. Dulling the pain wasn't an option. To solve this case, it would take full capacity. The withdrawals were hard, but the alternative was unacceptable. Lives were on the line. She could take a zap here and there.

Ana tried to write she could not make the words materialize in the midst of her withdrawal. Once the medication was out of her system, the words would flow like Rocky Mountain waters. Her mind would run free soon.

She switched to the latest Sally Hepworth book, looking for inspiration. Ana turned the pages, but she comprehended only about a third of what she read. She switched yet again to the candy-crushing game on her phone, her brain craving the little boost of serotonin it got with each explosion.

A weight hung over Ana. She hadn't posted much on social media lately. She just didn't know what to say and she was terrified that the wrong thing would cancel her in the land of public opinion. Or worse, make the FBI come calling again.

The longer she went without posting, the more guilt she felt. Her follower count had exploded in recent weeks - she was now up to nearly 25,000 fans on Instagram. The number attached to her name didn't matter, though. With not a single post shared in recent weeks, her engagement stats were in the gutter. There simply wasn't anything to engage with.

She opened Instagram and was hit with a slew of new notifications. The guilt she felt over not managing her following intensified.

The lighting was bad in her bedroom, but Ana fired the camera up and pulled her book into the photo. *Just laying low* she captioned the story and posted it so her followers could see that she was still alive. It was the truth after all.

She went back to the main feed and posted a picture of her, and Bex with The Serial Syndicate's logo screened over the image. She captioned the post, *New Episode*, with all the details. She should have created a prettier picture or included a clip from the show, but the logo was as good as she could do. It didn't matter anyway; people would listen either way.

Ana watched the likes rack up on the post, seconds after it went live. Her DMs ballooned to the point that Instagram stopped counting. She took a quick look through and found most were begging for an update on The Novel Killings. She didn't have anything to give them; she didn't bother opening a single one of them.

A new message popped up, filling Ana with dread. @anasnumberonefan was back. Ana clicked.

5:21 PM - @anasnumberonefan
> *Ha! A new episode? You two have learned nothing. I'm here for it though. Ana can do no wrong.*

Ana reread the message. She didn't even know what it meant but it sent her stomach rolling.

Her phone buzzed; she half assumed it was her number one fan again but then she saw it was a text message from James.

Hey, Ana. Urgent. Can I call? He sent.

Ana's heart sped up and she wondered what he needed. The latest podcast episode was already done. What else could it be?

Ana bit at her lip while she waited for the call to connect.

"Ana!" James said, in a stressed and tight voice.

"James. What's up? How's the show?"

"Oh, that's fine. Downloads are insane right now. It's going to crack the top one hundred of the day here soon," he said. Ana blinked. It was a dream come true. She shook her head; she couldn't trust James and she couldn't lose sight of what her real goal was.

"That's great news," she said at last.

"Yeah. I think people like it so far."

"Thanks for getting it done so fast."

"Yeah, sure. I saw your email with your latest story - interesting topic. I haven't seen anything like that in a while. I can't wait to dive in and give you some feedback."

She smiled. Maybe her plan would work after all.

"Thanks. So, what's up then?"

His pause filled the line.

"Well, this is going to sound crazy but hear me out, okay?"

"Okay..."

"I think I found something," he said. Ana could hear his excited breathing on the other end; he sounded like he'd just run a marathon.

"Tell me," she said.

"I was looking for everything I could find on Patricia Almont. I found some open-source footage from around when she was taken."

Muscles in Ana's jaw tightened. She had a basic understanding of open-source intelligence from research for a book she started writing a while ago. There were groups of dedicated computer people all over the internet who would compile and analyze footage from public sources, like uploaded social media posts or unsecured webcams. These obsessives spent hours a day, every day, combing through all of it, looking for everything from missing people to war crimes to illegal logging.

The tradecraft exploded in recent years as more and more footage ended up online and people joined the existing communities. It was becoming a viable way to track and locate people or expose things that people didn't want out in the open.

"Did you find something?"

"I think so. There was a red car parked near Patricia's neighborhood for hours."

"A red car? And?"

"A red Audi. The same make and model as Bex's car."

"How do you know what kind of car she drives?" Ana asked. It struck her how much he knew about their lives.

"She's posted it all over social media. She poses in front of it at least once a month. It wasn't that hard to make the connection."

Ana's mind refused to work. She couldn't process the information.

"I can't see the license plates from the angle I have but I'm working on it."

"James. We have to call the police. We need to tell them."

"I am going to, I promise. But I need more time. Open-source intelligence isn't exactly something the cops take seriously, and I don't have the plates yet. None of this stuff is actually valid to them without a warrant or chain of custody. Police don't trust everyday citizens to use technology this way, there's too much uncertainty and cops hate looking dumb. I've seen them fumble so many cases because they don't believe internet sleuths. I need to get evidence that they can't refute."

SEVENTY-SIX

Bex opened the door to the conference room. The head of HR, Sarah, sat on one side of the table, and her boss, Theo on the other. A man in a tailored suit sat next to them; Bex didn't recognize him.

"Thanks for coming," Sarah said as if Bex had any choice.

"Sure," Bex said as she sat down next to Theo. The long conference table was far too big for just the four of them. The room felt cavernous and quiet compared to the usual hustle of their meetings.

"Well, let's just go ahead and get started," Sarah said.

"Bex, this is Dan. He is our lawyer. Due to everything going on, we asked him here just in case there are any questions," Theo added. Bex swallowed a big lump in her throat. This was all so much more serious than she thought.

Dan waved but did not stand to shake her hand; she didn't either. Theo cleared his throat - his face was waxy, almost sick.

"Well, there's no easy way to say this Bex, but we're concerned about you," Theo said, his eyes searching hers.

"Thank you," she said, still not sure where this meeting was going. "I appreciate that."

"And we're concerned about the safety of everyone at the company," Sarah added.

Dan cleared his throat.

"The authorities have not confirmed it, but we fear that Aimee's death could be related to The Novel Killings. We have a responsibility to make sure that we take proper precautions to keep *all* our employees safe," Theo said.

Implication hung in the room. Bex felt a familiar wave of anger rise in her belly and land on her burning cheeks. None of this was her fault.

333

"I understand," she said instead, doing her best to keep a level head.

"And beyond that, our clients are starting to get a little nervous," Theo marched ahead. "I've had to have a couple of conversations with different accounts this week. People are talking. And the publicity hasn't done our firm any favors either. Unsolved murders and enterprise cloud marketing don't go together all that well."

Bex wasn't sure what they wanted her to do. She couldn't pick who her sister was. She couldn't control that a killer decided to copy her sister's books. She didn't wish Aimee dead.

"As far as your team goes," Sarah said, lacing her fingers together in front of her, "This is all hitting a little too close to the office. People are scared to come in."

Bex leaned back in her chair. She wasn't ready to give up. Work had once been her life. She was so good at it, and she thought they liked it. But now, at the first sign of problems outside of work, they were ready to throw her under the bus.

"Bex, you've been here a long time and it's no secret that you've contributed a lot to this organization," Theo said. "We don't want this to get in the way of the work we do here. We must balance everyone's needs. We need to let things calm down for a while. Honestly, we're concerned about you. You've got plenty of vacation days and we do have a corporate bereavement policy. We think it would be best for everyone if you take a break from work. We can reassess soon."

"You can't do this!" Bex said, "Punish me for finding my girlfriend's murdered body? What about my contract - you don't have cause!"

"You're not being fired, Bex. You just need to take some space," Theo said, sounding aggrieved. "And as for your contract, we're in

Colorado. At-will employment, remember? The company can do what we have to protect our stakeholders and the greater good."

Bex took a moment, controlling her impulse to yell and scream and accuse them of being unfair. "Okay, I understand," Bex said at last, in a small voice that rang defeated in her ears. It was all she could say. Theo clapped his hands together as if everything had been solved.

"Glad we're all on the same page," Sarah said; she tidied up her notebook and pushed her pen through the metal rings.

"Thanks," Theo said. He stood. The lawyer followed suit. Sarah went soon after, giving her a tight, sad smile on the way out.

Bex felt glued to the chair, staggered by the overwhelming sense of loss. She felt herself at a crossroads. Her job - the career she'd dedicated her life to - was on the line. Ana was changing and growing, she had new opportunities, ones that might not involve her. Bex could feel her pulling away.

And Aimee was gone.

Bex was alone. She wanted to cry. She felt like a child again: all alone.

She looked around the room and felt a sense of purpose take hold. In the heart of her despair, she found a familiar strength. This wasn't the first time she'd felt this way. Bex had crawled out of hell. She'd lived through the kind of abuse and loss that broke most people. She'd been given nothing, no resources or advantages, nothing but a vast reservoir of trauma and a basket case for a sibling, but, through hard work and determination, she had still built a fabulous life for them both. Out of nothing but herself.

She was Bexley fucking Adams. She wouldn't give up. With all her strength, Bex was going to hold on to what she had left.

SEVENTY-SEVEN

The paper was worn, the words began to smear. Ana knew what she had to do but the pen felt foreign in her hand. Her mind raced and jumped, zapping her whole body and leaving her twitchy. Ana's body was cold, but also very hot. She couldn't tell. Nothing was right.

Ana grabbed the pen and scratched James's name out. He couldn't be behind The Novel Killings. Ana saw the proof. When Patricia was killed, there was a red Audi TT just like Bex's parked near where she went missing. There weren't many of those distinctive little ice-skate-shaped cars in Colorado. It couldn't be a coincidence.

More than that, James had security footage of a red Audi TT passing through the E470 toll cameras on the way to Three Sisters Park. How long would it be until the cops pinged Bex's phone in that area?

Ana looked at her list. She had put so much stock in Aimee. Hell, in James. And even Caleb for a time. But Bex? No. Never her, not really.

With this proof, Ana could see it. It was hard not to. Bex had an intense ambition. Her drive never let Bex be satisfied; she was always looking for the next rung of the ladder. And there was no denying that being the co-host of one of the most popular podcasts in the country was a mighty big step up.

The walls felt like they were falling in on her. Ana struggled to catch her breath; Bex would be home from work any minute. Ana could not stay there. She could not face her sister, not under these circumstances.

She needed space and she needed to think. Fast. Bex already had Ana's latest story in her inbox. It was a race against the clock to get the police to arrest Bex before she used Ana's plot to kill some poor stranger again. Or even to kill her, the story was about sororicide after all.

Ana wished she could claw the words back; she wanted to delete the scene. She wished she never wrote about The Whistler. Ana sent the story thinking it would help her catch the killer, but now she had her answer. Ana couldn't be responsible for writing another deadly plot.

The guilt was nearly enough to knock her to the ground. Ana wasn't the killer, but it was her idea. If Bex killed again, Ana shared a portion of the blame, and Ana didn't want to be responsible for another death.

From the closet, Ana yanked down a green duffle bag. She threw in a handful of clothes and toiletries. She grabbed her book, iPad, and laptop. The only thing shakier than her mind was her hands; the chaos of the bag was akin to the chaos of her mind.

Ana looked around her room. Her eyes landed on a framed picture of her and Bex; they both held glasses of champagne, sisters celebrating the release of Ana's first book. They both looked so happy, things were so uncomplicated.

Her sister was beautiful, she had a glow in her eyes that made you want to drink her all in. Ana looked at the picture closer. She thought she might have seen something more behind the twinkle of her eyes. Was it greed? Had Bex known back then that Ana's success would be her own? Did Bex plan for the books and the podcast to explode?

Bex always got what she wanted. This was no different. The podcast and Ana's books were bigger than she ever thought possible. Ana was a bestselling author. They just got their first advertiser bonus with the podcast. Bex had turned Ana's words into success, into wealth.

It was poetic really. Since they were kids, Bex worked like a dog to support their family. There was nothing that motivated Bex more than a paycheck - the financial stability that they had never once known. Ana should have seen this coming. Bex turned Ana into a paycheck.

Ana put the frame back down and looked around to see if there was anything else she should take. A wave of sadness washed over her. This should have been her space to freely write. Instead, it was where the deadliest plot came to life.

She shut the door; it was time to go to the FBI.

SEVENTY-EIGHT

Ana pressed the pedal as far into the floorboard as it would go. She ran red lights and merged in and out of traffic like a drunk driver after a night at Red Rocks. While she drove, Ana unshared her location with her sister and turned off her phone. She debated throwing the thing out the window.

The big teal windows of the field office glinted in the sun. Three flags flapped in the wind. Ana recognized the American and Colorado flags; she wasn't sure what the third was, but she assumed it was the FBI seal. The building looked like a haven compared to her life.

When she got to the gate, the man sitting inside the booth looked at her with complete distrust; she could see his hand on the gun at his side. He stood and inched closer to the window, not taking his eyes off her.

She hand-cranked the window down and said, "I'm Ana Adams. I was brought here for questioning the other day. Delcore and Fredricks. I need to talk to them. I have information."

The man looked her up and down. He didn't move; he didn't open the gate.

"Please," she said. Her voice nearly broke.

He picked up a radio and turned his head to the side, speaking into it quietly. Over the rumble of her car, she could not hear him. He listened for a response and nodded his head.

"Park on the street, someone will come down," he said. His instructions didn't feel right. She wondered if they didn't let her car inside the fence in case it was rigged.

Ana parked where she was told and waited in the shade of the security box. As promised, Fredricks came out. He walked quickly; he wore a big smile. Her guard went down a little, remembering how he'd been the nice one the other day. She told herself to knock it off; he was still playing the part, he had to be.

He closed the gap between them and waved off the guard. "Ana. Good to see you. I hear you want to talk to me," he said. She knew better than to trust him, but she couldn't stop the feeling of relief that flooded through her. This would all end soon.

"Yes, I need your help," she blurted.

"Okay, come inside with me," he said.

The guard buzzed her through the fence. Inside, she went through the metal detector and her purse went through an airport-style X-ray machine. Once they decided she was clear, he brought her up to a room that was nearly identical to the one they brought her to before. Only this time, she noticed a red dot in the corner of the two-way window. It flashed once; they were recording this.

"What can we do for you, Ana?" Fredricks asked. He was still acting casual, just two friends talking.

"I know who committed The Novel Killings."

He raised an eyebrow. "Oh?" he asked.

Ana blew out a big breath of air. "It's my sister. Bex is The Novel Killer."

He leaned back in the chair and looked her up and down. His face didn't give much away. "Please explain," he said. He kept his tone light.

"Let me start over," Ana was desperate. "I have been trying to figure out who the killer is. I wrote a list, and I've narrowed it down. The only one left is Bex. The opportunity and motive, she has it."

Fredrick's eyes shot together, making his brows dance. "Okay, walk me through your reasoning."

"First, she has motive. We have been poor our whole lives; Bex figured out that our podcast and my books have real potential, they just needed some promotion and exposure."

"Okay."

"And Bex had the opportunity, she travels for work all the time and she was in California at the time of the bridge murder - when Ella was killed."

He rubbed his forehead.

"I know that's not enough. Patricia Almont. Bex murdered her because of my last story. It was about a woman in Denver and I only sent it to three people. Bex was one of them!"

Ana leaned forward on the table. Her words refused to keep speed with her racing mind. She couldn't stop shaking, she couldn't seem to make him see.

"Again, Ana - I'll ask you: why? Why would she do this? You really think her going on a multi-state killing spree was simpler than just hiring a publicist? And, of course, there are honest ways to make money, easier ones. Why would she do any of this?"

Ana was silent for a moment, turning the question over in her mind. A sense of understanding washed over her. "She wanted to get back at me," she said, "I'm the one that killed our mom." Ana didn't know why she hadn't seen it before, but it was the only explanation that made sense.

"What?" he said. He leaned forward, his eyes interrogating her all on their own.

"That sounds terrible. I know. I didn't murder her, but I did leave her alone when we were kids. She had very limited mental capacity and I should have watched her better. I know that now. I didn't want to babysit my mom. Dumb kid stuff. When I was upstairs, there was a fire. Our mom died. It was my fault."

He leaned back and crossed his arms. She could tell that he didn't believe her. Ana felt a desperate urge to make him understand.

341

"You have to believe me. I have evidence. I need you to see this," she said. She grabbed a piece of paper from her purse and pushed the receipt from the store toward them.

"I found this in Bex's desk. She bought bomb-making supplies at the hardware store. Here's the proof. Please just look!" Delcore pulled the receipt closer to him. His face still gave nothing away.

"And these photos. My friend James, our podcast engineer, used open-source intelligence to find these. Bex owns a red car, you know that right. Anyways, her car was parked just on the outskirts of Patricia's neighborhood. And then it was seen driving toward Three Sisters on the toll cameras. Three Sisters is our place. It makes so much sense. That's why Bex took Patricia there."

He picked up the photos and studied them. Fredricks set the photos down and picked up the receipt. He looked at it for a long time. He seemed skeptical but she noticed a line of sweat forming at his hairline.

"And what about whatever DNA evidence was stuck in the bomb box?" Ana said. Her voice was frantic, but she couldn't stop it.

He nodded.

"You have to run the DNA and track her phone. It's all there! You'll see!"

"Huh. I'll be right back," he said, standing. He did not wait for her to answer before leaving the room.

Sitting in that room alone was torture. She paced back and forth. Eight steps each way.

Finally, the door opened behind her, and he came back, along with another besuited man. He was older, his head nearly bald. His face was lined with wrinkles and popped with moles. "Agent Jansen," he said plainly. Ana nodded. She wondered where Delcore was.

They sat side by side opposite her. Fredricks opened a manila folder and extracted a picture. He turned it her way and pushed it toward her.

"Recognize this?"

Ana looked at the printout of a photo. It was a picture of a red leather laptop bag, lying on the ground.

"What's this?" Ana asked, not understanding.

"This was taken by one of the officers assigned to the bridge's security detail just after the woman was pushed into the water. We have reason to believe it was left by the person who drugged and pushed her."

Ana studied the photo. Nothing about it looked familiar.

As she set it on the table, Agent Jansen slid a set of black-and-white surveillance photos across the table toward her. The first was of a smaller person wearing a hoodie, their head was bent, face hidden. The hooded person was behind a woman wearing a dress. They looked to be on a bridge. The woman in the dress wore a look of confusion, her hair was scattered around her face, blowing in the wind. It was hard to see the person behind her, but they were close enough to be together.

Ana studied the next photo. The timestamp was just two minutes later. The woman in the dress was standing precariously on the railing of the bridge. The white fabric of her dress raced away from her body in the wind. The person behind her looked to be lifting her. Maybe holding a gun to her back. She couldn't see their face.

Ana's heart began to race. She understood these stills were taken from the security footage just moments before Ella was pushed.

The final photo called Ana's name. She picked it up and found the timestamp was just one minute later. Three minutes was all it took to end someone's life in one of the most terrifying ways.

The person wearing the hoodie looked over the edge in the last still. Alone. They were holding a bag in one hand and something dark in the other. The bag was the same red leather purse as in the photo they'd just shown Ana.

Photos fell to the table. They felt dangerous in her hands. Evil. She picked up the second photo again. Was it Bex? Was Bex the hooded killer? Ana couldn't tell. The person was built right, but in the dark of the evening and with the protection of the hood, Ana couldn't be sure.

Fredricks handed Ana another photo. This one was in color, and it showed the bag's contents. Lipstick, a pen, notebook. Normal things. Ana's eyes locked onto a photo of the two of them. The little Polaroid must have been in the purse. Understanding coursed through her.

"That's Bex's photo!" Ana cried. "That's us as kids. It's one of the few photos we have from childhood. She keeps it in her purse."

No one else would have a copy of it.

Bex was on the bridge. Bex pushed Ella.

SEVENTY-NINE

Bex felt the eyes of her colleagues on her all the way back to her chair. Her skin grew hot, shame bubbled in her stomach. Bex was supposed to be packing up her stuff to leave, but that felt impossible. She'd given so much of her time - her heart - to this place. How could she just walk out the door? Bex sat in her chair and swiveled her mouse to wake up her computer.

The screen barely switched from black to her ocean screensaver before, "Bexley Adams, front desk," was announced over the loudspeaker. She and everyone in the whole office turned to face the front door. Two men stood in suits. Were they about to escort her out of the building?

Her mouth went dry. She stood and smoothed her skirt; she took another walk of shame up to the front desk. She avoided making eye contact with anyone along the way. "Bexley Adams?" one of them asked as soon as she was within earshot.

She nodded. "Let's step outside," Bex said as soon as she reached the top of the stairs. They pushed the double doors open. She followed.

As soon as she was in the sunshine, Bex took a slow breath and worked to control her emotions. She already felt so close to tears, it wouldn't take much to completely break her.

One of the men said, "Hello, I'm Agent Delcore and this is Agent Fredricks. We're from the FBI." In unison, they held up their leather-encased badges. Delcore had a big scar above one eye; Bex wondered if he got in the line of duty. Fredricks was built bulky - she realized quickly she stood no chance against either of them. Bex stepped back. She put a hand against the brick wall to steady herself.

Bex slowly counted to ten in her head, working to keep her cool. She did not need to make a scene in front of her colleagues who undoubtedly watched all of this from the windows behind her.

"I'm sure you know why we're here," Fredricks said. He gave a smile; his teeth were perfectly in line and white.

She couldn't answer. He continued, "We just want to verify some things. Let's go to our field office, it's not far from here," he said. He still wore a smile, but it wasn't a question.

Delcore turned, she followed. Fredricks walked a few paces behind her; Bex knew why. His job was to make sure she wasn't a runner. Why were they acting so serious? Was Ana okay? Had they discovered something about Aimee?

Fredricks opened the rear door as soon as they got to a nondescript sedan, he held it open for her. Delcore got in the driver's seat and took them across the downtown area to somewhere near I-70. The ride was quiet save for the quick, loud heartbeats pulsing in her ear and the gnashing grind of her teeth.

Delcore pulled up to a gated security; a big metal fence looped the tall, glass-enclosed building. The whole thing looked imposing, contained, and steely. Bex could appreciate that, she was working to keep her face the same. A guard let them into the parking lot. Once inside, people in suits buzzed around the campus, each with a serious expression and purposeful walk. She was amazed at how much action there was here, just below the surface.

Following a thorough trip through a metal detector, they made their way up several floors and into one of those very television-ready interrogation rooms. As soon as the door closed, Bex felt another wave of fear. Why were they wasting time on her when they could be looking for Aimee's murderer? Or the killer? She took a deep breath, trying to calm her exterior. Could it be Ana? Could she be hurt? Or worse?

"Bex, we're just going to cut to the chase. As you know, time is of the essence, and we don't have any to waste," Fredericks said, in a friendly and cajoling tone.

"Yes, of course," she said. She wondered if she needed a lawyer.

"Okay then, we'll take it from the top," said Agent Delcore. "It's abundantly clear that someone is using your sister's books as inspiration to murder, someone with a lot to gain. We're looking at all the evidence and building a suspect profile. We're getting close."

Bex nodded. She felt sweat running down the small of her back. It made her annoyed that her body gave in to the stress so easily.

Fredericks continued in his friendly tone, "We're not going to bullshit you today. We're working many angles on this case. All kinds. And one of them is you, Bex. We're just trying to be thorough." She felt the blood drain from her face. This was the best they had?

"Bexley, let's be clear" Fredericks continued, "we're still in the fact-finding stage of this case, but we have some information about you that has proven quite relevant. We want to work with you Bexley, we want your help. Now is the time to tell us if you have something you want to get off your chest. This could all be over right now. Quickly and quietly. If you cooperate. Do you have anything you want us to know? Anything to confess?" Fredericks offered. The expression on his face was open and searching.

"I actually do," Bex said, fighting the urge to throw up all over the metal table. "Ana and I have a brother named Caleb. He was adopted as a toddler and has recently come back into our lives. He's done some very threatening things. I think you need to look at him." After a moment's contemplation, she continued "And James, our podcast engineer, needs to be investigated too. There's something off with him, something not quite right."

Delcore and Fredricks shared a look. Bex didn't know what it meant.

"Right now, we're focused on you, Bex," Fredericks said. "We think you might be the key to finding the killer. It could be someone close to you."

"Actually," Delcore interrupted, with a mean little grin, "I thought it might be you."

"You're making a big mistake!" Bex yelled, giving in to the emotions that had been building all day. "Why would I even do this?" She wanted to know what they had on her, but she wasn't about to back down now. Fear was quickly replaced by anger. After everything she'd been through, now this?

"Like I said Bexley, easy or hard. Your choice," Fredericks said in his calm and reasonable teacher's tone. He sounded like he was talking to a toddler, giving her a choice between shoes or a coat first.

The men waited her out, Delcore sneering while Fredericks gave her imploring puppy-dog eyes. The tension in the room was thick. It sucked up all the oxygen. She knew not saying anything would only confirm their suspicions, but all those years studying true crime taught her that saying something stupid during an interrogation could easily get her in trouble.

Sweat collected in her pits. Anger coursed through her veins. Bex just wanted them to get off her back so they could find the actual killer. So she could get home. So she could be with Ana.

"Okay, then," Delcore said. "We'll do it your way. We're going to go through this bit by bit, buckle up."

"Go for it. I have nothing to hide."

"Well for starters Bex, we did our due diligence. You were in Denver when Patricia was taken. You were in California when Ella was pushed off the bridge."

"Big deal. I live in Denver so, of course, I was here. And I travel for work. Do you think I sent that box, too? You can check with the hotel when I was in California. I was with the most annoying clients that whole week. I'll be on video coming and going from their stupid office on Mission Street. I was with my team."

"Don't worry, we're already on it," Fredricks said. "But we have more than that." Delcore opened the manila envelope in front of him. He slid out a piece of paper with a photocopy of a receipt.

Nothing about the image was familiar. Bex felt the tension drain from her shoulders. This wasn't the smoking gun they'd thought they found. She leaned back in her chair.

"Do you recognize this?" he asked.

"No. What is it?"

"It's a receipt from a gun and hardware store near your house."

Bex thought back; she vaguely recalled a grimy little shop called Pinecone Tools & Guns or something down the street. She couldn't remember the last time she went in it.

"Okay, and?"

"We verified. It's a legitimate receipt. Those purchases were made that day and paid in cash. And the receipt was in your desk." A tiny seed of fear took hold in her mind. She had no idea how it got there.

"So? What does that prove?"

"You purchased bomb-making supplies. Right before Ruth Banks was killed."

Her heart stopped. She shot up in her chair and grabbed the copy of the receipt. She didn't even recognize any of the products on the itemized list.

Her palms filled with sweat. "I did not buy these things. Was my card charged? Did you see me on camera?!"

"This was in your desk. It was filed away in a receipts folder along with many others. Paid in cash." Delcore pointed at the paper. "How did it get there, Bex?"

Bex wondered for a second if she somehow forgot that she'd been to a gun store. She shook her head and pushed the thought away. She wasn't Ana. She didn't forget things. She'd never been to that store. She'd remember.

"It's not mine. I have never been there. I don't pay for things in cash." She swung back to righteous anger. How much follow-up work had they done before accusing her of murder?

"Do you have footage of the cash register? Or of me at this store? I have never even stepped inside!" She was adamant. She would know if she ever purchased a spring or chemicals to blow someone up.

"Footage was not stored long enough for us to check but we will be talking to the clerk, you can bet that," Delcore said at last.

A thought suddenly hit her. "Where did you get this receipt? How do you know it's from my desk?"

"We're not at liberty to say, Bex, but it was brought to us by someone who thought you might want help, or even want to help," Fredericks replied, giving her a beseeching look.

"Why would someone I know go to you instead of asking me about this receipt?"

"As we said, we're still working many angles in this case."

Like a roundhouse punch out of nowhere, awareness hit her hard. They could have only got this from one person. "Ana gave this to you, didn't she?"

Neither gave her an inch. Delcore glaring and Fredericks pleading in silence Bex felt a wave of disgust roll over her, at the fear she'd felt before these mediocre middle-aged white men. Just another couple of assholes standing in her way. They meant nothing compared to Ana and her betrayal.

After all she had done for her sister, after an entire lifetime's work was this was how Ana treated her? How did Ana find this? Did she fabricate it? Would she frame her own sister for murder?

"I swear," Bex said at last, using the oath she never uttered, "on my mother's grave, I don't know where my fucking sister got this receipt, but I did not purchase these things."

"That's not all, Bex," Delcore said. His dark expression felt like a vice around Bex's neck. She could not breathe.

He slid something across the table toward her. It was a picture of a red bag on concrete next to some railings. It was nothing.

"Okay?" she asked. She didn't know what he wanted from her.

"This is your purse, right? We have it on very good authority, it was left on the bridge. Security found it just after the victim was pushed. Now is the time to explain how that could be, Bex."

"What? No!" She said, puzzled. "That is not my purse. Way too tacky. I've never seen anything like it."

He pulled out another photo. It was a picture of the contents inside the purse. A time-worn and faded picture of baby Ana and Bex stared back at her. She felt a pang in her chest.

"This is the photo you always carry with you, no?" Delcore asked.

"Yes, but that's not mine!" she cried. "I have mine with me. I'm sure of it. It must be Ana's!"

EIGHTY

The comforter on the hotel bed was about as soft as Styrofoam. It smelled like it had been washed a thousand times but, somehow still did not come clean. Every time she ran her dry hands over it, her cracked skin snagged on the fabric.

Just as her body began to relax, someone screamed outside. She jumped and tensed all over again. It was the middle of the day, and she was already scared; what would come of her at night? Alone?

Ana checked her phone; her location sharing was still turned off, but it was unsettling that Bex hadn't checked in yet. Ana chewed on the side of her thumb; her stomach growled, and her mind was littered with the remnants of two big thoughts crashing into each other - Bex is the killer and Bex is her sister.

No matter how she looked at it, Ana could not square this information in her mind. Sorrow and guilt crushed her. Anger tried to take over. How could Bex have done this to her? Why did she kill all those innocent people? There was no way to rationalize it. Ana knew Bex was driven by creating a better life for them than they'd had as kids, but would she go this far? Apparently.

And what about Aimee and Kyle? Were their deaths a coincidence? Or was Bex even worse than Ana assumed? A sob doubled her over. There were too many unanswered questions. Ana's mind didn't want to believe the truth staring her in the face.

Like an itch that just wouldn't go away, no matter how many times she scratched it, Ana looked at her phone again. Every single app was littered with notifications. Her news app was splashed with story after story about The Novel Killings. There was another news segment with the Francis family calling for justice for their son. It was all the media could talk about. It was all anyone could talk about. Somehow there was still no arrest though. Bex was still free.

Ana checked her email. Her inbox was cluttered with new requests from every news station and crime podcaster out there. She clicked on the first one. It was from a producer at *The View*; the subject line said - Tell Your Side of the Story! They offered to fly Ana to their studio in New York and pay for her accommodations. Ana considered it. If the cops weren't going to use what she'd given them, maybe they needed more pressure. Ana started a response and then thought better of it.

She deeply regretted sending Bex her last story. It would only be a matter of time before her sister killed again. Another innocent person would die because of Ana's words and Bex's action. Some part of Ana wondered if she'd be the victim herself. It was a sister story after all, and it would complete her arc.

Another big sob wracked her body. There was nothing she could do though and that feeling of helplessness was almost as powerful as her feelings of guilt. The cops didn't believe her. The only thing she could do was wait.

Ana needed a distraction. Her Instagram profile was full of notifications. She opened the messages tab, only to see @anasnumberonefan at the very top. She couldn't face another barrage of messages from them. She closed the app.

Ana went to her Kindle Direct Publishing account instead. Every time she logged in, Ana assumed it was a mistake; instead, her sales rocketed each time. She was now up to $130,121.59 in sales since this all began.

Based on how Amazon managed self-publishing payouts, she wouldn't see that payment for as many as ninety days. Ana didn't care. Knowing it was coming, knowing that her books were finally selling was enough.

That was another thing Ana could not come to terms with; she wanted to be at this level of success since she started writing. She never believed it would happen. Her joy and pride mixed with her guilt and sadness, and she couldn't stop her emotions from racing between all of them at the speed of a runaway train.

Ana leaned her head back against the pillow. Her head pounded and her hands would not stop trembling. Ana stood to go to the bathroom. A wave of nausea rolled over her and for a second, she felt like she might lose it. She felt paranoid and brittle like people were watching her from the corners of the room, waiting for her to crack. Her breath came in shallow pants.

Suddenly Ana heard a loud boom right outside her door. She ducked to the floor and covered her head. It was the police; it had to be. They were going door to door, and they would break hers down any second. She looked around the room; there was no way out but the front door - not even a window.

The room closed in on her. She was trapped. Ana's mind latched onto the only logical conclusion. Bex had somehow framed her. They were coming for Ana. The police were going to arrest her, and this would be all over. She would never have the chance to prove her innocence to anyone. The tears began to fall.

Ana didn't know how long she crouched on the carpet before the smell of pee and dust overwhelmed her and she stood again. The cops never came; she never heard another explosion of sound beyond the normal honks and sirens of the city.

It took all her mental energy to pull herself off the ground. She peeked through the stained curtains. There was nothing outside, save for two young boys who looked like they should have been in school instead of leaning up against a car, smoking joints.

The emptiness of the parking lot eased her nerves. The noise was probably nothing more than a backfire.

She didn't want to live like this - checking her back, waiting for someone to come get her. Ana had come far enough that she wasn't going to be the victim anymore. It was time to take matters into her own hands. It was time for all of this to end.

Ana grabbed her phone off the bed. She needed evidence the police couldn't refute. There was only one way to do that.

EIGHTY-ONE

Even if she had been allowed to, Bex couldn't go back to work. Not after the FBI came and demolished whatever sliver of respect those people still had for her. She went home and sat on the couch and stewed instead.

It only took one look at Ana's room to discover that her sister had left; her space looked like a tornado ran through it. Ana's green duffel was missing and so were all her electronics. There wasn't even a note. Somehow that hurt more than all the rest of it.

Bex couldn't explain how that photo of the two of them was left on the bridge - but neither could those agents.

The first thing Bex did when she got to her car was to look for the photo. It wasn't in the little slot where it had been for years. Bex's stomach dropped. Only Ana knew it was there. And Aimee, but she was dead. That meant only Ana could have left it on the bridge. But why? How? Ana wasn't there to drop it.

Bex waffled. There had to be an explanation somewhere, but she couldn't find it. How did a photo of them as children end up at one of the crime scenes? That photo was taken long before the days of social media and digital pictures. It was a real one - developed not printed - one of very few pictures of them from that time. Only Bex and Ana had a copy. It could have only been one of them who left it. And it wasn't Bex.

Anger and sadness and guilt swirled around her. She couldn't stop herself from hating Ana. Her sister was at the bridge and she somehow managed to give the cops a receipt that she had no recollection of putting in her desk. Sisters don't do things like that. Maybe Ana wasn't as innocent as Bex had always thought.

Bex doubled over, tears streaming down her face. She and Ana had lived through so much together and at every turn, they made a great team. How had things fallen so fast? As much as she hated herself for it, Bex just wanted Ana. She needed her sister. They could still figure this out together.

She checked Ana's location; her sister had stopped sharing it with Bex. Another longing pain shot through Bex's chest. It felt like the sensation people described with a missing limb. That phantom pain when some big part of your body is missing, you ache for it.

Bex forced herself to leave it. Ana couldn't be trusted and Bex didn't trust herself enough to call her sister. Ana betrayed Bex. And it was time Bex looked out for herself for once.

With every creak of the house or car out front, Bex froze. She could not understand why the cops hadn't arrested her. If they had a receipt of hers where she supposedly bought bomb supplies, wasn't that enough?

Bex had watched enough crime shows to know that they must have a plan. Were they watching them? Waiting for something to happen? Still gathering evidence? Bex was desperate for answers but the only thing she could do was wait.

Her eyes scanned her phone screen, looking for any kind of distraction. The red number '38' over her email app taunted her. Bex didn't want to see what was inside but knew that it would help her. Work always did.

The inbox was filled with client updates and questions from her support staff once she got the courage to open it. She flicked through them but didn't respond to anyone. The most recent message practically blared with neon letters.

It was from her boss. The subject line said, "An update." No one ever wants to get that kind of email, and given their morning, it wasn't good. Bex tapped the email before she could chicken out. HR was cc'd as well.

> *Bex, given the turn of events of the day, we must make this formal. At Product Xponential we have a responsibility for the safety of all our stakeholders and employees. Per our obligations, that sabbatical we discussed is going to be mandatory and in effect immediately. Please do not come back into the office. We will send someone to return your personal effects and retrieve your work laptop. We expect to circle back by the end of next quarter for a potential review but want to encourage you to explore other employment opportunities better suited to your lifestyle and needs in the interim. You have seven unused sick days and will be paid for those as well as for the remainder of this week.*
>
> *Best, Theo*

Tears formed in her eyes, not from sadness but from anger. White-hot anger that this was the best they could give her. Not a 'hi, how are ya,' or even a 'fuck you,' nothing but a cold dismissal with a vague follow-up. Bex had seen this happen before but she never in a million years thought it would happen to her.

Bex shoved her phone into the side pocket of her yoga pants and stormed into the kitchen. It was still early afternoon, but she poured herself a big glass of wine anyway. Her phone buzzed at her side; Bex assumed it was work again, but then Ana's name flashed on her wrist as her watch showed the text.

Want to record a podcast episode tonight? Ana wrote.

Every emotion hit Bex all at once. She was relieved to hear from her sister but hated that she still felt that way after everything Ana had done. Bex's feelings toward Ana were complicated and dangerous. And yet, Bex needed to see Ana. They needed to work through this, together.

Yes! Bex replied quickly.

EIGHTY-TWO

Ana's hands clung to the wheel at ten and two. The route back to their house was routine, the fear in her belly was anything but. Ana thought through her plan at each light. She'd get Thai food. And then they'd set up their recording equipment. Ana would suggest going live on Instagram so the whole world could bear witness as Ana confronted her sister.

Bex's confession would be broadcast to thousands of viewers. With a live recording, this purgatory would end. The waiting would end. Bex would be arrested, and Ana would be free to write whatever stories she damn well pleased without fear that someone would die with her words. In just a few short hours, this would end.

Not to mention, Ana's success as an author would be solidified by this legendary case. No matter what she wrote from now on, it would sell. Ana could finally live off her royalties and be free of her sister. She'd get a little place near Wash Park, and she would spend her days writing, drinking coffee, and building a life of her own.

As Ana dreamed of her future, one thing snagged. She would need to find a way to deal with their brother. It had always been Bex and Ana, but now she had to make room for him, too. Ana would need to find a way to build a bridge to him and help heal his trauma.

Ana knew that was wishful thinking. It probably wouldn't be that easy; she would need to look into a restraining order or buy some kind of protection. Their past had always haunted Ana. Caleb would be no different.

She turned; the Thai place was just ahead. Her hands rattled on the steering wheel and a cold sweat broke out above her eyebrows. Ever since Ana decided to stop taking her medication, her whole body was wet and shaky. The withdrawal was harder than she imagined but she didn't care. The price of freeing her brain from the chemicals controlling it was worth it. Next up, she'd free herself from Bex. Her life was almost hers alone.

Ana parallel-parked down the street from their favorite hole-in-the-wall and started walking back to it. On the sidewalk, people gave her a wide berth, and someone even took a picture of her. She ducked her head and made it inside as fast as she could.

As she pulled the door open, Ana caught sight of a dark sedan in the window's reflection. She turned and saw the tail end of the car driving by. It looked identical to the cars that had been following her for weeks.

She felt fear, deep in her belly. At first, Ana thought she was seeing things. Now she understood that the cops had been trailing her all along, gathering evidence - doing anything but catching the real killer.

That would all change soon. This was almost over.

EIGHTY-THREE

By the time Ana showed up with Thai food, Bex was a bottle of wine deep. The red cab was no match for the grief of losing Aimee and nearly losing her Ana. Not to mention her job. The only thing that pulled the corners of her lips up was seeing her sister. She didn't realize how much she needed Ana until they were in the same room.

Ana's skin was colorless. Her face was sullen and glossy with a thin layer of sweat, her hair matted into a low bun at the base of her neck. The plastic takeout bags rattled in her sister's hands. Ana looked as bedraggled as Bex felt. The last months had taken quite a toll on them.

"Hey, sis- I'm glad you're here," Bex said as Ana set up dinner.

"Me too," Ana said. Her voice was stiff, barely loud enough for Bex to hear. It didn't leave a lot of room for the conversation to continue.

They ate dinner in silence. Ana didn't look up from her phone and didn't give Bex any indication as to what they'd record, as was their habit. Bex didn't care. Seeing Ana across the table was enough.

"So, where'd you go?" Bex asked.

Ana cleared her throat but didn't answer. There was a block of ice between them and no matter what Bex tried, she couldn't thaw it. Bex wasn't deterred, that wine made her feel loose and forgiving. They had gone through so much worse together. It was all probably a big misunderstanding. Neither one of them left that photo on the bridge. They would find a way to get through this, too.

"Ana, you know that I'm here to help you, right? Whatever is going on, we will survive it as long as we have each other," Bex tried again.

Her sister didn't look up from her phone. That hurt Bex to the point that the pain sharpened into anger. Ana was in the room, but she wasn't there. It didn't have to be like this.

"So, what are we going to talk about on the show then?" Bex asked. She felt like a puppy begging for attention.

"We never finished The Denver Prostitute episode. I have the notes still, we can do that one," Ana said. Bex nodded.

"I was also thinking of calling Zane back," Bex said. "You know the advertisement placer guy? I bet they'd pay big bucks to have ads on this episode."

Ana still didn't look up. Bex's words were just bouncing right off Ana. Bex didn't care though; she knew they were about to have more downloads than those famous My Favorite Murderer or Crime Junkie chicks. The big time.

"Ready?" Ana asked. It didn't look like she did more than push her food around the container, but neither had Bex. Her emotions made her stomach a hard rock; there wasn't room for more.

"Yeah. Let's do it."

They set up in silence. The tension in the room was taut but that didn't keep Bex from being excited. They hadn't recorded in a few days and listeners were begging for more on all their social channels. So were advertisers. Bex's inbox was full of reach outs. She couldn't wait to turn them into a bidding war for access to a slot on this episode.

Ana sat at her microphone and adjusted the height to meet her mouth. Bex did the same. Bex clicked a few things on her computer to ready the recording. Ana took out her phone and set it up, facing them.

"Mind if I livestream this one? I haven't posted much in a while; I think people would like to see us in action."

Bex smiled; it was a great idea. "Yes, please!"

Ana leaned the camera up on the vase on the coffee table, with them at opposite ends of the table, the camera couldn't get both of them. They readjusted so they were sitting on the couch, side by side facing the camera.

Neither of them looked particularly good; Bex let it slide in hopes that people would buy into the real-life behind-the-scenes look at their life. She undid her pony and slicked back her hair. A rolling wave sensation hit her; she was a little drunker than she thought.

Bex took a swig of water and gave Ana a thumbs up. She pulled on her headphones. Ana started the Instagram Live and waited for it to spool up. Soon ten and then twenty people joined them. Ana slipped on her headphones and gave Bex a thumbs-up of her own. Bex started the podcast recording on her laptop. A thousand people watched.

"Hello, and welcome to *The Serial Syndicate* podcast. I'm your host, Ana Adams. Yes, that one if you must ask."

"And I'm Bex. That one, too. We're sisters and together, we give voices to the forgotten victims, those who time and racism and shoddy police work have let down, in a weekly format," Bex said. Ana nodded, she looked pleased.

A genuine smile crossed Bex's face. All was right in the world. Ana was home and they were doing what they loved together. After the recording, Bex would bring up her conversation with the FBI and Ana would have a reasonable explanation. They would sort it all out. Everything was fine.

"We're thankful for your support," Ana said. "Today, we're going to be discussing The Denver Prostitute Killer. But first, I just wanted to give you a little update on The Novel Killings since that's why you're all here."

Bex sucked in her stomach; all the muscles in her body constricted. She didn't even want to go there. Out of the corner of her eye, Bex saw hearts exploding at the bottom of the live recording on Ana's phone, people were watching, and they loved what Ana just said.

"No, there still hasn't been an arrest. The FBI has said very little about this case publicly, but I know they're working on it. They came and picked me up the other day and interviewed me," Ana said. "They've also been tailing me in black sedans for weeks. I won't lie, at first, I could have sworn it was the killer, about to kidnap me. I was terrified. Now that I know it's the cops, I'm relieved to know they're doing something."

Another round of hearts raced across the screen.

Bex debated adding what she knew about the investigation. Ultimately, she decided to keep her mouth shut. She needed to talk to Ana, and they needed to make a plan before the whole world heard.

"I couldn't take it any longer. I went to the FBI field office in Denver myself," Ana said. Her voice was firm. It contained a note of resolve that Bex didn't recognize.

"I brought them some evidence and I asked for their help. We have identified the killer," Ana said. Her voice was low and serious; it was clear, Ana believed every word of it.

Bex faltered. Was Ana about to admit she'd been on the bridge? Maybe Bex had it all wrong. The blood drained from Bex's face. Her hands broke out in a sweat. Bex looked at her sister, trying to gauge what was coming next. Ana didn't need to hang herself in front of the whole world.

Another thought hit her. Did this mean Ana had something to do with Aimee's death? Sadness washed over her. Cold, thick anger followed.

Had they not been live on Instagram, Bex would have stopped the podcast show and made Ana explain everything. Everyone was watching though. Bex knew anything she did at this point would just make this whole thing more viral.

"And that's why I'm live here tonight. I want you all to see it for yourself," Ana said.

Bex's mouth went dry. This felt like a bad idea. She put a hand on Ana's forearm; her sister shook it off.

Ana grabbed something from her folder; she held it up. "See this. This is a print of a still photo taken by the bridge security police," Ana said. She held up the photo of the two of them for the viewers to see.

"The picture is of me and my sister when we were kids. Bex kept it in her purse. This was left on the bridge, they found it shortly after the victim was pushed. There's only one person who could have left this there..." Ana said.

Bex held up a hand. She didn't want to hash this out on a live recording. Ana kept going.

"The FBI also found a receipt for bomb making supplies in Bex's desk," Ana said. Bex's eyebrows knit together. When did the FBI come to their house?

"If all that wasn't enough, my friend James found open-source pictures of Bexley Adam's car near where Patricia was taken and along the route to where her body was dumped. Bex drives a red Audi TT - the dumbest car for Colorado ever. It's not like there are many on the road. It won't be long until the police verify the plate and the driver in these images," Ana said.

Questions rushed through Bex's mind. Why did the killer have a car that looked just like hers? Why wasn't Ana letting the FBI do their job?

"It will take the police some time to gather murder trial-ready evidence, but you can all see it. We know who has committed The Novel Killings."

The whole world held its breath.

"The killer is sitting right next to me," Ana said in a low quiet voice.

The words finally registered in Bex's mind. Ana just accused her of being a serial killer. Shock hit and then anger. Bex could not believe that Ana set her up like this.

Defenses popped up left and right in Bex's mind. She didn't leave that bag or that photo on the bridge. She never drove through Five Points where Patricia was taken. Bex was innocent! Ana wouldn't do this to her. She couldn't. Fear ripped through Bex; she could barely breathe.

"No, Ana. Wait. Please stop this," Bex pleaded. "We need to talk!"

"What's there to talk about? The cops will arrest you in no time, Bex. The Novel Killings have come to an end. The press has stopped, the ink is dry."

As Bex was backed into a corner, something overcame her. She needed to prove to Ana and the world, she was no killer.

"Ana was interrogated by the FBI, too. I didn't leave that picture there. My copy is in my purse!" Bex lied. "The only other person that could have left it is you." Her voice was shrill.

"I wasn't the one in California," Ana said.

Bex slammed her hands down on the coffee table. "Ana! What motive would I have to do this? You're the one that has gained from all the news. If anyone has motive, it's you!"

Ana paused. Her eyes went dark and a look Bex had never seen crossed her face. It was only a split second, but Bex registered a shift in her sister.

"Ana, stop the live recording. We need to talk," Bex said. She put a hand on Ana's. "I had a chat with the FBI, too."

Bex saw something inside Ana snap. Ana flung Bex's hand off her. She stood and Ana pulled back her shoulders. Ana raised her arms, and a cruel expression took over her face. She sneered at Bex. Ana no longer looked like Ana.

367

Bex watched Ana set her microphone down. Ana stood, and deliberately walked around the coffee table, planting her feet in front of Bex. Bex threw herself back against the couch, but she had nowhere to run.

Something dark and vivid crossed Ana's face. She turned to Bex with an expression of cold loathing and intent that was utterly terrifying.

"What did you tell the FBI?" Ana snarled. Her eyes rolled back as she lunged at her sister.

Ana was gone.

EIGHTY-FOUR

Stars danced in her eyes. She pushed her palms into her eyes, not stopping when they began to hurt. Her head throbbed and her throat felt constricted.

"You have to answer us, Ana," someone said, their voice full of anger. She opened her eyes and looked around the room. Something about it was familiar. She recognized the men sitting opposite her. Ana didn't know how she got there.

Ana closed her eyes and felt shame wash over her. It happened again. She lost a big chunk of time. She couldn't admit it now; they would think she was crazy - or worse. Ana swallowed.

"Are you there?" he asked. She nodded.

"Just in case - I'm Agent Fredricks and this is Delcore. We've been working together on The Novel Killings," he said. He offered a smile which felt foreign in the midst of everything. Ana nodded.

"Something happened tonight," Delcore said.

Ana leaned forward in the chair. It all came rushing back. Relief flooded her. They finally had the killer. "You arrested Bex?" she asked.

They looked between them. "What?" Fredricks asked.

"You saw the Instagram Live show? I have all the evidence. Bex committed The Novel Killings. You arrested her, right?"

"Yes, we watched it. A lot of people called the cops as they watched it unfold. But no, we did not arrest Bex," Delcore said. Fredricks met her eye, he gave her an almost encouraging look.

Ana propped her elbows on the table and rubbed her eyes again. She felt shaky, exhausted. She couldn't fight this much longer. What were they waiting for?

"So tonight, you and Bex got into it pretty good, right? Got a flood of reports. Local PD called us. You really went after her, huh?" Delcore asked. He let out a mean little giggle.

"No, no. That's not what happened. We were recording, and I confronted her with all the evidence." Ana was growing frustrated. Why couldn't they see this? "I need you to arrest her. She's the killer."

"Ana, we know you are under an immense amount of strain," Fredericks said, sounding understanding. "Stress can cause people to act in ways that don't make sense. After you confronted Bex, your whole body changed. The anger in your eyes was concerning, your aggression triggered a lot of people online. It terrified them. The recording stopped - the final thing people saw was the look of pure terror on Bex's face as you lunged at her. People were very concerned, Ana."

Fear slid through Ana. The night was fuzzy. She couldn't picture what they were saying. People were scared of her? "Where is Bex?" Ana asked.

"She's at home," Delcore said. Alive.

"How come you haven't arrested her?" Ana demanded.

"There's a team with her. But, Ana, we want to talk to you. We need your help. You're the only one that can help us solve this," he said.

"Am I under arrest?"

"No, nothing happened. Bex was hysterical and in tears when the cops got there but you were just sitting there calmly. She didn't have a mark on her and didn't want to press charges. We came shortly after. You agreed to come down here with us."

"I did not! I would not! It should be Bex here with you!"

"We are talking to her, too. We promise," Delcore said.

"Ana, we understand this whole thing has been very hard. It must be so agonizing to know the killer is so close."

"I keep telling you this, I know who the killer is! Bex!"

"Help us understand, Ana. Please help us," Fredricks said. Ana leaned back in her chair and sighed. She could see she'd have to do it their way if they were ever going to believe her.

"Ana, we have some questions about your mental health if we may. With so much stress, we've noticed some things?"

She swallowed. Ana would do almost anything for a glass of water. "I don't have to answer your questions."

Fredericks nodded. "No, but we would appreciate it if you would. The whole world is hurting and you're the only one that can help, you can be a hero, Ana. Do you sometimes lose chunks of time? We spoke to your therapist, Dr. Daniels. He cited patient-provider-privilege but Bex told us that you black out sometimes. You have these fugue states where you may not be in control of your body. You don't remember what happened. He fears that during those times you hurt yourself, or worse, others. Can you help by telling us a little more about that?"

Ana shook her head so hard that a wave of nausea rolled through her. She didn't want anyone to know that she wasn't always in control. They would think she's crazy; they'd never believe her anymore. "No," she said at last, "I don't think I should answer your questions."

"Would you be willing to talk to our forensic psychologist about all of this?"

"Absolutely not! I don't black out or whatever you said. I don't hurt people!" Ana screamed.

The agents shared a look.

"Okay, we'll come back to that," Delcore announced. He laced his fingers in front of him.

"We've already looked at Bex," Delcore said. Ana disagreed but kept her mouth shut. "Let's talk about your brother, Caleb. Has he recently come back into the picture? You mentioned him the other day."

"Yeah," Ana said, eager to change the subject away from whatever they thought of her mental issues. Bex found him through one of those DNA sites. We lost track of him after he was adopted but now that he's found us, he's very interested in our lives."

"And why do you think that is?"

"He's just as fucked up as we are."

"How do you know that? Have you met him yet? Has he made any threats? We can help you, Ana. You just have to help us." Fredericks wanted to come across as sincere, but Ana knew he was just playing the good cop.

"Not yet, but he's been stalking us."

"From Chicago?" Delcore asked, his eyebrows raised skeptically.

"No, he lives in Wyoming. He's been driving down, I guess. I've seen him around."

"Huh." Delcore wasn't convinced. "Are you sure that's where he lives? How do you know?"

Ana chewed on her lip, welcoming the copper flavor of her blood, long past wincing at the pain. She hated the way they were talking to her. She was sure Caleb lived in Wyoming. That's what Bex told her. It wasn't that far of a drive, just two-and-a-half hours from Laramie to Denver.

Fredericks leaned forward, eyes wide. "Oh Ana, you've had such a hard life. I can't imagine."

"Mom dead, gone when you needed her most," Delcore added flatly. "That fire, a damn tragedy. A convenient tragedy, though. The first step is getting you out of the house. Still, a shame about your mom," he said. Ana couldn't let her mind go there.

"And now your brother comes back and stirs it all up. Oh Ana, all that stuff with your stepdad," Fredricks added. "It's okay to seek validation. It's a common and normal response. Makes sense."

"What do you mean?" she asked.

"It's not that special Ana," Delcore's eyes met hers and wouldn't look away. "We see it all the time - people who never got childhood acceptance and unconditional love, seeking it wherever they can find it. Sex, drugs, a tough reputation... fame. Maybe this is what it looks like for you. You're getting the love and attention and acceptance, what you missed as a kid, through fame and book sales."

"No. No!" Ana's mind refused the implication.

"Ana, it's okay. Given your childhood, we would understand if you just needed something your family never gave you. You should have had a stable childhood. Hell, all kids should," Frederick's voice sounded so heartfelt, that it was hard for Ana to remember he was trying to get her to confess. "If you would have had a safe childhood, you wouldn't be trying to fill the gaps any way you could."

"If you're saying what I think you are, the answer is no," Ana spoke in a tight voice. "No. I had nothing to do with this. I'm just trying to catch the killer. I'm as much of a victim here as the rest of them."

"Ana, we're not implying anything," Delcore spoke in a knowing tone that belied his words. "We're just saying that sometimes lack of love, stability, and family can come out in ugly ways as adults. Very ugly."

Ana closed her eyes and tried to do the same with her ears.

"Hell, I'm no psychologist," Delcore continued, "but I'm wondering if you might have blacked out tonight with your sister. It would make sense, given the stress you're under and your obvious confusion."

"Is that what happened Ana? Did you black out?" Fredricks asked.

373

Ana couldn't admit that she had been losing chunks of time since she was a child. She couldn't let the cops go there. It was too dangerous. Her head spun, desperate to talk about something else. She grasped at straws, trying to think of a distraction.

"What about the DNA evidence I heard about on Reddit?" Ana said, at last.

Fredericks cocked an eyebrow. "Yes, there was some DNA evidence left. Hair that may have belonged to the suspect."

"I knew it!" Ana exclaimed. "Whose hair was it?"

Fredricks leaned forward and wiped the sweat off his head. It was late, he looked tired. Ana checked her watch; it was well after eleven.

"We've done some testing. We're working on getting a DNA warrant to compare it directly to you and Bex. That can take some time, but we're getting there."

Delcore spoke up. "Of course, we were able to run that hair through the private databases - you don't need a warrant for that, just have to ask nicely. AncestryandMe was very helpful. We can't say exactly who the hair came from, but we do know it came from you or someone in your immediate family, Ana."

Prickles of worry ran up Ana's back as Delcore smiled at her knowingly.

"See!" she said, feeling dizzy. "Bex. It had to be Bex. Take another sample from her! It had to be her, compare it directly."

"We're working on it."

Delcore leaned down and picked up a folder from the floor. He opened it and plucked something out of it - a worn newspaper clipping. He looked at it for a second, and then turned it and pushed it Ana's way.

She studied the headline - *Deadly Fire Rips Through Family Home*. Nausea rolled through her. She didn't want to talk about her past anymore. They just need to let it go.

"Ana let's talk about your childhood a bit more. Do you remember this? Does it bring any feelings back, any memories of times you blacked out?"

Her eyes landed on the picture. It was small and hard to make much out in the faded black and white ink. There was a charred house in the background and a group of firefighters off to one side. Ana saw herself sitting in the front. A little boy sat next to her. A scared little boy, his face half-turned toward her and half-toward the camera. A scared little boy with the same pale blond hair as her and Bex. A scared little boy with an hourglass-shaped birthmark right above his eyebrow - where it would normally be hidden by a beanie.

The room spun. She would recognize that birthmark anywhere.

James.

EIGHTY-FIVE

Bex sat at the kitchen table. Alone. The night passed into that pallid hour after which nothing good came. Bex dreaded the idea of closing her eyes and seeing Aimee's face. Or worse, seeing the anger in her sister's eyes, a rage she'd never imagined from Ana. She couldn't.

Her stomach begged for food, but the thought of actually rising from the table, putting one foot in front of the other and walking to the cupboard and stove felt impossible. She imagined sitting there alone until starvation finally overtook her. It would be a welcome relief from the hellscape her life had become.

Something caught in the corner of her eye; it was pitch black outside. Just a cat or squirrel she told herself. No one would be near their house at this hour. The light changed, someone moved in front of the window. Bex's heart ramped up to Mach speed as she waited for them to come to her door.

Bex grabbed a butcher knife from the wooden block in the kitchen and held it by her side, she wasn't going to be a victim. She wasn't going to go down like Aimee. She waited. She held her breath. The knock never came. Bex tiptoed to the front door and looked out the peephole. The street was empty. The stillness of the night was the only thing that met her eye. Bex forced herself to relax.

She moved to the couch with the knife by her side. She rolled over and turned on the television. The 10 o'clock news was still playing. The weatherman detailed a late spring storm that could be in the forecast. She let herself zone out with the thought of something so normal.

His segment was interrupted by a chiming noise. A breaking news graphic covered the screen. Bex sat up and turned up the volume. "We have breaking news in The Novel Killings case," a woman with a full head of curly brunette hair said. She wore a green dress and a thick pearl necklace. Her eyes were wide with excitement.

"Ana Adams, the Denver author who has been embroiled in the serial killer case that has captured the world's attention has been taken into custody." The screen panned from the woman to grainy footage of Ana being led stiffly from their Denver home. It was surreal to watch her handcuffed sister walk across the screen.

"Reports indicate there was some sort of domestic disturbance at the home, but the police have declined to say more." The cop put a hand on Ana's head and ducked her into the back of a Denver Police Department vehicle.

The camera turned to a man wearing a 9News windbreaker. He was young and he looked hungry for action. Bex recognized her neighbor sitting on the porch in the background of the feed.

"I'm Reporter Aaron McFee, reporting live from the scene," he said in his cool anchor-trained voice. "We don't know much at this point, but sources are saying this could be the break this case needs. Ana Adams may have been arrested for her role in The Novel Killings case."

She sat up straighter and paused the television. Aaron's face froze with his mouth wide open, mid-sentence. Bex grabbed her phone and opened her Facebook app. Her notifications were exploding and nearly every post she scrolled past mentioned the case.

Bex landed on something shared just a few minutes prior by a former co-worker. She sucked in a breath, recognizing the man in the photo - Kyle, Ana's weird friend from inpatient. The post originated from Kyle's mom, Sherri Francis. She wrote - *I'm so thankful that this terrible woman has been arrested. May she rot in prison for her part in this and may Kyle finally have justice.*

Bex did a double take. In the comments, Ana had already been convicted in The Novel Killings case.

Two days ago, Bex would have come to her sister's defense and ripped them all a new one. Now, she sat alone, filled with sorrow on her couch. Before Ana came at her, before she'd made those wild accusations on a public livestream or turned her into the FBI, Bex would never have believed her sister could be a killer. But now she wasn't so sure. She realized there was a lot about Ana she wasn't sure of at all.

Bex saw the way Ana's whole body changed earlier that night, the way her eyes grew dark, and her voice dropped octaves. Bex knew that Ana was capable of more than she thought - Bex had experienced it for herself.

Ana had motive. Her author career had blown up and she was now a household name. She had the time and if Bex was honest, Ana was unstable. There were large chunks of time when Ana wasn't fully in control of her body. Maybe Ana's blackouts were serious. Deadly?

Bex closed her phone and turned off the television. Her mind couldn't take any more of the truth.

After running through every memory one more time, Bex finally crashed. Her dreams were filled with Aimee's lifeless body, visions of Ana standing over her. They weren't dreams, they were nightmares.

EIGHTY-SIX

Bex woke from her shallow, fraught sleep to a sudden noise. She rubbed her eyes and looked around the room. Her neck felt permanently askew from sleeping on the couch. The sun forced its way in through the curtains. Bex's head hurt. Her eyes felt grainy from all the tears.

Ana burst through the back door.

"I've got something, Bex!" Ana screamed. Bex shot up on the couch, fully awake.

Bex grabbed the knife that was still on the coffee table from the night before and stood, ready to defend herself this time. Bex didn't trust her sister. Not after Ana's anger. Not after the police flooded their house and took Ana away the night before. Bex backed into the wall, putting as much space between them as possible.

"I need you, sister" Ana said. Bex didn't move. "I'm sorry for what happened last night. I know it wasn't fair, I've been going through so much; it's no excuse though, I shouldn't have treated you like that. I know it's a lot to ask, but please... You've got to listen to me."

Bex opened her mouth to say something. The words wouldn't come.

"Please," Ana said, fumbling with her phone.

Bex looked her sister up and down. Her hair was once held in place in a bun, but strands of dirty, wild hair escaped. Her eyes were dark and darting, Bex didn't trust them. Ana's hands shook as they hit the screen of her phone.

Her sister looked like she had just broken out of prison. Hell, maybe she had. Bex didn't trust her. Not one bit. She clenched the knife handle harder.

"Look!" Ana said. She shoved the phone toward Bex. Bex squinted but couldn't register what Ana wanted her to see.

Ana took a step closer. Bex tried to step back, hitting the wall; she pulled the knife up, ready.

"Holy shit, Bex. I'm not going to hurt you!" Ana said, her face fell, and she stopped moving, her eyes pleading. After the crazy way Ana had come for her yesterday, though, Bex still wasn't sure.

"Then what was last night?" Bex asked coldly. She felt a sense of clarity that if Ana came any closer, she would be forced to do something.

"I'm going to show you a photo on my phone. I want you to look at it and tell me what you see," Ana said. "That's it. Are you ready?" Bex nodded.

Ana held the phone back up. Bex took a step closer. The screen filled with a black-and-white photo, turned yellow with age. The image was zoomed in, framing two kids sitting on a familiar curb. Bright lights and big trucks in the background. Bex looked at the kids.

"That's you," Bex said.

"Yeah, and who is sitting next to me?"

Bex looked at the phone again. "Caleb."

"Yep. Right after the fire. But look at Caleb's face. Really look at it."

"Okay." Bex did as she was told.

"Now look at this," Ana said. She turned the phone and looked for something else, her hands shaking. She held it back up to Bex.

Bex stepped closer for a better look. "That's James."

"Yes, but look at his forehead this time." Ana slid back and forth between the two photos. They both had a small birthmark above his right eyebrow. Bex looked up and searched Ana's face. Ana seemed so proud of herself.

"What?" Bex asked.

"You don't see it?! They're the same person."

Bex grabbed the phone from Ana and flipped between the images. She did a double take and then a third. The hourglass-shaped birthmark above his eye stood out like a beacon.

The sandy blonde hair. Bex's mind finally filled in the age differences. Ana was right. Same person.

How had she not noticed it before? She pictured James. That Carhartt beanie he always wore pulled low, like he was trying to hide his most identifying feature - a birthmark.

"Wait," she said at last.

"Yeah, that's what I'm telling you." Ana sounded relieved. "Caleb and James are the same person. Caleb has been pretending to be James all along."

"That can't be, it doesn't make sense. We hired him for the podcast."

"Yeah, but remember how we met him? We only chose him because he offered to help us master our podcast for free to build his portfolio. He reached out after our first episode. He reached out to us."

"Oh, shit," Bex said. "You're right. We need to call the police. Who knows what else he's hiding?"

"I'm sorry, Bex. I can't call them now. They're just looking for an excuse to call me crazy and get me locked up or institutionalized. I just barely got out. They're trying to say that I need to see their psychiatrist. They'll put me back in Hillside. We have to figure out what the hell Caleb... James is doing. We need proof that he's up to something before we go to the cops again."

"But why would he lie to us?" Bex asked. She looked between the two photos. It was all Bex could see - the resemblance between the two of them. James was a grown-up Caleb. "He's been messaging me on the AncestryandMe site. Why go to all the trouble?"

"I don't know? Maybe because you weren't answering. Or maybe because he's as crazy as we are," Ana said.

Bex snorted. She wondered if AncestryandMe had a genetic marker for 'batshit.'

"James - Caleb - whatever you want to call him has been giving me tips. He convinced me that you were the killer," Ana continued. "That's why I turned on you last night. I thought it was you." There was a note of sadness in her voice.

Bex laughed, bitter and hard. After everything Bex had done for their family, this is what she got in return. Ana and her little brother, so eager to put all the blame on big sis, so ready to believe the worst. Ana took a tentative step closer. Bex didn't move, not even to wipe the tears that had rolled down her face. Ana closed the gap and wrapped Bex in a big hug.

Bex let her. Ana patted her back and stroked her hair. Bex melted into the embrace.

"It's just us Bex, like always. Me and you. We have to catch James - Caleb," Ana whispered in Bex's ear. Bex nodded.

"Wait. What else is he doing?" Bex pulled back and searched Ana's face. Her jaw was set, and determination filled Ana's eyes.

"I don't know. But I think he's up to something," Ana said.

"Do you think he's The Novel Killer?"

Ana looked down at the floor. Her face went red, Bex didn't know what her sister was thinking.

"I don't know. Maybe. We just need to figure out why Caleb has been sneaking around pretending to be James. That's the first step."

"Yeah," Bex said. She sat heavily on the couch. Ana sat next to her.

"Let's invite him to be on the show," Ana said. Bex closed her eyes and pictured Caleb sitting in their living room. It was too much.

"We'll play dumb. We won't give Caleb any idea that we know he's James. We'll say we're doing a behind-the-scenes look at our pod. He'll come. I know he will."

"What, then we confront him?" Bex asked.

"Exactly. We'll be ready this time."

EIGHTY-SEVEN

The day drug on slowly. Ana tried to nap but the interrogation swirled through her dreams, she could barely tell what was real and what her mind conjured up. She shivered and her brain zapped again. She sat up in bed and thought of her brother, trying to force her mind to work.

The revelation that James was Caleb looped around and around. She ran through scenarios of their confrontation over and over again.

She wasted the rest of the day, wandering around the house in a nervous haze waiting for the evening to come. Ana was ready to write the final chapter, to close the book. Ana got out of bed to find her sister. She needed to be close. She needed Bex.

"I can't believe this worked. He's coming," Bex said. She paced around the kitchen and straightened the tea towel for the third time.

"His text said he would be here at 5 PM," Ana replied. Her nerves frayed one by one as the minutes passed. Ana looked at the clock. They still had more than an hour.

"We need to do something to protect ourselves," Bex said.

"You think?"

"I just don't trust him one bit," Bex said. She straightened the bananas in the fruit bowl on the counter.

"No, I think we'll be okay. He doesn't know that we know, remember. He's coming as James. I think he just wants to get to know us."

"Yeah, but as soon as we confront him... I worry it will set him off. And if he's involved in The Novel Killings, we really need to be careful."

"Maybe," Ana conceded.

"No offense, sister, but you've already sweetly confronted a bunch of people about this case. Has it worked out for you yet? This is going to take more than just a recording. I think it might get ugly and I don't want anything to happen to you."

Ana unlocked her phone and looked to see if there was anything new from James. Caleb. Nothing. Bex's words soaked in her mind. Her sister was right. Ana had tried several times to catch the killer with words alone. It hadn't worked yet.

Bex prepped the room; Ana watched. Her nerves frayed and she wondered if they were crazy for inviting him to their home.

"Read the messages again," Bex said.

Nothing had changed since they texted earlier in the day, but Ana did as she was told. "Here's what I sent - *Hey, Bex and I want to record a new show where we do a kind of behind-the-scenes look at our team and how we're all working together on The Novel Killings case. Would you be up for that? We can zoom you in or something.*"

Ana took a deep breath. "And then he said, *Sure - I'm actually in Denver this week for work. Want to do it in person?*"

"That's the part that gets me!" said Bex. "If he was James, he should be in Chicago. There's no way he's just casually in Denver."

"No, but remember Caleb lives in Wyoming. So, it's not that far of a drive."

"I know. I just can't wrap my head around it."

Ana didn't show Bex the rest of his text messages. James, Caleb went on to say - *Do you need my help pinning Bex? Is that what this is about?*

She didn't respond to that last part. Ana couldn't. James sent another; *I know that's what you were trying to do the other day with your Instagram Live. It was a solid idea. I'm glad you asked me. We'll get her this time.*

The bile rose in Ana's throat rereading the messages. Ana just couldn't believe James and Caleb were the same. She wanted to get this whole thing over with. She was ready to get both versions of him out of her life.

Ana picked at a thread on her shirt and watched it slowly unravel. Her mind couldn't hold all of the information in at once. James had given her a multitude of reasons to fear Bex - the receipt in her desk, sightings of her car near the place where Patricia was picked up, and the photo at the bridge.

All that aside, Bex was the one who had always been there. Bex was the one constant in Ana's life. Bex couldn't have done all of this. The FBI just told Ana that it was someone in their family. James had to be the killer. Caleb. And if it was Caleb, how did he have all that evidence against Bex?

She was about to find out. Ana pulled the string harder, watching a small hole form in the seam.

"So, what's our plan?" Bex asked. She pulled the blinds back and looked out the window again.

"I don't know," Ana said honestly. Her mind couldn't picture how it would go.

"I guess we just start the podcast recording and introduce him? At some point, I'm just going to come out and ask him if he's our brother. I'm hoping that if I catch him off guard, he'll answer honestly," Bex said. "It's a dumb plan but I don't have anything else."

Ana watched Bex take her apprehension out on one of the throw pillows, karate chopping it in the middle with a heavy hand.

"That's the thing about psychos, they love to talk, and they secretly want to be recognized for their cunning abilities. I'm hoping he's going to be so stunned we figured it out, he won't be able to resist at least bragging a little, finally getting some validation from his big sisters," Bex added.

Bex moved on to the next pillow. "I feel like we should film this... just in case," Bex said.

"Maybe we tell him we need clips for marketing the episode on social media?" Ana asked.

"We could go live again?" Bex offered.

"I think he'll be suspicious. I just did that, and I know he watched it. I'm not going to lie, that's how I thought I would catch you, Bex."

"Thanks for that, by the way."

"I'm sorry. I thought you were the killer. James. Caleb. He has a lot on you."

"He doesn't have anything. He's trying to frame me!" Bex yelled. "After everything I've done for you, I can't believe you bought it."

"I just don't know what to think," Ana said. Her heart wouldn't let her believe Bex would do this. Her mind couldn't square all the information. The evidence was damning.

"Well, I'm not a killer," Bex said with finality. Ana pulled another loose thread.

"I know," Ana said. She hoped it was true.

"Okay, so no live," Bex said, changing the subject.

"No live but if we hide a camera and film the whole thing, it will give us something to show the cops if he confesses."

Bex took her phone from her back pocket and started recording. She leaned it up against a book on the shelf and danced around for a minute. Bex retrieved her phone and verified that it got her. "Well, hopefully, he doesn't notice it," Bex said.

Ana stood and looked. The room was dark in the evening light and the phone kind of blended in the shadow of the shelf. "I think it will be okay," Ana said.

Bex took another lap around the living room. Bex watched her and picked up on her sister's frenetic energy. This was dangerous. Dumb. Yet, there was no other option.

A loud knock at the door interrupted them. Ana watched Bex's whole demeanor change. She pulled back her shoulders and slapped on a smile. Ana tried to do the same. Bex crossed the house with purpose. She pulled the door open before Ana could think better of it.

"James! You're here!" Bex said. Her voice was high, full of energy.

"I'm here. Sorry, I'm early. I just couldn't wait to see my favorite ladies."

"No worries," Bex said.

Ana saw her adult brother for the first time, really saw him. Her knees threatened to give way. The room started to spin. She forced herself to walk across the house and, for the first time in decades, knowingly join both her siblings.

"Hey," she said.

"Hey, you," James replied. She couldn't believe there was a time that she was in love with her own brother. She swallowed another round of bile. It burned her throat.

"So, you ready to get this party started?" Bex said. She motioned toward the living room where their podcasting equipment - the metal mics on their telescoping handles and the digital recorder they plugged into - waited for them, set up on the coffee table.

"Yeah, so what's this about?" James asked.

"Well, everyone is so interested in us and our lives now," Ana said. "We thought we'd give them a little behind-the-scenes look at it."

"No new case? You're not covering Patricia?"

"Well yeah. We should at the end, but people can get updates about this case anywhere. Everyone already knows all about her. I think this should be about us and our team - you," Ana replied. "I think that's what people want."

"Nice. Sounds solid," he said. Ana noticed how cool he was. A chill ran down her spine.

Bex sat down on the armchair. That left a space for Ana and James to sit side by side on the couch. Ana didn't want to be that close to him. She forced herself to do it anyway.

James smelled like beer and aftershave. Ana took a sideways look at him. He wore his signature beanie, but she could see just the bottom of the birthmark in the space between his hat and eyebrow. It was fairly faded by this age, but she couldn't stop looking at it. It was the same shape and location that she now remembered. It was cute, it gave him character. Their mom used to call it his 'angel kiss.' Hell, it was probably part of the reason he got adopted.

"Are we ready?" Bex asked.

James scooted forward, closer to his microphone. Ana did the same. Bex gave a thumbs up.

James gave Ana a wink when Bex fiddled with her microphone. A look passed between them; it was clear that James thought Ana was going to use the show to finally get Bex to confess. Ana offered a small smile, trying to keep the ruse up.

Bex pulled on her headphones and counted down from three.

"Hello, and welcome to *The Serial Syndicate*," Ana said into her mic. "I'm Ana."

"I'm Bex. And this is -"

Ana couldn't wait a second longer. "OUR BROTHER!" Ana shouted into the microphone.

EIGHTY-EIGHT

Bex's eyebrows shot up and she twisted in her seat to get a look at James. The room went still. For a single second, anger flashed in James' eyes. It confirmed everything for Bex. Ana was right. James and Caleb were the same person.

Ana laughed. It was cold and hard. She might as well have said, "Gotcha."

James rearranged his face into a smile. He spread his hands on his jeans. The smile was disarming; most people probably took it at face value, but it did not reach his eyes. Ever since they were kids and Bex became responsible for them, she'd developed a sense of hypervigilance. It kept them alive and now it was working in overdrive, Bex knew they were in danger.

"What?!" he said and laughed into the mic. "I'm not your brother, I'm your podcast engineer but that's a funny start to the show."

His smile grew. "I'm James Shaw. I'm the engineer for *The Serial Syndicate*. I live in Chicago and I'm a freelance podcast engineer. I help shows like this one get started and after each recording, I splice it all together. You don't see much of me on the shows, but I like to think of myself as the magic maker."

"No, no," Ana said, her words spilling out in a rush. "You're our brother; you've been posing as a podcast engineer. When we were first getting started, you reached out to us and asked if we needed help. That's how we got connected."

"It's true," Bex agreed. "You approached us."

"There's other evidence too," Ana continued. "DNA, physical resemblance, and, of course, your birthmark."

James swept his hand up to his hairline, covering the birthmark reflexively. "Ana, I..." he started to say.

"How long have you been watching us?" Ana spoke over him. "Was the show the perfect cover to force your way into our lives? Why didn't you just call us? Is this all because Bex wouldn't answer you?"

"No, Ana, Bex, no. This is crazy talk." James laughed stiffly, "Last I knew, you were in love with me Ana. You practically tried to kiss me that day at the lake. If I'm your brother, that's gross."

"Oh, shut up, Caleb," Ana said. A muscle tightened in James' jaw. "If I would have known who you were then, you'd have been kissing a knife."

Bex caught a look at Ana. Her fists were clenched, and her face bore a nasty half-smile. Ana and James had the same anger in their eyes. Genetics. It was the only explanation. Bex wondered if Ana was going to lunge at James like she had done to her the other night.

Leaning into her podcast mic, Bex said, "So, we're doing things a little differently today. I know things got a little dramatic during our last recording and it's probably a little bit hard to follow but we asked James to record with us today to give us a chance to get to the bottom of a mystery that hits closer to our home than our usual episodes. We have a suspicion that James the podcast engineer is actually our brother, Caleb."

Bex snuck a glance at her phone on the bookshelf. She said a silent prayer that it was recording.

"We lost our parents at a young age. Caleb was just a baby, so he got adopted. We haven't seen him since. Until now," Ana said. Bex watched her sister's face harden with each word. She didn't look like her baby sister Ana anymore.

James cleared his throat and spoke into his mic. "I don't know what they're saying," James said, flashing a high-wattage smile. "I'm not related to them. I'm just a podcast guy."

Ana grabbed her phone and unlocked it. "Here!" she announced. She pushed it toward James' face. The photo from the newspaper - the one with Ana and Caleb sitting on the curb - filled the screen. His eyes searched the page but didn't give anything away.

"This is us," Ana said. "It's you and me. You know how I know? Look at your birthmark, the specific shape - it looks like an hourglass. I don't know how I didn't see it the first time. Every time I've seen you since then, you've worn a beanie. It's almost like you covered it up on purpose. It wasn't until the FBI showed me this picture that I put it together," Ana said.

"For our listeners, we just showed James a photo published in the newspaper. It was from our hometown. We were just kids, outside the house fire that killed our mom. There's a big birthmark on the baby. James has that exact same birthmark. Same spot over the eye. They're the same. James is Caleb," Ana said. She felt the balance of power tipping in their direction.

Caleb shifted in his seat. This was working. They were breaking him down.

"So, Caleb - what made you come back after all these years?" Bex asked. She had to know.

"I'm not Caleb. I'm James," he said in a low monotone, barely containing his stifled rage.

"The podcast guy. So, let's podcast."

"I don't have a way to prove it yet, but we know you are our brother," Ana said.

"You don't have a way to prove it because it's not true," he shot back.

"There's one thing. The cops found a bit of hair stuck in the tape of the bomb box. You know what that means? DNA," Ana said.

Caleb's face remained placid. Bex twirled her hair around her finger and pulled.

"The results weren't conclusive yet, but they did figure out that someone in this family sent the box. Someone in this fucked up family is The Novel Killer."

EIGHTY-NINE

Caleb laughed. The sound was loud, out of place. The noise bounced off the wall and made it clear just how small the room was. Too small for all of them.

"Oh, ha! That's your big smoking gun?! DNA that will take them months to process?" Caleb asked. He laughed again, sounding like he was losing control. "We already know it's someone in this family. *It's Bex*. It's her hair. She had a receipt for the bomb-making materials. She sent the box. She was in San Francisco around the time the woman was pushed off the bridge and she left a photo of the pair of you on the bridge in her bag. And her red car was parked where Patricia was taken. What more do you need from me to understand that Bex is the killer?"

"You're framing Bex," Ana said. Her words were full of determination.

Bex watched something click in her sister's mind. "Wait. How did you know about the receipt?" Ana demanded. Bex knit her eyebrows together; she didn't know what Ana was reaching for.

"Everyone knows about that," Caleb said.

"No, no they don't. No one knows about it except for me and the FBI. I told them, but I never told you. I'm sure of it. It's not public information," Ana said.

Bex stood. The confusion was clearing. Caleb could only know about the receipt if he was responsible for it.

"The only way you could know about the receipt is if you planted it..." Ana said, quietly.

Caleb stood and paced the length of the room. "This is crazy. You invited me here to podcast about being your brother? To talk about some dumb receipt? This is nuts. You're as crazy as everyone says, Ana."

393

"Don't talk to Ana like that," Bex said. She stood and got between him and Ana. Bex didn't like where this was heading.

Caleb stopped; his whole body stiffened. "Don't tell me how to talk to my sister! You're not getting between us any longer!"

"Oh, so she is your sister? Are you going to finally admit that you're Caleb?" Bex said. She felt vindication.

"Little goodie two-shoe sisters over here figured it out. Whoop-de-doo. You're real detectives now."

The fog in Bex's mind finally cleared. It all made sense. "And you're The Novel Killer," Bex said. She stepped closer.

"Now that is crazy," he said, coolly.

"No," Ana said with a tone Bex didn't recognize. "You bought the bomb stuff using cash and somehow planted the receipt in her room. You already told us that you logged into our doorbell camera, you must have deleted any evidence. I know you've been lurking around. You're a creep. It's YOU! You committed The Novel Killings."

Caleb stepped back. He ran a hand through his hair.

"Why would I have any reason to be the killer?"

"I don't know but your lies are stacking up," Ana said.

"You know what I think?" Bex spat. "I think you're still mad about what happened when we were kids. We didn't rescue you or some bullshit like that. Is this your way of getting revenge?"

Caleb narrowed his eyes. "No, you dumb bitch," he growled. Anger rushed through her. She'd had enough of Caleb.

"No, I think that's it. Oh, poor baby Caleb. He got to be adopted while Ana and I had to endure life together with no one, but the foster system. No family. No money. And you know what? We made it. Together. The two of us. Does that just kill you a little bit?" Bex asked.

He lunged across the room and grabbed Bex by the shoulders before she could even take a step back. His hands were strong. Bex tried to bring her arms up to push him back, but she had no leverage. With a snarl, Caleb pushed her hard with both hands on her chest.

Bex was thrown backward. Her head hit the wall behind her with a thud that sent an explosion of pain all through her body. Her brain cracked against the hard bone of her skull, and a bright flash erupted behind her eyes.

Bex slunk to the floor. The room spun. There was another moment's pain and then a soft, thick blackness covering everything. She let go and fell into nothing.

NINETY

Ana watched Bex slam against the wall and then fall to the ground. Her head lay slack one way while her body twisted another. Her arms and legs flopped limply. Ana started toward Bex but the sharp rage in her belly forced her to face Caleb.

She grabbed Caleb by the arm, digging her fingers into his flesh. "What did you do?!" Ana screamed.

He smiled, shrugged.

Ana looked down at her motionless sister. Bex's face was white, her jaw hanging open. Her eyes were closed, and a small spray of blood formed a crown around her head. Ana let out a piercing scream.

"Don't let Bex fool you, Ana," Caleb warned. His eyes locked on Ana with a near-feral intensity. "She was behind all of this. Who left us in that house when we were kids? She's the real reason our mom died. And who killed my dad? It was probably her. She masterminded this media circus to earn you two some success, to make sure you'd never leave her. Our whole fucked up life is her fault."

His words snagged in Ana's mind. She looked between her sister and her brother. She was having trouble following the conversation.

"That day at the lake, when it was just you and me, Ana, that closeness," Caleb said. He loomed over her, his voice cracking. Her grip on his arm faltered. "That's how it will be when we get Bex out of the picture. She's a cancer. She's made both of our lives a living hell. You don't know what it was like. I was adopted into a horrible family. They've always treated me like an ugly little stepbrother. If it hadn't been for Bex, none of this would have happened," he said. He sounded close to tears.

The pieces finally smashed together in her mind.

"The lake. That day. You stole my hairband," Ana said. "It had my hair wrapped around it. Is that how you got hair in the box? Caleb, you're playing the long game!"

Caleb took another step, pushing Ana back. "No. You don't see it. You're blaming the wrong person. Look at your sister. Look at our sister. It was Bex, it was always Bex! Even as a kid, I remember how close we always were. It was you and me Ana. It can be like that again. We just have to get her out of the picture."

"What was your plan? Did you think the cops would think it was Bex if they had my hair?!" Ana yelled.

"Caleb! Don't you see how crazy this is? Just leave!" Ana demanded. She looked at Bex, praying he would go before it was too late. She hadn't moved.

"The hair band was just a first step, Ana, you needed Bex out of your life no matter what." Caleb was frantic. "Your DNA is close enough to keep the cops guessing for a while. You can get that evidence thrown out in court, hell Bex could have planted it."

"We won't need to. After tonight, they'll see who the real killer is," Ana said. "It's you, Caleb. You won't get away with this!"

With one hand he grabbed Ana's wrist and pressed tightly. She released her grip and felt her hand being bent backward, her arm exploding in pain. "Nooo!" she screamed. Ana twisted away from him, breaking his grasp on her arm. She turned back towards the kitchen and stumbled through the door, realizing too late that she was trapped. Caleb stood in the door frame, blocking the front door and cutting off Ana's view of Bex.

There was nowhere for Ana to run. Her sister still lay on the floor, motionless. Ana was on her own. And Bex needed her. It might not be too late.

With a growl, Ana lunged forward, clawing for Caleb's eyes. He seemed stunned by the ferocity, letting her rake his face with her fingernails before pushing her back again. In one quick motion, Caleb pulled something from the back of his pants. A gun was in her face. She froze.

"Let Bex go! She's gone!" Caleb screamed. He stood in the doorframe and kept his gun trained on Ana. A trickle of blood from the four sharp furrows her fingernails had left on his cheek mixed with sweat and ran down the side of his face.

"No! She's my sister. She's your sister!" Ana screamed, her voice cracking on the last word.

"She missed her chance for that! If she had just responded to my AncestryandMe messages, it could have been different. We could have been a family again! This could have gone another way! It's not my fault!" Caleb screamed.

He pulled the gun higher and aimed it directly in her face, the barrel shaking with his nerves. Ana stopped and put her hands out. She opened her fists to placate him.

"Ana! Why can't you see it?! You saved me when I was a baby. You got me out of that fire! Now it's my turn to save you from Bex. Please just listen to me! I've set you free!" he moaned.

Ana kept her hands open. She thought of the drying dishes by the sink. Was there something in the dish rack she could use as a weapon? "Caleb. I didn't need to be protected from Bex. She's all I have."

"She was evil! How can you not see that? She always has been!"

Ana took a slow step back. She let a hand drift behind her. She just needed to keep Caleb talking.

"Caleb. Why are you so mad at her? I don't understand. What do you even want? What's your endgame?

"You're my endgame, Ana. Bex is dead. We're family again, right? Nothing is standing between us. We can pin the killings on her, we'll get famous and rich. It's all so easy." Caleb's voice shook with emotion.

"Caleb. Just put the gun down, please. You need help. We can figure this out," Ana pleaded, her thoughts still on the possibilities of the dish rack. They'd used a serving fork last night to plate their Thai food, a sharp metal one. Was it still there?

His face fell. "Help, huh? You think I'm crazy - like you?!" His voice grew more unhinged as he seemed to notice her slow drift towards the sink. "Stop! Where are you going?!" he demanded.

"Nowhere. Ana lied. He hesitated. She was getting closer, but he was getting crazier.

"Bex ruined our lives! If she had never gone to prom, our mom would still be alive. None of this would have happened," he yelled. Ana heard the hurt in his voice; she also heard the crazy. They had all inherited it one way or another. "It's too late, isn't it? If Bex had died thirty years ago we might have had a chance. But now..." His voice trailed off.

"It would have been better for us all if we'd never been born," he roared. Caleb stood in a shooter's stance and aimed the gun at her head.

Caleb filled the doorframe. His expression was wild and crazed. "It's just too late Ana." He cocked the gun.

Ana yelped, then winced tightly, her head starting to fill with static.

"No one hurts my sister!" Bex cried. Ana opened her eyes and saw Bex, her face a mask of rage and blood and triumph. She was standing behind Caleb, thrusting a knife down between his shoulder blades.

NINETY-ONE

Bex had rolled onto her side as carefully as she could, aware at once that she was in terrible danger. Her head had throbbed and her vision was blurry. She bit her tongue, hard. Hard enough to keep her in the moment; hard enough to convince herself that she was still alive. Bex had tasted blood.

She'd crawled on all fours. She hadn't made a sound. She watched Caleb back Ana into the kitchen, fighting the urge to scream and fight. She had to be careful.

There was Caleb in the doorframe of the kitchen blocking Ana's exit. Ana was behind him; her hands were open. Caleb trained a gun on her sister.

Bex's whole body had lit up with adrenaline in a fierce protective surge that cleared the thick cobwebs from her mind and sent a rush of energy through her veins. It was now or never. Forcing herself to move quietly she edged towards the bookshelf. To where they'd stashed the knife before Caleb had arrived.

In a rush of dizziness, she stood, her head a merry-go-round of sharp pain. She gritted her teeth. She could do this. With a trembling hand, Bex grabbed the black handle of the knife hidden behind a photo of Ana and Bex smiling together at the lake. The blade glinted in the glow of the light.

"Caleb. What's your endgame?" Bex heard Ana shout.

Bex swayed a little, the room going dim. She held her breath and clenched the knife. Dizziness swept through her. All she wanted was to lie on the soft gray carpet and sleep.

The sounds from the kitchen were growing frantic. She was close. There were only a few steps left across the carpet, but they seemed impossible. Darkness threatened the edges of her sight. Her grip on the knife started to relax. The carpet called, soft and gray. The darkness.

Caleb was talking, it was hard to make out what he was saying though. She couldn't remember why she was standing when she was so dizzy. Why not just lie down and rest?

A voice tore through the gauze covering her eyes, a yelling angry man. "It would have been better for us all if we'd never been born" she heard.

Ana screamed.

Bex felt an electric bolt of strength travel through her. Bex had fought too hard every step of the way. She'd been fighting since the day she'd been born and wasn't going to stop now. Her life had never been easy, but it had always been hers.

A deep breath, a steadied grip, and Bex was running. For Aimee. For her mom. For Ana.

"No one hurts my sister!" Bex cried. With all her strength, all her countless frustrations, she plunged the blade into the thick of his back. His shirt bloomed in red.

Caleb staggered, turned, and pointed the gun right at Bex. "This is for Ana," he screamed, his voice laced in pain.

Bex smiled. "It was always for Ana," she said. And it always had been.

He pulled the trigger.

NINETY-TWO

The gunshot blew through Bex's face and tore through Ana's soul.

Caleb staggered back with the recoil; Ana pushed past him, to where Bex's body had landed on the floor in a pool of red spreading upon the white canvas of the carpet.

"Bexley baby! Bex!" Ana said. She crawled to her sister and pulled her body into her lap. There was just a mat of skull and blood. Nothing else. Ana stroked what was left of her sister's hair. The tears fell in wild succession down her face. "BEX!!!!!"

Blood seeped all around Ana. Brain matter littered the wall and the floor. Blackness swirled. She felt the familiar fugue state creeping up behind her. Ana didn't want to let go. She needed to stay present. She had to for Bex.

"What have you done?!" Ana screamed at Caleb. He stood in the doorway, his face twisted in pain. The knife was still pinned in his back, up near his right shoulder, the handle moving as he spoke.

"I did what I had to," Caleb said coldly. "Fair is fair. You saved me in the fire, and I saved you from Bex. She was never going to let you stand on your own. You'd have always been in her shadow. I got your books the recognition they deserve and now I'm going to be famous too. We're going to be famous together. I did it all for you Ana. I did it all for us. I hope you can see that someday."

Ana's vision went black. She felt her body and mind detach from one another. It took everything inside her to force herself back into place. She wouldn't black out now. She couldn't. It was the only thing she could do for Bex. Be here for her, one last time.

Blood seeped through her pants. Ana could feel the warmth of her sister's life on her skin. It was enough to ground Ana. She stood and grabbed the podcasting mic off the table by its telescoping handle and ripped out the cables. The heavy weight of metal felt good in her hands. She gave it a swing.

Caleb backed to the door. His face was pale white and layered in sweat. The scruffy innocent hipster was gone, a gore-soaked vision with rolling eyes in his place. Nearly the entirety of his shirt was red. Caleb trained his gun at Ana's middle. She held the mic up like a sword, weighing the distance between them. She waited for a bullet to sink into her abdomen. She prayed to join Bex.

"It's just us now, why don't you calm down?" Caleb said.

"Noooooo! I'm going to kill you," she screamed. "For Bex!"

Caleb tried to shrug, wincing as he raised his shoulders and jiggled the knife. "Don't you see? If you go along with it, Bex takes the fall for The Novel Killings. We can all win! You and I can be famous together, the podcasters who were betrayed by a madwoman. What other podcast has actually stopped a killer? We'll be the biggest ever. No one has to know we're brother and sister. We can live in the limelight - we can be together any way you want to be. We can be a family. We can *make* our own family... together. Let me help you write the final scene: our happy ending."

Ana heard sirens in the distance. Time was running thin. She just had to keep him talking and he could be stopped. "You're a killer and you're fucking crazy Caleb. How long have you been messing with our lives?"

"Since I found you again," he said.

"Tell me!" Ana demanded.

"I became Ana's Number One Fan," he said with a sad laugh.

"You were the one DMing me on Instagram?"

"Yes, of course. I *am* your biggest fan."

"And what about the rest of it Caleb, can you be honest?" The sirens grew louder.

"What do you mean? It was easy. After Bex sent her DNA test, I knew things had to come to a head. I couldn't wait any more. I wanted, more than anything, to finally admit who I was so we could all be a family. Once I realized Bex was going to be a problem, when I saw how rude she was and how her selfish behavior nearly killed you, I figured out there was a way you and I could both get the family and success we've always deserved. The Novel Killings were *my* art, Ana, it's like we're co-authors."

Ana laughed. "You're not an artist Caleb, you're just a psycho."

His face fell. "I'm not a psycho Ana, this took a lot of planning and work. After you went to Hillside, I knew it was only a matter of time before Bex crushed you for good and left you as nothing but an overmedicated shell. I came up with my plan. Once you were in-patient, I built the bomb and broke into your house and hid the receipt in her desk. For a pair of 'true crime experts' you two were shockingly dumb. You use the same password for everything. I could see where you hide your extra key on your security camera. I walked right in while Bex was out and then just deleted that footage from the app. I even went into Bex's car for a bit and decided to borrow her copy of our childhood photo because I was getting rid of mine. She never even noticed."

"What about the open-source pictures?"

"Oh, those were real. I just rented a red car that looked just like hers - kind of hard to find in Colorado but worth it. I planted it where I knew there would be surveillance footage. Easy."

"What about Kyle? And Aimee? What did she ever do to you?"

"Aimee? She was pushing you and Bex apart and putting you at risk. Bex was too obsessed with her, she forgot her responsibilities. If Bex chose Aimee over you again, it might have killed you. Aimee would have further ruined this family if she stayed in the picture. I needed her gone. We needed her gone," he said. His eyes swept frantically around the room.

Ana hated him more than she had ever hated anyone. Even her stepdad. She felt the blackness of anger threatening to overtake her.

She wanted to demolish him. She had a flash image of running him through with the podcast mic like a spear. He just kept talking, his face torn between the obvious pain and his pride at finally getting to share his work.

"And the photo at the bridge?" He continued, smugly. "That was easy too. A picture of you two was the only thing I was allowed to take with me when I was adopted. I had to plant it. I had to make you suspect Bex, Ana. I thought you would have caught on sooner. I thought you would have helped me. Soon you will see. Life will be so much better without her. Our lives will be so much better together."

She couldn't hear another word. Ana ran at Caleb, swinging the podcast mic with all her strength. She managed to smash the mic into his shoulder; he winced but kept coming at her. James grabbed her by the arm. Pain exploded in her face as he slammed the barrel of the pistol up into her chin. "I'm telling you to stop," he seethed.

A shot rang out and she closed her eyes tightly, fearing the end. Ana heard crashing. She waited to join Bex, but the room had suddenly gone quiet. She opened her eyes. James now stood in the doorway; door open to the night.

He had the gun pointed right at her. Another shot. This time, the bullet screamed past her ear. She knew he could have killed her if he wanted to.

He turned and slunk out the door in a limping run. "To be continued Ana!" he yelled behind him. She watched him jog away, his back covered in blood and the knife handle still stuck in his flesh. He moved with the desperate grace of a wounded coyote, soon swallowed by the dark of the Colorado night.

Caleb was gone. Bex was, too.

Ana was still screaming when the police finally arrived.

NINETY-THREE

@TexasTrueCrimeChick on TikTok

Suspenseful music playing in the background. A young woman is green screened over an image of a newspaper with the headline SUSPECT IN NOVEL KILLINGS CALEB DUKES BELIEVED AT LARGE IN DENVER

"Heeyyyyyyy there, true crime cats and thrill kill kittens. It's Becca here with your latest serving of the most piping hot true crime tea. I want to be the first to tell y'all about the latest twists and craziest goss in The Novel Killings saga. Things are definitely getting novel!

"You've all seen the newspapers, supposedly Ana and Bex had a brother named Caleb who was working secretly for them the whole time. Suspicious, much? The cops are claiming they didn't know he was their podcast engineer but come on now. Really? How stupid could they be?

"Police suspect that he's The Novel Killer, that this guy with no real record somehow embarked on this elaborate killing spree as some sick trick to get back at Bex for abandoning him as a kid. And now Bex is dead, this Caleb guy confesses on a camera recording, but then somehow evades the cops. And surprise, Ana Adams is now famous, her books are bestsellers, and you just know Hollywood wants to make a movie. It worked out awfully well for Ana. A little too well.

"I don't buy it. It doesn't sit right with me.

"Ana, Ana, just watch her. Something is not right there. She's a writer, she's spent time in a psychiatric hold, and that creepy doctor of hers claimed in an interview she had a habit of blacking out. You don't think she could have planned this all out?

"That chick stands to earn millions of dollars from all of this. Have you looked at how many book reviews she has now? Even with all the one stars, someone is still buying those books. She started at nothing. Anything she publishes from here on out will sell. She has it made. Those life rights are going to be worth a fortune alone. There will probably be a movie someday, too.

"I think Ana and Bex planned all of this. They were setting up their brother to take the fall for them both but lost the plot somewhere along the way. James is a convenient red herring if I ever saw one, just a patsy. A victim like the rest.

"There are too many unanswered questions out there. Too much pain. This sick family left a lot of bodies in their wake and sooner or later, the truth will come out. I'll make sure of it.

"I'll keep you updated as soon as the FBI starts doing their jobs.

"Make it make sense."

NINETY-FOUR

Low afternoon sun broke through the slit in the curtains, providing a single shaft of light that crawled slowly across the wall as the day passed. Ana thought about closing them all the way but couldn't bother. She just sat there, working her way through another set of episodes. Watching *Criminal Minds* was the only thing that made Ana feel like Bex was still there, like she wasn't alone.

The autoplay started a new episode and hot tears rolled down her cheeks when the reassuring voice of Agent Hotchner opened with, "The Taoist philosopher Lao-tze once wrote, 'He who controls others may be powerful, but he who has mastered himself is mightier still.'"

Ana was far from mastering anything, let alone her own mind. The tears came faster; she sucked in a breath and let the waves of grief crash over her one more time. It had only been two weeks since she'd been alone. Two weeks without Bex but it felt like she'd cried years of sadness already.

Bex had been everything to her. Their relationship was Ana's whole life. Even though it wasn't perfect, they were everything to each other. Now she had nothing. Bex was dead and the place still smelled of whatever cleaning concoction they used to get Bex's blood out of the carpet and her brain off the walls. She sat in Bex's cozy condo with only her grief.

Ana couldn't take another one of Hotchner's meaningful quotes. She flipped to the evening news instead. Denver's 9News show filled the screen. Kevin, the newscaster, was wearing a stylish tweed sports coat and had a grave look on his face.

"We've got some updates on The Novel Killings case for our viewers tonight. Ana Adams, the Denver author whose self-published mystery books have been linked to the nationwide murders of four people, remains in seclusion following the death of her sister.

Authorities are continuing to search for Caleb Dukes, the prime suspect in the killing of Bexley Adams. Caleb is believed to be their sibling who posed under the false identity of James Shaw.

"Caleb Dukes is also the primary suspect for the murder of Aimee Phillips and Kyle Francis of Denver, as well as the primary person of interest in The Novel Killings case. As the nationwide media attention abates, we urge you to report any man that may meet the description who also has a back injury. However, all of us at Denver 9News urge our viewers to remain vigilant, Caleb Dukes, also operating under the alias James Shaw, is armed and dangerous and viewers should take caution."

Ana fingered the remote and debated if she should change the channel. She didn't want to see her face on the screen, or worse, her sister's. She had to know if they had any leads on James. Caleb.

A picture of Caleb popped up on the screen. It was his headshot from the podcast production company's website. The only thing Ana could see was his birthmark above his eye. SUSPECT BELIEVED ARMED AND DANGEROUS, CONTACT THE TIP LINE OR POLICE IF SIGHTED, scrolled across the bottom.

Kevin wrapped up the details of the case before switching to something about the Broncos. Ana turned off the television; her heart sank. They were no closer to catching Caleb than they were the night he disappeared.

Bex was still gone and so was Caleb.

NINETY-FIVE

Days passed in a haze of reruns. Ana had never felt so alone. Whenever it got too much, she logged into her Amazon KDP account and checked her numbers again. They were still staggering. She had millions of page reads and had made more in the last two months than she ever thought she would in her lifetime.

Ana could finally afford a place of her own, but leaving Bex's condo would mean leaving Bex forever. She wallowed in the loneliness. She didn't think she could go on living without her sister by her side. She didn't want to keep facing the media, the police... hell, the whole world alone.

There was one other thing that buoyed her spirits. She had all of her old prescriptions and a brand new bottle of extra-strength Tylenol PMs. When she couldn't go on living any longer, she'd simply stop. No one would find her this time. Who would? No friends, no partner, no sister. She was all alone with no one to stay alive for. Sitting on the couch, working up the energy to put on another episode of SVU, she wondered how much longer before she'd take them. How much longer would she have to be alone?

"You're not alone Ana. You've never been alone, not really. I'm here, you don't have to do this by yourself," Ana heard the words distinctly. She looked around the empty, dark room. She was convinced someone was there with her. Adrenaline brought her up, she ran through all the rooms of the condo and checked the closets. No one was there.

"Ana, it's okay. I'm Sam," she heard the voice like someone was behind her, whispering firmly in her ear. Ana's eyes went all around the space. The voice came in clear as day but she didn't know how or where it was coming from.

"I don't want you to freak out," the voice said, "but I'm in your head. I've always been there. My name is Sam. I want to introduce myself."

Ana slapped her face, hard. She wanted the voice to stop. The pain shocked her, made her feel better. She raised her hand again. A tingle ran through it, her hand had gone asleep. Her arm fell by her side. She couldn't move it. "Ana, don't do that," the voice said.

She fell to the floor; her whole body shivered. Ana felt her sanity, the battered and frayed remnants of it, start to break. The voice was unrelenting: "Ana, let me try this again. My name is Sam. I'm someone else who lives inside your mind."

"No, stop!" she yelled back. The words echoed through the silent condo.

"Yes, I'm here Ana. I've been here a long time. I know you don't understand but I just want you to listen to me. When you were a kid, your stepdad did horrible things to you. Things no one should ever have to endure. I developed in your mind to keep you safe, to do the things you couldn't do."

"What do you mean?" Ana asked the empty room.

"You know how your stepdad died? That was me. I crushed up all those pills and hid them in his beer. I took over your body and got him out of the picture so you wouldn't have to deal with him anymore."

Ana pulled at her hair and screamed. She felt crazy. The voice was too loud, it knew too much about her.

Her hands moved back to her side, more forcibly this time. "Ana, baby. Please don't do that to us. It hurts." The voice sounded serious. "I just want you to know I exist. I haven't introduced myself before because we still had Bex. But after everything, it's time you know the truth. I'm Sam. And I'm here to help you. I mostly stay hidden in the dark corners of your mind, but when you need me, I come to your rescue."

"No. This isn't real. Who are you!?" Ana asked.

411

"Well, you know how people say you lose track of time here and there? Or ask if you have blackouts? That's when I take over. It's basically like I put Ana to sleep and manage your body for a while. Your mind doesn't remember, but it's a defense mechanism."

"No..." Ana said. She didn't want to believe the voice.

"I know it's going to take some getting used to it but I don't want you to feel so alone. I'm here for you," Sam said. Her voice was soft, it felt like a salve for her soul after everything Ana had endured. Ana wanted to melt into it. She didn't want to fight it anymore.

"I tried to save Bex," Sam said.

"I know," Ana admitted. "I did, too."

"But I did save you from Kyle."

"What? No!" Ana screamed into the void. "That was Caleb!"

"No, Caleb didn't kill Kyle. I did. He was going to do something very bad to you, Ana. I couldn't let him. I took over and gave him a chance to walk away. He wouldn't do it. So, I did what I had to do," Sam said.

"You stabbed him and left him to die in an alley!"

"Yeah, I know. I didn't have many other options. I tried to run but he kept following us. I grabbed what I could from your purse - that stupid little knife you keep with you. I turned and he ran right into it. I didn't think I killed him, but I must have hit an artery or something. I got us out of there before anyone saw."

"And you killed Henry?" Ana asked.

"Yup. Sick dudes shouldn't underestimate us, Ana. It doesn't work out for them."

A warm feeling ran through Ana's veins. She had felt Sam's protective spirit so fully in those moments. Hindsight was 20/20.

Ana had to know if this person knew more than she did. "Why did this happen? All of it??!" she moaned.

"I don't know Ana. You didn't deserve any of it. Neither did Bex. I thought you were getting better. Caleb surprised me too, by the time I had a chance to stop him it was too late for her. It doesn't have to make sense. Bad things happen to good people," Sam said. "I just wish I could have caught on to him sooner. I wish I could have saved you - and Bex - from all of this." There was a deep sadness laced in her voice.

"Me too," Ana said.

"Bex protected you one last time, though. She made sure that her phone recorded Caleb's confession. He won't get away with any of it now."

Tears rolled down Ana's face. She knew Sam was right, but it didn't make it hurt any less. Ana just wished she could have done something to save her sister instead.

"Do you want to give up Ana?" The voice sounded sincere.

"No," she said. She meant it. She wasn't alone, not anymore. She wouldn't be alone again. She still had some fight in her.

"Caleb has to pay," Sam said. Ana could hear the eagerness in her voice. "The FBI isn't doing nearly enough to catch him."

"I know," Ana said out loud. Determined.

"We have to catch Caleb. For justice. For Bex," Sam said.

Ana nodded her head and for the first time in days, she felt a tiny glimmer of hope. There was nothing like having someone on her side. It wasn't Bex but at least she wasn't alone. And she wasn't helpless either, she still had one more weapon - her oldest, truest one.

"Let's write another book!" Ana and Sam said at the same time.

Acknowledgements

How lucky am I that my acknowledgments could span pages and never fully encompass everyone who has helped me get to this point? When I use the word lucky, I mean it. I have the best group of family, friends, colleagues, and an online community who have endlessly believed in me and cheered me on every step of the way.

First and foremost, thank you to my love, Zachary D. When we dreamed of a life together when we were a mere 18 years old, I never thought it could be this good, and that is a testament to you. You have worked so dang hard to make it so, all while encouraging me to follow my dreams. Words could never convey how much I love you and this life we've built together.

To our daughters - Amelia and Penelope - everything I do, I do it for you. No matter the books I write or the milestones I reach, you will always be the best thing I've ever done. I hope that when you read this book (when you're much older) you realize that you, too, can do anything you set your mind to.

To my parents, thanks for instilling the work ethic needed to write a book and then rewrite it 100 times over. Without your examples of hard work, entrepreneurship, and dogged determination, I wouldn't be writing this page. 'Thank you' doesn't seem like enough, but know that you paved the way for me, and for that, I'm endlessly grateful. And side note: thanks for raising me in a way that gave me a healthy dose of material to write into the pages of my books.

To my Grandma Ardy who gave me a love for words and reading, you are a big reason this book is here. I love sharing stories and plots with you, but more than that, I love that you're just a call away. You have always been my biggest cheerleader and I'm so lucky to have you in my corner.

Thanks to my siblings, aunts, uncles, and cousins who have encouraged me every step of the way.

To my friends, who put up with me and listen to me complain, you keep me sane: Mary, Susan, Alex, Jaimie, Chelsea, Paige, Jen, Teal, and so many more - thank you. Thank you for doing life with me, loving my kids, and laughing at my jokes, even when they're not funny.

To my online friends, thank you for following along. Most of you I have never met in person, but that doesn't matter. Our friendship spans miles and apps, and you're as real as it gets for me. To my thriller-loving buddies, Chelsea, Tabitha, Emily, Alexandra, Erin, Krissy, and the rest of you - thank you. Thanks for reading my words and keeping me company.

Thanks to Erick Mertz for reading an early draft and providing the guidance I needed to help this book get picked up.

Most importantly, thanks to the entire Korza Books team for taking a chance on me and pouring into this book (and my writing skills!). Michael, I appreciate your guidance and hard work on this book. Katie, thank you for helping me shape this story into what it is. I am so grateful for all of you.

And finally, to my dear friend, Maggie. I still cannot understand your death and I probably never will, but I do know that in losing you, I found me.

If you've made it this far, thank you. Those two words will never be enough but they're all I have. Thank you. Thank you.

Until we meet again in the middle of a screwed-up story, all my love.

Kate Shelton, 2024

About The Author

Growing up in a loud and chaotic family, the only thing Kate Shelton could do for peace and quiet was to find some privacy behind a thick pair of glasses and the pages of a book. After graduating high school with a nerd designation, she attempted an engineering degree in college. When she failed to make it through calculus, Kate turned back to words. She got a very useful liberal arts degree from Colorado State University. A few years later, she earned a Master's of Creative Writing from the University of Denver. Kate now works as a professional communicator but prefers dark humor and emojis to crisis comms.

Like many others, Kate found herself restless and anxious during the height of the pandemic and reading was simply no longer enough. Coupled with the loss of one of her best friends to colon cancer, Kate discovered the strength to start writing a novel and the pure insanity that made her brave enough to get it published.

Kate lives in Fort Collins, Colorado with her husband and two (loud and wonderful) children. Find Kate at www.katesheltonauthor.com and @katesheltonauthor on social media.

Other Titles from Korza Books

Is It Just Me Or Are We Nailing This? Essays on BoJack Horseman
Published with Antiquated Future
Joshua James Amberson, Timothy Day, Jessica Fonvergne, Lauren Hobson, M.L. Schepps, Jourdain Searles and
Molly E. Simas
Illustrations from Eileen Chavez, Ross Jackson, Naomi Marshall and
Sarah Shay Mirk

Split Aces
M.L. Schepps

Poetry For People: Fifty Years of Writing
Dixie Lubin

How To Forget Almost Everything
Joshua James Amberson

Altogether Different: A Memoir About Identity, Inheritance and the Raid That Started the Civil War
Brianna Wheeler

The Last Grand Tour (Coming Autumn 2024)
Michael McGregor

Visit KorzaBooks.com or
Follow Us On Instagram @Korza_Books For More